# MISSING PEOPLE

# MISSING PEOPLE

## BRANDON GRAHAM

TYRUS
BOOKS

Published by
TYRUS BOOKS
an imprint of F+W Media, Inc.
10151 Carver Road, Suite 200
Blue Ash, OH 45242. U.S.A.
www.tyrusbooks.com

Hardcover ISBN 10: 1-5072-0052-8
Hardcover ISBN 13: 978-1-5072-0052-0
Paperback ISBN 10: 1-5072-0051-X
Paperback ISBN 13: 978-1-5072-0051-3
eISBN 10: 1-5072-0053-6
eISBN 13: 978-1-5072-0053-7

Printed in the United States of America.

10   9   8   7   6   5   4   3   2   1

**Library of Congress Cataloging-in-Publication Data**
Graham, Brandon, author.
Missing people / Brandon Graham.
Blue Ash, OH: Tyrus Books, 2017.
LCCN 2016034133 (print) | LCCN 2016043058 (ebook) | ISBN 9781507200520 (hc)
| ISBN 1507200528 (hc) | ISBN 9781507200513 (pb) | ISBN 150720051X (pb) | ISBN
9781507200537 (ebook) | ISBN 1507200536 (ebook)
LCSH: Middle class families--Fiction. | Life change events--Fiction. | Missing persons--Fiction.
| Domestic fiction. | BISAC: FICTION / Thrillers. | FICTION / Literary. | GSAFD: Suspense
fiction.
LCC PS3607.R33645 M57 2017 (print) | LCC PS3607.R33645 (ebook) | DDC 813/.6--dc23
LC record available at https://lccn.loc.gov/2016034133

Cover design by Frank Rivera.
Cover image © Chris Pritchard/Getty Images.

*This book is available at quantity discounts for bulk purchases.*
*For information, please call 1-800-289-0963.*

# DEDICATION

All my love to Michelle, Eliza, and Declan.

# THE PRACTICE OF MOURNING EVASION

Etta's disappearance, six years ago, had fractured Townes along his most brittle fault lines. In the months and years that followed, he'd been left to put himself back together, with no instructions or experience. No comfort came from those who should have cared. Not from his mother, not from his father, and not from his nonexistent circle of friends. In the absence of constructive guidance, he chose to make himself into something new, as well as he could. He considers good sleep an essential keystone in the precarious assemblage that defines the self-made Townes.

On this morning he wakes feeling rested and at peace. The gently ringing chimes of his digital clock call him calmly from slumber. He used to sleep horribly.

Violent dreams had begun a few nights after Etta vanished. He'd spent the next year avoiding sleep. Of course, there were times he'd grudgingly succumb to utter physical exhaustion. He'd be awake one moment; the next he'd plunge into a brutal cycle of fitful sleep interrupted at odd hours by utter terror. His nightmares were a recurring vision of a shadowy figure, a dark personification of his guilt. The blurry figure would descend slowly, unrelentingly, and from a great height. Townes would wait while the menacing presence came closer; his feet were rooted to the spot. Not because his dream self was incapable of movement, but because he was pinned between approaching danger and his older sister, whom he could feel trembling small behind him. If he ran, his sister would be lost. So he stood his ground and waited for death to take him, waking frightened at the moment he and the specter collided.

But that was before meditation.

As the last faint hint of the chime drifts out of the range of Townes's hearing he turns to sit at the edge of his bed and switches on a twenty-minute meditation timer. This is the first step of a ritual that evolved slowly, a self-prescribed course of treatment that is part of his approach to anxiety management. It's a temporary fix. He knows, someday, he'll have to come to terms with his guilt. But he tries not to think about that.

If pushed, he'd admit he doesn't put much stock in the beliefs behind his habitual routines but values them as a source of comfort from a life trapped inside his own head. This quiet life is a crutch, a way of hibernating from the world. He understands the day will come when he'll be forced to participate in his own existence, but not today.

He has wrapped himself in layers of daily procedure, like a glossy pearl forming around a painful irritant. He's far from ready to deal with the pain at his own center. He knows the process works, with or without his belief in it.

He comes back to the moment and concentrates on the cool air moving in through his nose and filling his sinuses, flowing into his chest and expanding his abdomen. His eyes close, not too tightly, and he imagines he can feel the air fill the cavity of his entire head, feel the refreshing purity on the inside of his skull and the backside of his face. He exhales and pushes the air from his head like a deflating balloon. This makes him happy and he allows himself a smile. He notes the wet sound when his lips stretch, curl, and slip over his teeth.

He considers the way his bare feet feel against the floor. The moist warmth of the underfloor heat seeps into his rough toe pads; cooler air eddies around his arches. He's grateful for the radiant heating under the bamboo planks. It's comforting, like being wrapped in a towel fresh from the dryer and then wrapped farther in the circle of a lover's embrace. Or maybe he's reading too much into the sensation. The term *hyperbole* comes to mind.

Etta once told him a joke: "Hyperbole is at least a billion times worse than understatement." He tries to bring his focus back. Still smiling, he recalls how Etta laughed at her own jokes; she never laughed as hard at other people's jokes. Her unrestrained cackling rings in his ears. He notes the memory rising and lets it pass.

His left big toe twinges, not painfully but inexplicably. It's not a good twinge or bad, so he acknowledges the sensation, careful not to worry over it and returns his attention to the moment. He wonders if his shoes are getting worn. Should he buy new shoes or buy insoles, perhaps the gel type he's seen advertised? He takes note of the distraction his monkey mind has generated and lets it drift through his awareness as a cloud passing on a clear day. He thinks *busy busy* and returns his focus to his body.

His muscles relax, giving in to gravity; his heavy feet spread across the floorboards. Some sharp grit is trapped between the outside edge of his left foot and the ground, something small that pricks his skin. The need to sweep his space floats across his overactive brain, and drags a distant memory with it.

When he was a tiny boy, maybe a kindergartner, he'd been lying on his back in the dry, prickly grass beyond the baseball field in Randall Park, Etta at his side.

"You see that cloud?" she asked, extending her arm and pointing into the blue sky. Her fingernail was covered in chipped, mint-green nail polish. "What's it look like to you?"

Townes thought about it. "Pikachu," he said.

Etta laughed and pointed again. "No. Really. That one. Not the stubby one, the long one." Townes saw the freckles on her arm and the soft hairs bleached blonde by chlorine and sun.

"I don't know? What does it look like?" He worked his body closer and tucked his hip to her side to look up her arm and spy the exact cloud she meant.

"A train. You see?"

"Yeah. I see it."

"What if it was a real train, a magic train that could take us to our favorite places," she said. She let her arm fall. "Pretend it could take us anywhere at all."

"Like where?" he asked, enthralled with her suggestion.

"Where do you think? Where would you want it to take us?"

"Navy Pier? No. The Shedd Aquarium."

"That's good. But we've been there. We should go somewhere we've never been. What if it takes us anywhere? Anywhere at all. Places you've only ever imagined. Places you've only read about."

"You mean like Willy Wonka's Chocolate Factory?"

"Yeah. Sure. Like that. Just like that."

"Then there, to the Chocolate Factory, but no dancing men. I don't like the dancing men."

"Okay. No dancing men. Just pink bubble gum grass, a river of chocolate, and a magic bubble elevator."

"I like Pop Rocks."

"And Pop Rocks."

"With Dr Pepper."

"And cans of Dr Pepper hanging from the branches like apples."

For a time they contented themselves running in switchback arcs, kicking the heads off dandelions, and baking in the sun until they were winded. In unison, they flopped back in the grass, and Townes said, "Look at that cloud." He pointed to a small one. "There's our golden ticket. Let's go!" He rolled over, got to his feet, and hopped in the air to snatch the cloud from the sky.

She laughed hard, got up, and played along. She giggled like she thought he was the greatest brother ever. Like she believed he was something special. She had laughed nearly as hard as she would have laughed at her own joke.

*God, I miss her.* He knows their relationship was fraught with tensions in the last years, like any teenage siblings. Or worse than average, because he so missed the preteen girl she had been. But they had been close, and she was his biggest defender and his best friend. He tried not to make her memory more precious than it deserved, tried not to elevate her into something unreal. She wasn't a symbol. She had been pretentious and bossy with a tendency to condescension and manipulation. She'd possessed an infuriating, self-centered obsession with fashion, music, and texting that made her absent even while sitting next to him. She liked to wear clothes a size too small and regularly failed to meet the school dress code. "The dress code doesn't know what's fashionable," she would argue. But she was generous and sweet too. Funny. She was his sister, the only person to ever make him feel remarkable. And now she is gone.

Townes has to admit today will be hard, harder than Christmas or even Etta's birthday. Those days were difficult. But the pain of those annual events dulled over time. Not like today. *Guilty, guilty.*

He's holding his breath, tensing the muscles that keep his heavy head balanced on his skinny neck. His shoulders are lifting toward his ears. He focuses on his exhale, allows his thoughts of Etta to flow away, push into his room, and dissipate along with the tension in his body.

He turns his focus to a spot near his Adam's apple and imagines a blue light growing there, swelling and radiating cool through his sparse room. In his mind's eye it washes from the bed, spreads across the floor, over his neatly squared columns of books and his yoga area. He designed the room like a monastic cell. His goal is to make his whole life an act of meditation.

Townes takes another breath, and as he exhales, he expands his attention to encompass his ankles and calves, acknowledging any sensations or lack of sensation, careful not to force his mind to generate sensations that aren't there. His pelvis and low back are tight from so much walking. *I need to do my stretches.*

Same as every morning, he works his way up his body, breath by breath, holding more of his body in his awareness. As his focus moves to his sacral chakra, his body's center of sexual energy, he thinks of Dory. *Distraction, distraction*, he tells himself. He goes on meditating until he holds all the physical sensations of his body in his mind.

He expands his focus to include the early morning light coming through the windows and glowing pale and pink through his eyelids. He hears water dripping from icicles along the gutters into the puddles of half-frozen slush on the driveway. The periodic snap and crack of ice falling from black tree limbs punctuate the scene. He accepts these things as part of his experience rather than separate from him.

Winter in Chicago is always tenacious. This year its tenacity is marked by cruelly teasing warmer temperatures, nearly giving way to pleasant 40s and even warm 50s, only to pull back into a sharp cold snap and layers of misting ice mixed with fairytale bursts of gentle, sparkling snow.

The day after Etta went missing, Townes had turned on the TV in his bedroom and left it on. The incessant buzz was a welcome diversion. His parents were too busy or too numb to tell him to shut it off. Maybe that was what he had really wanted, for them to yell at him rather than ignore him. He felt abandoned as they each moved around him through the house; the three of them tracing their own orbits like dead satellites trapped in the black hole of Etta's absence. Townes hoped for his mother, Meg, to check on him or for his father, Charlie, to hug him. But that never happened. Townes had been left to invent his own ways of coping.

*Loss* was the word reporters had most often ascribed to Etta's status, and Townes hated the term. The word was small and useless, generic. It said nothing and could be applied equally to the passing of an aged grandparent after a long illness, to an unmatched sock, or apparently to the life of a seventeen-year-old girl who went missing from her own block.

In those early days, he would leave his room only if told to, to sit at the kitchen table and man the home phone that served as a tip hotline, to talk to various detectives, or to trudge the neighborhood and staple up photocopied fliers. The utility poles were loosely shingled in thick, insulating layers of multicolored copy paper, each announcing some service, some event, some thing for sale. They were shaggy totems of microcommerce. Townes would select a spot, covering a notice about a missing dog or free kittens. The cropped image of Etta's junior prom photo, her hair in an updo with a few artfully placed tendrils framing her three-quarter profile, stared back into his face as he placed her image at eyelevel. Newton Parker, her horrible high school boyfriend, had been cut out of the photo, but Townes knew Newton had been at her side. It took a few swipes of an X-Acto knife, and Newton was purged from the frame, leaving the strange, lonely image of his sister.

Walking the sidewalks with his nose running, he'd thought how foreign her likeness was on the reproduction glamour shot. He barely recognized her. How would anyone else? They wouldn't. They didn't. *Worry, worry,* he tells himself and brings his attention to this moment, to his body sitting and his chest rising, his chest falling.

One morning, after the volunteers had quit searching, after his father quit speaking to anyone, and the detectives moved on to other cases, Townes sat alone in his room. When the sun was too much to ignore, he walked down to breakfast with his mother. She asked him a series of pointless questions to fill the silence. He gave his rote responses, barely listening. It was as if they were running lines from the script of a normal life.

He ushers his attention back to the moment. The past is the past. The future will come with the natural passage of time. There is only now. He can feel the air pushing against him; he doesn't fight it but is careful to keep his posture from slumping, his back not too rounded, so that anyone looking in would see his intention to attend to his focus.

He'd read that in Buddhist monasteries, during group meditation, a monk wanders among the participants and whacks them with a length of bamboo if their posture is incorrect. One needs to be active in meditation and if one's posture begins to slip, it's evidence one's mind is unfocused. He wonders what it pays to be a whacker of inattentive meditation practitioners. He grins and his lips make their wet sound. His mind is still playing tricks.

The memorial for the sixth anniversary of Etta's absence is today. It'll mess up his routine. He's opposed to the whole trumped-up event. But it's important to his mother.

Etta isn't dead. He knows it. If she were dead, he would feel it in his bones. *Siblings are connected*, he reasons.

Standing in a cemetery to say a few words may give his mother permission to move on with her life, but it will do nothing for him. It's an exercise in make-believe. Participants refuse to admit the obvious: Etta's body isn't in the ground. Neither is a coffin. The gravestone reads, *Etta Messenger*. No dates. No inscription. Just a cold monument, a placeholder for the space Etta should occupy. These are the games people play. It's an acceptable lie, harmless in some ways, not meant to honor the missing so much as comfort the survivors. But it's still an elaborate perjury of reality. *Anger, anger,* he thinks and tries to draw his mind to his breathing.

*An elaborate form of self-deception, an emotional sleight of hand.* His mind continues to rant despite his best efforts. He'd given up on trying to put all painful thoughts out of his head, learned from meditation it's best to admit such thoughts rather than fight them. The act of naming these feelings helps him exert a modest amount of control, which is better than no control at all.

Still, he feels like a failure when his brain runs free. He feels weak, helpless, and powerless. He's not capable of exorcising these disruptive thoughts. He can't help but replay certain moments, split-second, impetuous decisions.

By extension, Townes is forced to confess meditation is not intended to insulate one from reality, but instead to help one maintain perspective. His practice is an intentional misuse. He knows it, acknowledges it yet again, tries to let the thought float away.

He feels the rise of his chest, his skin stretches against his ribcage, but the movement is shallow. His body is being compressed. The hurt weighs heavily on him today, like somebody sitting on his sternum. *Let it all go, let it go,* he thinks.

The chime that ends his meditation sounds. He opens his eyes, letting the morning rush in. Unless some personal calculus is fundamentally changed, a great deal of life is out of his reach. Without a tangible resolution, he's resigned to this self-imposed, austere version of reality.

He rises and treads the warm floor to his bathroom. He opens the small window to let the frigid air fall in, drop around his bare feet, seep between his toes. He gets the shower running and starts the next step of his ritual.

# ATTEMPTED LIFE REBOOT

Meg never sleeps past six-forty. She tells herself it's her internal clock and a mark of her industriousness, but she knows better. It's her aging body's need for nicotine. *Aging* is the word that best defines her life in recent years. Between the loss of Etta, her strained relationship with Townes, her divorce from Charlie, she has aged rapidly and badly. The return to smoking hasn't helped, but she wouldn't give it up for anything. *Well, almost anything.*

She opens a drawer in the side table and takes out a pack of Native Spirit cigarettes. The black pack is more expensive, which is one reason she'd chosen it. She hoped it would force her to smoke less. It worked initially. Also the box is tough but mature, not fussy. She thinks she has those qualities: tough, mature, and easy-going. The logo of a Native American smoking a peace pipe in front of a rising sun does smack of faint stereotyping, but since it hasn't earned national ire, like the logo for that football team, she chooses not to worry over it.

As a teen Meg had been a committed smoker. She and her friends let their cars' engines run and turned up the radios until the cheap, brittle speakers split. They'd pass out Kools, swaying on the hot asphalt, getting sunburned shoulders, peeling noses, and drunk off punch-flavored wine coolers. Her unarticulated goal had been to project the perfect balance of beauty and recklessness. Among her clique she'd been the best.

That short phase of life ended abruptly when Charlie knocked her up. She let it all go: The recklessness, the smoking, and the beauty slipped away too. The cigarettes, she'd quit cold turkey when her belly began to swell, little Etta claiming more and more space within her. Meg resented the whole thing, as if she were being colonized by a greedy, invading force. She'd never made a conscious decision to get pregnant, barely remembered deciding to have sex. Next thing she knew, her body was changing without her permission.

She may not have known much, but she knew motherhood was supposed to be serious business. She did what was best for the creature latched to her innards. Truth is, the whole crazy ride had scared the shit out of her. But she was too insecure to admit that to anyone.

Charlie, for his part, was supportive. He had dropped out of school years earlier. One reason he'd caught her eye was he was young enough to be cute but old enough to make her parents uncomfortable. He had a regular paycheck and a tough car, a black '65 Comet with a double air scoop on the hood that reminded her of bull nostrils.

He'd worked at his uncle's hardware store when Meg got pregnant, quit there and took a job as an apprentice brick mason because the pay would be better in the long run. He even went to school on the weekends to get his GED. As if by cosmic design, neither of them had any idea what they were getting into, how parenthood would alter them. Nature had its ways of conning kids into adulthood.

About the time her debilitating morning sickness subsided, Meg's folks disowned her. Across the kitchen table, before heading to work, her father declared her " . . . a dirty little slut." Meg looked to her mother to defend her. Her mom had gotten pregnant around the same age. Hell, Meg had been born seven months after her parents married. But her mother sat there mute, letting her husband call her only daughter horrible names. After he left, Meg's mother made supportive noises, mostly so she'd get a chance to hold the baby when it came. Meg couldn't live under the same roof with them one more day. That night, she'd moved in with Charlie, in his family's unfinished attic.

Throughout the rest of the pregnancy, Charlie's mom, Daisy, had been primarily supportive and kind to Meg. Daisy's nurturing demeanor was interrupted periodically by hateful outbursts, seemingly to add variety. The subject of the outbursts revolved around her notion that Meg had " . . . destroyed any hope for Charlie to have a shred of happiness in his life." Then Daisy would regain control and add, "But it's not all your fault, baby," to take the edge off.

During pregnancy Meg's emotions were a grab bag. One day, when her belly was starting to stretch to grotesque proportions, and her feet were too swollen to jam in her shoes, Charlie arrived with a carton of fried chicken livers from some soul food place. She devoured them and demanded he drive to the city to get more. He refused on the basis that the place would be closed. She yelled and cried. She called him cruel. She collapsed on their rollaway bed, apologized, and agreed to wait for another delivery the following day.

Daisy claimed Meg needed the iron. Whatever the reason, her body dictated that she eat the livers, warm from the bag or cold from the refrigerator, as a chaser after every meal. She'd devour the greasy nuggets and kiss Charlie on the lips, making him shrink from the smell. When she was bloated with fried food and too uncomfortable to move, she'd stretch out and Charlie would lay his head on her tummy, feeling the lump of Etta's knee or rump shift around under Meg's skin, like a scene from *Aliens*. His whiskers would scuff against her pale, tight belly, and she was happy to be pregnant.

Some days her body ached; she was pissed, frustrated, overwhelmed, and wanted to kill Charlie. Literally, she spent hours considering the best options for homicide. She settled on slow poisoning, believing, with a little planning, she could get away scot-free.

The last two weeks of the pregnancy were torture. She tried a host of old wives' tales meant to induce labor: spicy food that gave her the shits, long walks that made her feet throb and her back scream. She even put a willing Charlie in charge of regular nipple stimulation.

Ultimately, Etta took her sweet-ass time. She came six days past the due date. The delivery was average, which is to say it was painful, unreal, and felt a little like a blessing but only long after it was over. Meg wasn't interested in holding Etta, just wanted some space and rest. The day Meg and Charlie got home from the hospital, they swaddled Etta tight and used an empty drawer for a crib.

Meg had tried to be a perfect girlfriend for Charlie back then, grateful and loving, pleasant, not too demanding. There was no money for dates, no energy for it either. They spent those evenings exhaustedly taking turns with Etta, laughing about every face she made, discussing her cooing little vocalizations, and celebrating every tiny milestone. They were in a tough place financially, but they were in it together.

A few years later, Meg pregnant with Townes, they had married and moved into a ramshackle rental home, and Meg had molded her life to the needs of her family. It hadn't felt like a loss of self. With Townes feeding at her breast and Etta hugging her around the knees, she was happy to make herself whatever they needed, like it was why she'd been placed on the face of the planet. Nature gave her the impression this was her purpose, even if it had been foisted upon her. It had seemed right. She'd embraced it. What choice did she have?

For close to two decades of concentrated homemaking, she'd been a zealot of the worst type for antismoking, really unbearable. Sharing all the latest health statistics with unenthused smokers, asking strangers in restaurants to stub out their cigarettes or move farther from her delicate family.

"Don't you know about second-hand smoke?" she would say. "Not good for little lungs."

After things with Etta and the divorce, she started smoking again. *What the hell* was as elaborate as her reasoning ever got. Inexplicably it had given her strength, a direct connection to the tough, foolish teenager she'd been. Smoking tapped a rebellious reservoir that had been dormant while she raised her children. Through the old habit of sucking hot smoke into her lungs, she'd rediscovered a willingness to flip people off in traffic and to say, "Why don't you bend over and fuck right off?" to her supervisor when she didn't get the schedule she'd requested.

"I realize you are under a great deal of stress these days, Meg, but I can't abide that kind of language" had been the very businesslike reply from the old crone who doled out assignments.

"I can't abide your fat ass," Meg had happily replied. "Eat a salad once in a while. Seriously. Have you taken a good look at your ass lately? It's out of fucking control."

That had gotten her fired from the temp agency. You don't badmouth another woman's body, at least not to her face. It is a rule of workplace sisterhood that must be obeyed. Somehow, with a cigarette bobbing in her mouth as she stormed out of the building, it didn't seem too bad. She was almost able to convince herself it had been her intention to quit. She was proud of herself. She'd wanted to stand up to that bitch for ages. Besides, her cleaning service was cheap to start, lucrative to run, and a natural transition. Motherhood had afforded her a crash course in cleaning up other people's shit, and it was finally paying dividends.

As a teen she had preferred to use paper matches, the kind she'd get at joints where she was too young to drink legally. She admired the orderly rows of stiff chipboard sticks stapled in the colorful booklets with their fold-top flaps. She had collected them as she barhopped with a poor fake driver's license that fooled no one but still got her through the door.

As she huddled with her girlfriends in a bathroom stall during her lunch period, she'd make sure they saw the matchbook when she lit up.

As they smoked, Stacey would act unimpressed. The other girl, some freshman ankle biter, would stare wide-eyed like she'd been invited backstage after an Aerosmith concert. They'd suck down half a cigarette, hear someone coming, and throw what was left into the toilet, the cigarette making a small pop and shush sound as the hot cherry end broke the water's flat surface. They'd flush and flap their hands to wave the evidence from the air. Stacey and what's-her-face would stand on the toilet seat and try not to laugh so a nosy teacher wouldn't catch three pairs of feet under the edge of the stall.

Meg shakes her head, remembering how stupid she'd been. The need to be willfully foolish, to seem unconcerned and distant, had been an overwhelming hormonal imperative, the same kind of driving urge that had led her to Charlie.

Thankfully, Etta had been much smarter at the same age. Any reasonable weighing of the life of teenage Meg against the life of teenage Etta can only yield one conclusion: It should have been Meg who didn't live into her twenties. Not Etta. Etta deserved better. Meg had been reckless, danger seeking, and petty. Etta had been self-confident without being overly self-centered. She had a mind of her own, which could be, at times, a challenge. She was determined her opinions be heard, which translated into arguments where Meg's advice was concerned. But Meg and Etta had grown up in different times.

Meg strikes a wooden match on the side of a pasteboard box and watches the glob of red phosphorus flare and burn to black, whiffs that sharp smell she loves. She flips open her cigarettes, suspecting there's no health advantage to smoking organically grown tobacco, but she doesn't want to hear it. Maybe there are a few less chemicals filling the hollow places of her body, the place Etta and Townes had stowed away; then again, maybe not. Her insides should sound a smog alert, her internal geography as hazy as a morning on the streets of Beijing.

Smoking isn't as acceptable now as it was in her youth. She smokes mostly at home and in private. Truthfully, she's ashamed of herself. The strident, antismoking know-it-all is still a part of who she is. And God knows Townes wouldn't approve, critical little bastard he's become, so superior with his new, chaste life. Clearly, he took her speeches about health to heart. He always had a tendency to be sincere and serious to the point of mild depression. *He's a downer to be around.* Still, she's his mother and she loves him. Most days. *Shit, he's practically all I have left. And I did help make him who he is. I still have a responsibility to him.*

Her own life has become a pattern of work and returning home, too much TV, toxic cleaning supplies, takeout food, and cancer sticks. Nothing more. Except breakfasts with Townes and a periodic evening meal together. She sometimes daydreams about sex, about riffling through some strange man's pants.

Inevitably, the generic man she gropes and rides in her mind takes on the contours and taste of Charlie. He is, despite the cliché of teen pregnancy and the mundane workaday life they'd lived for so long, truly the love of her life. The sexual daydreams usually turn her mind to darker thoughts: the death of a child, and the way Etta's loss had changed Charlie, had shut him down like grinding out a cigarette. In some ways Etta's absence had killed the entire family. In her heart of hearts, Meg has to admit she mourned the failure of her marriage more than the loss of Etta, but that's the kind of thing you can't say out loud. People can be such judgmental prigs.

The mourning Gestapo would accuse her of being heartless. Hell, given the scale of the attention Etta's story garnered, someone was bound to accuse her of being involved in the disappearance, using her apparent callousness as evidence of foul play. *It's always the family.* She'd heard it said a hundred times by so-called experts on some cable news roundtable. It was something to say. But it had planted a seed in her mind, a notion that Townes was involved. She'd never said anything to any living person, though she had asked the Etta in her mind about it, tried to seek her advice. Etta was so level headed. But Etta had no insight she cared to share.

Meg's guilt over the minor, momentary disloyalty was part of why she had gone to the expense of making Townes his own space over the garage, rather than forcing him to get out of the house and find his way after high school. He had been so morose, his behavior bizarre. She'd considered forced counseling or even meds. But she let it go, unwilling to alienate her only child.

Also, there had been her constant and deep loneliness, her need to have some remnant of a family left intact.

Charlie had pulled away abruptly and completely. Even if Etta walked in the door today, it was probably too late for her to mend her life, to knit all the parts back into a unified whole. Even without the issue of Etta, Charlie might reject the old woman she had become. She felt very much at home in herself now and had doubts Charlie would like the person she really was.

She recalls their first tentative kisses, pressing into one another in the alley separating the coin laundry from the grocery store. The slick way their fat tongues had coiled and rubbed together like chubby lovers skinny-dipping. Her smile had threatened to ruin the moment, until the insistent, hot urgency returned. His mouth tasted of Juicy Fruit and hers of nicotine. The combined flavor would be one she grew to long for. Who knows, maybe he remembers it the same way. If their mouths met again, perhaps some sensory memory would reboot their relationship, send it back to the beginning; time travel via taste-dependent reminiscence.

She knocks a cigarette out of the hard pack and works it between her dry lips, like a horse with a carrot. She uses the match quickly and shakes it out before it can singe her fingers. The warm smoke coils into the back of her throat. The familiar rush hits her brain and tweaks her nervous system, sending a euphoric burst of electricity tickling down her spine. She coughs hard. She flicks ash into an overflowing ashtray and takes another drag. She turns her head and makes a little spit sound, picks a fleck of tobacco from the tip of her tongue, makes the spit sound again.

A few minutes later, she lights a new cigarette off of the butt of the old one. She eyes the back of her left wrist where the skin is thin and her blue veins show. She imagines getting a tattoo there where she can see it every day, Etta's name in a feathery script, and maybe a flower. She has no idea what flower had been Etta's favorite. *Isn't that a thing a mother should know?*

In the bathroom mirror she probes the thin skin around her tired eyes. No amount of makeup, miracle eye cream, or moisturizer makes any damn difference. It's the one thing she hates about smoking—it deepens the lines in her face, makes her complexion sallow, her skin leathery. *I need Spanx for my face.*

Her monochrome box-brown hair is in points on one side of her head, the roots showing gray. She smoothes it the best she can, feeling how brittle it's become, like a granny's. She needs a better conditioner. She needs to color her hair. She'd like to do it before she sees Charlie, before the memorial.

She brushes her teeth, splashes cold water on her face, leaning over the sink and letting the excess dribble off her nose before patting dry with a worn hand towel. She allows herself one girlish act of vanity: She puts on bright lipstick and blots it with a square of toilet tissue. As she walks away, a perfect red print of her mouth falls carelessly into the toilet, like a drunken, open-mouth kiss.

# PAIN AVOIDANCE THROUGH VIOLENCE

Newton moves to sit up and immediately wishes he hadn't.

"Shit," he hisses.

He scrubs the heels of his hands into his eye sockets; the pressure sprays electric pinpoints across his vision and gives his throbbing head some relief. He takes the synaptic starburst as an opportunity to make a wish: "Make my aching head go away." He pauses a beat, waiting for a positive result. *No such luck.* He blinks until his vision clears. He's in his own bedroom. *That's good.* An image of the previous night develops as slowly as a Polaroid.

"Oh, hell."

He's a fit guy, but fitness is relative, and though he'd given a beating rather than taken one last night, his body doesn't know the difference. He hurts everywhere. In his defense, the beers and cheap vodka he'd polished off aren't helping.

A few weeks earlier, he'd gotten an invitation from Etta's mother, Meg, to attend a memorial. He was happy to be included, surprised but happy. In the intervening span of time, memories of Etta sent him on a bad spiral. At first he'd allowed himself to wallow, dwelling on the things he'd lost: first Etta, next his leg and his good friend, Albert, in one violent moment, a moment as lost to him as his missing limb. The final stop on his tour of self-pity was to imagine the alternative future that would never be realized, one in which he'd saved Etta from whatever transpired: a pervert in a creeper van, a drunken driver who hid his mistake down some deep hole. Hypothetical-Etta had been grateful, fawning over him. He'd been too in love to leave town and never considered enlisting in the army. Alternate-reality-Newton attended college locally, found a lucrative career, married Etta, made several chubby babies, bought a little house, adopted a boxer puppy named Diesel, and attended enough PTA meetings to kill the average man.

As the days passed, his mood became progressively darker and slipped farther from his control. He was self-aware enough to see things were getting bad. He tried to buck up. He started sleeping more, working out, and drinking less. He contacted the Veterans Administration to get on his shrink's schedule. The bitch had taken a better gig. Newton was put on a waiting list, but he knew from experience if they said six weeks, it would take twelve. As the memorial approached, his tenuous grasp on self-control gave out.

The night before, he grabbed his running shoe and his new leg in preparation for a long hike. He dropped his shoe on the floor and shuffled his foot in. When he started to lace up, his shoestring broke. He stared at the sad, frayed bit of string tucked in his curled fingers and took it as empirical proof he was still crosswise with the universe.

He didn't believe in karma proper, so much as a loose notion that what goes around comes around, that people got what they deserved. He'd taken about six straight years' worth of shit and figured he was due for a change in his luck. Maybe he'd been a shallow asshole in high school. But the hand he'd been dealt was overkill. If the universe planned to teach him a lesson, it had overshot the mark because he felt like more of an asshole than ever.

"Goddamn it," he said very soberly, letting the busted shoestring fall to the floor. It was the last sober thing he would do the rest of the evening.

He dialed his *Fear* album onto his iPod and plugged it into its station. He turned it way up. The singer barked out a call for war and Newton screamed along, bent the cap off the first of several beers. He sat in the living room, lights low, letting the angry music work on him as he replaced the lace in his shoe.

Listening to violent metal, punk, or thrash was the way he and Albert had prepared to go out on patrol, the same way they'd prepared the morning of the explosion on the edge of Kandahar

Province. Newton had chosen the Bad Brains; Albert's go-to was always Metallica. From the moment he started blasting the music the previous night, violence had been inevitable. He knew it, and he couldn't have cared any less.

Sometime between his second and third beers, his phone rang.

"What?" he yelled over the music.

"I think your music is kind of loud." The voice was barely audible. He knew who it was. The meek little man who loved to wear pastel cardigans and house shoes around the complex, his wispy comb-over floating above his head like the sun-bleached grass on a coastal dune. Newton didn't know his name, never attempted to find out. To Newton, he was a pathetic, weak loser and not worth Newton's time. "I . . . I . . . I think your music is a little on the loud side," he tried again.

"I know," Newton replied with a nasty grin. The little man was scared of him. Newton had watched him shy away when passing on the sidewalk. Newton was in the mood to take advantage of that fear. He took a perverse pleasure from dominating someone weaker; he always had. There was no answer through the earpiece other than the sound of a wet mouth working around an unformed reply. "Come turn it down if it bothers you so much," Newton added harshly. He jabbed the phone extra hard and reached over to scroll the music fractionally louder.

Newton props another pillow between his shoulders and the headboard. The gushing pressure in his temples matches the beat of his heart. He lets his bottom jaw hang open, working it side to side and listening to the grinding and popping. He's sore as shit and ashamed of himself. *Anger flares and issues of impulse control,* his psychiatrist had warned him to expect it, *a natural result of PTSD.* Newton had really liked her, felt they had a bond, but she had left him. Not before he'd been prescribed pills that were meant to keep his moods level. After a month the meds had run out and the rush of offers to hire a one-legged college dropout never came. He didn't refill his prescription, not enough money. Besides, the pills made him feel dead inside, hollow, strange, as if he were being operated from a great distance like a military drone.

"Shit, shit, shit," he says as he knocks his head back against the pillows. It hurts, so he stops.

While it's true he'd won the state wrestling title his junior year of high school, he never thought of himself as a badass. Not really. He'd spent time around too many formidable men. Though he'd often acted like one, he'd known it was a kind of bluff. Sure, he'd been a natural athlete, but generally hadn't cared enough about winning. Frankly, the wrestling title had been a fluke. After Etta's vanishing act, he'd picked up and moved to Colorado, where his dad had started a new, younger, cuter, and blonder family. There, Newton avoided organized sports and took up solitary rock climbing. His hands, forearms, and shoulders gained lean, hard muscle. A couple of years of ROTC at the University of Colorado, Boulder, had led to dropping out of school and enlisting. He was ready for deployment in time to be a part of Obama's surge into Afghanistan. He'd pretended joining up was due to patriotism, knowing full well it was a general lack of direction and dwindling financial options that drew him into the war. Plus a childish desire to shoot loud weapons at bad guys. Basic training, rapid deployment, and, they told him later, a roadside bomb that took his right leg above the knee had landed him back in Illinois, where his mother could keep an eye on him while he recovered.

He knew he wasn't the most dangerous twenty-something you could run across in a suburban bar. However, he was crazy strong for his size, fast, trained, and he was perfectly content to fuck someone up. The more pain the better; the more he hurt others, the more they understood how he felt. It was a basic psychological equation.

He surveys the path between the bedroom door and his bed. Among the discarded clothes, government-issued appendage, and wad of bloody bar napkins he sees an unopened bottle of beer. He wants the room-temperature beer in his dry mouth. He leans ever so slightly forward, testing the idea of reaching for the bottle. The effort causes his forehead to throb and his guts to churn. He belches, decides his thirst can wait, and lets his head sink back into his pillow.

His newest leg is something special and he regrets treating it carelessly. The army taught him two things: to hate authority figures because they are bent on abusing whatever limited power they possess, and the importance of maintaining your gear. His leg is a fine piece of machinery and deserves better. He'd failed to turn off its brain or snap on its magnetized battery charger. His doctors swore it could go for four full days without a charge, but he had his doubts and didn't want to put it to the test. The army had told him a lot of things that turned out to be dubious at best.

He considers shifting onto the floor and giving the leg a charge before the day gets rolling. Instead, he stretches his neck back and looks at the tea-colored evidence of water damage along the ceiling. He touches his fingers to his cheek, feels the crusty cut. It's tender, bruised. He's lonely and wishes for someone to care for him, for anyone to give a good goddamn about what he's going through. He thinks of Mara and then of Etta. He will never have either of them.

He gives his head a cautious shake of disapproval. The night before, when he got depressed, going out and finding someone to tussle with had made a lot of sense. Now, however, he sees the fault in his drunken reasoning.

He'd listened to the aggressive, gritty vocals of Lee Ving, thinking of Albert and their last patrol, honing his agitation into a razor edge. As "I Love Livin' in the City" finished, he scooped up his keys and wallet, shrugged on his winter coat, and shambled out the door. His new, high-tech knee moved smoothly at a steady walk or run, but at a slow saunter it gave him a slight hitch in his gait that looked to the casual observer like intentional swagger. He knew it and he liked it. He wasn't above posturing for effect.

Despite the low temperature, he'd worn cargo shorts. It would show off his aluminum and carbon-fiber prosthetic. It had a gyroscope and microchip stored in a calf-shaped housing and it was nearly as versatile as his flesh leg. Except it was hard to give someone a good kick with. He suspected a knee to the head with the hard angular hinge would be tremendously effective. He intended to find out.

Through years of observation, he'd learned if he hung out at a bar long enough, someone would say something he could pretend to be offended by. The music was still blaring, his iPod set to repeat, as he left the apartment. *Let that sweater-wearing asshole complain.*

Newton was only five-eight, built square. He thought of himself as compact. When he sat on the stool at Toony's Billiards, the toes of his shoes could just reach the brass foot rail that ran the length of the bar. He waited for his tumbler of vodka and tonic, watching the room in the mirrored back bar.

Toony's was a local hangout full of regulars: couples of all ages; clusters of men looking for women; clusters of women looking for men; lots of drinking, swearing, and the sound of pool balls being knocked around the felt tables. Once in a while money exchanged hands over a game won, a bet lost. There was no smoking, but there was a thick, sour smell, a mixture of body heat, talc, and sweet, spilled beer. Some asshole in a black biker vest was feeding quarters into the jukebox and seemed to have an inexplicable love for Willie Nelson. Newton did not love Willie Nelson.

When his drink came he nodded his thanks. "Keep 'em coming," he said. Then he swiveled halfway around, keeping his special right leg tucked next to the bar for the time being.

At a corner table he saw a tiny little thing he remembered from high school. She'd been a freshman the year he moved away, same age as Etta's weirdo little brother. Her name was something funny, maybe something with an N or an M. She'd barely grown an inch over the years, but he could see by her sweatshirt that she'd filled out nice. She was college age, but glancing at her and her friends, he could see she wasn't a college girl. Probably never left the neighborhood, took a job close by, maybe attended a few classes at the community college over in Naperville. She was definitely a townie. He liked that. He'd had enough of college girls in Boulder: too much work, placed too much stock in conversation, and always valued their own opinions' over his, even if it was on a subject he knew something about.

The cute girl caught him staring, met his gaze briefly, looked away quickly, careful not to encourage him. She'd made a split-second assessment and found him lacking. There had been no light of recognition in her gaze. She didn't remember him, didn't know he had been the boyfriend of the infamous Vanishing Etta. This was at once a relief and a disappointment. He hated to be looked on with pity, but he would happily use sympathy to get into some hottie's too-tight jeans.

He traded the empty glass for a full one and watched a group of tall, bulky boys chalk their cues and tell bad jokes too loudly while playing an unskilled game of eight ball. One of the largest and least skilled wore a cap with the flat bill cocked left of center. The kid kept missing his shots and laughing too much about it. The girl from high school, Mara was her name, kept her eyes on the kid and was laughing when he laughed, whispering with her girlfriends.

By the time Newton finished his third drink, he wanted to smack the cap off the muscle-bound gym rat. Mara was a cutie. She had a sweet face. She was short, short enough that Newton would be plenty tall next to her. It was perfect. *What is it with tiny girls always going for the tallest guys they can find?* He guzzled another tumbler of vodka and tonic, feeling nothing but the cold against his teeth.

He watched Crooked Cap miss the cue ball, leaving a blue mark on the green felt, rubbing it with his fingers to check for a tear and then laughing good-naturedly.

"Ha, ha, ha," Newton yelled loud enough to get the attention of half the bar. When he felt eyes on him, he smiled a feral smile, no humor in it. Crooked Cap and one of his buddies with a sleeve of bad tribal tattoos gave Newton a glare they thought was hard.

"What?" he called over.

He hung his compound leg out so it would be easier to ridicule. They turned their shoulders to him, their blocky profiles talked in a hush, glancing his way a few times, their eyes darting down to his metal leg. They pounded one another on the back and returned to the game, laughing like entitled frat boys.

They weren't much different than he had been: alpha males in the microcosm of high school popularity, drinking beer in the park and trying to get by with as little hassle as possible. They looked like they had ridden that straight into college, still hanging with the same guys and in the same places.

"Oh. What a cute couple you boys make," Newton called loudly, then cupped his hands into a megaphone, "You two going to get a room after this? Does winner get top or bottom?" The boys' v-shaped backs tensed, but they didn't turn to take the bait. Not yet.

He worked on them for half an hour. Heckling their skills, laughing when they missed a shot. He got progressively louder, the insults more frequent. None of it earned a response. That pissed him off.

When the bartender delivered the fifth drink, he set it on a fresh napkin, leaned forward, and said, "This is the last one, man. After this you need to take a break. And calm down with the bullshit or I'll ask you to leave." Newton nodded his understanding.

It was time to get the show on the road. He downed the drink, keeping one eye on the boys while they racked the balls for a new game. He took a detour to strut past Mara on his way to Crooked Cap's game. When he arrived at the pool table, he slipped a fiver from his pocket and slapped it on the rail.

"I bet you miss the cue ball," he said. He intentionally spoke slowly to give the impression he was more intoxicated than he felt, to lull them into thinking he was physically slow.

Tribal Tattoo was only a few feet away; the cue he held looked small wrapped in his thick mitts. "We're just playing a friendly game here." He said it like a threat. He stepped forward, picked up the five-dollar bill, and returned it by smacking it against Newton's chest. It stung. Newton's hands came up to snatch the bill before it could float to the worn floor. The two gym jockeys from the other side of the pool table stepped forward into the light, adding their slab chests to the conversation, their heads blocked by the stained-glass billiard lamp.

"Whoa," Newton said. "No need to get excited."

He calmly placed the five-dollar bill on the pool table, took the time to smooth it flat. The cash looked gray against the saturated green of the felt. He placed his hands on Tribal Tattoo's shoulders, leaned in real close. Tribal Tattoo was so tall Newton was forced to tip his face up, stand tiptoe with his flesh foot, his calf balled like a fist. His prosthetic foot couldn't make that particular movement.

In that moment, he was angry beyond reason. He'd found a way to blame those boys for all his hardship, all his loss. They were the reason his father left his mother; they had taken Etta; they'd built the bomb and buried it where he and Albert would drive over it. They were the gatekeepers who wouldn't give him a job.

Newton scratches what's left of his hairy thigh and turns to sit on the side of his bed, his solitary left foot dangling above the floor. He doesn't want to replay the whole thing. But he does want to understand that moment: his arms stretched up on the kid's shoulders, "Pancho and Lefty" playing on the jukebox, and the pale flash of Mara turning her gaze in his direction on the edge of his vision. He had never even considered bowing out, leaving gracefully. Now, sitting on a lump of crumpled bedspread, daylight building in his disaster of a room, illuminating his wreck of a life, he's concerned that he couldn't have stopped if he'd wanted to.

With his fingers curled over Tribal Tattoo's shoulders, he had pressed up into that broad, handsome face until their noses were almost touching. Newton knew his breath would offend so he exhaled a lungful.

"Sorry about all this. I think I'm a little messed up," he said with an intentional slur and sloppy laugh.

The kid's shoulders dropped their hunch. He looked to his friends, who laughed with him.

"Pocket-sized little fella," one of the beefy kids said from across the pool table.

"He's fun-sized," added his headless companion.

"What a cutie," Tribal Tattoo said and put his hand out to rough Newton's hair. Newton let him do it. "You're funny," he added.

"Yeah," Newton agreed. "I'm a riot."

"Leave him be. Can't you see he's on his last leg? He's got one foot in the grave," Crooked Cap's voice contributed. It was another in a string of insipid jokes he'd been making all evening. This one was different. It was only mild ridicule, but it was projected loud enough for the surrounding audience. Not too harsh a comment for public consumption, but with a dangerous edge. It was a locker room challenge, the kind of first-stage threat Newton knew from the barracks. They thought he was beaten and they wanted to tamp him down. *They don't know who they're fuckin' with.*

Newton let his hands fall to his sides, let his sharp teeth show. He leaned back just a smidgen and drove his forehead into Tribal Tattoo's face; he missed his nose but caved his mouth right in. The kid dropped like a sack of dirty laundry.

The rest was a blur. Newton was on Crooked Cap before Tattoo hit the ground and shoved him hard, making him drop his pool cue. The kid snapped back in Newton's direction, throwing a slow, sloppy roundhouse with everything he had.

Newton ducked and put his fists to work. When they connected they hit the kid's skull sharp and hard and from every direction at once, splitting the meaty brow and sending a sheet of blood into his left eye, bending his nose over to touch his cheek and putting a rip where his right ear met his square jaw. In the slow-mo stillness, the sound that accompanied the action was the hollow splat of a cantaloupe dropped on a sidewalk.

The ridiculous cap was knocked straight for a moment. Newton noticed what an improvement it was before it fell in the kid's face. The kid knocked the cap back up, and Newton chopped his clavicle with the edge of his hand, like swinging an axe. The bone made a satisfying snap. Newton drew back with the intention of caving in the ring of cartilage that formed Crooked Cap's trachea, knew it might kill him, and instead gave him a stiff palm jab to the sternum, tearing muscle and splitting the flat bone. The kid stumbled, windmilling for balance, exposing his torso.

Newton was in control. It felt good to be driving the kid back, his new leg moving smoothly under him, his feet light, gaining power from his stance with each concussive blow. He imagined his composite leg gave him an advantage, more unyielding power and cold, hard strength. He came around fast on the kid's ribs, pummeling the air from him, smacking his gooey organs together over and over until the meathead collapsed on his side and vomited a rancid spray of beer and half-digested hot wings. As Newton straightened, drawing deep, smooth breaths, he saw two things at once: one was Mara and her friends crowding forward, the other was one of the thick-chested pool players lifting a beer bottle by its neck.

Newton kicked the stupid fucking cap the rest of the way off the kid's head as he stepped over and moved around the pool table to dispatch his two friends. It had gone pretty much the same. The one connected hard with the bottle right along Newton's cheekbone. It really rang his bell. Rather than taking advantage, the kid stared at the bottle in his hand, stunned it hadn't shattered like a breakaway movie prop.

Newton blinked the tears from his eyes and kept driving, moving, ducking, and ramming his fists out until no one was left to punch. He was fortunate the space between the tables allowed him to face them one at a time. When it was over, the bartender appeared with a baseball bat to break things up. Newton stepped over bodies and avoided the puke before picking his fiver from the table and slipping it into his front pocket. "I win," he said.

He had a few terse words with the bartender, who claimed to have called the cops, though Newton assumed it was a lie. Most of the patrons lost interest and drifted back to their previous activities. No one would look him in the eye. On his way to the parking lot, Newton paused long enough to wrap his sore knuckles against Mara's table. He gave her a chin nod and a wink. She winced. He snagged a fistful of napkins to blot at some warm blood dribbling down his face. Before shoving the door open, he told the guy in the leather biker vest, "Willie Nelson sucks." The guy hadn't seemed interested in arguing the point.

Upon further reflection, Newton has to give himself credit. He had refrained from crumpling the kid's windpipe. He had shown a kind of restraint.

"Maybe I'm not a complete sociopath after all," he says to his dead best friend, Albert.

Albert laughs the way he always does at times like this and says, "Or maybe you decided killing someone in a bar fight might ruin your chances with Mara."

"Either way," Newton replies.

He had shown a spark of maturity, and that seems like progress. He also has to admit he is a little proud of himself for taking out four larger men.

"Imagine what I could do if I used my powers for good," he says ruefully.

Albert keeps chuckling.

From the side of his bed, it's two hops to scoop up his leg from the floor. He drops his stump in and feels the suction hold the prosthetic in place. He bends for the warm beer and carries it with him. He wants to slip his good foot into his other shoe, even up his leg length, but he doesn't see it anywhere.

He notices how cold the place is, and quiet. He figures he unplugged his music on the way to pass out.

He twists, taking one more scan for his missing shoe. It's his only pair and he'll have to find it before he goes to the memorial, if he decides to go at all. But first he needs to chew some aspirin and run warm water over his skull. He has another appointment to make before he decides about the memorial.

Hobbling to the bathroom, he thinks how little he misses his leg. He misses it. He also misses his friend, Albert, who'd been turned inside out by the same IED that took his leg, or so they told him. Mostly he misses Etta though, or the idea of her. Back in high school, Etta had been different from other girls. She'd seen something good in him, something no one gave him credit for. She'd made him a better person. But he'd lost all of that. Compared to the loss of Etta, he doesn't give a shit about the leg he left in Afghanistan. *Those Taliban fuckers can keep it for all I care.*

# DISPLACED RESCUE EFFORTS

Charlie turned forty-six the week before, and he feels bitter about it. *Late forties* is so much worse than *early forties*. Over the past few years, he'd managed to reverse many of the outward signs of his soft middle-agedness and the crushing loss of his baby girl. Since ending his marriage he'd slimmed down, uncovering the thick muscles of his chest and arms, built slowly and honestly through decades of manual labor. Though his hands weren't as strong as they once were, he'd been surprised how he retained most of his physique. He'd purchased clothes one size smaller and adopted a new hairstyle. With the combination of a full head of still-dark hair combed neatly, pointed sideburns, and his omnipresent jeans and work boots, it would be easy to mistake him for an aging bouncer at a rockabilly club. A look that is tinged only slightly nerdy by the Buddy Holly–style glasses he's taken to wearing. It's a look that puts him in the mix with every other male urban dweller he passes in the course of a day, and it echoes the kid he once was. It is a milder, mature variation of the Stray Cats–inspired look he sported in the mid-eighties.

Despite a program of healthier habits, there's no avoiding what sitting in a chilly car all night can do to his aging joints. He rolls his shoulder, shifts his ass around, rubs his eyes behind his glasses with the tips of his rough fingers and unscrews the cap on his bottled water. He takes a tiny sip, only enough to wet his whistle. He already needs to piss pretty badly.

He plunks the bottle on the dash and glances kitty-cornered at the gallery. The car's windows have fogged. He rubs a spot on the cold glass with the side of his fist. He spies through the hole to the half-illuminated storefront. It's early; still no sign of life. The cassette player snaps sharply as the Fapy Lafertin Quintet finishes their most recent tribute to Django Reinhardt. Charlie starts at the sound. The tape has been turning itself over for so long he's forgotten it was even on. He reaches up and turns the cassette player off. He loves gypsy jazz guitar more than the average guy, but even he has his limits.

Gallery Gauguin is owned by Professor Anthony Inch, a teaching artist and notorious misogynist. Inch came to Charlie's attention through an article in the *Sun-Times* about an unnamed victim of sexual assault.

At the time, Charlie was between jobs, had time on his hands, and had looked into it. Having failed to find any resolution to the heartbreak of Etta's disappearance, such situations felt like good places to direct his obsession. With a little research Charlie found that Inch was raised in Westmont, just miles away from where Etta was taken; his family still owned a home there. That was enough to give Charlie hope he was onto something.

These days, Inch lives above his gallery and studio in Pilsen. The word on the good professor is that he was forced out of a tenured position at Northwestern over an incident involving a young woman who accused Inch of drugging her, raping her, and holding her against her will for days.

Almost four years ago, after Inch had been fired, Charlie approached the custodian for the art building and got the official line: A student made unsubstantiated claims, the kid's parents were friends with the dean, it became politically too uncomfortable for Professor Inch to stay.

Charlie pulled his glasses off and cleaned them with the hem of his T-shirt. "Did you like Professor Inch?" he asked the custodian. "Good guy, I bet." He placed his glasses carefully back on his face and waited for the custodian to take the opening.

That slight prompt was enough for Charlie to get a less filtered version: The collective hive mind of the institution told that Inch was a prick to his peers, was especially hateful to adult women while being sickeningly attentive to a few pretty girls each semester. Inch had approached the sophomore, Olivia Wyman, in a bar adjacent to campus, slipped something into her drink, and drove her to a no-tell motel where he bound her to the bed with zip ties and a matrix of ropes. Not one person that Bill, the custodian, could think of was sad to see Inch go. The institutional community knew such situations could only hurt enrollment, so everyone kept mum. The university stood to lose tuition money if parents thought their precious darlings would be safer elsewhere. Even worse, the huge donations from alumni could decline with enough bad publicity. Sexual assault was something best handled as quietly as possible.

"Did you know Olivia?"

The custodian, who wore a neat zip-front coverall with a nametag sewn over his heart, spoke with a typical nasal Chicago accent, full of flat vowels and shushing *s* sounds. He could have been a character in the *SNL* Superfans skits from back in the day, except he didn't sport a Ditka-style mustache or a prominent sausage-and-beer gut. "No. Not really. The students don't talk to the facilities staff. Mostly ignore us. The one time I spoke to her, it was because another student left a lock on Olivia's locker. It happens all the time. I had to cut it off. She was polite, almost timid, you know, kind of mousy. I liked her. I can tell you, if Professor Inch did what they say, he deserved a lot worse than being fired. He got off with a slap on the wrist."

"So you remember the details pretty good?"

"Sure. It's all anyone talked about for weeks. I mean the professors got most of their information from students who had stories about Inch. They'd seen him at parties or at the bar the night he left with Olivia. It's unprofessional as hell the way they gossip. People are people and they love their drama. You know what I mean. And look at me. I'm really one to talk, right? Listen to me go on. You know?"

"Yeah. I know." Charlie could see Bill was getting self-conscious, about to clam up. He pushed his glasses up his nose and asked one more question. "You don't happen to remember the name of the motel where the girl was taken?"

A couple of weeks later, Charlie parked at a rundown and understaffed motor court motel on Chicago's partially gentrified historic Sin Strip. The *Yes! Yes! Motel* was a survivor of a past era, built during the heyday of America's car culture. It had served as a rest stop for paneled station wagons jammed with families traveling the country. Starting in the early seventies and on into the eighties, it had become a place for addicts and prostitutes to hole up for a few hours or a few days. In the nineties many similar places shut down; the land sold for huge amounts to developers looking to put up condos. The *Yes! Yes!* didn't sell before the recession hit and investors took their money to other parts of the city. Since then, it had been left to rot. Despite its evident decline, with the recent closing of so many single-room occupancy hotels across Chicago, the old place was half-full. The parking spots were filled with taxi cabs, folks trying to catch some sleep between shifts someplace that wouldn't eat all their income.

In a closet-sized office, Charlie spoke through a round grill set in clouded security glass. The motel's shoddy records were kept in paper ledgers, and the Pakistani kid spoke only broken English. He asked repeatedly to see Charlie's picture ID. He wore a pale-yellow, short-sleeved shirt worn thin with age, buttoned crookedly, and sticking to his bird chest. What became clear from the awkward conversation was that Olivia had been drugged, abandoned there, and left to fend for herself. The Pakistani didn't remember how long the room had been paid for, or how long Olivia had been left alone before she was found. The thing he seemed certain of was that the photo of Anthony Inch was definitely the man who had checked into the room where the girl was found.

"How did he pay? Cash? Card?"

"Only cash. Only cash."

"And you called an ambulance for Olivia when you found her?" The face through the safety glass clearly didn't understand the question.

"Never mind. Is the room free? The same room?"

"No. No. Ten dollars an hour. Not free."

"The room is available? The same room."

"Yes."

Charlie paid to rent room seven for an hour. The place was drab, forlorn, and reeked of hopelessness: mismatched furniture, unwashed bedspread, stained sheets, black mold peppering the ceiling near the bathroom, a drop light with a pull chain hanging over a medicine cabinet with a cracked mirror, busted tiles with sharp edges around the toilet, and masking tape used as curtain tiebacks. It took only a few seconds to get a sense of the place, two minutes for a cursory search. The insides of the drawers were scrawled with hateful graffiti. The dorm-style refrigerator housed a shrunken orange covered in pale green mold, a sunken tomato turning black, and half a bottle of Mountain Dew, the blue variety. Around a spindle of the headboard he found a loose loop of rope wedged down behind the head of the mattress. Charlie pulled it loose and rubbed it between his fingers: black braided polypropylene. He closed the motel door behind him. In the car he searched his floorboard for a squeeze bottle of hand sanitizer.

It took Charlie a while to figure out which hospital Olivia had been taken to. He finally found the right place, asked around, and was able to show up the Saturday of the following week at a time when the nurse who had treated Olivia was on duty.

After telling his innocent lie, that he'd been hired by a law firm looking into the case, he found himself standing at a side door during a smoke break. After a brief preamble the nurse said, "The girl had severe anal tearing and some deep scratches on her hips and back, not to mention abrasions on her knees, wrists, and ankles. She was confused and ashamed and tried to refuse the rape kit, claiming it was her own damn fault and forbidding me to tell her father." The cigarette gasped as she drew on it between her pursed lips.

"Based on your experience with this kind of case," Charlie asked, cleaning his glasses to control the pace, "did it look like the product of consensual sex? I mean, is it possible?"

She blew out a burst of white smoke in her rush to respond. "No way. Not likely. Whatever happened, it was rough and it happened repeatedly, probably for days. I know a little about bondage. This was not that. She was a captive, not a willing submissive."

It was a situation Charlie wanted to see resolved, and it frustrated him the way it had dried up. That was basically as far as his inquiry had gone. At the time, the girl was old enough to make her own decisions, and she and her family were unwilling to press charges. Charlie managed to meet them at their lakefront property in their Gold Coast neighborhood. They wanted to know where Charlie lived and what high school he'd attended. Once Charlie answered, they refused to let him speak to Olivia, made her go upstairs. But he had seen her, seen that she looked a little like Etta. They were suspicious that Charlie was trying to rip them off, take advantage, and asked him to leave soon after they let him in. They were born-and-bred Northsiders and thought of people from anywhere else as uninvited guests. He'd seen it before.

According to Detective Ruther, Inch had an alibi that met the initial smell test, and with no more proof than the cops already had, Charlie was forced to abandon the trail. Besides, about that time Charlie got a new job rebuilding stone retaining walls in an exclusive old neighborhood. It was good work for good money and he needed the cash.

But Inch was on his radar; he was a predator and Charlie would make sure he got what he deserved. He had Inch's number: He was an evil user with a messiah complex who leveraged his position to hunt vulnerable, impressionable young women. Women like Etta had been when she was taken. Inch wanted to be adored as a genius, worshiped, and catered to. And he was willing to snatch and restrain the unwilling.

Charlie worked while the weather was nice and went on with his search for Etta between jobs. He kept Inch in the back of his mind, followed the man's activities. After his exit from Northwestern, the prof had been hired as head of the digital design department at a for-profit art school start-up in the West Loop, where, by all accounts, he had immediately started scoping out new conquests.

Charlie reaches up and twists the car on, turns the blower up, and watches the pale film covering the window slowly crawl away from the hot air. He checks his watch. The professor has a class to teach and will have to show before long.

Up the street, a bakery turns on its lights and flips its sign to OPEN. Two men with floury aprons hanging below their coats carry trays full of hot loaves to a waiting delivery van. He catches the yeasty smell of fresh bread, a sharp contrast to the aroma his car has taken on during the long night. The thought of food makes his stomach rumble. He'd have to catch some sleep, clean up, and eat something before heading to meet Meg. *But that's a long time from now.*

He misses Meg nearly as much as he misses Etta. He even misses Townes. Though, like many fathers and sons, he and Townes had managed to obscure their affection with mutual disappointment over unmet expectations. When Etta was gone, he'd felt alone in his misery, as if Townes and Meg didn't give a shit about Etta. Of course, Meg had cried and been miserable. They all had. But Meg seemed to let it go so easily, fell back into her daily routines, and Townes had never seemed capable of facing it at all. It felt to Charlie as if they'd forgotten about Etta. And he couldn't forgive that.

Marrying that beautiful woman was the best thing he had ever done, that and the kids who followed. Meg had been bright and wild when he laid his eyes on her that first time. She challenged him, made him a better version of himself.

She fashioned a family for him under difficult circumstances, took formless chaos, and made a life for all of them. He questioned his decision to sign the divorce papers. *Maybe the separation was enough. We could have continued living separately without ending the marriage.*

He'd worried he was holding her back. She wanted to move on. She'd signed the papers. It was left to him. While staying married was a kind of lie, to divorce was a lie of a different sort: It implied he'd fallen out of love, but the opposite was true; his feelings for Meg were as deep and resonant as ever. Maybe he loved Etta too much to share himself with Meg, at least until there was a resolution.

His eyes begin to burn. He pulls his glasses from his face and tosses them aside to rub his eyes properly. He checks his reflection in the mirror. With his glasses off, his eyes are small, dark holes surrounded by crinkled skin. His hair is comb tracks running back from his forehead in dark furrows like tilled earth. The skin under his chin is starting to sag. He imagines what it would look like to grow a beard. He dismisses the thought. *Concerns of personal appearance are for fathers who know their children are safe.*

He fishes for his glasses amid the pile of debris in his passenger seat. He finds them in his shoebox full of cassette tapes and fiddles with the arms for a few seconds before sliding them back on his face and glancing up the street to the corner bodega. The neighborhood is beginning to wake, and people are hunching into the store empty-handed, walking out with go cups steaming into the frosty air.

Charlie often witnesses the dawn and imagines he should consider himself fortunate, but he isn't that taken with it. Winter mornings in Chicago are nothing worth writing a poem about.

Mute, weak shadows slowly shrinking into the recesses of dank alleys and pooling black under cars along packed curbs as shades of gunmetal and dirty off-white snow begin to dominate the overcast cityscape. Nothing like the beautiful, bright blasts of clean light he remembers from his youth, peering out to see piles of soft, snowy fluff and crystalline icicles blanketing the pines and bending the cedars.

Now that the windows are clear of fog, he snaps the engine off and yawns fiercely. He's so tired his hair hurts. He scrubs at his chin whiskers, considers using his electric razor, mostly to wake himself and have something to do, but decides against it. He doesn't care. He has no one to impress. *Not until tonight at least.*

The past few years, Charlie has simplified his life considerably, keeping his living expenses low. He makes enough money in warm weather to last through the long winter with no pressing need to have a job lined up. It gives him time to focus on Etta, to pursue what thin leads he can, and to keep the pressure on Ruther.

It's hard to explain, but parenthood rewires your heart. It's a nonreversible process; once one passes through that veil, there's no going back. Charlie had never thought about being a father until he was about to become one. He was a kid trying to find his way, and the next thing he knew, his beautiful, ferocious Meg was pregnant.

Holding Etta in the delivery room moments after she was born, kissing her on her warm, fuzzy hair, something churned in his body. It's a cliché, but that doesn't make it less meaningful, that on that day, holding Etta like she weighed nothing at all, afraid she'd float out of his grasp, he whispered a promise to his baby girl: *I will protect you, always love you.* And he had meant it; that's the part that matters. He'd meant it like a vow etched on his ribs.

Seventeen years later, a piece of him, the best part of him, died when Etta disappeared. "Disappeared" is the only way to describe it, as if she dissolved into air and blew away in a winter storm. Six long years with a piece of him missing, a ragged gap where his child should be. Hopefully, and with a little luck, he'll find some scrap of evidence that will link Inch to Etta and his excruciating wait will be over. *Maybe I don't want to know.* It's a long shot, he knows, but it's the only play he has. And he must see it through, wherever it leads.

Charlie's bladder won't make it another minute. He grabs his overcoat from the passenger seat, opens his door, and steps into the street. The morning air hits him like a kick to the head and makes his glasses fog. He wipes his lenses with his gloved fingers. His teeth chatter. His eyes leak warm tears to keep the lids from freezing. The skin across his cheeks clenches tight. He pushes his glasses up his nose, pulls his coat closed, and stretches his back, walks stiffly around the car, over the packed snow, and onto the sidewalk. He's feeling every bit of his forty-six years. He huffs the sharp air in and out, making white clouds around his head like a locomotive. He knows the bodega will refuse to let him use the toilet, so he turns down an alley and finds a likely spot next to a dumpster.

His bladder empty and his legs functioning normally, he feels better, even jaunty. He's thinking a hot cup of coffee will put him over the top as he exits the alley and nearly smashes into Inch.

"Whoa. Excuse me, sorry," Charlie says reflexively. He tries to look down and away to hide his face. Though there's no rational reason for concealment, the professor will have no idea who he is, hadn't even looked in his direction when they were in the same room.

"Watch out next time," Inch calls over his shoulder as he keeps going.

Charlie steps onto the sidewalk, pops his collar, and matches Inch's pace, keeping back. Inch is tall and dressed like a Southside Bohemian: dark cords over Redwing boots; retro coat with faux-fur collar; the hood from his gray hoodie flipped out the back; long, hand-knitted scarf twisted artfully around several times; and a messenger bag made of interwoven bicycle inner tubes riding against his low back. He has a full beard threaded with silver, trimmed tight on his cheeks and pointy at the chin, like a cartoon devil.

After a few minutes picking his way through the least-snow-covered portions of the sidewalk, Inch takes a right on 18th. Charlie's boots squelch in the packed snow at the same rhythm as Inch's. In the middle of the block, Charlie finds a covered doorway to step into. From this vantage point, out of the wind, he watches Inch climb a stairway adorned with a mural of powerfully muscled Aztec men and brightly plumed birds. The tropical colors are garish against the city's dirty smear of winter slush.

The stairs dump Inch onto the L platform, which straddles the street like a covered bridge. There are other commuters rocking back and forth against the cold. The Pink Line train rattles in ten minutes later. Inch walks on, turns as the doors close, and looks directly at Charlie. Charlie throws him a wave and a smile.

"See you soon, asshole," Charlie says. The train picks up speed and Inch is whisked toward downtown. Charlie turns on his boots and heads back to his car.

In the trunk he finds his pry bar and tucks it up the sleeve of his coat. He cuts across the street between creeping cars. There's a narrow alley next to Gallery Gauguin with a decrepit iron gate. A hard kick and the lock pops. The gate knocks hard against the water-damaged brickwork. Charlie notes how badly the building needs tuck-pointing and sealing. He steps in and closes the gate most of the way, careful not to engage the spring-loaded lock, in case he needs to make a quick exit.

At the end of the alley, nearly free of snow, three cracked and crumbling steps lead down to a tiny sitting area, a table and a couple of chairs piled with dirty snow and dead houseplants. There's also a vintage pedestal sink with a cracked outer face, the bowl intact, full of snow and empty beer bottles. From the pathetic back garden he steps down to the basement door, slips the pry bar from his sleeve, and easily levers the door open.

The basement is low ceilings and cobwebs, storage boxes and wooden stands for the gallery above. After his eyes adjust, he picks a path around the debris and moves toward the street side of the building. On his way, he takes note of a hand-crank press in one corner, its bed used as a workstation for a dismantled fixed-gear bike.

The steps are forest green, the treads worn from use, the dull wood exposed and cupped from a million footfalls. He listens carefully for a long minute before moving to the first floor.

The door opens into the gallery, a big rectangular room with oversize, dirty-white track lighting, circa 1980. There's no artwork displayed. A ladder, a tub of wall patch, a battery-powered drill, and paint supplies are spread around the room. A number of bubble-wrapped frames lean against one wall.

It's different than when he'd been here the previous Friday to scout the place during the closing reception of a mixed media exhibition. The work on display looked to Charlie like fibrous hairballs hacked by an enormous feline and stuck to stretched canvases. That night it had been standing room only, mostly twenty-something art students with neck tattoos and face piercings, drinking box wine and dividing their time between criticizing the artwork and trying to hook up with one another.

Charlie checked his attitude. He knew Etta would be the same age as these kids. Wherever she was now, she might be covered in Hello Kitty tattoos and have oversized gauges pulling on her earlobes. It wasn't the fault of any of these kids that they were going on with their lives while Etta's was on hold, as far as Charlie knew.

The opening had been hot and bright as Charlie worked his way through the space. He found Inch holding court next to a table of cheese and grapes, his face red from too much wine. He was pawing two different girls, physically pulling them back into the conversation if they turned or looked away. Charlie edged his way back outside into the frigid night before Inch could see him.

That night Charlie hadn't noticed the wooden floors were in a horrible state, refinished two times too many, the planking disintegrating at the edges, exposing large gaps filled with grime. Now the boards creak as he quickly moves away from the large window at the front of the room. He stays near the wall and moves into the shadows at the back of the space.

Charlie waits again, listening. He knows the layout. There isn't much to it: a kitchen at the back, a bathroom, a room converted into storage, and a gallery office. The back door to the garden is blocked by a beautiful old wooden flat file, and a closed door leads to the top floor.

He twists the knob and mounts the stairs. These steps are new, the walls freshly painted, the handrail refinished. His footfalls are silent as he moves. He steps into an open, modernly appointed flat: one big room with high ceilings devoted to living room, dining, and new industrial kitchen. There are paintings, photos, prints, and sculptures sprinkled among the blend of vintage furniture and new high-design pieces. His eyes are drawn with morbid fascination to several stuffed rats among the books and ceramics. *Morbid taxidermy must be a thing among Chicago's avant-garde.* It's all arranged tastefully over a new hardwood floor. The windows are thermal panes, and the lighting is a track full of tiny halogen pucks, midcentury tension lamps, and a funky drum-style chandelier over the dining table. Past the kitchen there are two doors, one open and the other pulled shut.

Charlie listens at the closed door but can't hear a thing. He searches the other room, a large bathroom, very masculine, with dark tiles, sparse decor, and a large rain shower fixture the size and shape of a chrome Frisbee hanging from the ceiling in a corner of the room.

It takes Charlie time to decipher how the medicine cabinet opens. He finds normal things: Band-Aids, Rogaine, clippers, tweezers, toothbrush, and bottles of prescription meds. He snags three unmarked pill bottles.

He hesitates, concerned what he'll find behind the closed door. He imagines one of the girls from the reception will be strung out and trussed up. There's nothing to do but get in there and see for himself. He turns the knob and the door swings wide. Charlie stands in the doorway to Anthony Inch's bedroom. It's dark, with heavily curtained windows that absorb sound and block the sun, richly pigmented walls, and deep earth tones on the rumpled and twisted bedspread. The hall light at Charlie's back falls across the bed, and Charlie's stretched silhouette casts a shadow that points at the center of the empty bed.

A few minutes later, Charlie exits by the basement door, tugs it closed behind him. He slips up the narrow alley and crosses quickly to his car. He drops the pry bar in the trunk as he thumbs the first number on his speed dial.

"This is Ruther," the familiar voice says.

"I stopped by the place I told you about," Charlie says.

"So you went through with it. Did you find anything to tie Inch to Etta?"

Charlie tugs his keys from his pocket and jams them in the ignition, waits to start the car. He's hot with fear. "No. You were right. The place was clean. I saw some pill bottles with the prescription labels ripped off. Could be illegal." He says it in a way that sounds as pathetic as he feels for mentioning it.

After a pause Ruther says, "Sorry. I know you wanted to get the case moving."

"You said I wouldn't find anything. And I didn't. You were right. Again."

"I'm sorry I was right. I wish I'd been wrong."

"It's just I really thought this was it. I thought I was onto something." Charlie feels like a fraud.

"You had a hunch you had to run down. It didn't pan out. It doesn't mean you were wrong. I have a bad hunch every month. Shit, every week," Ruther says. Charlie doesn't respond. "Okay. You think you should turn yourself in for breaking and entering? Or was the door open when you got there?"

"It was standing wide open." Charlie lies for Ruther's benefit.

"I thought so," Ruther says.

Charlie ends the call.

He lets the side of his head rest against the window. *What a letdown.*

Before leaving Gallery Gauguin, Charlie had searched through Inch's closet, dresser, and bookcase. There was nothing incriminating. Charlie had expected to find zip ties and black braided polypropylene rope but hadn't found any. It made him doubt Inch was responsible for Olivia. He didn't trust Inch, didn't like him. But being a middle-aged man who dates twenty-year-olds doesn't make you a rapist or a criminal. Dating your students makes you an unethical creep, but not necessarily dangerous. Maybe Inch's alibi was good. Maybe the Pakistani kid had been wrong.

He slips back into the cold and walks the block for a cup of coffee. He trudges back, settles behind the wheel. Before he turns the ignition, his phone buzzes.

"Yeah?"

"It's Ruther again."

"Yeah."

"You know, if you took a walk around his place in Westmont, it couldn't hurt. If he's up to no good maybe he uses it as a base of operations. You know?" Ruther is humoring him. But it helps to think there's still legwork to do. It's the slimmest of possibilities, but he has to run down every lead.

"Yeah. I will. I'll do it my next free day. But not today. Thanks."

"Right," Ruther says. "I almost forgot about today. Meg sent me an invitation. Maybe I'll see you there."

Charlie clears a space for his coffee in the cup holder. The engine comes alive, the heater starts to blow, and he thrusts a cassette in his tape deck, twiddles the volume until an electric guitar rumbles from the speakers. As he aims his car into the narrow street, The Reverend Horton Heat begins to testify.

# QUALITY TIMES

In the shower, Townes's mind does what it is prone to do, drift from the current moment and begin to plan for things to come. Through meditation he's learned to label such distractions, recognize them for what they are, and try to focus on immediate sensations, like the wet slick of warm water sheeting down his flushed skin. He doesn't judge the natural tendency of his mind to plan and organize; he acknowledges it and lets it run its course, washing down the drain along with the sudsy water.

He's anxious about the cemetery, worried his father will show up, and excited about seeing him. Townes modulates his self-worth based on how his father reacts to him, how he feels he measures up to Charlie, how he assumes Charlie feels he measures up. It's an affliction of young maleness he recognizes as both natural and counterproductive. He wonders if Charlie has received the gift yet. The book is a basic introduction to Taoist thought, but rich and wise in its simple way. When he found it, it reminded Townes of his father.

On some endless car trip, Charlie had folded himself into the back seat with Townes while Meg and Etta sat up front, distracted with their own easy conversation. It had been a surprise to have his father's company. Townes still sees Charlie's battered fingers, sucked dry by brick mortar, splayed wide to hold the small book. The book was red cloth with a missing dust jacket, going pink along the cracked spine from resting too long in the sun. When Charlie cleared his throat and began to read, a section of yellowed pages shook loose and fluttered to the floorboard. Charlie tucked them back in their spot and began to read *Winnie the Pooh* to Townes. He read loud, his voice a forceful monotone grinding, projecting over the road noise. He'd stop from time to time to show the illustrations.

Over several days he read the entire book. That undivided attention from his father was the most concentrated time they'd ever shared. Townes's love of books likely grew out of that trip. When they reached the last page, Charlie left the tattered copy on a bunk at a KOA campground some place between Chicago and the Grand Canyon. "For another dad to read to his little boy," Charlie had explained.

As distant as he and Charlie have grown, Townes knows his dad's gentle demeanor and quiet ways influenced his own interest in Eastern thought. *The Tao of Pooh* might be good for his father, might help Charlie understand, give them common ground, a starting place. It could help Charlie see Townes with new eyes. Ideally the book would be a catalyst to change Charlie's perspective on Etta's disappearance. With a little nudge, Charlie might take the absence less personally. He might not make it his responsibility. That would leave space for other people in his life.

Townes thinks of reading Hoff's book again. Taoism is intuitive, less intellectual than the Indian flavors of Buddhism, which have a tendency toward hopelessness and pessimism. Taoism laughs at itself, something Townes hasn't felt like doing for ages.

*Distraction, distraction.* Townes labels his mind's meandering and turns his focus back to the present. Every week he picks an action to pay special attention to, a way of extending his meditative state, and this week it's washing his hair.

He feels the weight of the wet bottle in his grip, hears the snap of the hard cap as he thumbs it open, the thick soap sliding toward the opening and gathering, waiting to be forced into his waiting palm; the pearly sheen, the clean, sharp scent, the thickening lather dripping over his ear and muffling the ambient sound of the shower enclosure. This is what is happening at the moment, not the event he is being cajoled to attend by Meg's skilled application of maternal guilt. Not memories of things past. Regrets. Not a hypothetical reconciliation with his father; those are the things he has no control over.

*Who am I kidding?* Charlie will never understand Townes's approach to life, never understand meditation or Buddhism. The book is a weak attempt to bridge a gulf. Charlie is of a different generation, blue-collar. He believes anything can be achieved through the application of effort and common sense. Townes admires him for it, wishes he were more like his father. Townes, on the other hand, believes most effort is just pointless busywork meant to distract from the fundamental truth of existence: Happiness does not come from what one accumulates, accomplishes or does, but instead from the recognition that there is no controlling life. Through acceptance, one can become comfortable with the cycle of life and death, and perhaps of rebirth.

Happiness isn't the goal. The goal is something closer to contentment through complete, perfect loss of self. For a flash, Townes thinks of Etta in this context, as if her absence is not negative, but the positive result of a transcendent moment. He imagines she reached a better place, left this mundane, physical plane. *But that's stupid.*

Townes finishes showering and steps onto the warm floor, begins to dry his body. He lost focus during his hair washing. The mere threat of being out of his routine is throwing him off. He tries to view the distraction as a means of testing his concentration, deepening his practice. He wraps a towel around his stomach and clears the round mirror with a swipe of his hand.

People often tell him he looks like Charlie. Staring at his foggy reflection, he doesn't see it. The idea that he reminds people of his father is fine. He likes his father, even if his father doesn't reciprocate.

Once, when Townes was four or five, Charlie had taken Etta and him to a fast-food joint. Maybe Meg was having a night out. He can't remember the details. What he does remember is that Etta had gone to snag a booth while Townes stood with his father at the counter.

Townes, from the time he could crawl, sought camaraderie with his father. He tried to walk like him, wear the same boots, the same belt and work shirts. He wanted to learn about bricks and trowels and mortar. He waited happily at his father's side, mimicking his stance with only slightly more fidgeting.

The girl who'd taken their order slid an empty tray across the counter. A minute later she placed a pile of hot fries on it. The fries were at Townes's eye level; the scent washed into his face. He reached over, picked out a crispy one, brought it toward his mouth.

"The fuck you think you're doing!?" A gigantic face, red with rage, filled Townes's field of vision. A huge hand smacked the fry from Townes's grip. Townes watched the morsel sail at half speed across the room and skitter across the floor to rest next to the condiment station.

This is what Townes remembers: One second he was lifting a hot, glistening bite to his mouth, the salt crystals large and sharp under the pad of his finger, the next a man he'd never met was striking him and cussing him. Startled and confused, Townes backed away. Before the tears could pool in his eyes or the cry could leave his throat, Charlie stepped in front of him.

He said, "Don't you ever lay a hand on my child." He didn't yell. He didn't cuss. He didn't make idle threats or raise his hands. He was deadly calm.

Leaning around Charlie's hip, Townes saw the big man turn white as a sheet of butcher paper, saw the man apologize to Charlie.

"Not to me," Charlie said.

"Sorry. Sorry," the man said in Townes's general direction. He left without paying for his food.

"You want these fries?" the woman at the counter asked. "We're just going to dump them."

Charlie shook his head. "No, thanks. We'll just wait for our food."

Townes realized, as he stood there, he'd taken food from the angry man's order. He felt guilty for stealing, for causing problems, and he felt overwhelmed. He looked up to his father to apologize, the tears rolling now. Charlie pulled Townes close to him, kept one hand reassuringly on his head while they waited.

"It's okay," he said. "It's all okay."

In the bathroom mirror, Townes tries to give a look that would frighten a full-grown man, a look that would stop a dangerous man cold or warn someone off, a look that promises impending pain and assures an embarrassing defeat. The expression that bounces back is serious, even dark, but with no heat behind it. It's defiant, not dangerous. If he were being harsh, he'd rate it as juvenile and sulky, with a smidgen of potential nausea sprinkled in. He gives up glaring at himself.

The thing about Charlie is that he means what he says, and he only says what he means. That gives his intention weight, his voice steel, and his glare authority. There's never a question of his commitment to follow through.

For Townes, on the other hand, there is very little he can think of worth getting upset about. The only thing he has control over in this whole damn life is how he reacts to the world. Everything else is a crapshoot.

He shakes his head and takes out his razor to shave his baby face.

# THE LAST NORMAL DAY

Charlie's car drives him to Oak Park and he knows he should feel blessed as he wedges into a parking spot reasonably clear of snow and directly in front of his rental. Instead he feels emptied out with nothing left to give. He needs to shower, shave, and catch some sleep before heading farther west; he's worn down to his core, and the car has warmed up nicely, making his eyelids heavy. Despite the fact that he's low on fuel, he lets the car idle and just sits.

Several minutes later, his eyes snap open and focus on a woman he knows from the far end of the block. Lee, her name is. His fingers feel the drool at the corner of his mouth, confirmation that he'd drifted off for a few minutes. Lee is a widow whose husband passed on the previous winter. She's bundled up like an Arctic explorer in a fur-lined parka and is vigorously yanking her stubborn snow blower to life. He considers dashing down the block to give her a hand, but his body demands he stay put. He watches her make a quick adjustment to the choke knob and pump the red bulb to prime the engine. She jerks the cord, and a puff of black smoke bursts from the side of the machine. The sound of the chugging engine follows the action.

*I need to get moving.*

Instead of exiting the car, he digs into the pile in his passenger seat and comes out with a manila folder, Etta's name written along the top edge. It's a photocopy of the police report of Etta's case. After the leads dried up, Detective Ruther had supplied Charlie with everything. Charlie had combed through it a hundred times. He doesn't need to open it to know what it says.

Based on the compiled interviews with anyone who saw Etta on the day she went missing, his own memories, and information gleaned over the years, he thinks he knows what her last hours looked like: It was a Wednesday morning and eight inches of snow had fallen overnight on top of the foot of snow from the previous few days. Charlie, referred to as the victim's father, didn't see Etta that morning. He was up at 4:30 to shovel the drive and dig his old F-150 work truck out of a drift. He was on the road around 6:00 with a full thermos of coffee and a sack lunch. He left a new pot of coffee brewing on the counter for Meg.

He made his way slowly, snow whipping in the wind, plows clearing his way and salting the road ahead of him, to Hinsdale, where he was laying another fireplace in a new housing development. When he'd gotten the job he was thrilled; steady inside work through the winter was always the goal back then. A few months in, he was sick of laying the same bricks in the same patterns in basically the same house over and over every day. It was early 2006. The economy was still solid, but he knew plenty of guys who couldn't find work through the winter. He'd bid the job a little low, wasn't making a lot of money, but he was working. Charlie knew his alibi matched Meg's version of events and was confirmed by the other tradesmen who were on the job that day. Most of them had worked with Charlie over the years, seen him around, seemed like they wanted to help.

About the time Charlie made it to the job site, Meg was slurping down her first mug of coffee and rapping on Townes's door, pushing it open without waiting for a reply. Charlie had heard Meg state the mundane details repeatedly to police, to detectives, to reporters, and to their grief counselor. That morning, the curtains were still drawn in Townes's room, the lights still off, but Townes was up, sitting at his desk, his comforter worn around his bare shoulders like a quilted cape, his lean face lit by a blue light from his computer screen.

"Are you up?" she asked, standing within the rectangle of his doorway, as if seeking shelter from an approaching tornado.

"I'm up," he said, deep and hoarse. His voice had changed recently, and it was startling for Meg to hear the new lower tone booming from his scrawny torso. His room smelled of body odor and oily male hormones. She wanted to throw back the curtains and open the windows, but that would have to wait until spring, or at least a warm snap.

"Why aren't you dressed?" It was meant to be rhetorical, but Townes answered anyway. Townes hadn't mastered the subtler nuances of social interactions. There were times she worried about her son, questioned if he had a disorder like autism or Asperger's syndrome. They called it a spectrum disorder, and she suspected he had one foot on the spectrum. At least a toe. Maybe he was just a typical teenage boy, and she was blowing things out of proportion, worrying like a mother was prone to do.

"I'm checking for school closings," Townes explained. "I bet the schools are closed. Did you see all the snow?" He tapped and pecked and scrolled, not bothering to turn around and look at his mother, not bothering to say, *Good morning, Mom.*

Charlie remembers Townes had been having trouble getting back in the swing of things after Christmas break. School was not his favorite place. He was a good student, but he wasn't a people person, not like Etta. He'd been a beast to get moving, according to Meg. Charlie wouldn't know, but he'd noticed the daily tension had been putting extra strain on his wife.

"The schools are not closed. The streets are clear and you have to hurry. You need to take the bus. If schools didn't close Monday or Tuesday, they won't close today. Where do you think we are? St. Louis? This is Chicago. A little snow won't slow us down." She snapped on the overhead light as she entered the room, set her empty mug on his bookcase, and began straightening the sheets, pitching his pillows back on the bed.

Townes made his eyes small against the light and turned to his mother in a petulant snit, his voice breaking with a childish squeak. "Why can't I ride with Etta?"

"Because Etta is going to take the bus today too. Roads are slick."

"What? That's stupid. The roads are good enough for school but not good enough to drive on? What kind of logic is that?"

She turned to him, dragged the comforter off his torso, and left him sitting in his boxer shorts, arms hugging his smooth middle against the cold.

"Mom Logic," she replied. Unmoved by his indignation, she whipped the comforter over the mattress like a matador twirling a cape. "The very best kind of logic. Now get dressed quick or you'll miss the bus."

Meg left the room, grabbing her mug and pulling the door closed behind her. "Get dressed," she said again over her shoulder and stepped across the hall to the bathroom, where Etta was up early and using a flat iron on her hair. She had bought it with Christmas money. She hadn't gone to school with frizzy hair for nearly three weeks and seemed determined to never do so again.

Etta was dressed, her makeup on, applied tastefully, not too heavy like with so many girls her age. It was only excessive if one considered she was so pretty that she needed no makeup at all. She was tall, taller than Meg, with fewer curves. "Statuesque" is what Meg called her. She was the best kind of heartbreaker because she didn't yet realize how beautiful she was to men, didn't know the spell she cast, or by extension, the power it gave her to wield. She was dressed in an eggplant-colored sweater over a dark-gray flannel skirt that stopped just above the knee, worn over heavy winter tights. Meg was able to provide a photo of Etta in the same outfit, sitting in front of a pile of presents with a Christmas tree in the background. It is clipped to the file folder, along with all the notes and photos Charlie had added himself, but Charlie doesn't want to look at any of that now. Not yet. He is too beat. He will save it for later, maybe before the memorial.

Down the block, he watches the snow blower kick an angry arc into waiting yards; a cloud of white powder drifts back toward the sidewalk on the constant breeze coming off Lake Michigan. The widow Lee, undeterred by the threat of snow down her collar, trudges forward. She dips her chin deeper into the circle of her scarf and keeps shoving the snow blower ahead of her. Women, Charlie concludes, are much tougher than men, better prepared for hardship. He had seen a brightly colored headline on the front page of *USA Today* at the bodega. It read, *Men Three Times More Likely to Commit Suicide.* He believes it. Women like Lee are strong as a leather strap. They are survivors.

For a moment his respect for Lee's gumption turns to pity. He knows she had been married for many decades when her husband passed away. She has only one child, who lives overseas, a daughter who married a Greek. Now she's left to live out the end of her life with no one to share it with, alone. *Not so different from me, I guess.* He looks away from Lee's progress and back to the folder he holds.

Meg had related to Charlie how Etta had caught her mother's reflection in the mirror and turned toward her, her head still cocked to one side as the hot plates pinched a length of her luxuriant dark hair.

"What's up?" Etta asked brightly. When she was in a good mood, she was a delight. When she was in a foul mood, she could be truly scary. Meg was grateful at least one of her teens was in a good mood. She was fortunate really; they tended to alternate. While that meant someone was always being pissy, it also meant that they were rarely pissy at the same time. It was a benefit of mixed gender siblings. She often speculated that if she'd had two boys they would have killed one another, and if she'd had to cope with two teen daughters, Meg would have abandoned ship. The situation didn't stop her from feeling torn by the clashing wants of her family, but it was better than it might have been.

Etta made her eyes big, an expression meant to urge an answer from her mother. "What is up?" she said again, with more emphasis.

"Listen. The roads are slick and I want you to take the bus today. I know it's a pain. But I need you to do it. Okay? You got the car stuck yesterday. I trust your driving. It's really the other kids that scare me. I would feel better if you weren't on the road. Okay? Yes? You understand don't you?"

Etta balanced the iron on the back of the toilet tank and ran her fingers through her hair, assessing her reflection, leaning toward the mirror to pinch a crumb of mascara from the bottom lashes of her left eye. "Okay," she said. No argument. Then she dabbed another coat of concealer onto a barely perceptible blemish. Meg wanted to tell her the makeup was more noticeable than the tiny pimple, but she held her tongue. It was important to pick her battles.

"Thanks," Meg said and turned to leave, anxious to refill her mug and get more caffeine in her system. "Bus will be here soon. See you downstairs."

"Quick question, Mom?" This was a typical Etta move. She always had one more question or one more comment that forced Meg to come back and listen. It was annoying. It was selfish. Sometimes they would laugh about it; other times Meg would lose her shit. On that morning, Meg figured it was the price paid for Etta's previous acquiescence, probably the reason for it.

"Yes?"

"Have you thought about the question from the other day?" Etta's long fingers gathered containers of mascara, powder, blush, eye shadow, and eyeliner into a plastic box.

According to Meg, the conversation was about getting a kitten. Meg explained that a retired neighbor had rescued some strays from the cold. Etta had gone to see them. The first Charlie heard about Etta's request was after her disappearance. It was one of the ways Meg tried to insulate him from the stress of family life.

"No," Meg had answered that morning. "I haven't thought about it because we settled it. Your brother is allergic to pet dander and so the answer is, *No.*"

"But I," Etta began to argue. She swept a pair of silver earrings into one palm before turning to her mother, exasperated by the unfairness of it all, looking like the precocious toddler she'd once been. The file indicated the earrings looked like silver screw heads and that Etta must have left the house wearing them.

During grief counseling Charlie had learned Meg had cut Etta off during the conversation. "Don't even start. No time for discussion. Get ready to go. When you get a place of your own, you can get a cat. You can get a whole litter of kittens, and pay for their food, and change their box, and clean the fur off of every surface in your very own place. You can pay the vet bills and watch them claw your furniture to shreds. Until that time the answer is IN OH spells NO! No argument. Get ready to go."

Later, Meg would be upset about the exchange. She blamed herself for driving Etta away. Miserable that the conversation had turned heated, that she'd raised her voice, lost her cool. To Charlie, it sounded pretty tame and not worth the weight Meg gave it. He'd told her so under the guidance of Dr. Shirley, the counselor.

"She was just parenting. Putting her foot down. It was no big deal," Charlie said to Shirley.

"Not to me," Shirley said. "Tell your wife. Share your feelings with Meg."

Charlie felt foolish turning to repeat himself, but he did it. "You were just being a parent. Just doing the work of being the bad guy when you had to. It's no big deal. We all have our roles to play. And parenting isn't an easy one. Really. You loved Etta. She knew it. There was never any question about your love for Etta."

"I had to be firm, to put an end to the debate. She needed to hustle. The bus was coming soon," Meg explained to both Charlie and to Shirley, as if she needed to justify herself.

Back in the hall that morning, Meg had banged on Townes's door again. "Let's go, let's go. Don't forget to brush your teeth." Then she went down to the kitchen to finish making breakfast. The menu was instant oatmeal with dried fruit and brown sugar. The food was shoveled with no conversation. Both Etta and Townes were irritated. Minutes later, the kids trudged into the snow in time to wave down the bus. This series of events was confirmed independently through questioning of both Townes and Meg.

Lee the snow-clearing widow rumbles up the sidewalk, the auger blades scraping the uneven sidewalk where roots have heaved the cement sections into peaks and valleys. Charlie waves out the window as she passes, but she doesn't notice, despite the cloud belching out the back of his car. He watches her rounded shoulders shrink in the rearview as the sound of the blower diminishes with distance. *Looks like she's clearing the whole block.*

The police report had a write-up on the bus driver, Danny Ahearn, a retired Chicago cop who sported an overgrown, woolly beard like a member of *Duck Dynasty*. He had a habit of stroking it, like a blue-ribbon show dog. He confirmed that both Messenger kids were on the bus that morning. They sat separately. Etta talked with another girl, April Stein. Townes sat alone, his back against the side of the bus, his feet stuck out in the aisle and dripping melting snow. This was usual for them, to sit apart on the days they both took the bus. Etta had been driving to school only a few months, and Mr. Ahearn knew her fairly well.

After school that day it was much the same. He dropped both kids back at the corner next to their house, thirty yards from their front door. Everything seemed fine. He hadn't noticed anything out of the ordinary. No strangers on the street, no cars parked along the curb, and no vehicles tailing the bus. After asking around, it was concluded that Ahearn had been a good cop with a solid record. No reason to doubt him, other than his compulsive beard-stroking.

Charlie catches movement and glances to his rearview mirror. At the end of the block, the widow manhandles the machine around and leans over to crank the chute. Pivoting its mouth back toward the yards, she squeezes the throttle and engages the auger while heading back toward the place where she started, cutting a wider footpath into the snow as she returns.

The file doesn't say that April Stein had been a classmate of Etta's since kindergarten. But Charlie remembers. He knows they weren't close friends as teens, though they had been close in grade school. April had been to the house a dozen times back then, and Etta to April's house for a number of sleepovers. The file did hold April's opinion that they'd grown distant as they hit middle school, still liked each other, just different interests, different friends. They got along and often spoke in passing around the school. During her interview April cried, snot streaming over her top lip, too wrapped up in how Etta's disappearance affected her to be helpful. Her memories supported the bus driver's recollections. She couldn't remember what they spoke about on the bus. Nothing important: school gossip about teachers, stupid assignments, and mutual friends. How much they disliked the gym teacher, speculation about the sexuality of the band teacher. April mentioned Etta's boyfriend, Newton Parker. This fact was freely confirmed by anyone the police chose to ask.

Charlie had been asked and acknowledged it too. Charlie liked Newton, had a good impression of him, but mostly tried to keep his nose out of Etta's personal life. That had been easiest for both of them.

Etta had once asked Charlie his opinion of a boy she had a crush on in eighth grade. "He seems fine," he replied.

"Fine? What do you mean 'fine,' Dad? Huh? Why can't you just like my friends?"

It went on from there. Charlie had tried to find the right words to calm Etta, and Etta had gotten more upset, eventually locking herself in her room to post vague references to her sad life on social media. Since stepping into that emotional torrent, Charlie had tried to form no opinions whatsoever of Etta's social circle.

Meg had more difficulty letting Etta manage her own love life but had learned that giving Etta space and time was what worked best where these issues were concerned. Etta was smart about people, made good choices eventually.

Etta's school day was uneventful. She attended classes. She turned in her work. She seemed normal. Happy in some classes, bored in others. A Mr. Randall, her honors English instructor, related an exchange. He'd dismissed class and started to yawn. Etta was there loading her backpack. He'd said, "Oh, man, I need a nap."

Without missing a beat, Etta replied, "I just had one," apparently critiquing the liveliness of Mr. Randall's lecture. When he recounted the story, he'd seemed delighted by her ribbing. In other interviews given in the days after she disappeared, her teachers were upset and as helpful as they could be, which was not at all. No one supplied a likely culprit or mentioned suspicions or illicit activity on the part of the victim. All of her teachers checked out on paper and in person.

Outside, Lee passes by again, moving at a steady clip, the bottom half of her dark coat now white with snow, caked up like the spray texture on a ceiling. The engine rumbles loud and deep, and Charlie feels it deep in his chest as he draws a shuddering breath. The machine passes down the block and the vibrations subside.

The school counselor for female students whose last names start with the letters G through M was a young kid right out of college by the name of Darren Brown. He'd been working at North since the beginning of the school year and had only met with Etta once. He had no qualms about revealing every last detail of their conversation; however, it was largely pointless.

According to Mr. Brown, Etta was "unusual in the fact that she seemed to have no significant problems. She was socially well adjusted, a good student. According to her own judgment, she was happy at home, parents still married and generally supportive, one sibling, a younger brother, whom she liked but worried about. That's normal, even healthy, for an older sister to be concerned for a younger sibling." When prompted during her visit with Mr. Brown, Etta revealed Townes was being bullied and didn't know how to cope. Mr. Brown and Etta had mostly talked about applying to colleges. Deadlines were in mid-January and she seemed interested in applying wherever her boyfriend was going but was open to pursuing other schools. Seemed interested in seeing the world. Even mentioned traveling in Europe. Mr. Brown took that as a good sign. She wanted to study biology, maybe pursue veterinary medicine. Was worried because her parents weren't helpful on the college search front. She would be the first person in her family to go away to college. She claimed her parents ignored her when she tried to fill out forms in November so she could be considered for certain grants and scholarships. She felt more and more financial pressures, as the reality of college expenses loomed closer.

"But all very normal kinds of anxieties," Mr. Brown concluded. "She was bright and well spoken. She seemed to be managing."

The snow blower goes silent, and Charlie snaps out of his train of thought. He really does need to get going. He takes his glasses from his face, cleans the lenses with his gloved thumbs, his mind still elsewhere. At the end of that day, Etta's last day in Charlie's life, she walked on the bus with her backpack full of books and settled in to chat with April.

According to the bus driver, Etta and Townes stepped off the bus and moved toward the house as the bus pulled away. Townes told Ruther he reached the front door first and went in, kicked off his snowy boots, and headed straight to the kitchen to make a snack. He left the front door standing open, the storm door closed. When he found it still open on his way to his room, he assumed Etta had forgotten to close it when she came in.

"Close the door next time," he yelled up the stairs. Then he slammed the door and went to his room to fire up his PlayStation.

That was the last anyone, anyone in the family at least, had seen of his baby girl. No neighbors saw her that afternoon; no one saw her on the street.

It is hard to take.

Charlie can't come to terms with it and he doesn't think he should. Why should he feel comfortable with a completely unexplained disappearance? Why should he let it go? Why should he move on with his life? This is the seam that tore open and unraveled between Charlie and Meg, leaving only a raw feeling and a frayed edge.

His windshield has a light dusting of new snow settling on it. He puts his glasses on. When he opens the car door, he's shocked by the muffled silence. It pushes on him, the way the snow absorbs sound, giving the morning a forced calm, like the whole world is being smothered by a soft, white pillow.

The afternoon Etta left the bus, there had been piles of snow sucking up the sounds of her footsteps, maybe absorbing her cries for help as someone dragged her into a car, into a basement.

He jostles the things he carries so he can pull his windshield wipers out, leaving his car looking like it has insect feelers. This way the rubber won't freeze to the glass and rip when he tries to use them.

He steps up the sidewalk, stomps his boots, and works the key. Inside, Charlie sits on a bench by the door and drops his armful of crap onto the space beside him. He removes his boots, lets them *thunk* onto the sodden mat, lets his tired limbs hang loose and legs splay out, wrists upturned in his lap, head back against the wall. He's tempted to sleep right where he sits.

Bootsy, a longhaired calico and Charlie's roommate, appears and begins weaving a figure eight around Charlie's ankles, rubbing her face on his pants in an act of greeting and possessiveness. When this gets no response, Bootsy meows loudly and leaps onto Charlie's lap, begins painfully kneading at Charlie's crotch.

"Okay, okay," Charlie says. He roughs Bootsy's head and scratches her scruff. Bootsy was one of five kittens of a local bookshop cat. The momma cat he didn't know, nor did he frequent the dusty little store. But it was next to his favorite record store, and he had watched the fluffy orange-and-white shop cat sunning itself in the front window for years, had watched as she got larger and larger with her litter. One day after shopping next door he dropped in and asked about the kittens. He left with Bootsy in his coat pocket and an old George Clinton album under his arm. He thought, in a moment of defiant confidence, that when he found Etta, she would be happy to know he had a cat she could come visit.

The familiar feeling, that he has all the pieces in front of him, all the information he needs to lead him to Etta, takes hold. Maybe he's too close. The perspective to see properly requires distance. Bootsy butts Charlie's palm and begins to purr.

"Okay," he says again. "Let's quit sitting around."

He sits a few moments longer, his body still not persuaded to go. Shifting his dry eyes in their sockets, he sees a small package and some mail on the floor inside the door. He lets Bootsy ride his shoulder as he gathers his mail and riffles through it on his way down his shotgun hall into the kitchen. It's mostly junk mail and bills. Bootsy jumps off Charlie's back, lands lightly, and trots along behind him.

Charlie pauses over the package, his address in a familiar scrawl of blue pen. He thinks it might be from Etta, communication arriving on the anniversary of her disappearance, but it's not her writing, too masculine. Maybe it's something he sent himself, but he knows that's not right either. Close. But not right. Eventually he recognizes it as Townes's hand. He wonders on the genetics of handwriting as he tears into the brown paper.

It's a book called *The Tao of Pooh* by Benjamin Hoff. There's no note. Charlie turns it over in his hand, as if it will reveal its meaning with closer scrutiny. He flips through the book, catching glimpses of vaguely familiar black etchings. He wonders if he'd read this book before, a lifetime ago, when the kids were young. He pauses over a passage somewhere in the center of the book:

Why should we live with such hurry and waste of life? We are determined to be starved before we are hungry. Men say that a stitch in time saves nine, and so they take a thousand stitches today to save nine tomorrow.

The meaning isn't clear, so he searches for more information. The sentence that precedes the passage attributes the quote to Henry David Thoreau. He knows the name, but that's about it. Charlie has never had time for fiction. Townes is the reader in the family.

Townes is trying to tell him something, to reach out in some way. Charlie's too exhausted to understand, no concentration left. He'll have to remember to thank his son at the memorial, talk to him about the book, ask what it means, what it's for.

He loves his son, but Townes has never been easy. He makes things harder than they need to be, complicates them. Charlie would love to sit and have a beer with his son, catch up like men. Maybe split a cord of wood, or fix Meg's busted snow blower together, something not too talky, something to do with hands and grease and tools, an experience they can share, a project.

After paging through the book a second more, he drops it on the table to join the general landslide of neglected bills and seasonal catalogs. The messy table reminds him of his messy bed. To sleep in his bed would require cleaning, and he doesn't think he can manage it. He finds the couch instead, lets Bootsy settle in the crook of his arm, purring at the attention. He takes off his glasses, lets them fall on the floor next to the couch. He closes his eyes and sleeps like the dead.

# A MEAL SHARED

Meg hears her son stomp up the back steps and walk through the mudroom into the kitchen. She has her back to him, pouring coffee from the glass pot of the drip coffee maker.

"So, how'd you sleep?" she asks without turning. This is always the first thing she asks. It's tradition.

"Fine," is his expected reply.

She hears him slip his bag from his shoulder and hang it over the back of his chair, following it with his long coat.

Meg slides into her chair at the small kitchen table. Townes takes his place across from her. She brings the black coffee to her face and slurps a little off the top, nestles the mug between her hands.

"Well, let's get some food in you," she says, nodding to the half grapefruit and glass of unsweetened almond milk she's already set at Townes's place.

"Thank you," Townes says.

Meg watches him take a teaspoon and scrape out a section of citrus. She has, like always, cut the grapefruit apart for him. She doesn't know how he can eat a cold breakfast on a winter morning. She's said as much many times. She sips at her coffee to prevent herself from repeating the comment. When she exhales, she can smell cigarette smoke on her own breath.

Townes glances at her. The flare of his nostrils tells her he smells the cigarettes too. His eyes tell her he wants to scold her. He knows as well as she does that there's no use. Their relationship is formed of the topics they avoid and the safer, innocuous things they choose to say. It isn't the close relationship she might hope for, but there's affection in it.

He says, "Good grapefruit. Aren't you eating?" She never eats until he's gone, and he knows it, but he asks anyway.

"No. I have to keep my girlish figure," she replies, as always.

"Okay."

Meg watches her son work his way around the grapefruit. His hands look longer than Charlie's, thinner, but there's a way his fingers walk as they turn the citrus, the prominent crescent of white at his nail bed, the curve of his fingers around the spoon, the tone of skin across the back of his lean hand as it flexes to reveal knuckles, bones, and veins that echo Charlie's strong hands. Of course, Charlie would never wear a red beaded bracelet like Townes has on his wrist. She thinks it's religious, like an Eastern rosary, but she's never asked him.

She gets the urge to dash away and find a photo of Charlie at that age, hold it up next to her son. She doesn't know where to find such an image, so she sits, fighting the need to hack loudly to clear the smoker's phlegm from her throat.

A spark of regret flares in her mind: There are no good photos of Charlie and her together. Part of it is logistical. It was always Charlie snapping pictures while she forced her children to bunch up and act like they were happy together, with her taking her place once they had met her standards. There are grocery bags full of photos of the kids doing fun things like building snowmen, holding their noses in the primate house at the Brookfield Zoo, walking along the lakeshore, and of course, opening Christmas presents under the tree. Meg is often there in these images too. Charlie is implied, the eye behind the camera, the one who chooses what to frame. In this role, he was the family historian. He caught the moments that defined the family he wanted. He was rarely the subject of a snapshot and never next to Meg. They'd never even had a wedding photo taken.

Maybe his absence was intentional. Perhaps he had always wanted out, even when the kids were small. Maybe his mother had been right; Meg had robbed Charlie of his chance at a better life.

In truth Charlie liked mechanical things, liked to make things work. It was as simple as that. He loved the combination of cold science and chemical magic that a camera provided.

Or was it more? Was it that they weren't ever a happy couple? Their courtship had been hot and brief, cut short by her pregnancy. Was the lack of couple snapshots proof that when Charlie stood with his arm around her, all the joy drained from his face, and knowing this, he couldn't risk being recorded?

She knows this isn't true; they had been in love; he had been her man. She may have been lost in parenthood, but so had he. They had been a real couple, happy to be lost as long as it was together. As real and contented as any couple she'd ever known, as happy as the toothy couples in wedding catalogs. They had weathered nearly two decades of minor hardships. Only something as enormous as the ordeal of Etta's loss could have knocked them off course.

It isn't like Meg to think these thoughts. Especially when she isn't working. She often has imaginary conversations as she cleans. Maybe it's a sign of her age, the way her mind drifts. But it's probably just the occasion. She's feeling morose and wistful.

She rubs her rough hands on her face. Cleaning products and the dry heat of the house in winter are bad for the skin.

"Oh, Townes," she says, reaching into the pocket of her robe. "Can you call Newton and remind him about the memorial?"

"Why?"

"He was a part of your sister's life."

Townes's head is over the grapefruit, and he looks at her with the tops of his eyes, unconvinced.

She tries to explain again. "It's a ceremony, like a wedding, to acknowledge the loss of Etta, a chance for people to share their memories. Lean on one another. A time to regroup and move on." She slides a slip of paper across the tabletop.

"You know how I feel about this," he reminds her.

"I do."

She watches him battle to control himself, and fail. "It's a naked pretense," he says, his voice loud. "You can't memorialize someone who may be alive. You can't honor Etta's memory if Etta is still walking around out there."

"Sure you can."

"No, you can't."

"She's gone, Townes."

"You don't know that."

"Is she here? Look around. Do you see her? No. You know why? Because she's gone. All we have is her memory." She scoots her chair closer, and her ribcage bumps the table's edge, sloshing her coffee.

"That's the whole problem." Townes waves his spoon in a broad circular motion. "The memory of Etta is better than Etta ever was. She was mean and moody and used to make you nuts. She was always in my business. Dad barely even spoke to her. But in everyone's memory, she was the perfect daughter. How can I compete with that? I'm just human, flesh and blood. I'm right here! How can I compete with a memory?"

"It isn't a competition."

"Yes, it is."

"You're wrong. We are the survivors and we can do what we think is best. You aren't being compared to Etta. Etta is gone. You are here."

"Yes, I am." He points his spoon at her accusingly, voice raised another notch. "I'm here. I just said that. That's my point. And that makes me guilty of something. Right? That's how Dad acts. Even you treat me that way. I'm here but Etta still gets all the attention. Dad wishes I was the one missing. That Etta was still here. Admit it."

"No. No one thinks that. Your father is doing his best." Her voice rises above his. She takes a few moments then adds more quietly, "We are all doing our best."

Townes returns to his grapefruit, turning the waxy skin, the white pith clinging to a section as he puts it in his mouth. He chews, swallows, speaks. "It's not right to put up a gravestone."

"Maybe not. I wasn't sure about it. But it's paid for. Besides, when people suffer loss, they mourn, they mark the loss. It's like a punctuation mark. The ceremony signifies the end of grief. It's a time to heal and rebuild. People suffer loss every day, and they get on with their lives the best they can. It's time for us to do the same. Past time." She pushes the scrap of paper closer to her son.

"I disagree. I mean, I agree with some of it. But I disagree with most of it." He snatches the paper from the table.

"You have told me so, many times. Now do me a favor and just fucking call Newton," she says. "Remind him about today. Encourage him to come. He should be there, don't you think? I mean, Etta was a big part of his life. She doesn't just belong to us."

Townes glares at the paper he pinches between his fingers. He exhales.

"Why me?" he asks more calmly. "If it's so urgent, why don't you do it? You can call him just as easily as I can. More easily. We are not friends you know, Newton and I. We are not the same. We don't get along. I never liked him. He hated me. Used to call me names. He called me 'sissy' and 'wussy' and 'little weirdo.' He called me 'fag' and 'queer' and 'butt muncher.' He is not a nice person. Never was." He drops Newton's number on the table between them.

"That was a long time ago. Time passes. People change. Especially teenagers. I bet he regrets the way he acted." She picks the paper up, shoves it back at Townes's hand. He just looks at it.

"Besides," she adds, "I already sent him the invitation. He knows I want him there, but he doesn't know you want to see him."

"I don't want to see him."

She ignores him. "It'll be encouraging. I bet that as strongly as you don't want him there, he feels just that unwanted. Make him feel welcome and wanted, Townes. I spoke to his mother. He's having a hard time. He was hurt in Afghanistan, lost a close friend.

He was injured. He always liked you. He was young. He didn't know how to show it."

Townes looks doubtful. But she knows her son, knows a part of him secretly looked up to Newton. He takes the paper and puts it in his front pocket.

Satisfied, Meg drinks more coffee and lets time pass. In the stillness, she watches Townes's wheels turning. He takes the last bitter, acidic bite of the grapefruit in his mouth and holds it without chewing. The tightness in his shoulders and across his chest seems to ease. He exhales, stretches his neck side to side, and she watches him relax.

"You need another grapefruit? The other half is right there. It's no problem." She knows his answer. He doesn't want any more grapefruit now. She knows he will want half a fresh grapefruit tomorrow morning, not the uneaten half that she will cover with a thin sheet of plastic wrap. It's something to do with enzymes.

Townes checks his watch, chugs his almond milk. "No, no. I'm good. I need to get walking to catch the train." He stands, leans to kiss his mother on the forehead. She pats at his arm as he pulls away. He slings his coat on and grabs his bag before heading out the door.

"Don't forget to be back in time, Townes. We can ride together," she says.

"I know," he says without turning.

"Wait," she calls.

"What now? I've already missed my usual train. I'll miss the other one too if I don't hurry."

She comes to him and puts a wool stocking cap on his head. "You can't go out in this weather with nothing on your head."

"Mom," he whines, like the teen he used to be. "I don't like hats. They make me look funny. You know I don't like hats." He yanks it off and passes it back to her.

"You think too much. You always have. Don't complicate things. It's not a manifesto. It's a hat. It's so cold. You need to stay warm."

"I'll be fine." He turns away and lets the door slam behind him.

When he's gone, she pitches the cap on the table, takes his dishes to the sink, and tops off her coffee. She takes a microwave sausage sandwich from the freezer, slams it in the microwave. She sets it to heat and walks heavily back up the stairs to get dressed, careful with her coffee. As she reaches the upstairs hall, she feels unusually winded and barks a harsh cough, her body bending forward. She straightens and stands between the bathroom where Etta used to get ready and the room Townes used to occupy. She takes a sharp, scalding sip of coffee and keeps going. If she's learned nothing else over the years, she's learned you have to keep moving or risk never moving again.

# LADIES' MAN

Townes walks down the block and around the corner, passing from cleared and salted stretches of damp, pitted sidewalk onto crunchy sections of compacted snow. His breath comes in white bursts as his pace quickens.

The sun is fully up, the air brisk, flurries beginning to fall. If the forecast is accurate, by midday everything will start to melt, and his commute home will involve slogging through gray slush. His trip to the cemetery is likely to be a soggy one. *Another reason not to go.*

They're calling for the evening to bring a hard freeze with more snow by morning, but he can worry about that when he needs to, or better yet, accept it. His morning walks are reserved for counting his steps, not letting his mind run loose.

It's a waste to consider if he is happy or not, what his wants or expectations are. The day will bring what it will. He is like water in a stream, when obstacles spring in his path, he slips forward and around. If he's in tune with the rhythm that underlies all life, then no random event can come as a surprise.

He inhales deeply, counting his footfalls, calming his mind, puff-puffing bursts of air with each exhale. One and two and three and . . . counting is his mantra. This practice makes space in his cluttered mind for being Townes, nothing more, nothing less, accepting honestly who he is, his limitations as well as his natural abilities. His mistakes of the past are behind him. Only through honest self-assessment can one hope to understand the true path of life.

Townes has always had a forceful inner voice, always lived with his thoughts nattering at him. He's curious if others have the same problem, or is his mind especially tangential and random? He quietly concedes that the question is itself random and pointless.

It used to take nearly fifteen hundred strides to get from his back door to the train platform. He'd made a project of increasing his stride length. Lately his trip takes just over a thousand strides. Of course, today his count is off. He hadn't started counting right away and is halfway to his destination.

He's reassured when he turns a corner and sees he's gaining ground on a business commuter he often passes on his morning walk. The man in the charcoal pea coat must have gotten a late start too. They usually take the express train together. Now they will be stuck on a local, which will stop at every neighborhood along the way.

Normally, Townes's weekly schedule is blessedly uneventful. He'd go weeks in which the only things that changed would be the weather and the number of layers he wore. Today he's running late, has an errand and an unwanted appointment to attend to, will be stuck on a slow train, and will have to cut his visit to Printer's Row short.

At least he'll get to spend a short time with Dory. The social ritual known as dating, for Townes, is a challenge for numerous reasons. In no small measure it's due to his stunted emotional development and social inadequacies. He admits it freely. Not all of it can be blamed on the loss of Etta during his important formative years. He was unusually inept at human interaction before Etta's absence altered his life so thoroughly, and placing blame wouldn't solve the problem anyway. Though, it must be said, with the happy exception of Dory, the only women he feels he has room for in his tightly structured life are the memory of his missing sister and his damaged mother.

Dory's hair changes colors with the seasons; in the fall and winter it's like the turning leaves of a deciduous tree. It had been maroon last week, orange for a month before that. As spring approaches, it will be shades of blonde or neon pink or electric blue.

In the years after Etta went missing, hormones and teen boys being what they are, a new girl would catch his eye on a weekly basis. He would make initial contact, hesitant and strange though it may have been.

The summer between his sophomore and junior years, he approached Alicia Worth when he found her waiting for her dog to poop in his side yard.

"Hey, Alicia," he said.

Alicia was fair skinned with sun-kissed cheeks and freckled shoulders showing around her rose-colored tank top, a popular girl, smart, athletic, universally liked. What Townes admired most was that her big eyes and upturned nose made her look like a manga heroine. Townes knew she was on a sports team, but he paid little attention to such things and couldn't guess which sport. Maybe volleyball. He knew she sometimes wore a girl's letter jacket, and she was not as good at geometry as he was. Despite the fact that they existed in parallel realities, each walking their own sliver of social strata, Townes felt he might have a chance with her. Not out of ego, but because his family's recent tragedy made him more interesting to girls. They wanted to take care of him. He was ashamed of banking on this subtle manipulation. Not ashamed enough to prevent him taking advantage of any edge he could get. Besides, Alicia had hugged him in the hall in his first week back to school after Etta disappeared. She pressed her body to his, and he liked it and wanted more of that kind of thing.

"Oh, hello, Townes. Is this your house? I didn't know." Alicia looked a little guiltily toward her dog, hunched up and straining at the end of the tether she held.

"Yeah, this is the old homestead." He wished he hadn't said *homestead*. He didn't know where that came from. "What's your dog's name?" he asked.

"Kim," she said. "As in Kim Possible. I used to love that show."

"Oh, yeah. I still watch it. Watch it all the time." They both stared as Kim's whole body tensed and pushed out a rank turd that was roughly half her size.

"What kind of dog is she?"

"Just a mutt, really. Mostly terrier is what my dad says. I think she's at least half pit bull. He doesn't like to say that because of the stigma."

"I understand," he said, though he didn't know to what stigma she was referring. Kim finished her crap, stood, stretched, scratched the grass once with each back paw, and took a few steps as if ready to leave. Then she found a new spot and hunched up again.

"So, what are you doing Saturday night?" he forced himself to ask. Kim left one little round poop in the new spot. She shook herself and started sniffing for anything of interest, pressing her nose into small depressions in the lawn.

"Why?" Alicia replied defensively. She began to pat her shorts pockets in a fraudulent attempt to find a plastic bag for her dog's heap of wet shit.

"I . . . I . . . I was wondering if maybe you would like to see a movie. I have this coupon for the Tivoli. Saturday night is the After Hours Movie Club. I'm a member. They're showing a short documentary about female genital mutilation, with a discussion to follow."

She winced and started tugging Kim down the sidewalk. "Sorry, I can't."

"It's a serious problem." He could see his mistake. He knew he was fighting a losing battle. He blamed the movie theater for its selection of disturbing docs. Why couldn't they show something uplifting, like that Canadian comedy *Starbuck*? Now that was a great date movie. "Or just some coffee. Or frozen yogurt. There's that new place. They sell self-serve with a bunch of toppings. It's not fattening. Not that you need to worry about that. My treat." It was clear he'd lost her. "You know, it would be nice to talk," he added in a last-ditch attempt. "Because of everything with my sister and all."

"Sorry. But not interested. I have to go. Also, I don't have a bag for the poop. Sorry." She trotted away, letting Kim pull her down the block.

"I got it," he said, waving at her back. "No problem. Thanks."

He knew he would not get another hug from Alicia. He had felt especially filthy after that exchange. The reeking pile of shit hadn't helped.

Though many of his interactions with the opposite sex had been similarly awkward, they had not all ended in rejection. Teen girls and hormones being what they are, the girls often seemed willing to overlook his lack of conversational skills, stylistic quirks, and skin problems and would, to his utter surprise, agree to go out with him.

Acceptance by a cute girl would fill him with a euphoric surge of conceited self-satisfaction. The inflated self-worth would lead to guilt. Why should he be proud of himself while Etta was gone to who knows where? What had he done to help her? Wasn't he, in part, responsible for her absence? Here he was, manipulating girls who felt sorry for him, using Etta's tragedy to get lucky. Or at least, for a chance to get lucky. He didn't know the bases. First base, second base, third. He was no good at sports and didn't understand the metaphor, but he was pretty sure a home run meant sex, and sex seemed like an idea worth exploring.

His brain would start in on him, attacking him, preventing him from being a normal teen. Before a relationship could develop, he would inventory all the ways these girls were like his sister. They were similar in age to Etta the last time he'd seen her, wore clothes of the same brands or had hair the same color, turned their faces up when they laughed, or tucked their hair behind their ears in the same nervous gesture. Recalling Etta in these specific, tangible ways would make him feel distant from the day-to-day concerns of adolescence. It made Etta's absence feel fresh. A part of him cherished the pain. Because he deserved it, or because feeling strongly toward Etta meant he hadn't forgotten her. He missed her.

Dwelling on Etta's absence led to more guilt, and his sex drive would take a back seat to raw pain. He often bailed out before the first date. For some reason he was certain should be clear to him, young women would never say *yes* to a first date a second time. While most kids his age were hanging out, eating fast food, going to see bands, and sneaking beer, he'd spend his evenings alone, safely behind a wall constructed of poorly interpreted Eastern philosophy and other cerebral distractions, like reading his way through all the great books of the Western canon.

It's not like that when he's with Dory. She's different from girls he grew up around, and he never thinks of anyone else while in her company. Her skin is the color of butterscotch. He imagines it's warm to the touch, and it smells of exotic spices. He sees his fingertips tracing along her jawline, working into the fine, jewel-colored hair at the back of her neck, bringing her mouth to his.

*Distraction distraction.* He clears his head and focuses on the details of the moment, the steady pace of his footfalls, the wind whistling around the bare branches. He will see Dory soon enough.

He approaches the back of Business Man. *The world's most boring superhero.* He veers off into the snow of someone's lawn, his feet leaving deep punctures in the previously unmolested snow. Back on the sidewalk, he throws his hand up in a courteous acknowledgment to a fellow traveler, stomps his feet a bit while bringing his mind back to counting his steps. Two hundred thirty-four, two hundred thirty-five . . .

# MEMORIES UNPACKED

The aspirin and beer leave a bitter taste in his mouth, but augmenting it with a stream of hot water down the back of his neck makes Newton feel better. He wraps a Pac-Man beach towel nearly twice around his waist and goes back to his room to find his phone.

Sitting on the corner of his bed, his stump sticking out, swaddled in the towel like a blunt-headed baby, he swipes and taps his phone until he dials up Cranky Thomas. The hot shower loosened him up, but the cold apartment makes him want to get dressed fast. Around the fourth ring, he wonders what time it is.

"Who the fuck?" Cranky Thomas says, his speaking volume turned too high for Newton. It's Thomas's standard phone greeting, but he sounds more irritable than usual.

"Newton," Newton says. "I got a little cash and some time to kill. You want to do some work?"

"Newton who?"

"How many Newtons do you know? Wiseass. Newton Newton. That's who. Do you have time to do some work?"

"What kind of work? I can't accomplish dick in a few hours if you got something elaborate in mind." Cranky Thomas is picky about his clientele, if not his manners or personal hygiene. He only works on vets, and only if he feels like it. He's retired and does this as a hobby or as some kind of veteran outreach, personal penance, or something. Newton's been talking to him about getting work done for months.

"Just words," Newton explains. "Real simple."

"Where you want it?"

"My calf."

"Which one? Oh, never mind." Thomas makes an amputation joke.

"Smart-ass."

"Yeah. I got fuckin' time. But if you call me this early again, I'll rip you a new one." Cranky Thomas is forever threatening people. Newton doesn't take it too seriously.

"Fair enough," Newton replies. "What time is it anyway?"

"How the hell should I know? I just woke up. See you here in thirty minutes. Bring cash and black coffee, or don't come at all." Cranky Thomas hangs up.

Newton checks his phone for the time. It is early for a mean old drunk like Cranky Thomas, but he doesn't feel bad about it.

He had met Thomas while standing at a trough urinal at a bar that's been torn down since. He had glanced at the tall man as he moved into position and drunkenly believed a malnourished and baldheaded Lee Marvin was fishing his prick out in his presence. He was so excited and inebriated that he followed Thomas back to the bar and bought him drinks until he was broke.

It takes Newton three minutes to find his shoe, stick his leg back on, slip into some relatively clean clothes, and brush the sharp, foul taste out of his mouth. In the living room, he finds his keys in the front door, the door standing half-open. "No wonder it's so damn cold in here." He can't find his iPod anywhere. *Shit!*

He does pushups on the linoleum floor, each exhale sending dust into the air and making his nose itch. He hops up when the microwave goes off and pulls the cellophane-wrapped breakfast croissant sandwich onto the counter. He runs cold tap water into a dirty glass, rips open his steamy breakfast, and takes big, scalding bites while standing at the counter, looking around his derelict little place. *It's like a crack house with none of the sweet sweet crack.*

He spots the invitation from Meg on the floor, and it gets him thinking. He finishes his sandwich and goes to his bedroom closet. He drags a box out. It'd been stored at his mom's while he was at college and while he was deployed. After rehab, when he moved into his own place, she'd asked him to take it with him.

He rips the packing tape and opens the flaps. He throws out a high school yearbook, a rolled-up letter jacket, and a balled backpack. There's a long object protected in a twist of bubble wrap. He lets the heavy object unroll into his hand and grins at his old bong. He sets it aside.

He sifts through the loose pile of junk that remains, looking at some items, ignoring others, until he finds what he's searching for: a strip of black-and-white photo booth images. He takes the curl of paper in the palm of his hand, sees himself and Etta staring up at him, four times. *She really was beautiful.* He can't recall the last time he looked so happy, the last time he acted so goofy. Maybe not since Etta left him.

He folds the strip of photos carefully so the seam forms in the gutter between two images, and the pictures go in his wallet with his cash. His phone's clock tells him he's already late for Cranky Thomas, but on a whim, he snatches up his yearbook and flips through it. He finds a candid snapshot of Etta smiling while crowded onto the bleachers for a pep rally. Maybe he'd been out there on the floor, taking credit for the wrestling team's record. Maybe not. He lets the book drop open on his bed, grabs a coat, and heads to the door. He sees his iPod sitting next to his TV. He takes it and drops it in its dock, dials up some Danzig, leaves it loud. He's careful to lock up on the way out.

# HARD DETERMINIST

Townes walks onto the cement slab along the tracks as he reaches a count of four hundred and fourteen steps. He works his way among the clusters of commuters to find a clear spot. Leaning to gaze down the tracks, he catches a glint of metal or headlight sliding through the evergreens at a distant curve. The train is running roughly on time, probably just coming into the Main Street station.

In his bag he finds his smartphone and headphones. He taps at his screen to make a show of selecting a song. No one seems to be watching, but he continues the pantomime. He doesn't have music on his phone, other than a dreadful recording of Tibetan monks throat singing. He tucks the phone in his inside pocket and trails the wires to his ears, where he inserts the buds. This completes the subterfuge. With earbuds in, he can pretend not to overhear others' conversations, can dissuade unwanted interaction. It's an effective way of creating a bubble of privacy while crammed onto public transit.

Townes sees public transportation as a great equalizer, forcing cross sections of society that would otherwise avoid one another to interact civilly. The train is humanizing. A businessman is just as haggard from the weather and the rush to snag the train as the art student or the groundskeeper who works around Millennium Park. Public transit gives complete strangers an opportunity to commiserate over shared hardship. *And commiseration is a balm that soothes the downtrodden masses.*

Townes's thought is interrupted when a dented metal speaker pops with static and a heavily accented woman makes an announcement. He can't decipher it; she sounds like an Eastern European cyborg from a technically backward future. The people around him begin to debate what she might have said.

"Is the train late?" two men nearing retirement age, sporting matching beards and competing amounts of aftershave, ask one another at the same time.

"Did she say mechanical problems?" a nice-looking woman wearing a wine-colored scarf, dark tights, and damp running shoes asks a short, round Hispanic grandmother. The grandmother shrugs, not having understood the question, and lets her granddaughter tug her closer to the tracks.

Townes watches the granddaughter, drawn to her for some unknown reason. She's in a green sweater and brown corduroys. She has earmuffs clapped on her head in a green that clashes with her sweater. Her pants are tucked into cheap knockoff, wool-lined boots. The boot tops are folded over so the nappy sheep wool makes a cuff. They're covered in a black, suede-like material that isn't meant to get wet. A series of dried, horizontal white stripes mark the wet-dry cycle of her little feet tromping through the bad weather. The boots look new, a size too large, and probably a Christmas present. They are decorated on the outside of each ankle with a cheap and useless buckle. As she moves toward the tracks, the toes of her boots catch, one of her boot buckles snags in the opposite wool cuff and she trips. He reaches toward her from three yards away, but he doesn't move his feet to close the distance. Her grandmother is there to help, and the little girl recovers and continues on her way. His attention is pulled to a stocky student in checkered chef pants who speaks to a man with an unwashed salt-and-pepper ponytail trailing down his back. "Was it delayed?"

"Who knows, dude?" is the reply. "Probably."

"Right on," says the culinary student and turns away to continue tearing hunks from a dry bagel with yellow goat teeth.

"I bet someone stepped in front of the train. Damn inconsiderate," a whiskey-harsh voice says just behind Townes. The comment may have been meant for him, but he ignores it, bobs his head as if to music.

No one knows what the announcement said, but that doesn't curtail the ritual of guessing. The pointless conjecture trails off as the train rolls into view, its horn blares two blasts, the gates flash red and close on Fairview, and the engine clatters into the station, trying to come to a stop.

Townes listens to several variations of "Here it comes," mumbled all along the platform, paired with corresponding gestures and nods. He shakes his head and tries not to begrudge the predictability of human behavior, only recognize it and acknowledge it. It, too, is a part of the natural way of things. His long coat swirls around him and he turns his face away from the flecks of salt melt stirred by the train.

A set of doors just to his right come open, and a youngish man in an oversized uniform leans out. His clothes are so baggy Townes wonders if he's lost weight. Perhaps he's ill. He's a new conductor, one Townes has never seen on the express train. Maybe he needs to have the uniform altered, maybe he can't afford to have it done. What salary do Metra employees make? *Maybe it would be a good job, riding the rails and watching people.* The scattered crowd of individual commuters bunches up and forms clumps in front of each door, like mercury molecules pooling together. The orderly swarm begins to jostle forward to find spots on the train, as if seats will run out.

Two train cars to his left, an obese man in farmer-style bib overalls and an unbuttoned work coat uses an aluminum cane, the adjustable kind from a medical supply store, to pitch his girth toward another set of open doors. His swollen knees, apparently taxed to their limit by his weight, don't seem able to flex as he stumps forward. Townes trots in that direction.

The big man is Mr. Stephanopoulos. He's the father of Tansy, whom Townes had been in elementary school with. Tansy was a funny little tomboy who eventually grew into an Upper-Midwest version of a Kardashian-style hoochie, but without a trust fund or a TV show. When Townes and Tansy were in first grade and Mr. Stephanopoulos had been only very fat, he had come to their classroom to read poems from a Shel Silverstein collection. He'd hunkered down onto an undersized chair. He used funny, expressive voices. Some were his own improvisations and others were perfect impersonations of various Muppets the kids recognized immediately. He'd done a good Grover and Cookie Monster and an absolutely perfect Oscar the Grouch. Combined with his broad facial expressions and flamboyant gestures, the poems came to life. Mr. Stephanopoulos, like a large, gregarious toddler, smiled a lot and laughed during his own reading. The assembled six-year-olds had been drawn in, having a great time. For Townes it was one of his best memories of first grade.

Townes reaches the doors as Mr. Stephanopoulos is using the shiny handrail to hoist his mass onto the train. He turns and drops his ass onto the steps, in a move that reminds Townes of trying to lower onto the toilet of a cramped airplane bathroom. This leaves Mr. Stephanopoulos, red with exertion, facing the opening he has just passed through. It's not the first time Townes has seen this move. Mr. Stephanopoulos often rides the train. Townes mounts the stairs next to him, gives a friendly nod as he goes by. Mr. Stephanopoulos doesn't acknowledge Townes. He knew he wouldn't. He never does, but Townes always nods anyway.

Townes assumes that Mr. Stephanopoulos is too slow to get back to the exit doors from a seat in the passenger car. At least in the amount of time allotted for a stop. He's too unstable on his damaged knees to walk when the train is swaying, maybe too wide to fit down the aisles without turning sideways. So he plants himself on the gritty steps and waits for the doors to open onto the downtown platform. Townes wonders what Mr. Stephanopoulos does for work. Some morning he'll follow him, to satisfy his curiosity.

Ghosting Mr. Stephanopoulos to his job feels less stressful than starting a conversation. Townes has done this in the past: followed someone through Chicago neighborhoods just to see where they end up. He has no ill intentions, no nefarious plans. Some days he lets his feet take him where they want to go.

In the vestibule between passenger cars, Townes checks his options. One direction, the coach is old with brown seats, the padding worn thin so one's ass hits hard on the frame when the tracks are rough. The other direction is a car with blue seats. Not the newest version of blue seats, but still only five years old or so. The blue car looks pretty clear, so he toes the kick plate that activates the sliding door and pushes into the car; the warning bell clangs three times to announces the brakes are being released, and the train makes an initial lurch forward, rolling toward the next stop.

He mounts the narrow twist of steps that take him to the upper half deck and sits in a place toward the center of the long row of single-file seats. From here he can watch the tops of people's heads through the luggage rack while nesting amid the cold throbbing of the too-bright fluorescent lighting.

He supposes his commuter voyeurism is slightly pathetic, though watching people is a kind of puzzle for him, as if he is an alien come to observe the inhabitants of a strange world. A part of him believes that with enough data points he will break the code of the human condition, design an algorithm that will unlock social acceptance. Another, more pessimistic portion knows the confused muddle and isolation he feels most days is, in fact, the definition of the human condition. No amount of observable behavior will change it or make it easier to navigate. If trying harder is no solution, it follows that trying less is a possible answer. At least that's the simplified version of the theory on which he currently operates.

The train builds speed, its steel frame creaking in the cold, and almost immediately it begins to brake. A voice calls, "Next stop,

Westmont," over the public address system. This voice is completely decipherable. Of course it helps that he's heard the names of the platforms called countless times. Townes settles in for the long ride, unzipping his coat. The slow commute allows him time to think, which is no bonus. The memorial flashes across his mind and an image of Etta, falling out of view, the person he had been that day and the person he is trying to become.

Six years ago to the day, he had been sitting outside the principal's office waiting to explain his involvement in a scuffle.

• • •

It had been an innocent remark to Andy Adair that led to the altercation. The bell rang, ending second period. Townes slid his books from his desk and tucked them under his arm, pushed himself into the flow of kids, raced down the too-narrow hall to his antiquated locker. He twiddled his combination and yanked on the slide; his locker failed to open. He started again.

Andy's locker was next to Townes's. They weren't friends, but Townes liked Andy. For a wrestler he was nice; he'd always been decent. Not warm, but not dismissive either, and never mean. So when Andy sidled up, Townes said, "Hey, Andy."

"Wassup, Townes."

"I'm beat. I was counting on a snow day. I was up late."

"Yeah. It sucks."

Townes popped his locker open, shoved two books in, and pulled two books out. He tunneled through the remaining pile, uncovering a spiral notebook with the words *American Pistory* scrubbed into the cover with an angry eraser. As he slammed his locker, he saw something on the top of Andy's ear. It looked like a twist of paper, but that didn't make sense. It also looked like a moth that had settled, unnoticed, on the side of Andy's head.

"You got a bug," Townes said and reached to shoo the moth away.

Andy jerked back and caught Townes's wrist. He squeezed it hard and came at him, turning him and shoving Townes against the lockers. Townes didn't attempt to resist. He'd found compliance often took the steam out of teen boys. They got bored if you didn't resist.

"Very funny, asshole," Andy said, twisting Townes's arm behind him and pressing his face into the locker, his smooth cheek scrubbing along a hinge.

"Really. You just have a moth on your ear," Townes tried to explain through the side of his mouth.

Andy smacked Townes in the back of the head. He drew his hand back to do it again. The pressure on Townes's shoulder increased. It felt like something would snap. He could see the blow coming in his peripheral vision, closed his eyes tight.

"Whoa, whoa, whoa," said a new voice. It was Newton Parker, Etta's boyfriend. Another wrestler. A typical, mean, boxy, sweaty little man hopped up on inflated self-image and competitive rage. Townes didn't think much of Newton, but Etta wouldn't listen. Besides, he didn't know what exactly he didn't like; he had a feeling his sister could do better.

"Andy, man," Newton said in a persuasive tone. "You don't need to do that. You know Townes. Take it easy. He didn't mean anything. He's just stupid. Right, Townes?" Then a little quieter and next to Townes's ear he said, "Say *right*."

"Right."

Townes tried to turn his head. He saw a dense crowd gawking and grinning and talking among themselves, expectantly awaiting violence or tears or anything to break the monotony of sitting in another classroom for another forty-six minutes of test prep.

Andy abruptly released Townes and slammed his own locker closed. "Fucktwat," he said. He stormed off. Townes relaxed and watched him go, confused, embarrassed, and relieved. Only a few strides away, Andy was stopped by Mrs. Bennis.

"What's all that about?" she asked. She was five-two in her ever-present heels, her hair a severe shell of black dye and hairspray. She had a reputation for being a hardcore bitch. Her eyes darted between Andy and Townes, settled firmly on Andy, demanding a response.

"He was making fun of my fucking ear," Andy explained, still irritated.

Townes winced, both from his sore rotator cuff and from Andy's word choice. He was a popular kid, an athlete. Maybe he would get away with it.

Newton quietly asked Townes, "What's the idea, dumbass? Why you want to give him shit about his cauliflower ear, you gaywad? Don't you know that shit hurts? You gotta learn to just be cool about people's shit, Townes. It's none of your fuckin' business to talk about his fucked-up ear, you know? You fucking fudge-packer."

"What? I thought it was a moth," he replied honestly.

"Dumbass. That's a drain for fluid or something. Shit for brains."

They, along with the entire crowd, kept their eyes on Andy and Mrs. Bennis. His simmering temper crashing against her inflexible attitude was enough to capture everyone's attention. It was bound to be the most interesting thing to happen the whole day.

"I don't like your tone," she said warningly. She seemed willing to let his language go, once.

"My tone isn't the issue," he snarled.

Mrs. Bennis was not a fan of back talk and she turned nasty fast. "Did your precious feelings get hurt? Is that the issue? Did the little freshman scare the big senior?"

"No, goddamn, you don't fucking get it." Andy was a foot taller than Mrs. Bennis in her heels. He scowled openly, trying to use his height to intimidate.

"That's enough," her voice snapped like a whip crack, and she suddenly seemed larger, Andy shrinking. "We'll let Principal Greene sort this out." She grabbed Andy by his shirt and led him to the office. Open-mouthed teens cleared the way ahead of them.

"Get off me, bitch. I gotta get to the gym," he protested.

"And he just keeps digging his own grave," Newton said.

Mrs. Bennis called over her shoulder, "You, too, Townes." Then she quickened her pace, her heels tapping out an emphatic staccato warning.

"Be cool in there, Townes. Andy took most of the heat off you. Act stupid like you didn't know better."

"I didn't know," he said.

"That's perfect," Newton replied. "I told your sister I'd look out for you. Put in a good word with Etta, will ya? Maybe I'll get laid later." Newton laughed crudely. Townes didn't join in.

Townes bent to gather his books. He walked through the gauntlet of giggles and stares, into the office to wait in a seat designated for those about to be punished.

During the long wait, Townes found he wasn't angry with Andy. Townes had made a faux pas. He was willing to take the blame. Instead, his anger was for Etta. Maybe because they were siblings and it was safe to blame her. High school was hard enough without her interference. He could figure it out on his own, handle his own business. Why the hell did she have Newton sticking his nose in? He wasn't even family.

• • •

The train brakes hard, nearly overshooting the Westmont platform. Townes digs in his bag. He grabs *Rashomon and Other Stories* by Ryunosuke Akutagawa, takes a moment to admire its cover, brushing his fingers over the traditional woodblock illustration of a samurai warrior. The multistep process and the resultant beauty appeal to him. He tries to see the individual layers, pull apart the color impressions, and deconstruct the picture one press run at a time. He'd like to have a print studio. There might be room in the garage under his room, if his mother would sell Etta's car. *That is a big IF.* He thinks of Meg's claim that *it's time to move on* in contrast with her refusal to let the car go. *She is as trapped as I am.*

He cracks the book open and pretends to read, another useful conversation deterrent. He makes sure his monthly pass is handy for the conductor, tucks it into the back pages of his book.

A few dozen people with similar computer bags file into his car; the vestibule doors open and close several times and let in gusts of frigid winter air. The train passengers are resolved to the toil of another commute. Some sit in friendly clusters, flipping the seat backs so they can face one another, their knees touching, talking casually about their kids and drinking coffee from travel mugs or hot tea from sleek metal thermoses. Others turn their backs to the car, staring out the windows, watching the slippery reflections of neighborhoods slide across the windows. A woman with a Bluetooth device in her ear has a loud, one-sided phone conversation.

"I'll tell you exactly what I told him, 'No, I will not redo the report,'" she says. After a few moments she continues, "Well, no. I didn't say it in so many words, but he got my meaning. And I will tell him to his face if he asks me. I used the real numbers. The only numbers. Numbers are numbers. This isn't a fucking Karl Rove situation. And if he doesn't like the totals he should do a better job. He expects me to turn a pile of shit into a chocolate pie. I'm not a character from *The Help*."

Passengers stop staring at their phones to glance at her, smirking or laughing at her, not cruelly. A few paper readers look put out by the volume of her conversation, flicking their pages to peek at her, then flicking them back with irritation.

Melting snow leaves wet glitter winking on shoulders and caps as light flashes in through the windows. The clicking rhythm of the train's wheels on the tracks increases, and the slight surge of g-force pushes Townes back into his seat. The rocking of the train feels organic, like waves on a beach or fluid rolling in a mother's womb.

Below Townes, the Mexican grandmother from the Fairview platform gives her granddaughter a coloring book and a four-pack of waxy restaurant crayons. The girl tugs off her minty-green earmuffs and drops them on the seat. They twist in on themselves and take the form of a hamburger in a Dr. Seuss diner. In the reflection from the lower windows opposite, Townes sees the little girl tuck her chin toward her lap and start right to work. The grandmother smiles tiredly and lets her eyes close, her left ear ever so slowly leaning closer to her left shoulder. The little granddaughter, maybe five, scooches her rump on the seat and bumps the earmuff beside her. He knows who the girl reminds him of: little Etta. As she was in his earliest memories of her, complete with round cheeks and blunt-cut bangs; summer-baked Etta before puberty changed her body, her mood, and her priorities.

The automated announcement declares, "Clarendon Hills" through hidden speakers. The poorly tailored conductor hustles through the car to the next vestibule to open the doors. Moments later, a tall man in a faded army coat and mismatched, green pocket pants passes heavily down the aisle, the toes of his worn boots clipping the legs of seats as he passes. He's looking for something, a seat of his own, maybe a friend. It's not clear. It's predatory, the way he swings his gaze, a hunter searching for prey. He spots the little girl, eyes her dozing grandmother, and slows his pace to a stop. He takes a seat across the aisle from the girl. He unwinds a scarf and pulls it off over his head, drops it on the seat next to him, and crosses his arms over his chest. His gaunt face is a long feral nose; dark whiskers in sunken, angular cheeks; tiny, deep-set eyes;

and high forehead crowned with dark hair parted hard down the middle. His body has the lean, loose look of someone young, with the face of an old man.

The bell clangs, stealing Townes's attention. The train moves and the conductor enters the car and barks, "Tickets, please. Please have your tickets ready." He unholsters his spring-loaded ticket punch, clicks it rapidly to test its action, and more quietly says to the first passenger, "Ticket, please." The man flashes a monthly pass and the conductor says, "Thank you," pointing his silver punch at the passenger and clicking it for fun. "Tickets," he says as he moves through the car, periodically making change from a coin dispenser and shoving a fist full of bills deep in his pocket.

Townes gauges the number of passengers and guesses it'll be two stops before the conductor reaches him. Double-checking that his ticket is still where he put it, he holds his book higher, puts his back to the window, and peeks over at the people below. He closes his eyes as the train accelerates, aware of his breathing. His brain is everywhere today.

Minutes later the conductor raps his punch on the metal bar near Townes's foot and repeats more loudly, "Ticket, please."

"Oh. Sorry." Townes pulls his pass from the back of his book and shows it. The conductor barely acknowledges it, ducks his face down.

"Tickets, please," he says to the next group of passengers.

A round man in a banana-yellow trench coat comes up the steps, unbuttoning, the coat's belt swaying loose against his legs. He smiles broadly and slouches into the seat in front of Townes. He pulls a woolly cap from his head, revealing a burst of white hair like dandelion fluff. He looks less like a tired commuter and more like a Dick Tracy character with an alliterative name like Rex Rotund. The man rustles around in his inside pocket and tips a silver flask to his lips. Drinking on the train is perfectly legal, as long as you're of age.

But Townes rarely sees it on the morning train. On an evening train, people regularly crack open beers. He'd witnessed good-natured ribbing from fans of rival baseball teams end with a shared six-pack. He'd also seen fistfights and sloppy grappling broken up by Metra police.

The round man turns halfway and offers the flask to Townes.

"What is it?" Townes asks.

"Irish coffee," the man says loudly.

Townes remembers his earbuds and tugs them out, curls the cord around his hand, and tucks it in his pocket with his phone. He starts to shake off the offer. He hasn't had alcohol in years. Caffeine is out of the question; it interferes with his clean-body-strategy. Of course, if he ever needed an excuse to drink, this anniversary would qualify.

"Minus the coffee," the man adds. His big, fleshy cheeks look flushed. If it's from the booze or the cold, Townes doesn't know, but it makes him look cheery and kind, like Santa if he had a deep tan and a fresh shave.

"Thanks," Townes says, surprising himself. He takes a quick swig, not even bothering to wipe the mouth of the flask. It's a potent mouthful and Townes swallows it fast, trying not to wince or cough. He feels it burn when it hits the back of his throat.

"Name's Stoddard," the man says, taking back his flask and offering his hand to shake.

Giving his best shake, he replies, "Townes."

"That's an interesting name. Can't say I've ever met another Townes. What you think about these school closings? Any opinion on the subject? They just announced it. You must have heard."

"I haven't seen the news," Townes explains. "I actually don't own a TV."

"Well, they're closing a lot of schools in Chicago. The most schools any city has ever closed at one time. They say, and by *they* I'm talking about politicians and the crooked school board, so you know how reliable it must be. They say they're closing underused schools and consolidating resources to better serve neglected communities. They sweetened the pot by investing in computers and books for these consolidated schools. What they don't say is that the schools that are closing are full of sweet poor brown students. The schools with all the white faces are staying open. The schools that are closing have been underfunded, on purpose, for decades." Stoddard gets loud. "It's outrageous how they treat people. They got the money to wage a pretend war for fake reasons in distant countries. They rebuild the schools they blew up overseas. But they can't fund the schools in our own country. Run our country on credit for planes and bombs? Hell, yes! Thank you very much. Raise our taxes to educate our little brown babies? Hell, NO!" He catches glances from passengers below and calms himself. "Anyway, Townes, is it? What a great name," he says more quietly, but still louder than Townes is comfortable with. "Excuse an old man. Happy Tuesday," he says, throwing back another belt of whiskey. He turns his bright yellow back to Townes.

"Happy Tuesday," Townes responds. He can feel the whiskey warming his stomach, similar to when he focuses his attention on his *swadhisthana* chakra. *Maybe booze is a shortcut I've too blithely disregarded.* He grins a lopsided grin. *Is it possible I'm drunk already?*

A man wearing spandex biking pants and matching athletic coat takes a seat below. He digs something from his nose, inspects it closely, and swipes it across his opposite sleeve. He flicks his eyes up toward Townes. Townes feigns interest in his book until the man turns away and begins digging in his nose again. The train picks up speed.

Stoddard turns back around. "All I am saying is there's a reason the shootings are up this year. There is a reason we have the most violent city in the country. It isn't because broke people are inherently violent. It's not because they are too stupid to stop killing each other. It's because they're out of options, and tired and hungry. Politicians look out for their best interests; the system is standing on the throats of poor people." He jangles the flask toward Townes. Townes takes another swig.

"Do you know what a food desert is?"

"Thanks for the drink. I really should get back to my reading," Townes says. He gestures with the open book. "For class," he lies.

"Sure. I understand. Say no more. I'll just have a sit and enjoy the view. We can save food deserts for another day." Stoddard turns away.

Below, a man who looks Chinese or Korean stops next to the man in the army coat. He stands, rocking in the aisle, waiting politely to be acknowledged.

"I'm holding this seat for someone," Army Coat says without looking up.

"Are you a soldier?"

"What?"

"I see your jacket is of soldier and I wanted to thank you for service to country."

Army Coat snatches his coat front and looks at it. The color of his scalp along the part is like the damp shell of a boiled peanut. "It's just a coat, man. To keep warm. Fuck off. Seat's saved."

The Chinese man bows a little, looks prepared to leave. But he takes a deep breath and says, "If you were to die today, do you know where your soul would reside in the afterlife?"

"Huh?"

"Would you like for me to share the story of Jesus Christ? If you let him into your heart and accept him as your Lord and Savior, he can wash away your sins with his cleansing blood."

Army Coat stands. The buzz of conversation through the entire car dies. The thump and creak of the rails fill the train. The grandmother's head still lolls, but the little girl looks from her coloring to watch the two men standing inches from her.

"Go the fuck away, Hop Sing. Get your yellow ass back to the Ponderosa," Army Coat says. His arm whips out quick and Townes thinks he's just hit the Chinese Christian. But he's only pointing a finger down the aisle. "Get to stepping." His raised arm pulls his coat open and reveals a long hunting knife in a stamped leather sheath.

The Chinese man bows again. "God bless," he says.

"Fuck you."

The train begins to brake. The speaker announces "LaGrange Stone Avenue." The conversation in the car burbles back to a normal level. Army Coat stays standing until the Chinese man exits the car.

This kind of behavior is why Townes prefers to take the express. The express is all business. The local is too colorful. To have something to do, Townes turns the page in his book and pretends to read. He feels his pulse in his neck, his breath held tight in his chest. He ignores the world around him and counts his breaths.

Over the next fifteen minutes, Townes barely notices the slow shift from the homogeneous suburban collar of politically right-leaning white families to the progressively more ethnically mixed group of residents who now fill the remaining seats of the car below.

A crayon rolls onto the floor and the little girl slides off her seat, crawls around, reaching for it and dropping her coloring book and the other three crayons in the process. The grandmother is sleeping, her face down in her scarf.

A woman from somewhere at the back of the car comes striding down the aisle in yoga pants tucked into rubber boots; a tight athletic top with no bra shows her small breasts. She passes by quickly and slides the door to the bathroom closed with a metallic slam followed by the sharp click of the lock. Anyone who tries to sit on that public toilet does so at their own risk. It's always covered in piss from men trying to aim their dicks while standing on a rocking train and is rarely flushed. Townes only enters when he needs toilet tissue for his nose and only finds the supplies he needs half the time. He's heard the Metra is spending a portion of its increased fares on staff to clean the trains, but he has yet to witness any improvement.

The man in the cycling getup abruptly unzips a pouch at the small of his back. He pulls out a bandana, puts it to his face, and hacks loudly into it. He inspects the result, like cupping the blossom of a large, paisley flower, folds it over, and tucks it back into his zippered pocket. A smattering of other people cough and clear their throats too, unconsciously cued by the cyclist's wet rasp.

Army Coat is still alone. Despite the crowded conditions, no one has been willing to sit with him. Townes watches Army Coat's gaze follow a high school girl's ass as she passes, then goes back to watching the little girl, who is resituating herself to color a new page. Army Coat turns his fox face up and catches Townes watching him.

Townes focuses on the window next to his seat but still watches the man in the reflection. Army Coat glares at the side of Townes's head. Townes pats his pockets nervously, trying to look preoccupied. He takes out the slip of paper with Newton's number. He fumbles for his phone, opens his contacts, and thumbs in Newton's cell number. Townes checks the reflection in the window. Army Coat has turned his attention elsewhere.

The woman with the Bluetooth is still on her phone, and her voice carries as if she's sitting next to Townes.

"After dinner he asked if I wanted to see his apartment. I told him he wasn't all that fine, dinner wasn't all that good, and I wasn't all that desperate." There is a pause as she listens. "I didn't say it in so many words but I said enough. He knew what I meant."

Townes tucks his book in his bag. He feels Army Coat's eyes on him again, so he bobs his head and lets his eyes close momentarily.

He touches the place the wires from his headphones normally fall, remembers he tucked them away, and stops bobbing his head. He cracks his eyelids. Army Coat is squinting at the little girl, like he's trying to suss out a solution to a riddle.

Stoddard, having noticed Townes put his book away, turns around to offer his flask again. Townes takes another hit, bigger this time.

"So I was saying about food deserts, police violence, and school closings," Stoddard begins.

Townes passes the flask back, watching the scene below. Something is about to happen. He can feel it like static in the air. "Just a second, please, Stoddard."

The girl's earmuffs roll into the aisle as the train slows for another stop. Army Coat pulls his scarf up and wraps it around his neck a few times. He scoops up the muffs and waggles them so the girl can see. When he's got her attention, he takes a few steps toward the vestibule.

Townes can't understand what Army Coat is doing. Taunting the girl by taking her earmuffs? Luring her to follow? He knows, deep down, Army Coat plans to take that little girl. The grandmother will wake up with no granddaughter and no idea what happened. For all practical purposes, she will vanish like wood smoke on a stiff breeze.

Army Coat wiggles the muffs, grins bad teeth at the girl, and cocks his head toward the vestibule while taking a couple more steps. Townes looks to the other passengers, all lost in conversation, staring out the windows, reading the *Sun-Times* or staring at their phones. No one sees the girl slip off her bench and shuffle her boots, her loose buckle slapping, toward Army Coat. Townes stands, leaving his bag unattended, and brushes past Stoddard, stepping on the tail of his yellow coat in passing. Army Coat catches the movement and stretches the earmuffs over his own greasy head, smiles again to the girl like they're playing a game, starts walking to the doors.

The woman exits the bathroom with a loud *thwack* of the heavy sliding door and waits for Army Coat to pass. Townes thinks, *This is it; either she helps the little girl back to her grandmother, or I have to do something. I have no choice.* The thought makes him sick. He takes little sips of air and watches the scene unfold, keeping pace with the girl below. The alcohol is making his forehead perspire, his armpits slick.

The woman walks to the girl, they sidestep one another, and the woman heads back to her seat, placing her hands on each seatback to steady herself as the train brakes.

Townes can hear Army Coat kick the vestibule door to open it, sees the girl as she surges forward. He takes the narrow stairs, sticks his hands between the doors before they can close, and wedges his body through.

The air between the cars is cold and close, shut off from the passengers and eerily isolated. Mr. Stephanopoulos is still on the stairs, his massive round form blocking half of the steps. Army Coat stands on the remaining bottom step, his back to the train's exit, ready to leap off when the doors come open. He's taken the muffs from his head and holds them out, arm half-bent so the girl has to get closer. The little girl edges closer, hand outstretched to grab the offered earmuffs. From the train car, he can hear the grandmother call out in Spanish, suddenly aware of her granddaughter's absence.

The train stops at the platform. Townes lets his body lurch forward and steps between the girl and Army Coat. The doors open. Townes yanks the muffs from the guy's dirty fingers and pitches them behind him, half-leaping down the steps as Army Coat turns to leave. Not intending to tackle the man, not knowing what exactly he intends. They land in a tangle on the cement.

"The fuck's your problem?" the guy says and strips Townes off as he stands. Townes gets to his feet and before he can straighten, he's laid out like a corpse in a casket. He never saw the blow, not sure what hit him. Probably a fist, but it felt harder. The pain is unique to Townes's previous experiences with being punched: immediate, bright, and completely overwhelming. Splinters of light stab his eyes.

A voice calls to him amid the spray of sparks.

"I'll settle up with you someday, pretty boy. I'll take this out of your hide."

Heavy feet run sloppily away.

When he uncurls, he finds the poorly tailored ticket taker staring at him from the train door, Mr. Stephanopoulos on his feet, in some pain with the effort, but using his bulk to hold the door until Townes can stagger back on board. Behind them, the grandmother has hoisted her grandbaby onto her shoulder and looks confused, and something else, perhaps grateful.

A Metra police officer, dressed in tactical black topped off with a bulletproof vest, enters the vestibule as Townes tries to get his legs moving. The officer speaks into the mic at his shoulder and moves down the steps toward Townes.

Townes tastes salt. When he runs his fingers around his gums, they come away bloody. No passengers exit the train. Everyone is waiting for him. He stumbles farther away and looks over the rail to the neighborhood below. He sees Army Coat making fresh tracks through the deep snow covering an abandoned lot. He lets the officer lead him back to the train.

# LIFE LEAVES MARKS

Twenty minutes later, Newton uses his good foot to kick the door to Cranky Thomas's place. His hands are full. He can hear Thomas grumbling and bitching to himself as he moves across the creaking floors. While Newton waits he looks above the plain, filthy-white exterior door. Along the overhead trim a quote is written in black magic marker. Thomas once clued him in on the joke, but Thomas was too drunk to be understood, and Newton was too Newton to care. It reads, *What Fresh Hell Is This?* The penmanship is thoughtfully done, in some kind of old, slanted script with little flicks of the pen leaving intentional caps and tails. The door has a similar but less lovingly made scrawl that reads, *Fresh Hell Tattoos.* Then in red pencil and underlined repeatedly, *By appointment only! Assholes!*

Cranky Thomas opens the door. His droopy eyes study Newton's injured cheek a moment. He walks away with no comment, leaving the door standing wide and not offering to help Newton with the coffees and paper bag. Thomas is a gangly, arachnid of a man, wearing greasy Levi's that are falling off his flat ass. A lot of old men are diminished by the years, turning into soft, miniature versions of their younger selves, but Thomas still looks lean as a snake, if a little hunched over. At his kitchenette, he turns and stares with eyes like dirty ashtrays. He's really old. Newton doesn't know his age but knows he was in 'Nam. He has a thick, expressive face that wrinkles into strange troughs and lumps when he's thinking hard or telling a story. Instead of turning into topiary like other men's, his eyebrows are nearly hairless and meaty.

"Bring that shit over here and let's talk," he says, his face bunching up tight then going slack.

Newton walks over and drops the bag, carefully passes a tall paper cup of hot, black coffee to Thomas. Thomas pries the lid off. He takes a deep smell, tips it to his lips, and slurps.

"Ahhhhh," he says appreciatively. "That's the good shit." He sips again and sets his cup down. "What's in the bag?"

"Boston cream doughnuts."

Thomas's brows roll up his bald forehead. "How'd you know that was my fucking favorite?" he asks, not waiting for an invitation to dig into the bag.

"One of my skills is to know people's doughnut soul mate. You are a Boston cream. Closed off on the outside, but soft and sweet in the middle."

"Fwuck you," Thomas says around a mouthful of fried dough, yellow cream squishing from the corners of his mouth. Newton sips his own coffee and watches Thomas take huge bites until all three doughnuts are gone. He wipes his long fingers, covered in old, crude tattoos, the black ink gone blue, and the lines blown out and fuzzy. When he's done, he tosses the balled-up napkin onto a pile of dirty dishes in the nearby sink and says, "Let's do this shit."

Newton explains what he wants and where. "This is first piece for a kind of sleeve, but for my leg. Is there a name for that? A sleeve running up a leg?"

"Fuck if I know. Probably. A sock? A stocking? A leg sleeve? I do tattoos. I don't talk about tattooing."

Thomas makes some sketches, gets one he likes, and walks over to a light table along one wall to refine it. His expression is even more exaggerated by the up lighting, his face working as hard as his wrinkled hands. Newton walks around the place to kill time.

The studio is located above Tommy's garage, a tire and muffler shop owned by Cranky Thomas's son. Tommy is older than Newton by a lot, but he's half Vietnamese, so it's hard for Newton to judge his age exactly. The whole place smells of rubber and oil, and he can hear the hard clang of metal tools dropping onto a hard floor now and then, sending a shock through the bones of the building.

The way Thomas tells the story, he lied about his age to enlist in Vietnam, flew over in sixty-eight, and was shot in the ass, low back, and thigh near the end of his first tour of duty. He'd already decided to avoid a second tour if he could help it. He was taken to some military hospital and patched up. Told he'd likely be given an honorable discharge and would get to fly home within a few weeks. But he had other plans. Once he could get around, Thomas got dressed and walked away from the hospital. *I heard how things were going for returning soldiers.* Besides, he wasn't sure America was really his home anymore.

He learned to tattoo over there, lived there, married his wife, had Tommy, and would have stayed. But his wife got sick and died. He moved with Tommy back to the States in the roaring eighties. Thomas's sister had offered to help with Tommy. In school, Tommy couldn't speak great English, but he took to shop class.

"Thomas," Newton calls out.

"What?"

"Why don't people call you Cranky Tommy? It's got a nice ring to it."

"Bullshit!" Thomas declares with his back turned to Newton. "My name is Thomas. Abbreviations are for kids and men in collared shirts with those fucking itty-bitty buttons to keep the collar from sticking out. Do I look like a collared-shirt motherfucker?" He waits for an answer.

"No. You do not. But nicknames are okay?"

"What? I'm busy."

"I'm saying you don't mind being called Cranky."

"Why would I?"

"So abbreviated names bad, nicknames good."

"Yes. I guess. Now shut the hell up."

"Yes, sir." Newton stands as tall as he can and snaps off a smart salute like he means it. Thomas doesn't pay any attention. Newton figures the subject is dropped, gets distracted taking stock of the place.

Then Thomas pipes back up, "How would you like it if everyone called you Newt? Like that puffy politician? Newt Grindstead or some such. The one that looks like uncooked dough. Would you like to be called Newt like that asshole?"

"Some people called me that. But no, I don't like it."

"See," Thomas says, as if his line of reasoning is unassailable.

Newton walks the perimeter of the dark and dusty space and can't find a portfolio of Thomas's work nor a book or poster of flash art. It concerns him a bit: all the dirt and lack of materials that might mark Thomas as a professional.

"You've done this kind of leg sleeve before, right?"

"I've done it all. You want me to make your pecker look like a candy cane?"

"Let's start with the leg."

From the garage below, Newton hears the mechanics calling back and forth in Spanish, the sound of an air wrench twisting or untwisting lug nuts. Upstairs, the only sounds are Newton's own sauntering gait and Thomas scratching out marks on paper.

"You sure you want it in this kind of typeface?" Cranky Thomas calls from across the space.

"Yep."

"You know that tattoos are made with permanent ink?"

"Yep."

"Well. It's your leg, I guess." Thomas bends back over his work.

There's a low leather couch, part of some old sectional, with its legs missing so the dust flap splays out on the floor around it. In front of the couch is a coffee table piled with porn magazines and an overflowing soup bowl that's been recruited as an ashtray for stubbed-out cigars. Newton moves the magazines to read the titles: mostly old *Hustlers*. He scoots a few around and looks at the covers. He recognizes one of the women from a centerfold Albert had kept hidden in his footlocker. Under the top layer of porn he finds a layer of ten-year-old tattoo magazines. These too are adorned with mostly naked women.

"I didn't know they still printed porn magazines," he calls over to Cranky Thomas.

"Of course they do. Dumbass. As long as men will pay to gawk at naked ladies, they will keep printing them. Besides, those are for research."

"Are you trying to remember what a woman looks like?" Thomas just grunts a grudging acknowledgment, intent on his work. Newton tries again to get a rise out of the old man. "Haven't you heard of the Internet?"

Thomas doesn't look over when he says, "Fuck, no. What is that? I'm old and senile and don't know shit." After two beats he adds, "Wiseass."

"I'm just asking a question. Calm down. Don't let me distract you."

"Fucking considerate of you, you shithead. All you've done the past ten minutes is distract me. But good for you I'm talented. I'm done. Let's get this show on the road, soldier."

Newton follows Cranky Thomas's saggy ass into a room at the back of the place. He's surprised by what he finds. It's clean and bright, with a comfy-looking pallet on the floor.

"Well, this looks like it's ready for inspection," Newton says.

"It's SOP. What kind of outfit do you think I run here?"

Thomas walks to an old porcelain washbasin. It has dark bruises around the rim where the enamel is chipped. He grabs a matching oversized pitcher and pours the basin full. He takes soap and washes his hands like a field surgeon. When he's done, he carefully picks a white hand towel from the top of a stack and ritualistically dries his hands, one finger at a time. There's a full-length mirror propped in one corner, and Thomas has Newton stand in front of it.

Thomas gathers a few things, snaps on some black surgical-style gloves, and squats down to shave the back of Newton's leg. When he's done, he takes a piece of paper and transfers his line work onto Newton's smooth skin.

"Take a look at the placement. Tell me what you think."

Newton turns his back to the mirror and looks over his shoulder at the purple ghost image. It reads *ONE FOOT IN THE GRAVE*, in a typewriter font, running in a line down toward his Achilles tendon.

"Looks good to me."

"It best look good, 'cause I'm not going to change it," Thomas replies. "Now lay your ass down and try not to cry like some pantywaist."

Newton stretches out on the pallet, his chin propped on his fist, while Thomas rolls a cart over and gets his machine fired up. Newton would guess the tattoo contraption Thomas uses is handmade. It rattles and vibrates loud enough to mask any of the garage sounds below. Thomas nods, his face clenching up tight as he bends over Newton's lower half.

"Now you didn't drink or take any aspirin this morning, did you?" Thomas asks as he dips his needle into a little plastic thimble of black ink.

"Why?"

"'Cause if you did, you're gonna bleed like a son of a bitch and that won't make this any easier."

"Nope. No aspirin. No booze. What kind of degenerate do you think I am?"

"The U.S. Army kind. Now hold still and try to act like a man."

Newton knows that needles are punching into his skin, pushing a line of ink below the surface, but he feels like he's being scraped with the tines of a hot shrimp fork. After a few minutes, Newton gets over it and is able to half relax. Thomas runs the machine, wipes away some blood with a gauze pad, cusses a little to himself, just for fun, dips his needles in the ink, and pushes a little more ink into Newton's leg.

"Aren't you supposed to chat me up to keep my mind off what you're doing?"

"If you want. What's with the tattoo?"

"Well, I made a new friend last night, and he gave me the idea."

"Is it the same friend that gave you that cut on your face?"

"Nope. Different new friend. Same social gathering."

Thomas doesn't respond, just keeps working, settling into a rhythm. The sensation on Newton's calf evolves from specific jabbing pain to a general raw heat that moves down and starts to make the bottom of his foot tingle. It does a little trick to his brain and makes the bottom of his missing foot tingle too. It's unnerving, so he starts talking again.

"I think I'm going to eventually get my whole lower leg covered. You know, everything below the end of my stump. So it's like a matching set." Newton turns his head to see if Thomas is listening.

"Uh huh," Thomas says. "Now stay still."

Newton lies still for several long minutes, staring at the baseboard a few feet in front of him. It looks like it's been wiped down with Murphy Oil Soap, shiny and clean. He sees the floor is swept spick-and-span, too.

So many of his friends over in Afghanistan had tattoos. Hands, digits of each hand etched with letters to spell out compound words when the curled fingers of both fists were lined up, scalps, full sleeves, back pieces, *MOM* on a shoulder in an old-school heart, a girlfriend's name on a pectoral, or maybe the name of a child on a forearm. There was ink everywhere. The army had regulations about tattoos, but they were mostly overlooked.

He'd seen so many tattoos it seemed like a pathetic cliché. Ridiculous really, the way his generation of men and women had turned themselves into living sketchbooks. It was his generation's rattail or mullet, *Members Only* jacket, parachute pants, blue eye shadow, and pastel sweater tied jauntily around the shoulders. *And here I am getting my first tattoo. Hypocrite. But that is just how life goes.* Finally he says, "I got an invitation to this thing. Not sure if I want to go."

"Uh huh. What kind of fucking thing? If this is the conversation part, you're gonna have to do a better job." There's a smile in

Thomas's voice, a peace backstopping his gruff words. Newton gets a sense Thomas is enjoying his work.

"Remember I told you about Etta?" Newton says after a moment. "About her going missing? I think she was kidnapped, but there's no way of knowing. That was six years ago. Six years today. Well, her mom invited me to a memorial or something. I'm not sure what the hell it is. But she invited me and I want to go. Just thinking about it has fucked me up pretty good. No telling what seeing her family would do."

"Yeah." Thomas wipes down Newton's leg again. It's bleeding more than it should. Thomas leans back a bit to get a good look. Decides there is nothing to do but keep going. Then he settles back into his job. "What's the worst thing that could happen? If you go to this thing?"

"I guess I could turn permanently mental. Start shooting people at the local Whole Foods. I do half hate those people. Just on general principle."

"Amen."

"You know, I'm chickenshit about feelings. When everything happened with Etta I couldn't cope, so I bolted out of state. Then I bolted to Afghanistan. Shit. If I could, I'd run away from what happened to Albert and my fucking leg too, but every time I look down I see what I lost over there. I think of Albert." He starts to get choked up, waits a few breaths to get his feelings in check. "It's crushing me," he continues. "It's not like I've gotten any better at dealing with this shit. If anything I've gotten worse. It's just I don't have the option not to. So I thought, what the fuck, maybe it'll help to go to this thing. Being around people that are torn up over the same shit could be good." Thomas doesn't reply. "You know what I'm saying?" Newton adds.

"There's this guy I used to work on. He was a medic in Iraq. He's older than you. A reservist. There was this boy who got blown to hell.

Lost a hand, lost a lot of blood. When this medic got to the boy, the boy barely had a pulse, nearly dead. This guy started to work on the kid. Before he could do squat, the kid died. That day the medic saved four other boys. But the one he lost, the one that was already gone when he found him. That's the one he has nightmares about."

"Yeah," Newton says.

"Thing is, I asked him how many people did he work on. How many people are alive now, walking around, eating tasty groceries and drinking skunky beer while they play grab ass with their sweetie pies? And he told me, 'Maybe a hundred or more.' But he can't give himself any credit for those happy bastards. He can only think about this one-handed kid. It's classic PTSD. That's what they call it these days. They used to say *shell shock* or *Gulf War syndrome* or other shit, but it's all the same. He was traumatized. War really is hell. People aren't made to live that way. I lived through it forty years ago. No . . . wait. More than that. I've heard a hundred variations on the same story from men laying right here on this mat."

"So how does he deal with it? The medic. What does he do to get along?"

"He doesn't really. He drinks and he gets married. When that doesn't work, he drinks and he gets divorced. When he was in last, I gave him a tattoo of a black widow on the side of his neck, and he gave me an invitation to his fourth wedding. Stupid, sad fuck."

"Did you go?"

"Hell, no. Why would I do that?"

Thomas swipes at Newton's raw skin again, assesses his work, dabs a bit more blood away, and hunches over some more. "The point I'm making is he's never been able to let go of something he could never have changed. He lets it eat him up, ruin his life. It's corrosive, the guilt of being alive. Now I understand you feeling shitty about your friend Albert. He died. You didn't. It's the oldest story when it comes to boys and war. It's called survivor's guilt. It's a real thing. I've had it. Maybe I still do. You've got it. The good thing about survivor's guilt though, and it took me a long time to come around to this, the good thing is that you're still able to feel guilty. It wouldn't do Albert a fucking bit of good for you to be dead. It wouldn't make him alive. Would it, soldier?"

"No, sir. Though maybe if we'd piled in the Humvee in a different order. Or maybe if he'd sat his ass on a flak jacket. Some of the troops had started doing that. Using whatever extra body armor they could find as a seat cushion, just in case."

"Maybe, maybe, maybe. Maybe is bullshit. There is reality and there's the fantasy you concoct in your messed-up head. Stick with reality. That's enough to deal with. You have to stifle that *maybe* bullshit."

"Yes, sir."

"And the same is true with this girl, your Etta. The world is full of loss. There are bad people everywhere and stupid mistakes made every day. If Etta cared about you the way Albert cared about you, it's because she knew there was something worth caring about. If you piss your life away feeling guilty, getting in fights, drinking, and smoking weed or whatever drugs you do, then you're being a selfish shit bird. You're pissing on their memory." Thomas takes an especially rough wipe at Newton's aggravated flesh. It feels like running sandpaper over a sunburn.

"Ow, Jesus fucking Christ! What the hell are you doing to me?"

"Quit your bitchin'. I can tell by how you're seeping blood you had at least one drink this morning, or you're still drunk from last night. So just lay still and let me finish."

Newton works hard not to fidget. The discomfort jolts through his skeleton with the pulsing of the tattoo machine. Thomas can see he's about had it, so he tries to get Newton's mind off his body.

"You know," Cranky Thomas says slowly, trying to formulate a thought he's never put into words, "I still live with my wife. Her name is Anh and I loved her a lifetime ago. She saved my life in a way, gave me something to live for. She comes and sits with me in the evenings. Don't get me wrong. She's not a ghost or anything New-Agey like that. It's how I don't forget. I let her come and sit with me. She gives me advice about Tommy, tells me to take better care of myself, reminds me of meals we ate, the old straw mattress we had in our first place. I recall her so clearly, it's almost like she really is still with me."

"I know what you mean."

"You do that with Etta then?"

"No. Not with Etta. But once in a while Albert shows up to call me a dumb ass or laugh his laugh. He used to come around a lot, but it was too hard. Just lately, he's been coming back around. I never thought about it much. Just my mind playing tricks. But now that you mention it, I'm always happy when he shows up. But never Etta. I'd like to talk to her too."

"I don't really believe in any of that spiritual bullshit. But who knows. Maybe you don't hear from Etta because you can't cope with her memory. Or it could mean she's not dead. That she's out there still in the world. That's why she can't come to you. Now relax a few more minutes, will you? You're acting like a twitchy little cunt."

Newton does as he's instructed. He thinks about Etta still being alive. It hurts to imagine she went off and left him behind. But what if she was taken somewhere, not given the chance to get in touch? Like one of those POWs that are held so long they forget who they are or how to speak English.

The tattoo takes quite a bit longer than Thomas had led him to believe. Newton's hips start to ache, his back feels like it might cramp up, and the red heat from the scraping sensation continues to build. About the time Newton feels he's had enough, Thomas leans back and declares, "That about does it."

Newton stands carefully and takes a look in the mirror. He's no expert, but he thinks it looks great. The phrase has one word stacked on top of the next, the spacing looking like someone took an oversized typewriter and punched each letter into his round calf. The ink is mostly dark, slick black, with some lighter, grayscale edges here and there, as if the typewriter didn't strike quite square. It's much better than he expected.

"Wow, Cranky Thomas. You know your shit."

"What the hell did you expect?"

Thomas bends down and slathers a layer of A&D ointment over his work. He's careful but it still hurts. He bandages it and pulls Newton's pants leg into place. Newton fishes in his wallet for some cash. He finds the pictures of him sitting cheek to cheek with Etta. He decides right then to go to the memorial, say his goodbyes.

"Take a look," he says. He unfolds the pictures and holds them out for Thomas to see. Thomas pulls his head back, tries to focus. His mouth draws down hard like he sees something distasteful; his lips relax; his eyes go calm; his bald brows unhunch. He almost smiles as he realizes what he's looking at. He sees Newton, younger, clean-cut, all teeth and eyeballs and angular cheekbones, nearly unrecognizable in his shiny newness. He's squeezed next to a girl about the same age, kind face, pretty, confident, maybe a bit mischievous in the curl of her lip and the squint in her eyes. In the last image, Etta is about to kiss Newton's cheek, her puckered lips held forever a fraction of an inch from touching his skin. Thomas thinks about that thin gap, that tiny distance between the two kids and he lets it break his heart a little.

"Etta, I presume?" he finally says.

"Yes. Etta."

"Well, she looks nice. You look nice, too."

Newton takes the pictures and tucks them safely away. "You ever do portraits?"

"Huh?"

"Tattoos of people. You know. Portraits. Memorials."

Cranky Thomas gets the grit back in his voice, shakes his head as he talks, "I used to. But I would worry about fucking it up. It's too important. You want a likeness of Etta? You get one line wrong and it just doesn't look like the same person. But I know a guy. I can give you his card when you're ready. Just don't tell him I sent you. He hates my old ass."

"How come?"

"I think I slept with his old lady."

"That'll do it," Newton says knowingly. Then, "Okay. Thanks again. How much do I owe you?"

"The ink is free. The advice is sixty bucks."

"I think that's cheaper than the shrink at the VA. Advice was better too. And you didn't ask me about my mother." He hands over the cash, sticks his wallet in his back pocket, and starts to leave. Thomas takes a sip of room-temperature coffee, scowls at the mouth of the cup, pours the rest down the sink.

Newton halts near the door. "Hey, Thomas. What rank were you anyway? When you were over there?"

"I made it to sergeant. They were giving field promotions like they were going out of style."

"Sergeant, huh? Well, I won't hold that against you. You weren't an officer, huh?"

"Hell, no. I believe in working for a living."

"Why isn't your nickname Sarge? And why do they call you Cranky?"

"Sarge is fucking disrespectful. I fucking hate it. The title is Sergeant. Not fucking *Sarge*. Now get the fuck out of here, Newt. Okay, smart-ass. What was the other question?"

"Never mind. I think you answered it."

Newton walks down the steps and across the lot to his old, snub-nosed truck. He'll drive back to his place, change clothes, press his slacks if he can find an ironing board, and maybe get a haircut before the memorial. At least that's his plan.

# EMOTIONAL HOUSE CLEANING

Meg drops her robe and strips off the shirt she slept in, slides on a pair of comfortable jeans and a ratty sweatshirt. She doesn't bother with a bra. She has become very antibra lately. The sweatshirt has a map of Michigan printed across her unrestricted breasts. It reads, *MI happy place*. She bought it from a shop in Saugatuck. She used to vacation there with Charlie and the kids, early every August. They'd rent a cabin in Douglas, just a few miles away. Douglas isn't on Lake Michigan, but Charlie thought it was cheaper, nicer, and less crowded. Meg didn't disagree. They would spend days on the beach, swim in the lake, rent kayaks or Jet Skis and generally eat and drink too much. They'd come home exhausted, broke, happy, and tan.

The warm days of summer, the bustling life of a home filled with young children, the sun-warmed body of Charlie leaning over her for a secret kiss are distant memories now. She stands at her closet's mouth and guides her sock feet into one tall winter boot, then the other.

She tugs them into place and tucks her jeans inside. She pulls her hair back into a nubby ponytail and tromps downstairs to the kitchen. She pulls the sausage sandwich from the microwave and eats it over the sink. Out the window, a bright male cardinal swoops across the yard and lands in the branches of her dying ash tree, like a single drop of blood splashed in a cement sink.

When she's done eating, she rolls her napkin and pitches it in the trash on her way to the hall closet. She dresses in her long winter coat and her scarf. The cap Townes refused to wear is still on the tabletop; she pulls it on her head. *He'll freeze his scrawny ass.*

She retrieves her keys from the bowl on the kitchen counter, searches her coat pocket for gloves. It's going to be bitter out, and she wants to do all she can to brace herself.

The moment she steps outside, an impish blast of wind comes over the house and brings a swirl of dry snow off the roof and down the V in her coat front. *Good morning, Chicago.* She follows a trail Townes left. It leads her to the garage's side door. She enters and walks to her car. When she opens her car's door, its edge bumps into Etta's car, stored under a fitted car cover. She climbs in and twists the ignition. She holds her breath. The cold weather is hard on car batteries. It seems like every other year she has one die on her. The car turns over. She lets it run, leaves the garage door shut. She wants the engine to warm before she lets the cold air in. Townes would disapprove. He complains about the exhaust getting into his room above. *Asphyxiation.* The term pops into her head. *A lack of oxygen that leads to blackouts and ultimately death.*

Etta took swim lessons at the Y when she was in preschool. The graduation certificate required her to jump off a diving board. She was scared. Her tiny little legs took short half steps out to the end of the board. Meg sat in the bleachers watching, far enough away to have a good view. Townes was there, too, in a stroller, trying to put his whole plump foot in his wet mouth. Meg clapped and yelled encouragement to her daughter, but the sound was lost in the cacophony of the immense, chlorinated echo chamber.

The trapped humidity made Meg's hair droop and her shirtsleeves stick to her shoulders. The atmosphere was thick and oppressive and unpleasant.

Etta reached the end of the board and curled her toes over the edge. She looked around for Meg, for comfort, but couldn't see her. Meg yelled and waved louder.

Etta looked down at the instructor treading water below. He waved her in. She closed her eyes and stood blind for ten or fifteen long seconds. She let herself fall. The side of her head struck the board. She tumbled loose, slapped the water hard and at a bad angle. She went under like a rock.

Meg left Townes, didn't even think of him really, raced around the pool, ignoring the signs that read, *No Running*. When Etta was lifted onto the pool deck, Meg was there. Etta had gone blue around the mouth, she was turned on her side, and she coughed out a gallon of water. Meg picked her slim, wet body up, hugged her tight to her chest as her little girl cried.

Meg often recalls that moment. In her worst fears of what happened to Etta, she imagines Etta drowning, her body thrashing as some stranger holds her head just a fraction away from the air her body needs. Eventually, Etta breathes in, fills her desperate lungs with stagnant water, and asphyxiates.

The whole point of the memorial today is to put a stop to the unbidden speculations. To accept that Etta is gone. To accept they will never have more details. No fresh news in six years. When it comes to missing persons, they say you have a few days to find the trail. If it takes longer than that, your odds drop to almost zero. Everyone knows that. *She is gone and isn't coming back.*

After the engine has run for less than two minutes, she pushes the remote on her visor, and the garage door rattles open. She backs the car over the crunchy snow, aims the front bumper into the street, and drives the car toward Ogden Avenue.

At the beauty supply store, she spends a long time looking at hair coloring. She considers making a change. But after weighing the pros and cons, after picking up and reading a dozen boxes, she buys the same color as always.

She checks the time. She could get her fingernails done. She wants to look nice for the memorial. Wants to look her best when she sees Charlie. Not that she expects to rekindle a romance. Though she wouldn't discourage him. She wants to feel good when she sees him. It can't hurt to make him regret having left her, if only a little. After a moment's consideration, she concludes her nails will have to be good enough. Besides, she hates to work after she gets her nails done. It's like throwing her money away.

Instead, she drives to the nearest place to buy cigarettes. She parks in front and walks straight to the counter. The clerk is middle-aged, his gaudy franchise shirt is too small, and his attempt at facial hair is uneven. So much so that if his face were a dog's hide, she would think he had the mange.

"May I be of service?" he says, his formality out of place.

"I'll take a pack of the Native Spirits in the black box. Just one pack."

"We have a sale on the cartons," he says. He points to a sign that reads, *Sale On Cartons!*

"Just one pack, please."

The man has trouble finding the pack right in front of his face. While he searches, Meg notices an old Slushy Pup drink machine on the back counter. "You sell many of those drinks in the winter?" she asks.

"No. Never really. I haven't sold one," the mangy man replies. He drops the hard pack on the counter. "Will that be all?"

She doesn't answer. She watches the fake blue and vibrant red concoctions tumble in their see-through cylinders. She asks, "Why's it back there behind the counter?"

"You'd have to ask the manager."

On a whim she says, "Okay. I'll take a cherry one."

"Are you serious?"

"Yeah. I couldn't be more serious," she says in her best deadpan. The Mangy One can't tell if she's joking.

He gets a cup, puts it under the spout, and twists a handle. The cup fills fast, the fake cherry slush running over the side. He takes a plastic lid and mashes it on. He sets the drippy cup on the counter next to the cigarettes, sucks some cherry flavor off his fingers, and starts to ring her up.

She stares at the cup. She points at where it sits. "I can't take it like that. It's a mess. Can you clean it up or something? Dump it in a different cup?"

"Oh, I'm sorry. That was the last regular-sized cup."

"Really? You haven't sold one all winter and you still ran out of cups?"

"It seems silly to order more if we don't use them. Don't you think?"

"Can you put it in a bigger cup?"

"I could, but I'd have to charge you for the larger size," he explains slowly, like he's speaking to a child.

"Are you fucking serious?"

"Yeah, I'm serious. It's the rules," he says. "Did I mention our TRU brand e-cigs are on sale today?"

Meg ignores his sales pitch. "What are the rules about giving a customer a Slushy Pup that's dripping all over the fucking place?" She picks it up, gets sticky red syrup all over her fingers. She sets it down and shows him her fingers. "Look. Look at that. You see that? You made a mess of my drink. Can you fix it? That'll drip all over if I try to take it. It'll stain my clothes, my car. This cup is a lawsuit waiting to happen."

"I will have to charge you for another one," he says again. His tone makes it clear he believes she's being very unreasonable. "Also, e-cigs are very popular. They are an excellent value. I smoke this brand myself."

"Fuck e-cigs. E-cigs are for assholes." The Mangy One gets red and blotchy under his patchy beard, places a delicate hand over his heart. "I was just doing you a favor," Meg continues. "Ordering this stupid fucking slushy for fun. I used to buy this crap for my kids. So I thought, what the hell. I'll get one today. It's a special fucking occasion."

"You are mom of the year. Do you want me to charge you for two? Or not?"

"I got an idea, you scruffy baboon's ass. You just keep it." She grabs the cup, leans over the counter, and dumps the contents on Mangy's ugly shoes. She takes the pack of cigarettes without paying and walks away. The Mangy One, for his part, stares wide-eyed at his feet, at the mess she made, and wonders who the hell is going to clean it up.

The ten-minute drive back to her neighborhood takes twenty minutes because she gets stuck waiting for two freight trains. She worries the sad freak will call the cops for assault with a sticky weapon. She keeps her eyes in the rearview, but no patrol car materializes. She smacks her cigarettes against the heel of her hand to pack them tight. The trains pass, traffic moves, and she turns onto her street. "That was a smooth getaway, huh?" Meg says to Etta. Etta doesn't respond.

She passes her house and keeps going down the block to the home she needs to clean. She parks on the street. The driveway has yet to be cleared by the kid who works for the realty company.

She piles out of the car. *It's starting to warm up.* Across the street is the house of Mr. and Mrs. Temple. Even though the holidays have passed, the colors flash on the crisscross lines of festive Christmas lights that form an elaborate cocoon around the clapboard abode. The lawn is full of plastic reindeer, drippy with a hard shell of frozen drizzle and a cap of softening snow, and several birdbaths are filled with green and red Christmas balls.

She shakes her head at the things people do to occupy their time once their children have moved away. *People need to fill their lives up, never an empty moment.* She grabs her vacuum in one hand and her tote of supplies in the other and breaks a fresh trail to the back door of the house.

It's a modest ranch, like many in the neighborhood. She fumbles in her tote for the place she stores her keys. She finds the right one, pushes into the house. After she sets her armload aside, she slips out of her boots and leaves them just inside the door. She uses one hooked finger to tuck her feet into a soft pair of fitted slippers. She claps her hands and gets to work.

The house used to be home to a kindly old couple. Before they moved away, ages ago, the man could be seen going on a brisk walk every day. He would step out smartly, long strides, businesslike pace. He was the image of an efficient man with a job to get done, dressed neatly in a button-down shirt with the tails tucked into chinos, the waist belted too tight and pulled too high. The thing she most remembers is how he'd have a good head of steam and then come to a complete stop when he came to a tree in bloom or a baby in a stroller. It was as if he were transfixed. He would say something kind in his mildly French accent to anyone who was close by, like, *Spring is finally here*, or, *Cherish these days. They grow so quickly.* Then he would step out again, eating up sidewalk.

The rumor among the neighbors was that the couple had lost their only daughter to illness. They had moved after the tragedy from whatever country they were from. The Chicago suburb was to be a new place, a fresh start, but the wife had gotten sick too, with something chronic and aggressive and unrelenting. A few times Meg had seen the man carry his wife, like an empty dress draped over his arms, and place her carefully in the passenger seat of their old, yellow sedan.

Meg takes her supplies to the kitchen counter, unpacks them, lines them up. She has cleaned the house once before: mopping floors, cleaning windows, scrubbing toilets, even emptying the fridge and scouring the oven. This would be easier than the last time. She removes her gloves, tucks them in her coat pocket. Her fingers are still gummy with Slushy Pup. She removes her coat, pitches it, along with her scarf and hat, onto the counter. She goes to the sink and lets the water run until it's warm, then uses pump soap to wash her hands. Standing in her sweatshirt and jeans, she realizes how cold the house is.

It has been vacant for many years. As Meg understands it, the property has been repossessed, but the ownership is tied up in court. The bank held onto the property, hoping the last heir would come forward, pay the taxes or whatever was owed, and take over the home, perhaps simply put it up for sale themselves. The heir never surfaced. Meg is fuzzy on the details. The bank, at the time, had its hands full of foreclosure properties, short sales, auctions, and new federal regulations. The empty ranch must have been a low priority. But the bank finally put it up for sale in the past year. There has been no interest on the part of buyers, though Meg doesn't understand why. It would be a good starter house for a young professional or a young couple. She and Charlie would have been giddy to find a house like that twenty years ago.

She takes up the bottle of toilet bowl cleaner, the glass cleaner, and the foaming surface disinfectant. She moves to the only bathroom in the house, snaps on the lights, and begins by squirting blue gel under the rim of the toilet to let it soak. She pumps the squeeze handle of the glass cleaner, lightly spritzes the mirror. Immediately the liquid begins to gather and run in rivulets down the smooth surface, drip on the vanity beneath.

"Oh, shit. I'd lose my head if it wasn't stapled on," she says mildly to her own runny reflection. She hustles into the kitchen and finds the roll of paper towels and a plastic grocery bag to drop them in. She stands in front of the mirror and starts wiping.

With her likeness obscured by swirls of drying window cleaner, Meg can pretend she's looking at Etta. She misses her girl. The teenage years had been rough. Etta was forever rifling through Meg's closet and makeup, taking things without asking. Later, just before she left, things had fallen into a good pattern. They shopped together, shared clothes, liked the same movies. Meg had learned to parent a little less, to appreciate the person her daughter was turning into.

Meg finishes the mirror, catches the last drips on the bottom edge, then sprays cleaner over the vanity top, around the bowl of the sink, and over the old gold-colored faucets. The house has been empty as long as Etta has been gone. *The house knows how I feel, vacant and abandoned.*

Her memory of the time when Etta was taken, understandably, is selective. She recalls the overwhelming exhaustion, the constant worry, the rage and hurt. She was oblivious, not only to what was happening in the rest of the world, but also to what was happening to her own husband, her own son. She lost a full year. During that year she did what was needed, went through the motions, operated on muscle memory and instinct. Her internal life was the only real thing. Everything else, everyone else was like static on a screen. "No wonder the details of what happened to the old couple escape me," she says conversationally. She says it to Etta.

As she cleans, she continues to chat with Etta.

"You never told me what you think I should say at the memorial," she says, continuing the conversation from the last time they spoke. "You think I should speak directly to you? It seems like there's some confusion. Townes, Charlie, Newton," she starts to say, then she amends it, "Your brother, your father, your boyfriend. They seem reluctant to say goodbye. They're treating me as if your death is my fault. They can be so weak. Not strong like you and me. When men cry, they are devastated. Defeated by it. But women, we find reasons to cry all the time, then we wipe the mascara from under our eyes and keep going, stronger than we were to begin with. As strong as it takes."

She finishes with the sink and vanity, pulls back the curtain to the tub. As she grips the material and tugs it, there's a momentary panic that something scary will pop out: a stranger with a knife, a dead animal, a corpse. But it's empty, like last time. "Too many horror movies when I was your age," she says.

She sprays all the tiles, the soap dish, the built-in porcelain shelf. She grabs a fresh rag and begins to scrub and wipe.

"If you were here now, I think I'd tell you: It's simple to be a high school girl. You do what you want. You look good doing it. You wait until one particular boy comes along, then you show your boobs and wiggle your ass the way he likes until you get his attention. You are happy. You play house. You make some babies. You create a whole world for the two of you. Once you get there, if it lasts, you spend the rest of your life trying to hold the entire fabric of the universe together. If you're like me, you stay exhausted with the effort. You become stretched thin and worn through. You see? So, in one way of looking at it, you got to do the best part. The beginning. The middle part is long and not nearly as fun. Trust me."

Meg finishes with the tiles, takes a few minutes on the chrome faucet and knobs. She finds it unfortunate they don't match the sink or the other way around, but that's not her concern. When that's done, she carefully steps out of the tub, squats down on the bathroom floor, and sprays the sides and bottom of the tub. She leans her body as far over as she's able and starts cleaning again.

"The end years, they aren't likely to be any easier than the middle years. Don't get me wrong. I wish you were here. I miss you all the time. But you did get to do a lot of the fun stuff, got to skip a lot of the drudgery. You were happy and beautiful and strong. You went out on top. You understand my point." Her nose begins to run from the cleaning fumes or her emotions. She sits her rump back on her heels, finds a clean rag to use on her nose.

She thinks of saying these kinds of things out loud at the memorial. She realizes it's a question of audience. "Do you think I should be talking to you like this, like we usually do? Or do I need to try to say the things that will make your dad and brother feel better? Because this kind of thing will only get them upset. But if it's about you and me, it's a different ball game."

She moves into the kitchen and finds her oversized plastic cup. Leaning into the tub, she runs a little water and begins rinsing away the residual cleaning product.

"For me," she says, "the big question of life, the one you need to decide as a woman, is how do you fill a life with people to care for, people to care for you in return, and still have any room left to make yourself happy? How do you get what you want from the life you have? How do you make room for *you* once you make your role to be a caretaker for *others*? It's the crux of the problem. If I were starting out like you, I'd think hard about how much you really want to take on, as you build your life, because each thing you add requires time, money, and maintenance. A man: time and constant attention." She turns the tap off, uses the flat of her hand on the smooth tub bottom to squeegee the remaining water down the drain.

"A child demands time, decades' worth. Time for the rest of your life. And money. Tons of money. And constant maintenance. Babies come out as need machines and the only thing that changes as they grow is the specific needs. A pet, a houseplant, a car, a home. It all requires maintenance. Hell, your own body, the thing that carries your secret desires across the face of the earth, it requires daily maintenance. No matter how well you take care of it, it gets older, wrinkled, and out of control. Your cells fly apart and grow things they weren't meant to grow; they become confused and senile. They kill you with tumors and cancer and arthritis and heart disease." She stands, her low back protesting the movement.

She goes over to the toilet. There's a brush stored in a decorative vase in the corner. She grabs its long handle and goes to work. "As a kid you build yourself up, fill your head with goals and aspirations. The rest of your life becomes a slow acceptance of loss, a release of all the things you hoped for, of all the things you planned. A long series of compromises. Life is one big goodbye until you die." She flushes the toilet.

"If I were you, I would think twice about this Newton boy you have your eyes set on. Trust me. He might be cute. He may be popular, but he isn't the kind of guy you want to spend too long with. He will ask a lot of you and not deliver the same in return. He's a taker. Sure, given time, he might come around, but life is short. Trust me on this. Shit, look who I'm talking to. You know firsthand. Don't you? Life is short and you don't have decades to wait for a man to blossom. You have to start out with a good one. On that count I got lucky. And that is all it was. Luck."

She shakes the toilet brush off and returns it to its perch. She squirts a little of the blue cleaner into the clear toilet water, so when the real-estate agent comes and opens the lid, he'll know the toilet was cleaned. She gathers her supplies, returns to the kitchen.

"Of course, Etta, I see the hypocrisy of this advice. When I was your age I made all my decisions on pure guesswork and sex drive." She shares a little laugh with her missing daughter.

"Libido and gut instinct. That's it, that's all. I just made it up as I went along. I suppose it's not fair to expect more from you. But I do. I expect you to be smarter than I was. All the time I've spent making a life for you, you damn well better take advantage of it and make better decisions. Be smart. Be safe." She finds another clean rag and blows her nose. She goes around the house gathering little throw rugs and laying them across the backs of the kitchen chairs. She starts sweeping in the kitchen and moves around the circular floor plan, one room at a time, gathering grit and dust bunnies as she goes.

She doesn't speak for a while, just passes time with her work, feeling comfortable in Etta's quiet presence. She remembers she'd intended to ask Etta something but can't remember for the life of her what it was. Eventually she says, "Sex is a powerful part of our interior life. It's easy enough to find someone to satisfy you momentarily. It's really easy. It's good to want someone who wants you right back, just as hard. But it's rare to find someone who can leave you feeling content, happy, safe, and fulfilled. Leave you feeling like you are the best you. Like you are connecting, sharing who you are in all the right ways. It's bizarre how such a basic thing gets so complicated, but it does. And the longer the relationship, the more complicated it can get. Or if you are smart and lucky in the right proportions, if life cooperates and doesn't screw it all up, maybe you can have a love that goes on being joyful and pure. That's what I would want for you. If you were here."

Meg stops talking, because the hard truth is, Etta isn't there. She won't have to traverse the transition into adulthood. She won't navigate the shifting landscape of a long-term relationship. Meg's advice, hard-won though it is, will never come in handy for her only daughter. Not only that, but Meg is no closer to knowing what she will say at the memorial.

She realizes she's been humming quietly to herself, a tune Etta used to love as an infant, a tune she used to hum as she nursed her daughter, sliding back and forth in the silent glider, with Charlie snoring at the other end of the room.

"You remember this one?" she asks.

Etta doesn't respond. She's drifted off.

Meg sweeps and dusts. She vacuums and replaces the throw rugs. She sprays Lysol in the trashcan and checks that the fridge still smells clean. She gathers her supplies. She reaches for her coat and remembers she wanted to check the thermostat. Down the hall, the old-school, rounded dome is set on sixty-eight degrees. The little bent wire that indicates the internal temperature of the house reads sixty-two. She wonders if the furnace is working right, or maybe the thermostat is too ancient to be accurate. *Things wear out, same as people.*

She opens the door to the basement. With each step down the dark stairway, the air temperature drops a degree. At the bottom she finds a pull chain and gives it a tug. There is a giant iron furnace that occupies the far end of the basement. She walks over to it, tries to find another light, but doesn't see one. She takes a quick trip around the basement, looking for a flashlight. She passes a locked cage with two shelves of storage. Mostly what looks like old camping gear: a metal disk canteen, a rolled sleeping bag, a cot, a backpack, and a brand-new covered litter box. Nothing valuable, but she's surprised the items have been left in storage. She strolls past a huge, two-compartment cement utility sink sitting on rusting, angle iron legs, and a pegboard with a few tools dangling from hooks. No flashlight.

She guesses the furnace is working well enough. Besides, furnace repair is not her responsibility. She pulls the chain to switch off the light and tromps back up the steps. She bundles up, switches into her boots, and gathers her tote and vacuum. She's careful to lock the door on her way out. The day feels even warmer than when she went in. Water drips from the trees, the power lines, and the eaves of the house. She follows her own sludgy trail back to her car and rolls down the block to park in her garage. She barely notices any of these actions, her body just going through the motions.

# PRINTER'S ROW RESPITE

Townes sleepwalks through the rest of the ride to Chicago Union Station. First he stands in the vestibule with the Metra officer, giving a required incident report. The train jostles him back and forth as it switches tracks, slows to stop at a platform, and speeds on to the next. When the force of the movement threatens to knock him over, his hand stretches for support on the nearest handrail. Mr. Stephanopoulos, the grandmother with the little girl at her knee, and the poorly dressed ticket taker each contribute to the report the officer takes. Each of them supports Townes's version of events and defends his actions. They add to his version, explaining that the man in the fatigues and army surplus coat pulled a knife from his belt in a flash during the fight and used the pommel to strike Townes in the side of the head. At the news, Townes feels the knot above his left temple and knows what they say is true.

Even the grandmother, in her broken English, manages to cast Townes in a positive light. She reaches over and hugs him before she walks away. The little girl, who is called Esmeralda, her big round cheeks reminding him again of photos of toddler Etta, gives him a happy smile and a wave when she leaves. She's holding her green earmuffs loosely in her other hand. The sight of the tiny person walking away, oblivious to the tragedy she barely avoided, gives Townes a deep satisfaction. A peace deeper than he's found through meditation.

Townes is given a business card with the officer's name and told to call if he remembers other details, then the officer marches his tactical uniform down the central aisle of the train to request a statement from the Chinese Christian, if he can be located. Ticket Taker heads in the opposite direction to punch holes in more tickets and sell more fares. Townes says his goodbyes to Mr. Stephanopoulos and wanders half-dazed, back to his seat behind Stoddard.

"I kept my eye on your stuff," Stoddard says, passing his flask over the seat.

"Thank you," Townes replies, taking a sip. It stings a cut in his mouth, and he can taste the salt of his own blood. He tries to pass the booze back.

"You keep that. You might want another nip later."

Townes doesn't argue. He slips the flask into his pocket with his phone and headphones.

A new passenger takes the seat in front of Stoddard. The two start talking about school closings, about school kids crossing gang boundaries, about parking meter rates, ride-sharing companies, the rise in police shootings of black men, and eventually food deserts. Townes barely notices until the conversation gets heated.

Stoddard says, " . . . the schools with little brown babies get shut down, but the ones full of bright white faces get to stay open."

"Well," the new passenger says in a reasonable tone, "CPS has a student population that is around ten percent white. In nearly any scenario in which a large number of schools are closed, it would have a disproportionate effect on minority students. Nine out of ten students are not white. It's just the way the numbers work."

"I'm not talking about numbers. I'm not talking about a system and how it has failed. I'm talking about people, about good families and their sweet babies. Little brown babies aren't numbers." Stoddard waves his yellow arms and pitches his voice for the passengers below. "Brown babies need as good an education as white children. They are not, as you think, numbers on a spreadsheet. I know we live in a free market. But that doesn't turn everything into a commodity. It doesn't mean children should be moved around like credits and debits on a ledger. Little brown babies are worth more than a few tax credits. Black lives matter too." He goes into full-on preacher mode. "They did not fail the system, the system has failed by not educating them, not lifting them up. The system is setting them up to fail. The system has failed them. It is the failed system keeping them down."

"No. You misunderstand my . . ."

"Oh, I understand. I understand better than you think. You think because I disagree with you, I must lack the capacity to understand your point. I will not be condescended to. I think we are done." With that, the conversation ends but a strange monologue continues. The new passenger turns his face forward, frustrated but at a loss as to how to fix the problem. Stoddard continues to mumble, clearly agitated, behind the back of the new passenger.

"Try and tell me about statistics and numbers. I'm not missing the point. He's the one missing the point. He thinks that just because . . ." He doesn't speak loud enough for the new passenger to feel the need to respond, but loud enough that he can hear every point Stoddard enumerates.

Townes half listens for a time, then tips a few more sips from the flask, puts his earbuds in to deaden the sound, and waits for the train to come to a complete stop on the dark platform beneath Union Station.

All the passengers stand and begin jockeying for position before the doors are opened. They don their winter gear, secure their bags and backpacks. They look at their seats to confirm they haven't left a glove, a cap, a wallet, a phone, or their monthly pass clipped to the seat frame. They carry their travel mugs and water bottles. They try not to touch the people packed next to them. Townes joins the queue, shifting his weight from one foot to the other.

When the train doors open wide, he files slowly down the stairs, waiting his turn to step into the vestibule again. As he edges forward, he spots something shiny on the ground. He reaches down and holds the square of cold metal between his fingers. He knows it as the buckle from Esmeralda's little boot, finally turned loose as she left the train. He doubts he'll ever see her again to return it, so he lifts his coat and slips it in his back pocket, happy to have a keepsake. Then he waits for his turn to take the steps onto the platform. He merges and lets the crush of pedestrians push him along until the escalator dumps him onto street level.

He crosses the Chicago River, the bridge swaying and bucking like the deck of a ship as the car traffic and foot traffic beat out competing rhythms in opposite directions. He walks a zigzagging pattern along the sidewalks and across the streets, moving away from the heaviest commuter routes to less traveled areas. The sidewalks in the city's center have been cleared of snow, but the piles along the curb make the way narrow.

He passes beneath a block-long array of scaffolding built the previous summer to protect pedestrians from construction debris during the stone and glass building's architectural face-lift. Summer storms and an early, unusually harsh winter curtailed their progress and interrupted their schedule. *Now*, Townes thinks, *the scaffolding is a rusty metal promise, a physical reminder of the intention to complete the renovations.*

*Busy busy.*

As is his habit, Townes notes that his mind is wandering, that he isn't focused on his steps, on the sensations of the moment. Instead his thoughts range and leap from place to place. He doesn't see the things around him; he's living too much in his head, not connected enough to his body and its place in the world.

On this occasion, he makes no effort to correct himself. An hour ago, he believed that walking forward one step at a time and taking life as it came would expand his existence like the expansion of his ribcage when taking a deep breath. But now, that seems foolish: thin, pathetic, and easy to dismiss. It's petty to care about trivial things like his meditative practice. How can he spend his time on self-centered activities when there are people out there intent on doing wrong? How can he count breaths when some little girl he's never met needs protection from a monster? He willfully lets his mind go. He lets his thoughts run their course and doesn't try to reel them in.

He knows, with no proof to back it up, Army Coat and his hunting knife will be out again. That man with the prowling eyes will not let go of a thing like losing Esmeralda. He could be watching her now, tracking her, his pointed nose sniffing the air like an urban coyote to catch her scent in the wind. If he isn't watching her, some similar girl will cross his path. He will cruise public places where families gather. Maybe walking together, bundled in puffy layers against the weather, like colorful waterproof marshmallows, milling around the Museum Campus, and no one will be there to stop him. No one will notice how he lures a child away. The mother will be preoccupied with another child. The father will be gawking at an exhibit. Who will be there to look out for the girl? What's to stop her from vanishing? Vanishing as Etta vanished.

He answers his own questions. *I could be there. I could be there again.*

Ahead of him, the foot traffic is being funneled into a single file around a sign warning of falling ice. Most people take the warning seriously. Townes watches one college kid, the furry earflaps of his hat bouncing like those of a puppy at play, ignore the warning and cut down the open path under the overhanging ice. A fist-sized hunk comes loose, tumbles thirty feet, picking up spin and speed, and glances off his shoulder. He flinches from the impact, keeps moving as if unhurt, but his hat flaps less as he gets over to the recommended path as quickly as he can, glancing at the ledges above.

Instead waiting his turn, Townes ducks into a revolving door and cuts through the cavernous, warm hall of his favorite building. The floor and wainscoting are thick slab marble, the vintage hanging fixtures are ornate and Art Deco with a gorgeous patina of age. The newel posts and doorknobs are convincing replicas of the originals.

They'd been formed from massive hunks of brass that, he was told, scavengers used to pop loose and sell as scrap.

Compared to the harsh noise and reflected light outside, it's another world in here. It's calm. No traffic noise penetrates the thick walls, and it's dark with ancient cast-iron radiators spitting moist warmth into the air every hundred feet down the hall. As he walks, he passes the espresso shop, a throwback barber shop, the vintage clothing store, a sandwich shop, the handmade hat shop, a tailor advertising suits made to order, the imported-leather shoe shop, the cigar shop, and the shoeshine stand at the far end.

Townes once stood near an architectural bus tour and learned that the building is on the National Register of Historic Places. At one time it encompassed more square footage than any other building in the country. It's the kind of building where a noir-era, hard-boiled gumshoe might have rented a small office in some back corner of a top floor, his catchy name painted onto the frosted glass and covered in gold leaf. Something like: *Jack Dart Investigations*. For breakfast, he'd drink whiskey from a heavy, diner-style mug with his feet up on his desk, waiting for the next leggy dame to come in and beg for his help to solve her hard-luck story. At least, that's what Townes imagines.

The building is a place separate from the stream of time outside. The elevator is the kind with a hinge-cage door and designated operator who greets you as you enter and knows your floor by memory. He convincingly wears a maroon uniform with gold-tasseled epaulettes and matching pillbox hat. Townes imagines, if he had the compulsion and the funds, he could walk in, in his street clothes, and leave an hour later looking and feeling like a different person: new suit, shoes, and hat, new haircut, and a new sense of self.

Wanting to be someone else, someone different from Townes Messenger, is a familiar longing. He's always felt he didn't measure up to his father, wasn't growing into the kind of person his mother had hoped for, didn't have a place in the world. He wasn't what girls his age were looking for. Mostly, he was a disappointment to himself. In the end, he'd been a poor brother to Etta. *If it was truly the end.* Perhaps that is what his meditations are about: personal transformation. In the absence of significant change, at least the practice helps him live with himself.

He pushes the revolving door on the opposite end of the block-length hall and steps back into the modern city in winter. The L rumbles overheard, raining down snowmelt droplets and stirring a cloud of crystalline snowflakes. Cars honk at pedestrians who continue to cross the street despite the flashing *don't walk* sign. He has an urge to retreat into the anachronistic space he just left.

But his destination is only a few more blocks. A couple more crossings, and he will be in Printer's Row. He will be with Dory. He feels freed by his experience on the train; he'll be able to express his feelings, explain himself with a clarity he's never managed. He waits for the crosswalk sign to change, crosses between cars that have tried and failed to push past before the fresh rush of foot traffic. The streets are less crowded the farther south he moves.

The first time he saw Dory, her hair was yellow with black tips, like a bumblebee. He was waiting to get an order to go so he could sit in the little park and watch people walk their dogs. She grabbed his food and left the store. When he realized the mistake, he followed her to the bookstore where she works. They traded bags, and she invited him to have a cup of herbal tea. They shared a meal; they discussed philosophy and religion. When he had no excuse to continue standing there, he said, "Well, nice to see you."

"We should do this again," she said.

"That would be nice," he replied. "When?"

He thought he had ruined it, being too eager, but she replied, "Same time next week." And he has been coming back ever since.

He steps into a final crosswalk. A car honks, nearly hitting him. He hops away from the bumper. He hadn't even seen it, hadn't thought to look. Had stepped right into oncoming traffic. He runs on across the street, the driver yelling from inside his warm car, his rage muffled by the sealed windows. Townes leaps a pile of black snow and lets his heart slow on the empty sidewalk. For the second time in the past hour, the spike in heart rate leaves him feeling spent. *Maybe this is what shock feels like.*

It's no wonder Townes's emotions are off, no wonder he's distracted. Saving Esmeralda was the first time he'd actively engaged in the world in years. It was the first time in his entire life he'd initiated a physical confrontation. It had hurt, being bashed in the head, but a part of him liked it. It hadn't been as bad as he feared. Having survived it, having chosen it, is an accomplishment, something even Charlie would be proud of.

Meg would disapprove, not because he fought, but because he put himself in danger. Because he took an unnecessary risk and Meg has become overprotective when it comes to Townes, her only surviving child. That doesn't matter. His mother wasn't there. Today, he was a participant rather than an observer, and he is impressed with himself.

He plays his tongue along the inside of his bottom lip. The skin is torn and ragged from being pushed against his teeth, but the bleeding has stopped. His lip, he realizes, is a bit puffy. He probes it with his fingers. It's definitely tender. The sensation makes him smile. He has done something bold and managed to survive. He feels something unfamiliar: pride. Pride for taking initiative is a new phenomenon.

He walks the last few paces to the building with a low-relief sandstone frieze of a group of printers working a giant hand press. The image runs overhead the entire length of the storefront. It's the kind of craftsmanship and attention to decorative detail that would never be reproduced today. Garamond's, the ground-floor business, is named after a famous type designer, back when all printed books were hand set.

He moves past the glass front of the print-themed coffee bar, sees art students spread around the tables, drinking frothy cappuccinos and mochas and typing on their MacBooks, surfing the web, listening through their big, soft headphones. He pushes the heavy door next to the entrance and takes the long stairway to the business above, his destination, Second Story Books.

Every stair creaks on the way up. He turns into the space and immediately lays his eyes on Dory. She has shaved her hair down to fuzz and dyed it a pale pink. It looks stunning against her skin tone. She's talking to a customer, makes a crooked face at him when the customer can't see. He smiles the kind of smile that makes his whole body feel light. He browses the shelves of used books to wait for Dory.

Townes has learned over the past year or so that Dory's immigrant parents opened Second Story Books in the late seventies when this part of the South Loop was an area filled with unoccupied buildings and unused commercial spaces left behind when Rand McNally, RR Donnelley, and Franklin Printing & Graphics all abandoned the area for cheaper spaces near better schools out in the suburbs. The store began as an eclectic assemblage of Hindu statuary and books on various world religions. In the eighties, developers turned their eyes to the old buildings as likely spots to convert into lofts, condos, and storefront businesses. The foot traffic in the area changed, and the bookstore morphed into a place for crystals, incense, candles, and tarot cards. As universities expanded into the neighborhood, students began to frequent the store, and it eventually arrived at its current incarnation: a general used bookstore with an emphasis in esoteric religious material and hard-to-find and out-of-print art books.

As is his habit, Townes migrates to the shelf of Buddhist and Taoist texts. Dory will know to find him there. He picks up an edition of *Zen and the Art of Motorcycle Maintenance* that he's never seen before. The cover has what looks like an abstract interpretation of the red leaf of a Japanese maple. It is not, strictly speaking, a book about Buddhism, but it is a book he loves, about a father and son who take a motorcycle trip on an old BMW from Minnesota to Northern California. Robert Pirsig, the author, is not a perfect father, but he is the kind of thoughtful, sincere man that Townes has always hoped Charlie might evolve into. Perhaps Charlie is exactly that kind of man. Townes wouldn't really know. They barely see one another.

The book is in good shape. He checks for the price, written in pencil in Dory's light script on the inside front cover. It's only five bucks. He decides to buy it, give it another read. Maybe he will gift it to Charlie once he finishes *The Tao of Pooh*. *If he ever reads it.* He thumbs the pages and tucks the book in his armpit as he browses some more.

It only takes a few moments before Dory finds him.

"Hey there, stranger. I didn't think you were going to make it. You're late." She self-consciously rubs her freshly sheared hair. She moves closer to him. Her body smells like chai tea. Her voice is musical, a soft, lyrical soprano with a slight British enunciation to her words.

"Your hair looks so good. Is it cold?" His hand lifts to touch her, but he stops it, leaving it as an awkward gesture. *Still too timid to touch her.* He decides, that moment, it is time to act. Just like on the train, take a leap.

"It is! It is so very, very cold." She laughs and rubs her hair some more.

He smiles with her and explains, "I got a late start, missed the express, and there was an incident on the train." He is biding his time for the right moment.

"What kind of incident?" She looks concerned.

He, uncharacteristically and bravely, takes her hand and says, "I'll tell you all about it. I want to tell you, but let's order lunch. We can talk when I get back with the food." He says it like a love note.

She looks down at the place where they are touching. He has the impulse to release her, but he holds tight. She flashes her happy eyes at him, glances away with mild embarrassment. After a long moment, he lets her warm hand go so she can call in their standard order.

Their bag of food isn't ready when Townes endures the wind and cold to hustle the two blocks to the little raw-food restaurant at the back of what was once the Dearborn Train Station. He takes out his phone as he waits. He almost never surfs the web, too many distractions. He turns his Wi-Fi on and accepts the terms set by the vegan place. He remembers he's supposed to call Newton but doesn't want to. He sees a QR code on a display of bottled coffee and shoots it with his QR reader. His screen flashes to a video about a new coffee roaster and bottler located somewhere in the West Loop. They fire-roast their beans in small batches and tumble the beans over a flame by pedaling a bike. He watches the short GIF of the bike turning the beans, of the flames licking the perforated cylinder.

His food is set on the counter. He pays and walks back. Despite the warm sun on his head, the wind has a bite. He keeps his head down against the cold. Back up the stairs in Second Story Books, they share their meal, as always, standing at the end of the counter.

He takes a bite of his avocado and tomato sandwich on almond-based uncooked bread. It is delicious, as always, and messy. He sets the sandwich down, wipes the edges of his mouth as he continues to chew.

"How do your parents feel about the new hair?" he asks Dory, once she has swallowed her own bite of food.

"Oh. Same as always. They love me no matter what. As long as I am a devout Hindu, they allow me to make my own choices when it comes to my hair."

"They sound so great. Maybe, sometime, I could meet them." He is surprised by his own presumptuousness. Pleased, too.

"Yes. Perhaps." She glances away from his face, shy for a moment. "Though they would insist you come to our home so my mother can cook a traditional meal. It would be very formal. My brothers and sister would be there too. They would be curious about you. You would have to endure my father's scrutiny. Also, it would be best if you were willing to say you are considering becoming Hindu." She makes the last statement with an apology in her tone.

"You mean it will be best if I lie?" he asks.

"Yes. That would be best," she says. They smile. They eat and discuss the weather. "Perhaps it would be easier if I met your mother and father first," she suggests after a while. Then adds, "I don't mean to invite myself. I know your parents aren't together. I just meant, easier than you surviving my parents." She finishes her last bite of sandwich.

"That," he says kindly, "would be a whole different kind of challenge. Maybe we should put off the whole meet-the-family step. Maybe something easy to start. How about a movie some night?"

"I'd like that."

Townes doesn't know how to respond in words, so he grins his grin at her. He is still grinning as he tries to eat the last of his sandwich, so much so that it's difficult to chew. A customer comes in and asks for books on Jewish mysticism.

"Right this way," Dory says. She walks away from the counter. Townes does three fist pumps when he's certain she can't see. He munches on some carrot chips. The customer and Dory return to the counter. Dory punches buttons on the register, inserts a bookmark into one of the books, and slips the stack into a paper sack. The customer leaves happy.

"Another satisfied customer," Townes says lamely.

"So," Dory says, only acknowledging his comment with a crooked little twist of the lip. "You promised to tell me what happened on the train."

He washes the last of the carrot down with some room-temperature tea. Then he recounts what happened on the train. He starts with Esmeralda nearly falling on the tracks and how he was drawn to her, how she looked like his sister. He described her coloring while her grandmother nodded off. He ends with Army Coat striking him and scurrying away through the snowy lot.

When he finishes, she says, "Oh my goodness, Townes. You really did that?" She looks on him with wide hazel eyes. She tries to keep it out of her voice, but he can hear he has impressed her. "What possessed you to do such a thing? I mean, besides the obvious, there was a little girl that needed you."

Townes considers the question. He wants to tell Dory about the day Etta disappeared, wants to share a secret he has never uttered, but he fears Dory will hate him if he comes clean. He's not certain how to make her understand that his actions today are to compensate for guilt he carries. Another incident comes to him, another thing he's never spoken of, one that he harbors guilt over.

"During my sixth-grade year," he explains, "I was on a school bus, a field trip to the Museum of Science and Industry." She shakes her head that she knows the place well but doesn't want to interrupt.

"The bus stalled. The driver radioed for assistance, and we parked on the side of the road. It would be a twenty-minute wait before a new bus could arrive. The teachers let the driver turn on music to keep us occupied. In the bus, a kid named Roger, a flamboyant and powerfully personable gay kid who everyone loved, started showing off his best new dance moves." He watches Dory's face. He decides it is safe to be frank.

"To be frank," he says, "I wanted to watch Roger dance too. He was a good dancer, and funny. A natural entertainer. All the other kids stood and crowded out my view. They were inconsiderate and I was insulted. To be even more honest, I was a little jealous of the attention Roger was getting. So I sat staring out the window and wishing I had taken dance lessons." Townes gauges Dory's reaction. She nods for him to go on.

"Across four lanes of traffic was a brick apartment building. Out from a doorway in the building ran a naked woman." Dory looks surprised, riveted.

"It was obvious she was running scared," he says. "I mean, she was outside naked. But also, she kept looking back at the doorway as she ran, tripping over her own toes. Her breasts jangled in crazy directions and it took me a moment to understand what was happening. Honestly, I hadn't seen a lot of nudity and it was distracting." Dory makes a rolling gesture with one hand, to indicate he should keep going. Maybe talk faster. *She wants to know what happened.*

"Well, I was kind of stunned. As you can imagine. I started to notice little details. Like she wasn't actually naked. She was topless, but with flesh-tone pantyhose on her lower body. The control-top kind, pulled way up under her chest. And the hose had a tear in the outside thigh closest to the bus. Her body kind of welled out of there as she ran, as if the uncompressed skin was swollen."

"Oh my," Dory says, unable to contain herself. She smacks a hand over her mouth to keep herself quiet. Townes sees her big eyes peering over her hand, and he falls for her a little more.

"This naked woman kept looking back over her shoulder, like she was expecting someone to come after her." He's gesturing, getting into the storytelling. "I remember I looked around me in the bus. No one else was seeing what I was seeing. Not the teachers, not the driver, not the other kids. Roger was really putting on a show. He was kind of an attention slut, really, but he was good and the whole bus was clapping. The music was up. All the kids were whooping and doing that raise-the-roof move." He demonstrates the move. She nods her head, her hand still over her mouth.

"When I looked back out the bus window, a man in jeans and a sleeveless T-shirt came out of the apartment building, sprinting full speed, covering the distance between him and the woman in no time. His arms pumped, and I remember how he made his hands into blades when he ran, cutting the air." Townes shows Dory the hands he means.

"I watched as he reached out his arm, his body stretching like an athlete in a relay. He gripped a hank of the woman's hair right on top of her head, then he put on the brakes, yanking her back." Townes pantomimes the man's movements.

"It was crazy. Her feet just flew up in the air. He had her whole body just by the hair. She fell on the ground, but he still had her. He started dragging her back to the apartment, like one of those old shows of a caveman finding a wife. He just pulled her by her hair, hose-covered legs getting runs and holes as she kicked and bucked against him. Her hands grabbing onto his hand where it had her head. Not so much to pry him off, as to keep him from ripping the top of her scalp off." Now he calms down, thinking of the confession he is about to make. He speaks more softly, soberly.

"I looked around, hoping someone else would see it, wanting the teachers to do something, but I was the only one who noticed. Then the naked lady was gone. Back into the apartments. And I sat there with my mouth open like an idiot. I never said anything to anyone." Dory drops her hand from her mouth. She reaches across the counter and pats his hand to reassure him.

"We sat there much longer than twenty minutes. I stared at the apartment the whole time, trying to get some clue about her situation. I never saw her come out. Never saw the man who caught her. Never told anyone what I'd seen, even as I filed off the bus; even as I passed Mr. Busby, the science teacher, and Mrs. Hefner, his student teacher. I didn't say anything." Townes feels bad now, ashamed.

"You were a little boy, Townes," Dory says.

"I was young, but I regret not having tried to do something. At least told someone. Better yet, made a fuss, raised a stink. I could have done something. Anything. I was embarrassed, scared, and I guess I didn't think anyone would believe me. To be honest, again, I was not the kind of person who would do something about a situation like that."

"But today," Dory said. "Today you could have sat quietly, but you didn't. Even when that little girl was safe, you still tried to stop that man from getting away. He'd already given up the girl. Had already left the train. She was safe. You were safe too, on the train, but you still tried to stop him."

"Yes." He hadn't thought of it quite that way. He realizes she's right. Dory seems a little awed by his selfless bravery. He hadn't thought about what he was doing. He'd just done it.

"So now you are the kind of person who would do something." Dory, with her new, short hair the color of pale roses, is the loveliest sight he has ever witnessed. Her big eyes draw him in, her smooth skin contrasts with her bright, perfect teeth. He's in no position to judge the merits of her statement. He simply feels compelled to agree with anything she says.

After an uncomfortably long pause, he snaps back to reality and says, "Maybe so. I like to think so." He looks down to where his hand rests on the counter, to where Dory's fingers rest lightly on his hand. He doesn't move his hand away, although he's finished his story. Dory doesn't move away either, and that feels very good.

# ABRUPT CHANGE OF PLANS

The truck's interior is nice and toasty as Newton makes it back to his place. There's a patrol car parked across his assigned and numbered parking slot when he pulls into the apartment complex. He slows his car to a crawl and rolls down his side window to stare in disgust at the cruiser. *That's some bullshit!*

It's a common sight to see the cops here. Low rent and young couples are a recipe for frequent domestic disturbances. Over the summer there was a kid who got arrested three times. Each time his girlfriend called the police, he'd storm out and march across the undeveloped dirt lot across the street. When the officers approached him, he'd rip off his shirt and beat his narrow chest, screaming, "What? What?" Newton always suspected *Cops* was his favorite TV show. That couple finally got married and moved away.

The kids that live under him now fight often, mostly shrill screaming matches. He doesn't know them, doesn't know their names. What he has noticed is the girl wears flashy yoga pants that read *Pink* across the low back and has blonde, perpetually rumpled hair, as if she's been napping on it. It's likely Rumple Head and her husband who the cops are here to visit. Maybe she got hold of a pair of kitchen shears and pulled a Lorena Bobbitt on that little redneck of hers. But there's no ambulance yet, so not too likely.

A ridiculous surge of jealousy rises in Newton's chest as he lets his truck continue to creep ahead. *I wish I had someone to create a domestic disturbance with.* He thinks again about Mara and wonders at his minor obsession. *Why do I want her so much? I don't even know her. She could be a crazy bitch, a horrible person; she could have one of those accents that drive me crazy or face-melting halitosis.* He shakes off the introspection, chalks it up to blood loss from the tattoo and a residual hangover. He cranks his window up against the cold, continues to pull slowly forward.

With so many parking spots piled with mounds of snow from the plow, it's not at all alarming that his parking place is taken. Hell, maybe it was the first empty spot. Cops always take liberties that they would ticket your average citizen for. He's amazed when he watches cops drive while looking at a laptop mounted at eye level, and then pull someone over they suspect of glancing at their smartphone. He can feel the blood rising to his face as he thinks about it. *I have a problem with authority figures*, he admits. Again, he notes his internal voice. *The memorial for Etta and the talk with Cranky Thomas have me all stirred up.* His emotions are out of control, and he doesn't like it. If he broke the cop's taillight he might feel better but quickly decides it's not worth it and drives on around the corner.

He passes two buildings and slides his truck into a visitor spot near the manager's office. When he slips off his seat, his raw calf bumps the doorjamb and he winces. He hitches his pants up and lets the cold air clear his head. The day is warming up, getting above freezing. The cement is dark with moisture; the snow is crawling back from the edge of the sidewalk, exposing a fringe of brown grass below. Now that he's decided to attend the memorial, he needs to get himself in check. He doesn't want to lose it in front of everyone.

When he makes it upstairs, his apartment door is wide open and he hears the familiar voice of Arthur Heller, the rotund property manager.

" . . . don't feel right about all this," he's saying.

Newton stands in his own doorway, unnoticed. Arthur is speaking to a little milksop in a pale green cardigan, the sleeves too long and covering everything but the tips of his fidgety fingers. One worried little hand grips a balled Kleenex, slowly unfurling it like a damp flag of surrender. His bald spot looks huge and sickly from the back, like a meat yarmulke. As the twerp begins to reply, he moves a foot in and out of one of his fuzzy house shoes.

"Well. He is aggressive and unpredictable," the Cardigan Man says in a chirp chirp chirp that raises Newton's hackles. "When I called him about the music, he threatened me and turned it up even louder."

"Yes. You told me last night," Arthur answers a bit testily.

"What do we have here?" Newton booms. He strips off his coat and lets it fall on the floor as he enters his living room, taking joy in their startled reaction. His hands make fists and he feels his body coil to strike. All he needs is an excuse. There must be some law, some stand-your-ground bullshit that will allow him to beat these two men to the ground just for being in his home uninvited.

"Oh, uh. Hello, Mr. Parker." Arthur turns and his flat palms come up in a placating gesture. His hands are huge and pink, like slabs of pork belly but not as lean. His piggy eyes keep darting off toward the mouth of Newton's bedroom, like he might make a break for it.

The Cardigan Man turns and his face goes a tint whiter. He brings the tissue up over his thin lips and takes a couple of steps back and to the side, so he's half-behind the bigger man. *That won't keep you safe, you simpering little bastard.* Cardigan makes a sharp intake of phlegmy breath as if he hears Newton's thoughts.

"You left your music blaring again," Arthur says calmly. The man in the cardigan nods vigorously. He stabs his eyes over to Newton's bedroom too, back at Newton, finally settling gravely on Arthur as he continues his speech. "Last night. When you didn't answer the door, I came in and turned it off. Your music. The iPod. I used my keys to get in. I didn't mess with your stuff or look around. I just turned the music off. Well, I couldn't find the right button, so I took the iPod out and put it where you could find it. Then I locked up when I left. This morning, you left it playing again. The music. It was very loud. Again. I got calls."

Newton inches forward at the thought of Cardigan having the nerve to rat on him. His hair trigger is pulled taut. At the sudden movement, Arthur speaks louder, pitching his voice off to his right. Newton hears rustling sounds from his bedroom. "Again," Arthur nearly shouts to get Newton's attention. "I came over to turn it off. The music. I had no choice. Your neighbors are getting fed up with the music lately. Not just Mr. Gray here. Others too. All the neighbors called. They called last night and I had to come out in the cold. Then they called this morning and I had to come out in the cold again."

Newton isn't really listening. He thinks about how huge Arthur looks in his puffy vest and unlaced duck boots, about the way his fat arms rub against the sides of his chest as he continues to speak with his hands up, as if Newton is pointing a gun at him. He thinks how the Cardigan Man's too-long sweater and stooped shoulders make him look wet, or like he's made of wax that is slowly melting. There's something sickly and larval about his skin, like a grub or a mealworm. He barely registers Arthur telling him that he is being evicted, that the cops have been called, that Arthur doesn't want any trouble.

"You two make a cute couple," Newton interrupts.

"What?"

"I said, you two make a cute couple." He jangles his finger at them. "It's sleazy to take your lover's side in this. I get it. You're in love. But just 'cause you are butt buddies doesn't mean you should shirk your duties as manager. You should still be fair-minded. I've lived here for a while now. I pay my rent on time." His voice notches up, and he moves in a bit closer. "I'm a goddamned wounded veteran. I gave my leg for this country. What the fuck did you do? Stay here and make out with your little cookie butt?" Arthur drops his hands, seemingly flummoxed by the scale of the apparent misunderstanding.

Newton sees his chance and goes off. He steps forward smoothly, uses his shoulder to ram Arthur to the side. Arthur is off balance and tips right over onto his ass. Newton is face to face with the little wormy man now. He notices, for the first time, that Cardigan is actually a bit taller than him. This irritates him. He gives the other man a two-handed shove in the center of his sunken chest. He also falls over, curling up immediately like a roly poly, protecting his soft underbelly. Newton pauses, confused by the lack of resistance.

There's a rush of movement in Newton's peripheral vision and he turns with his fists up. Two police officers rush out of his bedroom. The man has his sidearm drawn and starts yelling, "Get down on the ground, get down on the ground." The female officer has her hand on her gun where it's holstered at her hip. She's waving him down, gesturing and bending her knees a bit to indicate what he's supposed to do. "Show me your hands," she's saying. "Get on the ground." He recognizes her, thinks they were in the same junior high science class. *Wendy? I'm being arrested by Officer Wendy, who doesn't like to dissect fetus piglets and makes me do all the work?* Everyone is screaming. Both cops keep shouting simple, terse orders. Arthur is advising him at the top of his lungs, "Just listen. Just listen." And Cardigan is making a high-pitched squeal like a cheap home security system.

Next thing he knows, he's lying on the ground and Officer Wendy is securing him. She drives her knee into his good calf and mashes his tender tattoo. His eyes go wet with pain.

"What the fuck," he screams. "Not so rough. That hurts."

That gets his face squashed into the floor by the other officer, who says, "Tough tits. Now be good."

He does as he's told, because he has no other options. He blinks his eyes, his face still in his carpet. He notices a sour smell. *I should try to set some money aside for a vacuum cleaner.*

As Man Cop reads him his rights off a little business card, he thinks how it only takes a moment for everything to change.

One minute Etta is bopping off the bus; the next she's a fucking ghost.

One second Albert is playing air guitar on his M4; the next he's ground meat.

*And now here I am; all the roles have been reversed.*

Arthur and Cardigan are up on their feet, standing over Newton where he lies with his hands cuffed and resting on his tailbone. Cardigan openly smiles at the way things have turned out. When Newton is hauled to a standing position, he stares the little whelp down.

Man Cop pats his body, turns his pockets out, checks around his waist, tosses his wallet to Wendy. He watches Wendy flip through his wallet, riffle his cash with gloved hands, look at his pictures of Etta. Her eyes widen just a fraction before she drops the wallet into one Ziploc bag and the photo booth images into another.

Man Cop feels the back of his calf, notices the bandage there.

"What's this?"

"A bandage."

"What for?"

"A wound."

"Does it hurt?" Man Cop asks and squeezes his leg. Newton jerks away. Cardigan tries to hide a grin with his Kleenex.

Man Cop feels the top of Newton's prosthetic, feels the carbon fiber calf, knocks on it a few times. "What's this?"

"My leg." The officer pulls his pants up, takes a good gander at the prosthetic, tugs the pants back in place.

Wendy steps toward him, scrutinizes his face, the cut on his cheek. He smiles at her. She mostly ignores him, maybe grimaces a bit as she points at his face.

"You got a cut and a bruise up here?" She phrases it like a question.

"Yes I do. Correct," Newton replies.

"What happened to you, Mr. Parker? Were you in a fight?"

"You can call me Newton if you want."

"Answer her," Man Cop says and yanks the cuffs up, sending a bright flash through all the nerves from his shoulders to his wrists.

"I cut myself shaving," he explains. "I'm really bad at it."

Officer Wendy drops the subject. Man Cop uses Newton's cuffed hands to steer him toward the door. Newton takes a step in the opposite direction, bringing him closer to Cardigan and Arthur.

"See you around," Newton says. Giving them a meaningful look.

"Keep moving, tough guy," Wendy says. She sounds angry.

The cops walk him out of his apartment, past the rumpled blonde and her little redneck in his Wrangler jeans and International Harvester trucker cap. They are huddled together against the cold. They look worried yet supportive of one another. Like they are witness to some national tragedy, like they can't wait to save enough money to move the hell out of this shit hole. Newton feels that stab of jealousy again.

Man Cop tucks Newton's head as he's deposited in the back of the cruiser. Once he's settled, the officer reaches over Newton, stretching past him. Newton thinks the guy is about to crawl in with him. He's surprised, at a loss. Different scenarios play through his mind. In one, the cop plans to sit with him, keep a close eye on him. Another one involves police brutality. The last involves unwanted advances. He's unnerved. The side of the officer's face is in front of Newton, his chubby left ear lobe is within reach of his teeth. In basic training he'd gotten into a scuffle over someone sitting on his bed after he'd made it. He'd gotten a grip on the soldier's ear with his teeth and yanked until the ear started to tear away from the skull. This is his chance if he wants to make the first move, but he lets it pass. The officer draws himself out of the car and pulls a seat belt across Newton's lap, clicks it into place.

"Sit tight," he says.

"Hey, this is my parking spot, you know."

Man Cop closes the door on him. Newton watches Wendy carry his old high school backpack, now stuffed full. She also carries the bong and a one hitter that he misplaced months ago. His winter coat is tucked under her arm. The male cop talks into the mic at his shoulder while Officer Wendy walks out of Newton's view to drop his stuff into the cruiser's trunk. He feels it shut, sees the change in light as the glare from the pile of snow behind the car fills the back window like the spotlight in a prison yard.

"And this," he says, "is why I don't like authority figures." Then he thinks, *I should have busted their fucking taillight when I had the chance.*

# GIRL TALK

Meg puts her car back in the garage, pulls up as far as possible without crushing her busted snow blower. She maneuvers far enough away from Etta's car to squeeze her ass out of her own vehicle, but close enough not to hinder the side door to the garage. She checks her parking job, thinks it could be better centered between the various obstacles, but shoves it in park anyway. The engine stops; the garage door rattles its rectangular segments around the curve in the overhead track until it's stacked in place like a solid wall over the opening she just drove through.

It's pitch black. The last of the forty-watt bulbs housed in the frosted plexi nose of the garage door opener has died. She'll have to back out the cars, drag out the ladder, and replace the bulbs. *Maybe in the spring.* Sitting in the dark, she's momentarily crushed by the addition of another task to her to-do list, and she lets her chin drop to her chest.

Managing her life since Etta left has felt like driving in a violent storm on a starless night. All of her focus is on moving forward, surviving the trip, keeping it between the lines. And everything else, all the things she passes along the way, the historical markers, the roadside attractions, the amusement parks, her health, a lover, her dreams of travel, those are beyond her capacity to acknowledge, make time for, or enjoy. The light bulbs are just one of the things she's let drop.

She carefully opens her car door until it touches Etta's car cover. She slides out, leaves her supply tote and vacuum cleaner where they are. She firmly closes the door, remembers her bag of beauty supplies. She opens the door and reaches across until her fingers find her shopping bag. She slams the door tight.

Meg feels her way like a blind woman, her hands out in front of her. She moves between the back bumper of the car and the garage door. Her boots splash through water that has seeped under the rotten weather stripping to form a shallow puddle. *Something else that should be fixed. These are the kinds of small jobs that Charlie would never let go, the kinds of things he would get to the moment he noticed them. But Charlie isn't here.* She finds the wall, which leads to the door. Its handle turns and she's back in the glare of the day.

Inside her kitchen, she's hot. The day is the warmest in a month. When she returns her coat and cap to the hall closet, she sees that her answering machine is flashing. *Probably someone trying to shift the time or date of a house cleaning.* It's a constant juggle. Money is tight for people after the holidays. Some of them ask if they can skip January and February altogether. Or it could be a thoughtful old friend, maybe Trish or Debbie or even drunk old Stacy, calling because it's been six years since Etta went missing. She doesn't have the strength for that kind of emotional outpouring. She lets the machine keep blinking. She remembers her stolen pack of cigarettes.

Meg drops the smokes into the bag with her box of hair color and walks to her bathroom. Just for the hell of it, she swings the plastic bag like it's a fancy wristlet, swings her hips as if she's in a tight black dress heading out on a hot date.

She settles her butt on her unmade bed. She thinks about the things Drunk Stacy might say in a phone message. Something like, "Hey, Meg. It's Stacy. I was thinking of you today. Wanted you to know you were on my mind. We should have a drink sometime. Take care." *Pointless. Awkward. Difficult.* Essentially, there is nothing useful anyone could say. So, understandably, most people don't even make the attempt.

When she was on the other side of this situation, back when she would read about a kidnapped child, of course her heart would go out to them, but, she always suspected parents whose children went missing from the park or the grocery store or movie theater were at fault. She was certain a momentary lapse in attention, a poor series of parental choices had led to the tragic incident. Back then, she held a conviction that good parents, smart parents don't lose children. She would stop short of openly indicting those poor destroyed souls, but just barely. *I mean, honestly, children don't just vanish.* At least, that is how she thought about it. And even now, a small part of her is convinced that somehow, in some way, she could have made different choices, and doing so would have led to a different outcome. An accumulation of better decisions would have unquestionably led to different results. It would have led to Etta, right now, sitting in her own room down the hall, listening to too-loud music, lying back on the bed, her bare feet leaving dirty toe prints on the wall.

She opens her side table drawer and drops in the pack of cigarettes. After her sausage sandwich this morning, she'd wanted to smoke. In the car, stuck at the tracks and worried about being arrested, she wanted a cigarette. After she finished cleaning, she wanted to smoke. Sitting here now, missing Etta, she really, really wants to smoke. But doesn't want to overdo it, and her rule is to only smoke two a day. She closes the drawer and starts getting ready.

She strips off her cherished sweatshirt and comfortable jeans. She stands in her socks and underwear, absently letting her hand fall on her soft belly as she goes to her dresser. She finds a sleeveless T-shirt she always wears for messy jobs and slips it over her head.

In the bathroom she opens her box of L'Oréal semipermanent hair color and gets her supplies in order. From under her sink, she removes a deep Rubbermaid bowl she uses to mix the color. It holds her brush with the long, tapered handle, her wide-tooth comb, some rubber gloves, and a shower cap, all remnants of a time in her life when her looks were a higher priority.

First, her process to keep the color from sticking to her skin: she takes a small tub of Vaseline from the medicine cabinet and dabs some on her fingers. She carefully traces a thin, greasy line around the perimeter of her hairline, careful not to touch her hair because it can keep the dye from sticking. She begins at her slight widow's peak, where the gray is showing at the roots. She works around her forehead, down along her wispy sideburn, and on around her hairline at the back of her neck. She does it by feel, barely using the mirror. She notices how she holds her mouth open and contorts her tongue with concentration, recalls how Etta liked to mock her for the habit. She brings her finger on around until the slick circuit is complete, creating a protective border. Satisfied, she carefully washes the residue from the tips of her fingers.

She wishes she'd shared this trick with her daughter. Etta had never had much interest in coloring her hair. Why would she? Her hair was beautiful, rich, and full. The same color Meg now tries to dye her own. But Etta had a general interest in all things related to makeup, hair, nails, and beauty. Meg can hear Etta respond, "I will add that to my arsenal of womanly arts." Meg smiles a bit.

She takes the tube of color from the box and pierces the opening with the back of the cap, squeezes the tube from the bottom. She's always mildly concerned by the fact that the dark hair color comes out of the tube white. She mixes a similar amount of developer and starts to whip it up with her hairbrush. When it's the consistency of mousse, she stops stirring. It almost immediately begins to oxidize and change color.

"Okay," she says. "Here goes nothing." She pulls on the thin, oversized rubber gloves before she gets started.

She holds the flat brush, takes some of the color onto the synthetic bristles, and pushes the color into the roots along the hairline. Her bent elbows stick out, like she's trying to take flight. She watches the brush in the mirror as she once again traces the perimeter of her hairline, this time working the dye into her hair, careful not to touch her skin too much.

"This process is time-sensitive, and you have to work fast once you start moving." She doesn't speak loudly; no need to project her voice for the Etta in her mind. She is casually conversational. It's nice to have company for this kind of mundane ritual.

"Damn," she says. "I forgot to turn on my radio."

She takes the pointed end of her brush handle and makes a line down the middle of her scalp. She paints the color onto the roots on both sides of the part. When that section is saturated, she makes a new part, using the tail of her brush to grab a new section no more than a half inch closer to her left ear, and she leafs each hair section like flipping the page of a book. She slaps on color, tries to be generous, but not wasteful.

"Sometimes, if you're not careful, you can run out of color before you get to the ends. The ends can soak up a lot of color. So you don't need as much there. But still, try to judge it so you have plenty."

"Okay," Etta says. "I hear you. That sounds like good advice, a regular pro tip."

"With age comes wisdom, I guess," Meg says.

"Also gray hair and wrinkles," Etta adds.

"That's cold," Meg replies, smiling. She hears Etta's distinctive laugh join hers. Meg finishes half her head and starts from her center part again, moving down the other side. She asks, "What color do you think you'd want to dye your hair? If you decided to dye it? Not that you need to. Your hair looks lovely."

Meg's hair is getting a little out of control. Her gloves are covered in goop; the brush handle wants to slip from her fingers. She keeps stacking the wet hair on her head as she goes, but slick tendrils slip loose to leave marks where they brush along her collarbone, neck, and the tops of her shoulders. It tickles.

"Oh, Mom," Etta says. "You really think my hair is pretty? It's pretty ordinary. That's for sure."

"No, no. It's a rich, dark color. It has good body, is easy to work with. You don't know how lucky you are to not have to fight it all the time."

"Really? It wants to curl up and get bushy. It's a hassle."

"It's beautiful. Trust me. What about a hair color? What do you think?"

"I don't know. They say blondes have more fun."

"That is a lie. Blondes do not have more fun. Blondes are preening, needy prima donnas. Blondness is a warning to the world: Stay away. This hussy is no good. Blondness is like that red mark on a black widow. Nature's way of warning the wise."

"I see I've hit a nerve," Etta ribs her mother.

"Maybe you did."

"Okay. No blonde hair for me. How about some kind of red?" she asks.

"Yeah. I can see that." And Meg can see it: Seventeen-year-old Etta is the one she speaks to. She's never managed to see her daughter as the twenty-three-year-old she would have become. Her gorgeous, fair, youthful face is flawless, framed by fiery red hair. She sees it in curls, though she knows Etta would prefer it straight.

"Why red?" she asks.

"Remember taking me to *Annie*? I loved that. All I could do was sing and dance around the house for weeks."

Meg remembers. Etta briefly had Broadway aspirations. Asked to take voice and dance lessons that cost a fortune. Threw big fits until Charlie finally capitulated. Quit after a few weeks. But she doesn't mention that sad episode to her daughter. No need to foul her mood.

Meg moves down the back of her head, one section at a time, adding color in horizontal lines. She brushes the color on nearly the whole shaft of the hair.

"Almost done," she says.

For the last step, she takes the remaining color from the bottom of the bowl, scoops it with her gloved fingers, and massages it into the tips of her hair. She goes in for a last scoop of color and drops a big glob on the floor.

"You didn't see that," she says.

"See what?" Etta asks.

"Exactly."

Meg's nose itches, but she ignores it. When all the color is used, she sets the filthy brush into the empty bowl. She takes up her big comb and makes tracks through her hair to triple-check that the color is evenly distributed. She piles it back up and drops the comb in the bowl. Gravity pulls at the wet arrangement, threatening to spill the whole sticky jumble down her face. She packs the sodden mass against her skull, pats it into place, and stands with her chin tilted up a little. She carefully removes the gloves and disposes of them. She takes up her hair dryer and the shower cap.

"This stuff is heat activated. The heat from my head is enough to do the job, but I like to take a cap like this and trap a little extra heat in it, just for good measure."

She warms the inside of the plastic shower cap with the hair dryer. She carefully slips the cap on over her slimy, heavy hair.

"Pretty cool, Mom. Another pro tip."

"Thanks, kid." Meg likes it when Etta calls her cool.

"But also, you really stink." Etta often follows her compliments with a zinger to soften the sincerity of the moment.

"Nice," Meg replies, like it's not nice at all. "So now, we just let it sit."

She carefully leans down with an old, damp washcloth to scrub the dye from the cold tile floor without tilting her gaze enough to actually see where the spot is located. She manages to find the mess and wipe at it. She checks the clock on her bedside table and thinks again of how badly she'd like to smoke. She wonders if the fumes around her head are flammable. Then she goes down to the kitchen to warm some soup, before jumping in the shower to rinse.

# CHANGE IS THE ONLY CONSTANT

Three university students, two girls and a guy, walk into Second Story Books with paper cups from Garamond's. Dory greets them, but they don't seem to notice. They point to different book covers and laugh loudly at the titles or illustrations. They have opinions about design. They say words like *kerning* and *leading*. They say, *Emigre typeface, sans serif,* and *humanist font*. They agree strongly with one another's assertions and are self-assured they could have done a superior job. Eventually they migrate to the section on sex magic and the Kama Sutra. Their conversation becomes more subdued.

Townes cleans the counter of their lunch trash while Dory goes to check on the students. He takes his copy of the Pirsig book and leaves money on the cash drawer for it. When Dory returns he says, "I have to go. I have to meet my mother. It's something that matters to her. An event."

"Go. Be with your family. Family is important. It's the most important thing. I'll see you next week." She hooks his pinkie finger with her pinkie finger. Their conjoined arms swing in unison for three beats. Then she releases him and turns back to start stocking shelves.

Townes opens the door at the top of the long flight of stairs.

"Wait," Dory says. She's there next to him again. "You can't go out in this weather with nothing on your head." She takes a dark-plaid driving cap by its short brim and works it into place on his head. "It fits," she says happily. She kisses his cheek. It's a quick peck, but euphoria washes over Townes's entire being. His body flushes from his scalp to his toes, like being dangled upside down and dipped in warm honey.

"Stay snug," Dory says, unaware that she has taken his breath. "It has earflaps if you should need them. Stay safe. See you soon."

He recovers enough to say, "Thanks." He doesn't mean the hat. He can't decide if he's more stunned or elated.

Townes walks the flight of stairs from the bookshop to the cold street one slow, creaking step at a time. Today was big for his relationship with Dory. He impressed her. They held hands, touched more than once. They talked about meeting one another's families. They planned an actual date. They spoke as if they had a future. *And she kissed me.* His hand comes up to feel the place her lips touched.

Normally, he'd have stayed with Dory longer, would have said less. On a normal day, his time with Dory would have gone differently. She would have talked about her siblings, sharing the things that weigh on her. She would share again that her older sister is pregnant and unmarried. Or she would say that her younger brother is gay and has his first serious boyfriend, but that the rest of the family is keeping it secret from their traditional father.

"Father is a small, kind man," she would explain. "But he was, at one time, when he was a young man, a volatile person. Very passionate in his beliefs, fierce in his convictions about religion and family." Townes would nod his understanding.

Dory might even say something about her oldest sibling, Ishan, the doctor. He is married with two children and a Caucasian wife. He converted to Catholicism when he married. Dory had been forbidden to contact him, warned not to mention him at all. Ishan is officially dead to her family, by edict of her father. The odd absence of her favorite older brother has been especially hard on Dory. They had been close as children.

Dory might say again how she set money aside for a tattoo but is waiting for her own place. Or she might talk about books that have come in, books she has read. Sometimes she will talk about her fantasy of driving across the country as a book hound, finding valuable books and selling them to collectors over the Internet. "Though I'll have to get a car, learn how to drive, and get a license.

Small details," she always adds. "Besides, the market for rare books is not what it once was. Because of the Internet."

He would have listened a lot, shared little. Even today, he didn't feel compelled to tell Dory the details of the memorial. In the beginning days of their relationship, he had sometimes filled the quiet moments with monkey chatter about Etta and her disappearance. He had hoped to seem more interesting by his association with tragedy. As he meditated more deeply, refined his practice, and simplified his life, he had refrained from such brash manipulations. In his most recent visits, he had kept his feelings and memories in check and had left Second Story feeling relaxed and calm. The relationship with Dory had remained in a pleasant stasis, and he had tried not to expect it to ever be anything more.

The sun is out when he hits the sidewalk. The wind is comparatively still. He loosens his scarf, bunches his cap, and sticks it in the pocket of his coat. Instead of turning to the north and working his way west, as he normally would, he turns farther south toward Dearborn Station; on the way, he hangs a right, not really thinking much about what he's doing or where he's going. He lets his feet show him the way.

A mass of kids about his age come down the sidewalk toward him. They gesture broadly and laugh freely, seemingly untouched by life's losses. As they approach him they stop talking and in a choreographed movement, they form into an orderly line and snake beside him on the narrow sidewalk. When they've passed, they spread back out and continue their animated conversation.

If Etta hadn't gone missing, perhaps Townes would be a kid like those: a college student rushing to class with friends. Exhausted from having been out bar hopping or attending some black box theater production or at least studying at a coffee shop like Garamond's.

*What if, what if,* he reflexively reminds himself. He has tried to refrain from such speculation, as a matter of habit. He believes it's a pointless exercise that only leads to depression, but today, he doesn't attempt to stop himself.

He passes Blackie's South Loop, closed at this time of day. He's read that at one time Dearborn Station was the hub of Chicago's rail system. Back when it was common for people to commute across the country on the train, Blackie's was a local hot spot. Supposedly, in the mid-forties, it was common for Sinatra to walk from Dearborn Station when he came through town, have some dark liquor over ice in a heavy tumbler, then sit in for a couple of sets with whatever jazz quartet was wedged on the tiny stage. He'd drink free booze and smoke cigarettes while he sang, until he eventually had to be helped into a cab.

Townes's feet turn him back to the north. He's the only person dumb enough to walk along this particular wide stretch of street, where the wind cuts right through his clothes, the traffic spitting salty mist and stirring the air into thrashing whirls. He barely notices the wet or the isolation. His head is running fast.

He had left the bookshop without confirming a time for a movie date, but he had asked Dory out. She had said yes. He is going to have a date with a girl. The best girl he's ever known. He wishes, for an instant, Etta were here to share the news with. She would smile and tease and scrunch him with a squeeze around the shoulders until he couldn't breathe. She would laugh and force sister smooches on his cheek.

He physically winces at a fresh stab of grief. He kicks an icicle that's dropped from the edge of a cloth awning, watches it skate down the sidewalk, spin into the street where it is crushed under a bus tire.

He's frustrated he failed to nail down the movie date, but he's also impressed with how quickly their relationship has changed. *Dory has just been waiting for me to work up the nerve to ask.* He's tired of the effort it takes to ignore the fact that he's a twenty-one-year-old virgin. *It's not a race. It's a matter of individual choice.* He is agonizingly aware that his entire peer group has been gleefully sexually active for ages, and he worries it might never happen for him. He doesn't want to get ahead of himself, is careful not to think the impending date with Dory will become a prelude to sex. *But it could be a prelude to sex with Dory!* He stops at a crosswalk. When he gets the signal, he steps into the street and strides to the next stretch of sidewalk.

Something is definitely changing in his mind, his body. It scares him. Without his daily beliefs and rituals, what's he left with? The sensation is frightening and liberating all at once.

After a series of twists and turns and fifteen minutes of walking, he crosses the street in front of Willis Tower and moves quickly to the raised median, a part of the ramp down to Lower Wacker. He can't beat the cars all the way across, so he stands stock-still, stranded on the urban island while the traffic streams around him.

Townes gazes back at the tower. Some people refuse to use the new name, Willis Tower, still calling it by its longtime title, the Sears Tower. For some, it's force of habit. For others, it's a stubborn refusal to honor the deal that was struck to change the name, as if they should have been consulted. He's heard the name may change again soon. *People will be calling it by all three names.*

He can make out the Skydeck, jutting out of the building over a hundred floors above. One of the transparent cubes is closed for repairs, a layer of its clear glass having crazed inexplicably. He has stood in that very glass box and looked down at the city traffic between his own two feet, felt the panicked rush of his reptile mind's evolutionarily ingrained fear wrestling with his higher logic as he levitated over the tiny pedestrians. He can't imagine the fear of seeing the glass floor seem to shatter under him.

He hears the break in the traffic before he sees it. He turns his attention back to the street, finds it clear, hops down, and moves the rest of the way across Wacker.

In the fall he'd been crossing in nearly the same spot when a storm front punched in off the lake. The sudden change in air pressure caused a glass pane to pop out of the side of Willis Tower, like a cork forced from the mouth of a champagne bottle. People around him stopped and pointed. His gaze followed theirs up the tower. The street and the traffic grew still as his eyes found the square of glass, free falling. He saw the pane twisting, swooping lightly at first, like a silver leaf winking in the sun, floating gently on the breeze. Then it turned and dropped thirty stories, like a guillotine fired from a rocket, shattering on the busy pavement but managing to miss all the people and vehicles. It was a miracle, if Townes believed in such things, that no one was killed or injured. It would have been so easy for the glass to slice through a person, leaving one piece of their body on one side of the pane, and the rest of their body on the other.

At the time, he'd pondered the randomness of life: the beauty and the dead seriousness of it. He took that unpredictable occurrence and tried to fit it into his understanding of the way of things. He couldn't quite make it go, no matter how he turned it, so he just let it drop.

"A dollar for my cell phone bill," a homeless woman sitting on a mashed box outside the Walgreens yells right at Townes as he tries to slip past. "A dollar for my cell phone bill."

He ignores her and jams himself into the foot traffic that is increasing with each step back to Union Station. He rides the escalator into the building, passes by the places to buy sugared almonds, pizza by the slice, cold bottles of beer, and magazines. He rides the next escalator down to the level where the Metra and Amtrak trains depart; the thick, humid, diesel-scented air meets him.

He finds the sign with the train schedule lit in lines across the display board. The express is on track four, departing in ten minutes.

It would get him back to Main Street, where he would have a short walk back to his house to meet his mom. The line above the express is for the local. Leaving now from track two. It would stop back at the train station where Army Coat ran off.

He doesn't think. No time. He runs for track two. He hitches his messenger bag over his head, adjusts its fit on his shoulder, and reaches one hand back to stop it swinging as he moves. He pounds down the platform, zigging around milling commuters, trashcans, and massive support pillars. He makes it to the nearest car of the train and jumps into the vestibule as the doors begin to close.

"Close one," says the Metra employee Townes finds in the vestibule.

"Yeah." Townes pants. The train starts to roll.

"Ticket, please," the man says. He removes his punch and clacks it a few times.

Townes shifts his bag to his front, rummages through, finds his monthly pass, shows it to the ticket taker. The guy nods and passes into the train car, calling out, "Tickets, please! Please have your tickets ready! Tickets, please!"

Townes stays in the vestibule to catch his breath. He feels a sense of destiny, standing here now, riding toward the man in the army coat. As the train pulls from under the gray shadow of the station and passes into the bright daylight, Townes realizes what this decision means. He will definitely be late for the memorial, might miss it altogether. He has no idea how long it will take to find the man, doubts it's even possible. One thing he knows for certain, Meg is going to kill him.

# BIG MISUNDERSTANDING

For the first several minutes of the ride, Newton just looks around the back seat of the squad car. They've left his hands cuffed behind him, which seems wrong. He's forced to lean forward and bend over to prevent his body from crushing his fingers into the deep plastic bowl of the seat.

The seat has seams where the molded sections are linked together. The seams are secured with rivets, each rivet marked by a big, flat, shiny silver button. There are sixteen buttons he can see, contrasting in color and texture with the dark-blue matte plastic. One of the buttons has an oily fingerprint on it. Another has what looks like dried blood around its edges. The space has been wiped mostly clean and smells like disinfectant and fake lemon. It makes his nose run, but he can't wipe it.

He sniffs loudly and declares, "Your subtle torture tactics will not stand. This isn't the Bush era. Obama is president." The officers stop their conversation, wait for him to get quiet. When he's done, they continue talking in hushed tones.

The clear plastic partition that separates the officers from the criminals is worn and scratched, leaving random white cross-hatching that gives the plastic a frosted look. Under other circumstances it might look festive, like that aerosol snow people spray on windows in those fortunate places where winters are mild. There is a series of small round holes in the plastic divider to allow air and sound to pass through. The cops mumble to someone through their radio.

The cruiser hits a pothole straight on, and Newton bounces back in the seat, crushing his hand and banging his calves. His tattoo throbs and his government leg knocks hard against the seat. Both officers glance his way at the noise; seeing nothing out of the ordinary, they continue as they were. Man Cop gives a smug nod that Newton catches in the mirror, realizing he'd hit that pothole on purpose, just to rough his helpless passenger up a little, rattle his cage. Newton shifts his ass forward to get his weight off his hands. He hears a name: Officer Wendy says, "Ruther will meet us there."

Realization begins to dawn: This ride is not about loud music or drug contraband; it's not about knocking down a couple of douchebags in his living room. It has something to do with Etta. It's about his backpack stuffed full of high school crap and the photos from his wallet. He can't imagine what. Even more than that, it's about that a-hole detective taking another crack at him. He hates Ruther. Old memories surge up fast and make his face hot with rage.

He wants to start kicking the back of the seat in front of him, to yell and cuss and hurt someone. *We've already been over all of this. I didn't do it. Etta was my girl. She was the one good thing I had. We've already been over all this shit.*

The anger and confusion come so fast and make so little sense, he has to wonder about it. In that slow moment in his apartment, as he floated forward and carefully applied the right amount of force in the right spot to clear portly Arthur from his path, he had felt calm, sure of himself, quiet. His mind was focused. Now, hearing the name Ruther, recalling how he'd been accused of doing something to Etta, his brain starts buzzing so loudly he can barely breathe. It's like he has one of those fucking fat cicadas rammed in his ear, making that incessant screeching sound. Like a high-speed drill bit going through a steel plate with no lubricant, or even worse, like the squealing of that little cardigan-wearing wussy stuck on repeat in Newton's head. He wants to act out, to make the noise stop. So he can breathe, feel in control.

Instead of kicking the seat with the flat of his good foot, he clears his throat and tries to speak calmly. "Excuse me, please."

Officer Wendy glances over her shoulder. Man Cop glances in the rearview mirror from the driver's seat. "What?" he asks gruffly.

"I was kind of shook up earlier. Kind of distracted, you know, with having armed militants streaking out of my bedroom and waving guns in my face, screaming at me. You know, like a military coup in my own fucking home. So I missed it when you told me what this is about. Could you clue me in? Now that I can think half-straight. What am I charged with?"

Man Cop glances over to Officer Wendy. Officer Wendy turns her profile to Newton, pitches her response to one of the circles in the Plexiglas.

"Your landlord called because he feared you would be violent if he approached your apartment and requested you turn down your music. He claimed you have a history of erratic behavior and of making threats to some of your neighbors."

"Just one neighbor," Newton mumbles too quietly to be heard. He feels the best strategy is to listen. Get the lay of the land, while not pissing anyone off.

"So officially," she continues, "we were there for disturbing the peace. Mr. Heller had us accompany him to your apartment. You were not home."

Officer Wendy glances back to check that Newton's listening. He nods his grim understanding. Man Cop stabs his eyes into the rearview again, looks back at the road. Wendy shows Newton her profile some more. "Heller let himself in to turn down the music. There was drug paraphernalia in plain sight. Mr. Heller invited us in, alerted us to your bong. Without opening any doors or digging through anything, we found photos and mementos from an open investigation. We contacted the officer in charge, gathered the things we saw, and were about to put out an APB when you came in and attacked Mr. Heller and your neighbor . . ." She pauses to look at something in her lap. "A Mr. Gray."

"That was poor timing on my part. I overreacted. That's on me. I accept that. My bad. May I ask why Mr. Gray was wandering around my place uninvited? As best as I can tell, he has no right to stick his nose in."

"He showed up. Said he wanted to give his side of the story. Was insistent we take a statement. Mr. Heller asked him to leave, but he was hard to get rid of."

"Like an STD."

Now she turns and looks him in the face. "I knew Etta," she says, the official tone leaking from her voice and replaced by something close to grief. "I knew you too. I don't want to believe this. But . . ." She doesn't quite cry, but her voice breaks and her face twists. "If you did this, I hope you rot in hell. I hope you get the death penalty. I hope you get a lethal injection with that fucked-up cocktail that doesn't work so you die long and slow."

"That's enough," says Man Cop.

"Are we clear?" she asks, the rage uncontained.

"You have made your position clear," Newton replies.

"You got anything else to say?" Officer Wendy asks.

In response, Newton stares down at his kicks in the foot well, tries to stretch his back and relieve the tension in his shoulders. He thinks, *What's so fucking earth-shattering about having old high school shit around?* He knows his reputation as a general asshole in high school makes it pretty easy for people to assume the worst. Hell, he's still a fucking asshole. Nothing has changed much. Maybe he has better reasons for it now. *Well, not reasons, but at least better excuses.* He doesn't even believe the thought as he forms it. *No evolution at all.*

He notes the police cruiser doesn't have floor mats in the back. He guesses they must have them in the front. He tries to look over the back of the seat into the front floorboard, but can't see past the floating laptop. He settles back to wait out the rest of the ride.

When Wendy sees he isn't going to respond, she turns the back of her head to him. He mumbles and stares at her out of the tops of his eyes. "Next time you can dissect the fetus pig yourself, bitch."

# A RUDE AWAKENING

Charlie wakes with a start. Bootsy nips him hard on his earlobe, the points of her teeth clamping with enough force to draw blood. Charlie reacts instinctively, knocking her to the floor before he knows what's happening. He rolls off the couch. His knee comes down on his glasses with an ugly crunch.

"Goddamn it, Bootsy!"

He hears his phone ringing where he dumped it on the bench next to the front door. Bootsy had been trying to get his attention. She'd probably meowed and bumped him with her head. Biting was a last resort.

"Sorry, Bootsy," Charlie says.

He doesn't make it to the phone in time to answer, but he sees it was Ruther, so he calls right back. It's busy. His phone makes the tone that indicates someone has left a message. Rather than listen to the message, he thumbs the phone to dial the number again.

"This is Ruther," Ruther says.

"You just called?"

"Yeah. Charlie. Hi. Did you get my message?"

"No."

"Listen, Charlie. Listen close. We might have a break in Etta's case. It may be nothing, but it looks like it's going to be something."

"Tell me." He freezes in place, holds his breath, as if the good news is a small animal he could frighten with the slightest movement.

"It's the old boyfriend. Newton Parker."

"No. Newton?" He starts moving again, turning a circle in the little entryway as he talks and listens.

"A patrol was called to his apartment to oversee an eviction notice. They found some things that set off alarms. They're taking him to the Downers Grove PD right now. They'll get him processed and sit on him until I get there."

"Can I meet you there?"

"That's why I'm calling. Your place is on my way. If you want a ride, I'll swing by and get you in twenty minutes."

Charlie's brain gets in gear. Newton. Newton was her boyfriend. Was an athlete. Charlie had taken that as a good sign. He assumed he was a kid with aspirations, directed, goal-oriented, part of the high school community, in possession of a work ethic. Or at the very least, he wasn't always idle and therefore was too busy to hatch cockamamie, half-baked, addle-brained teenage schemes that might involve Etta in mischief. Frankly, if Newton was good enough for Etta, that had been good enough for Charlie. He had trusted her judgment. *Look where that got her.*

"Charlie? You want me to come by and get you?"

"Has Newton said something? Did he say anything about what he did with Etta?" Charlie asks, still twisting in place.

"No. No. No confession, no incriminating statements. But there's a bunch of evidence he'll need to explain. It's definitely worth a talk. He had some things, things that Etta was carrying when she stepped off that bus. Stuff he wouldn't have had a chance to get hold of unless he lied about the last time he'd seen her. If it means what I think it means, we can prove he was the last one to see her and that he lied about the timeline. If we can prove he was hiding something, we can build on that."

Charlie stops spinning. "Tell me." Bootsy butts her head against his ankle, walks circles around his feet where he stands. She wants to make up for the bite, but he doesn't notice her.

"Let's not get ahead of ourselves. All I know for sure is I never liked the kid. He's a hothead. I had a feeling he was involved, or at least that he knew something. I went at him hard last time. His story held up. But now, this could give us an opening. That's all I want to say for now. Do you want me to pick you up?"

"What did you find? At his place? What things did he have?" Charlie starts twisting again. He steps on Bootsy's tail. She yowls and runs away.

"That is all I'm saying. Seriously. You want the ride or not?"

"You bet your ass I do."

"Twenty minutes or so, depending on traffic." Ruther ends the call.

Charlie drops the phone. There is a haze on his brain, like smoke hanging over Navy Pier after the Fourth of July fireworks, thick, heavy, acrid clouds clogging his mind.

"Twenty minutes," he tells himself. He walks back to his living room and checks his glasses; busted arm, one lens popped out, another one crushed. *They are done.* He's barely fazed. Glasses can be replaced.

He moves to his turntable and drops the needle on a yellow vinyl album. He hates when he forgets to store an album properly, especially when it's a limited edition reissue. "Goo Goo Muck," the first song on the B-side from *Bad Music for Bad People* by The Cramps, starts to play. He was always a sucker for the distorted psychobilly riffs of Poison Ivy and the vocals of Lux Interior. It blows away the fog in his head and gets him in gear. He rushes upstairs to shower and dress before Ruther arrives.

It takes him less than fifteen minutes to run back down the stairs, just in time to hear the last chords of "Uranium Rock" before the arm of the player lifts and returns to its cradle. He slips into his oversized work coat, finds a cap and gloves. Before he steps outside to wait for Ruther, he finds his keys. For the hell of it, he slips the paperback Townes sent him into his coat pocket.

Ruther is double-parked when Charlie walks out. He slips into the low seat of the sedan and pulls the heavy door closed.

Charlie looks to Ruther expectantly. Ruther reaches forward and turns down the chatter on his police scanner. He turns down the blower on the heater too.

"Did you eat yet?" Ruther asks.

"No. I forgot about food."

"I haven't eaten either. I spent all day processing a big bust. There was this trucker carrying a dozen Mexican girls. The girls all got sick and he tried to stop at a Jewel-Osco and stock up on cold meds. He mashed a car when he was leaving the lot. Cops were called, coughing was heard, truck was inspected. He's in all kinds of trouble. I think he's going away behind this one. But he wants to deal, give us a bigger fish. Anyway, never-ending paperwork."

"Ruther, you are getting off track."

"Well, as I was wrapping that up, I got the call from the DGPD. So now I'm here, hungry and in desperate need of caffeine." Ruther looks to his rearview mirror. Puts the car in drive and starts to roll down the block.

"Shouldn't we get on the road?" Charlie asks.

"No hurry really. We might as well let this Parker kid sit. Let his nerves start working on him."

"I guess."

"Besides," Ruther says, "it would be a shame to be this close to Jitters and not stop and get one of those spicy mocha drinks." He glances at Charlie, can see the tension in his face. "Listen. We need to eat, get caffeine in our systems. This could take a while."

"Okay," Charlie concedes. "Jitters it is."

Ruther steers the big car back to a main street and takes a few turns, parks right in front of Jitters Café. The parking is metered, but Ruther never feeds those things.

They walk in and stand in line. Ruther orders a Mexican Spice Mocha with two extra shots of espresso and a piece of coffee cake. Charlie orders a Black Eye, no sweetener, and grabs a cup of Greek yogurt, plain. They don't really talk, just shift from place to place near the front counter to let customers come and go around them.

An attractive woman in her forties comes in, waits to be seated. Ruther turns his face away, pulls a plastic comb from his back pocket, and runs it through his mustache a few times. He gets the comb put away and turns back as the woman passes on her way to a table. Ruther gives her a nice smile, his tidy 'stache spreading over his white teeth. She smiles back, very friendly.

"I love it here," Ruther says, watching the woman walk away.

They take their order to go and slide back in the car. By the time they speed down the ramp to the freeway, they've eaten their morsels of food and are taking appreciative pulls through the sippy lids on their coffees.

# PROCESSED LIKE SAUSAGE

After Newton is roughly extracted from the squad car and led into a holding area within the station, his hands are cuffed in front and he's instructed to sit until he can be processed. He watches Wendy and Man Cop pass his possessions to another cop, an old white guy with a tight white beard and mustache. Newton watches his winter coat piled on top of an armful of his stuff, remembering his phone is in the pocket.

"Hey," he calls over to the cops. Wendy and Man Cop hear him but walk away, stab at some buttons on a keypad for a secured door, and let the heavy door slam behind them.

"Hey," Newton calls to the cop across the counter, who is filling out forms and labeling the bag his bong went into, checking the pockets of his coat. The cop looks up.

"Just sit tight," the cop says, obviously bored.

"I just have a question. Hey. What time is it? Can you just tell me the time?"

"Time to shut up and be quiet," the cop says flatly.

"I have an appointment."

"Not anymore. Now shut up."

"No. Really. It's important. I have a real appointment."

"Your ass has an appointment with that chair. Now shut the fuck up so I can work, will ya?" The cop walks into a room full of metal shelves, taking Newton's things with him.

Newton gives up.

After twenty minutes, a short black woman in a tight-fitting uniform comes to stand in front of him.

"Listen," she says.

"I'm listening." He meets her gaze.

"Good. I am Officer Harris. I am here to process you through. That way you can go talk to the detectives and maybe get the hell out of here. You understand me?"

"So far so good."

"Good. You just keep up that good attitude. If you need something, you address me as Officer Harris. If I respond to you, you listen. If I tell you to do something, you do it."

"That was very clear. And I hear you. I'm not a troublemaker. I'm a bit shook up. But I'm not a troublemaker."

"Hmm. That's not what I was told. But you play it cool with me and I'll make my own assessment. Is that agreeable?"

"Yes, Officer Harris."

"Good. You got some Eddie Haskell b.s. going on. But you stick with that and we'll do fine. Now stand up and walk toward that door over there." She steps back and he stands. She's really tiny. Maybe five feet tall, with round features and glossy, blue-black skin; her hair is pulled back tight and smooth in a bun at the back of her head. He can see a few dry skin flakes sticking to her hair along the top of her scalp. It's very human, the dandruff and the snug uniform belted tight in the middle. She passes his personality test, and he decides to be cooperative. She nods toward the door and he walks to it.

Officer Harris takes his hands and instructs him: "Just relax and let me move your fingers. If you tense up or smear the prints, we'll have to do it over. You understand. The longer this takes, the longer you're gonna be here. You got me?"

"I got you."

She takes his fingers one at a time; she presses down on his nail bed and rolls his finger pad across the wet, cold ink. Then she moves his hand onto a paper with two rows of five rectangles, each labeled for one of his fingertips. She pushes each finger firmly down and rolls it again, leaving a record of the finger's passing. She continues the practiced dance, controlling his every movement, like he's a dangerous marionette and she is his wary master.

After a time, he says, "Officer Harris?" His mouth is very close to her ear; he speaks quietly, as if they are dance partners.

"Yes."

"I have an appointment I hope to keep. People are expecting me."

"Well. We will do our best. You just keep cooperating, it will go fast."

"Yes, officer. I just wondered about a phone call. If I'm not going to make my appointment, I'd like to let someone know."

"Well, once you're processed, you will get your phone call. I'm not in charge of that." She plucks a fistful of wet wipes from the top of a dispenser, one at a time, and passes them into his hand. He rubs the ink from the tips of his fingers, just as Cranky Thomas had done with the blood and ink on the back of his calf.

"Officer Harris?"

"Yes."

"It seems outdated, this kind of fingerprinting. Don't they have digital printing now?"

"Not here we don't."

"Seems odd for a rich suburb like this."

"Nobody wants to spend a dime they don't have to," she replies.

His calf hurts and he doesn't know if it's a normal amount of pain for a tattoo or if it's damaged from being kneeled on, squeezed, and banged around. Maybe it's all fucked-up now. *Like everything else.*

When his fingers are mostly clean, Officer Harris takes the dirty wipes and leads him in to have his mug shots taken. He's instructed to stand in front of a set of marks that indicate his height. He looks over his shoulder at the check marks and stands as straight as he can.

"I used to be six-foot-two before I lost my leg," he says.

Officer Harris looks at him from behind the terminal with a digital camera mounted to the top. He watches her replay what he's just said, then shake her head in mild disapproval, not falling for his joke. The reaction disappoints Newton. She taps a place over the top of the lens, all business, and says, "Look right into the camera."

Initially he gives a hard, criminal glare, but at the last moment he flashes his most winning smile, like a model in a Sears summer catalog. He's decided he must make her smile. *It's important to have goals.*

"Really?" Officer Harris says, unsmiling. She clearly doesn't approve of his antics, but doesn't want to give him the chance to answer her question, so she hurries and instructs him; "You are not allowed to smile in these digital snapshots. They are a legal document and the face-recognition software in the federal database is only effective with a forward facing, unexpressive face. Now hold still and try again."

He holds still and lets his face relax.

"Thank you. Now turn to the right." He wants to ask her what's the point of the profile image, because of what she just explained, but he lets it go. He turns and she captures his sullen profile. He's disappointed she wouldn't smile. *Another goal unrealized. No job, no girl, no smile from Officer Harris.* He hears the roll of Albert's laugh somewhere in the back of his head.

When Officer Harris is done, he's passed to a kid, about twenty with acne on his forehead and a crisp new uniform. Newton is led into a room the size of a supply closet, just a narrow wooden table, two folding metal chairs, and a camera mounted on pipe sticking through the drop ceiling. No one-way glass. No windows. A door, thickly painted cinderblock walls, and a buzzing fluorescent light fixture set flush with the dirty acoustic tile squares. His handcuffs are removed, and he's given a plastic Solo cup with water.

"Can I get my phone call, please?"

"You'll have to talk to the detective. He'll be in soon. Just relax." Newton looks at a busted pimple leaking oil onto the kid's brow. The kid catches his gaze and self-consciously probes his head as he leaves the tiny space, securing the door behind him.

It's a long wait. Newton has no idea how long. There's no clock. He drinks his water. He beats out a rhythm on the tabletop with the bottom of the empty cup. He fiddles with the cup, pinching it flat and letting it spring back into shape until it cracks. He splits the rigid plastic all the way down the side. He rips the cup in half, his strong fingers making precise movements. He continues to shred the cup into ever-smaller pieces until there's a pile of sharp confetti littering the table. He looks for a trashcan, but there isn't one. He considers brushing the pile onto the floor but chooses not to.

Periodically, he hears people passing down the hall outside, muffled conversations. He has to pee. He moves the bits of plastic cup around and tries to form a trash mosaic. He makes a car-shaped thing and scrambles it up. Then makes a gun-shaped thing. Finally he spends a long time on a penislike thing complete with two jagged testicles. He really works on it, crafts it. He uses the red outside of the cup for the phallic foreground and the white inside of the cup to form a high-contrast negative-space border. He runs out of plastic and wishes they would offer him another cup to pull apart. When he's completed as much of the picture as he can, he leans his body back so the camera can get a good look. He flips the camera off and smiles his prettiest smile. Then he scrambles the bits and stands to do some stretches.

He tucks his ass on the corner of the table and pulls up his pants leg to inspect the bandage over his tattoo. There's a little pink, greasy seepage visible through the gauze. *Not too bad.* But it is definitely tender. He can't remember what Cranky Thomas said about taking aspirin or Tylenol or something, or if he said anything at all.

He switches his attention to the other leg, rolls up his pants, and removes the prosthetic, lets the tip of his stump stick out in the air and breathe. His brain tells his missing foot to wiggle its phantom toes. Without any effort at all, he can feel the air between the memory of his toes, feel how glorious it is to let those piggies out to play. He takes his time.

For months after part of his body was ripped off, he had searing pain in a leg that no longer existed, like a hot, blunt railroad spike was being pounded through the meat of his missing calf. Many nights he would wake, reaching for the place the calf should be, trying to grasp the place where the sensation radiated, and his hand would only close on itself. Those days had been rough ones, the rehab was excruciating. How weak and helpless the incident had left him. How he'd sworn to never feel that way again.

He stays like that a long while, his stump out, his mind in the past, his body at ease in the tiny, cold room. *It's good to just be.* Eventually he remembers he has to pee.

He hears more people in the hall, men's voices. Shadows break the light that leaks under the door. He puts his leg back on and sits in the chair farthest from the door. He tries to be patient for a count of thirty.

"Fuck it," he says, brushing the ravaged, two-tone cup litter onto the floor.

"Hey, assholes," he yells. "I gotta take a piss and get my phone call. I had other plans for the day."

He turns his face to the camera on the ceiling and flips it off again. He steps onto the chair, guesses if he gets on the table he can rip the camera right off its mount. He looks around for something to swing at the camera, remembers his leg, starts to jimmy his stump from the prosthetic as he balances on the chair. Then the door opens.

# PREPARATIONS ARE MADE

Meg watches the dark water run down the center of the tub and twist into the drain. She wrings her hair with her hands and applies the heavy conditioner that comes in the box of hair color. She works it through her hair to the tips, massages the ends for a long time. She tries to force the moisture into the hair, banking on the outside chance it will give her newly darkened locks the appearance of youth and health.

"My hair will be nearly as pretty as yours," she calls to Etta. No response.

The conditioner sits while she lathers and shaves her legs, her armpits. She rinses the razor and hangs it in its spot. She rinses the conditioner and wraps a towel tightly around her head.

Once she's dried off, she blow-dries and styles before passing judgment on her reflection.

"Not too shabby," she finally declares.

"It looks great." Etta is back. Meg knew she would be.

"It feels so soft when I color it, but it is such a pain in the ass."

"The sacrifices we make to be beautiful," Etta says knowingly.

"You are wise beyond your years," Meg replies.

Meg applies the full contingent of makeup; it takes a while, but when she's almost done she takes a hard assessment and thinks she looks pretty damn good.

"Pretty damn good," she says.

"Why am I not surprised you said that," Etta jokes.

Meg applies lipstick and blots. She leaves her makeup supplies spread around the vanity top. *Who is going to complain?*

At her dresser, she steps into a thong and straightens all the seams. She rummages through until she finds her most serious bra, the black one with the underwires and good padding, and the touch of lace running around the top edge. She hates this bra. It picks her girls up and shoves them high and tight where they once lived on her body, but it's uncomfortable as hell. She puts her arms through and fastens her instrument of self-bondage firmly at her back.

"Good God, I hate bras."

"Amen," Etta replies.

At her closet she takes out a lovely, long black sweater dress and some long black zipper boots with chunky heels. She doesn't want to look like she's going to a funeral, but she feels good in black, looks good in it.

"Black is slimming," she tells Etta.

"So you keep telling me," Etta replies. "It's also a little drab. Maybe you should try some color."

"No, thanks," Meg says dismissively. "I feel too old to pull off color; it makes my skin look even older. Besides, if I handle it wrong, it reads less like youthful attitude and more like eccentric old lady."

Etta doesn't have anything to add.

In a plastic bin, Meg finds an old pair of tights the right color. She rams her fist all the way to the toe of one leg, splays her fingers wide, and pulls the tights over her hand to check for runs. None. She checks the other leg. She finds two small holes, both high up on the left thigh. She remembers snagging them on something the last time she wore them, can't recall what. Fortunately, the holes will be hidden by her dress. She wiggles into them, tugs them up, runs her hands down the length of her legs to smooth them. She twists them a bit at the toe to fix the way the seam falls. Then she smacks herself on the ass.

She slips the dress over her head, careful not to smudge powdery deodorant against the fabric. She sucks in her middle and zips the dress. She exhales.

"Hey. Look at that. Still fits."

"Looking good," Etta says.

Meg tugs her boots on, zips them snug to her calves. She stands a few inches taller, feels strong, formidable. She takes a long look at herself in the full-length mirror. She turns to see how the dress looks from behind. She pushes her colored lips out and gives a little nod of satisfaction.

Etta says, "Damn, girl."

"I know, right?"

"Mmmm-hmmm."

She glances at the clock. If she hurries, she can run an errand and get back to pick up Townes before the memorial. She puts a little extra swing in her hips. It's been a while since she's been so dressed up, so put together. She's proud of herself.

She says, "I think I can finally see a little light at the end of this long tunnel."

Etta mumbles, "Sometimes that light is a train bearing down."

Meg tries to ignore her.

# AN INEXPERIENCED STALKER

The train stops and Townes willingly steps through the open doors to stand at the very farthest end of the covered platform, nearly as far away from where he tackled Army Coat as is possible. Strange to think it had happened only a few hours earlier. He feels different now, like a new version of his old self.

He hadn't been certain he would get off at this stop, not until the train doors opened and he walked out. He had clung to the idea that he could exercise agency, demonstrate his belief in free will, and change his mind at any moment, but standing outside the safety of the familiar train car calls his long-established stance on determinism into question.

It's true he'd been considering this possible course of action since he watched Army Coat getting away from him. With his head still ringing from the blow of the knife handle, the thought of following Army Coat had crossed his rattled mind. For a split second, staring over the rail at the man below, he'd even considered not getting back on the train, just hounding him on foot. He pictured the pursuit in his mind's eye. Standing face-to-face with the dangerous man, watching him lunge with his long knife, and taking him down. The details were unclear, but once the notion had formed, it was hard to shake. True, he'd been too out of sorts, had forgotten the thought nearly as quickly as it had come. He'd been confused and preoccupied by the questions he was asked, by trying to recall what had transpired.

Standing here now, in this strange place, setting this circumstance into motion, he doesn't have any intuition about where it will lead. As he's thinking, the doors to the train close behind him. Townes looks toward the engine at the front of the line of silver cars. One other person has exited at this platform. A man, overly bundled against the increasingly mild weather, supple leather glove gripping the pull handle of a suitcase on rollers. He turns away from Townes and starts walking toward the stairs. The train lurches forward, then *clack clacks* out of the station.

Townes is alone on the platform, his back exposed to the wild elements loose in this unfamiliar neighborhood. *What the hell did I just do?* He takes the cap from his pocket and places it on his head, more for security than warmth. He tugs the brim down, just as Dory had done when she gave it to him.

He takes out his phone. An announcement that it's low on battery is showing. This surprises Townes. He opens the phone, investigates. He had turned on his Wi-Fi in Printer's Row. It has been roaming, trying to connect every few minutes ever since then, constantly draining his battery. He needs to warn Meg he might be late, might not be there at all. It's the right thing to do. He calls her, even though he dreads speaking to her directly. He's relieved when the machine picks up. He leaves a message. When he's done, he texts Newton rather than call. He definitely doesn't want to speak to him.

He crams his phone back in his pocket, hitches his messenger bag into place, and walks over to the rail. He looks at the place Army Coat crossed the empty lot. The deep holes left as he trudged through the virginal snow are still clearly visible.

The man pulling the suitcase is crossing the street below, moving at a good clip, lugging his suitcase over piles of snow and potholes full of gray, slushy water. The man swivels his head around and moves like he wants to get off the streets. Townes decides it's time to move too.

His nerves are getting the best of him as he starts down the stairs. His mind is on what comes next, instead of what is right in front of him. On the third step down, he fails to see the place where the concrete corner has cracked and snapped away. He misses his footing. His shoe turns at a bad angle and his hands grab at the handrail. His messenger bag flies away from his body, pulling him farther off balance. He barely avoids slipping farther down the steps and cracking his tailbone. He gets his legs under his body, walks down slowly, careful with the tender, swelling ankle.

A few cars drive by. Once they've passed, he limps over to the lot and follows the trail left by Army Coat. It is peaceful there in the abandoned lot between empty buildings. The snow sucks up most of the city sounds; the structures block the wind. The rattle of the train has died far in the distance. The fresh blanket of snow serves to cover the trash and debris, hide the frozen mud holes and piles of busted asphalt. The cold kills the smell of rotting garbage and masks any number of other sins, hidden beneath the surface.

Townes tries to step in the prints left by Army Coat, but his stride is too short, especially as he attempts to pamper his fresh injury. Instead he shuffles through the snow, creating his own path in the wake of the one left by Army Coat.

At the back of the lot, he steps over a low spot in the fence, the top rail bent nearly to the ground in a rusted V-shape, a heavy object having crushed it violently some time in the distant past. He crosses a similar lot that opens onto another street. Townes waits for cars to pass, tries to hide his white face between his collar and his cap after a dark-skinned driver looks at him suspiciously.

His ankle throbs and feels dead as he eases across the street, moving in a straight line from the last of Army Coat's tracks. In the alley he enters, he sees more footprints, left in patches of snow that haven't been blown away by gusts or driven through by tires. Where he enters the alley, the opening is a normal size, wide enough for a couple of bent dumpsters to sit, staggered across from one another, with space for a compact car to push through the remaining gap. The buildings on either side don't sit square to the world. As he walks, Townes is funneled into an increasingly narrow space, the walls moving in on him, compressing the humid air. Army Coat's tracks are gone. The sliver of sky overhead gets thinner and thinner, letting in less and less light, less air. The sky is getting darker, too, storm clouds rolling in. He can feel the cold radiating off the bricks on either side of him, has to twist his left shoulder ahead and shuffle walk until he exits through a space about a third smaller than an average doorway.

He comes out in a commercial district with a lot of traffic, metered parking, cars filling most of the parking spots. The street has been plowed and salted. Stores are open along both sides of the street. Bustling people walk in little groups up and down the block.

He has no idea which way to go, no clue as to the direction Army Coat might have turned, but he's drawing attention simply standing and gawking, so he turns and starts his feet walking. He tries to guess which business brought Army Coat to this block. The stores are like none he's seen before. Across from him is a wig shop full of Styrofoam heads and a window sign that reads: *Lingerie, Wigs and Hair Food.* Next to it is a patriotic-themed payday loan joint with the whole building painted poorly in gaudy red, white, and blue stripes. A few doors away sits a store dedicated to frighteningly large and realistic Catholic-themed statues. The largest is an adult-sized, alabaster Jesus, complete with crown of thorns and crucifixion wounds, being cradled in the lap of a weeping Mother Mary. The giant Jesus has skin pale as a frog's belly, wounds splashed with red, half-closed eyes bright blue, and cheeks rosy with round smears of rouge. In the window of a five-and-dime, a sun-bleached display of Mr. Bubble Bubble Bath makes Townes smile. He passes a bail bonds office whose logo is a cartoon convict in an orange jumpsuit giving a double thumbs-up. Near the end of the block, he finds a store with a giant, green-and-brown, Western-boot-shaped sign over the front door. He crosses the street on his tender ankle toward a place dedicated to prepaid phones.

He still has no idea where to go. A very old couple comes toward him, walking arm in arm, leaning on one another. As they approach he asks them, "Is there a good place to sit and get some tea?"

The old man wears a vintage faux-fur hat, the brim a tight curl, with a red feather tucked into the band at one side. The hat turns sideways when the man looks to his wife. He pats her hand where it rests around the forearm of his coat. She says, *"No lo entiendo, no Inglés."*

"A place to drink some warm tea?" Townes repeats a little more slowly, tipping a pretend cup to his lips. He rubs his tummy in a yum-yum gesture.

"Oh. Café," the man says.

"Yes. *Sí,*" Townes replies.

"*Sí. Allí,*" the woman says. She points behind Townes. When she tips his way, her bright eyes flashing toward his face, he notes a Blackhawks logo on the front of her stocking cap. "*Dos bloques,*" she says to him.

" *Sí. Dos bloques,*" the old man contributes, pointing down the block in a mirror of his wife's gesture. Then he holds up two gloved fingers. "*Dos bloques,*" he says. "Two *bloques.*"

"Two blocks that way," Townes repeats and smiles. They smile back and nod and wave. They lean a little closer to one another and totter down the sidewalk. Townes gives another wave as he passes them. He's lost Army Coat's trail. He wants to rest his ankle for a few minutes, decide what to do next. Decide how to get himself home, if that is the next step.

Two blocks down, the businesses thin out, most of the storefronts covered in pull gates, but he finds a corner diner with windows along the street and booths along the windows. He walks through cigarette smoke as he nears the entrance; it drifts from around the corner. Townes isn't a smoker and normally finds the scent of cigarettes offensive, but on this cold day, it reminds him of wood smoke and summer nights on the beach with Etta. He makes little puffs of air out of his nostrils before the carcinogens can make his nose twitch and run, then limps through the door.

The place is moderately busy and smells of fried meat. He moves to the first empty booth, but it's not been cleaned; it's full of napkins twisted into knots and half a plate of biscuits covered in congealed white gravy, flecked liberally with black pepper like flyspecks. He keeps moving and finds a booth near the back corner and happily sinks onto the worn bench. He props his foot in the seat opposite and opens the oversized menu. Something sharp pokes his ass cheek. He fishes the metal buckle of Esmeralda's boot from his back pocket and tucks it into his front pocket, where it feels more comfortable.

There's no food he wants to eat, and he isn't hungry. A waitress steps next to him. She is too old to be working, too old to be alive. She is skeletal-thin and her skin is see-through. She has two ballpoint pens stuck into her silver hair and a pair of reading glasses bumping around on her chest. Her back is so bent it's as if she's leaning her face down to eye level with Townes where he sits.

"You know what you want?" Her voice is strong and direct. She has her order pad poised, her pen resting on the page, ready to write. She means business and has no time for nonsense.

"It says here hot tea." He points at the open menu. "What kind of tea is it?"

"Tea. Regular tea. Tea in a bag," she explains. It's clearly not a question she usually gets and not the kind of question she has patience for.

"So just black tea?"

"I don't know. It's dark. It's Lipton, I think." She taps her pad, looks around the diner at her other customers.

"Is the orange juice fresh?"

"Harlan just mixed it this morning. If that's what you mean."

Townes scans the menu a moment longer. "Okay. Can I have an orange juice and a mug of hot water?"

She does not write on her pad. She tucks the pad and pen into a pocket at the front of her apron and says, "Is that all?"

"Yes, please."

"Sure. Give me a minute. Can you get your foot off the seat?" She points a tuber finger at his shoe.

"I twisted it. I'm trying to elevate it," he explains.

"Okay. You leave it. But you're melting all over the place." She looks back down the diner. She makes a sour face. She calls, "I'll be right there."

"Oh, I didn't know," Townes says, talking about his wet foot. He starts to sit up, pull his foot down.

"Stay put. Don't worry about it. I'll get a dishrag."

He nods his gratitude, but she doesn't notice. She hurries away. Townes folds his menu closed, slips it back in the holder, and thinks he sees the back of Army Coat's head three booths ahead of him. He's sitting at the table with all the knotted napkins and half-eaten biscuits and gravy. *Maybe he was in the restroom. Maybe he was the one smoking around the corner.*

Army Coat holds his empty coffee mug aloft, rocking it back and forth, impatiently waiting for his refill. The waitress goes around the counter and grabs a glass pot of coffee. She shuffles to Army Coat and fills his mug. He doesn't say anything. She doesn't act like she expected him to. Then she moves through the diner, topping off coffees, chatting lightly, dropping a bill at one table, and removing plates from another.

Townes tugs his cap down farther on his head. He's grateful to Dory for forcing it on him, for caring for him enough to make him wear it. He hopes the cap changes his appearance enough that Army Coat won't recognize him.

Townes sinks lower in the seat to make himself small. The waitress sets a glass of orange juice and a mug of hot water on his table. Townes nods his thanks but keeps his eyes on Army Coat.

"Lift your foot," she says.

"Huh?" he grunts, without looking her way.

"Lift your melting foot," she says loudly. She slaps at his shoe with a clean dishrag. He's worried she will draw the attention of Army Coat.

"No, no," he says quietly. "It's all right. I'll just move it."

"Lift your foot," she repeats more loudly. A Mexican man with a bushy mustache and a cowboy hat throws one arm over the back of his booth and turns to see who the waitress is fussing with.

Townes lifts his foot, and she mounts the bench seat opposite him with her knees so she can wipe the snowmelt from under him. Her rump waves in the air. She's making a spectacle of the booth cleaning. The Mexican is still watching, shaking his head, his expression hard to read. Townes shakes his head right back at the man, trying for the same blank look. The waitress folds the cloth and places it under his foot; she pushes his foot so it's at rest and backs out of the booth.

"There," she says. She straightens her apron but not her back. "So, how is it?"

"Huh?" Army Coat is still turned away, perhaps wringing the life out of more helpless napkins.

"Turn up your hearing aid, gramps. How is it?" The waitress jokes.

Townes doesn't know if she's asking about the orange juice, the hot water, or his foot. So he says, "Good, good, it's all good."

"Glad to hear it. Wave if you get hungry." Then she's gone, leaving Townes feeling very alone and very concerned that his only path to safety is blocked by a man with a knife and a grudge.

# A PRELUDE TO INQUISITION

In the car with Ruther, Charlie asks questions and Ruther repeats the little he knows. Charlie knows Ruther is trying to sound understanding without saying too much. Charlie knows it would be best to just sip his strong coffee and bide his time, but he can't help himself.

"So, tell me again. What was the deal with the apartment? Why were the police called in?"

Ruther's mustache gets ruffled, but he doesn't let it creep into his voice. He says, "How long have we known each other, Charlie? I don't mean when we met. I mean when we started to get to know one another."

Charlie thinks about it. "Four years. Maybe more. Four and a half years? Something like that."

"And in all that time, have you known me to play it loose when it comes to an active investigation? Have you ever known me to run my mouth, to speak out of turn?"

"No. You are professional. Even when drunk." And it is true. Charlie had attempted to get information from Ruther early on. It was the reason he had first invited Ruther to grab a beer. He'd plied him with drinks, graduating from bottles of 312 Urban Wheat to sampling various whiskeys and vodkas from a local distillery. It cost Charlie a small fortune. When Ruther seemed sloppy and happy, Charlie started complimenting him: "You must be good at what you do to be the lead on so many high-profile cases. So accomplished." Or "Wow, it's impressive you're the head of this task force. Next stop, chief of police." Or "The way you move all over and interact with so many departments, you must have a nimble mind. A mind for politics. I bet you make all kinds of intuitive connections, have all kinds of theories. You are a regular Kojak, but with hair. James Rockford with a badge." Ruther had accepted the compliments. He let Charlie spend his money, but he never drifted into conjecture about Etta's case. Even when he was so drunk he had to lean on Charlie to walk to his cab, Ruther had never let anything slip.

"So you know, I've already said everything I can about Newton, his apartment, and what it means. You know I'm not likely to say more," Ruther continues.

"Yeah, I know, but it's Etta. You know. You know how long we've waited? Do you understand how long I've been trying to find anything new, any lead, any answer? Do you know? Do you know how many times I've followed bad leads to dead ends? You understand. I can't help myself. She's my little girl. I don't know how to let it go, how to stop pushing on it. And you're all I've got right now. And we got time to kill. So, you know, try to understand." Ruther accelerates to the rear bumper of a tanker truck, jams his big car into a space in the next lane before he gets boxed in.

He says, "I do understand. You know I think of Etta nearly as much as you. And if she ever moved off my radar, you would remind me." Ruther rides the bumper of a silver Toyota Prius. The Prius driver shows his eyes in the rearview, taps his brakes, and begins to slow, just to demonstrate his displeasure. Ruther flips the switch on his police lights, allows them to flash red. The hybrid changes lanes and lets Ruther surge past.

"Yeah, I know," Charlie says.

"I will humor you. We can keep talking about it, but don't expect to learn anything new from me. Not until I know something new. I'm protecting you. I don't know if this will be anything real. I can't keep you from getting your hopes up. I can, at the least, try to be realistic with you. While it's the first new, *possible* lead." He puts obvious emphasis on the word *possible* and then says, "And I emphasize the word *possible*. It could be nothing at all. Nothing. It could be something, but not what we think. So please. Understand. This. This is not a homerun. We are not about to make an arrest. We have no smoking gun. We just have a little shot at something. I know it's hard not to get your hopes up. My hopes are up. But try not to get your hopes up. Because if it turns out to be nothing, it'll be hard to get over. You understand me?"

Charlie knows Ruther is right. He says, "I know you're right. It's okay. You just drive. I'll pipe down." He casts his eyes around at the traffic. Ruther jams the accelerator again, urging the car down the road.

A couple of minutes later, Charlie pulls *The Tao of Pooh* from his coat pocket. He flips it open. He has to hold the book farther away from his face than usual in order to get his eyes to work. He misses his glasses. He reads the first lines his eyes can focus on:

Do you really want to be happy? You can begin by being appreciative of who you are and what you've got.

Charlie lets that sink in. He thinks of Meg and Townes. He even thinks of Bootsy. He puts the book back in his pocket and taps a number into his phone that used to be his. Meg's canned voice speaks into his ear. Charlie eyes Ruther and thinks of what to say. He leaves a brief and appropriately vague message. Ruther takes his eyes from the road for a moment, gives a little nod of approval, and switches lanes without using his blinker.

"You mind if I try to find some music on your radio?" Charlie asks.

"Knock yourself out," Ruther replies.

Charlie spends the rest of the drive twiddling the radio knobs, trying to find anything worth listening to. He never does. It only takes thirty minutes from the time Charlie buckles in at Jitters until they are parking in the lot outside the police station.

"Okay," Ruther says. "You keep quiet. You are my guest. Let me do the talking."

"I understand."

Ruther exits the car, leaves the keys in the ignition and the car unlocked. Charlie slides out too. Ruther hitches his pants and retucks his shirt as he crosses the parking lot. He fixes his tie and combs his mustache before going through the doors of the police station. He walks straight to the front desk and shows his badge. He says, "Detective Ruther. I'm expected."

The officer at the counter wears a uniform like a cop's, but she's a civilian, a professional administrator for the city. Ruther's apparent self-importance, brusque manner, and sense of urgency send her into high speed. She checks her clipboard, types on her keyboard. Then she pushes a hidden button that causes a sound like a giant wind-up joy buzzer to rumble from a nearby door. Ruther pushes through, Charlie on his heels.

They pass down a long hall, feet clopping, and are greeted at the far end by two police officers. Ruther introduces Charlie. The female officer looks familiar. Charlie thinks she must be around the same age as Etta. As Ruther and the male officer go over the situation, the female officer pulls Charlie aside.

She says, "Mr. Messenger, I was in school with Etta. I was a year ahead of her. We were in a school musical together. *Sweeney Todd*." She waits for the information to register on Charlie's face. He remembers.

Charlie and Meg had sat near the front of the school auditorium Etta's sophomore year. He had never attended a musical before, other than Etta singing about Thanksgiving one year while dressed as a carrot. He'd been puzzled by the macabre choice of material but impressed with the performances, the theater space, and the overall quality of the production. It wasn't his kind of thing, but it struck him as fairly professional. It was a little disconcerting to see all those young, fresh kids singing their hearts out and dancing in syncopated steps while describing cut throats and victim's bodies being baked into meat pies. After the initial shock, his strongest impression was that Etta was more talented than he'd ever realized.

"I remember," he says.

The officer, still just a young girl, looks into his face, seeking a connection. "I was only in the crowd scenes. Wendy Zwick," she says. She taps her chest where her name tag is fastened. "But it was fun. Etta had a very pretty voice."

Charlie notes the use of the past tense: "Etta *had* a very pretty voice." He hates that. He normally corrects people who talk about Etta in the past tense. But the officer is being nice and is referencing a past moment. He lets it pass.

He says, "Yes. She surprised me. She did a nice job. She gets her talent from her mother. I love to listen. But I can't carry a tune in a bucket. The whole production was wonderful. You were great, Wendy. Everyone was great." His eyes cloud, like his glasses are smudged. He moves to take them off and clean them before realizing he's wearing no glasses. He sniffs, clears his throat, rubs his eyes.

Wendy waits for Charlie to get it together. "I just wanted you to know, Etta is not forgotten. Not by me. Not by a lot of the people here. We remember her."

"Thank you." Charlie can't stare into that sincere face any longer and looks around the room instead.

"When she was taken, that's when I first started to think about law enforcement. I wanted to be of help, if I could."

Charlie doesn't know how to respond. After an awkward silence, he brings Wendy in for a hug. He wraps his arms around her, feels the warmth of her, and wants to hang onto that sensation. She is the same age as Etta, the same size. He can pretend he is holding his daughter. The hug lasts too long. Charlie releases Wendy, who seems both moved and embarrassed. She fidgets with her heavy belt and checks to see if anyone is staring.

Ruther and the other officer watched the hug but go back to their conversation when Wendy glances their way. They finish their hushed conversation, and Ruther gestures for Charlie to follow. He says goodbye to Wendy. They are escorted by a round black woman through a door with a keypad lock, through another long hall. They stand next to a closed door and huddle together.

She says, "This is where Mr. Parker is waiting. He was cooperative with me. But he's starting to get agitated."

"That's good," Ruther says.

"We have you set up over here." She leads them into a room just opposite.

There's a laptop showing a bird's-eye view of a black-and-white, grainy, and distant Newton Parker sitting in a small room, fiddling with something on a small tabletop. As they watch, Newton sits back to reveal the likeness of an erect dick and balls. It's hard to tell exactly what he's made the image from, but he seems proud of his effort. He looks into the camera and flips them off.

"Classy," says Ruther.

Charlie is reminded of a famous image of Johnny Cash.

Newton, through the little screen, mixes the picture up and hops up beside the table. He starts stretching this way and that.

"I'm Harris," the woman says to Ruther. "Officer Zwick is bringing the box from the evidence locker. She'll be here shortly. You want me to get you coffee? There's a machine downstairs that makes it by the cup. Powdery cappuccinos, hot chocolate, even beef broth. You want something? Water? Beef broth?"

Charlie isn't listening. Just staring at the screen. Newton sits on the corner of the table, leans down to tug one pants leg. After a moment of closely scrutinizing something Charlie can't make out, Newton drops his pants leg back in place.

"Yeah," Ruther says. "I'll take one of those cappuccinos. I'm a sucker for those things. Charlie? You want a drink?"

"Nothing for me."

Harris leaves on her errand. Ruther joins Charlie to hover in front of the screen. Newton pulls up his other pants leg. One moment he bends over, blocking most of the view. The next, he takes his leg off, pitches it on the table beside him, and sticks a thick stump out into the room. He leans back, looking relaxed.

"What the hell?" Charlie asks.

"He lost it in Afghanistan."

"I had no idea."

Newton sits like that a long time. The two men keep staring, because it's on a screen. They don't speak. After a time, Officer Harris returns. She hands Ruther a paper cup. He takes a big swig, getting the corners of his mustache wet. He rubs the back of his hand across his mouth.

"I gotta get back to work now. Officer Zwick should be here any moment, and another officer will come by to see if you need anything. His last name is long and Welsh and impossible to pronounce. So we just call him Davie. He'll be here in a minute, too."

"Thanks," Ruther says.

He and Charlie keep watching. Newton finally puts his leg back on. He sits a bit longer, eyes closed, chest rising and falling in a slow rhythm.

"What are you waiting for?" Charlie asks.

"I want to look through the box of evidence before I go in," Ruther replies.

Newton hops to his feet and draws a breath. They hear his voice through the weak little speakers and coming from across the hall at the same time.

"Hey, assholes," he yells. "I gotta take a piss and get my phone call. I had other plans for the day."

Then he turns his eyes to the camera and flips it off again. This time it reminds Charlie of Sid Vicious.

The two middle-aged men watch as Newton steps up on one of the chairs. He reaches for the camera, his hand sweeping close to the lens, his fingers filling the screen. He stops his assault and looks around the room.

"Shit," Ruther says. He swipes a folder from the desk and leaves the door open as he shoots across the hall. Charlie sees the proud look on Newton's face when Ruther walks in. Charlie closes the door, finds a chair, and takes a seat and listens.

# PLAYTIME WITH GRANDMA MEG

Meg has a hard time digging through the coats in the overfull hall closet, but she eventually extracts her heavy winter trench coat. She hasn't had occasion to wear it in years. She also finds her supple leather gloves and a dark floral scarf with some shimmer to it.

She starts to bustle through the kitchen but comes back to write a note for Townes, just in case. When she closes the back door, she's careful to leave it unlocked, so Townes doesn't think she's already gone. She knows he's likely to take the slightest excuse to bail out on the event or decide he should walk on his own.

In the garage, she listens for a sign of Townes's presence but doesn't hear any movement above. She starts the car, lets the garage door rattle open, and backs out. The weather is overcast; a front is coming in. She gets stuck behind another train, an Amtrak racing into the city from points west. It blasts by in a self-generated cyclone of swirling snow, flashing red lights, and silver cladding. It only slows her down a couple of minutes.

She parks at the Feldman's Fresh Mart, a high-end fruit market combined with a nice flower department, cheese shop, regional wine bar, and artisan bread bakery. The prices are high, the fruit is the best in town, but she's come to visit the florist.

"Hi. Welcome to Feldman's. We have a special on roses today." The woman has a spritely, prepubescent build that is hard to age. She takes her apron and wipes it between her hands like it's a dishtowel, leaving it wet and crumpled, even after she smoothes it down.

"Hi. This is a little strange. I'm not sure what I want. I need an arrangement for a twenty-three-year-old young woman."

"We can do that. Do you know what she likes?"

"I should. I should. But I don't. I can't remember for the life of me what kind of flowers were her favorite." Meg's voice breaks a little. The woman's expression morphs from helpful salesperson to thoughtful caregiver. She's clearly caught the use of the past tense in Meg's phrasing, a sad look pass over her face.

The apron has a name embroidered on it in a hard-to-read, loopy script. Meg thinks it reads *Kimberly*.

Kimberly reaches out and takes Meg's hand. She holds it reassuringly between her two hands, gently, like it's fragile and might shatter. "I can help you with whatever you need. You just tell me what you need. We'll figure this out together."

The kindness threatens to undo Meg. She takes her hand back, takes a moment to compose herself. Finally, she says, "Thank you. I'm sorry to be short, but I have to get to an event. I need something pretty easy. Something to leave at a gravesite."

"I understand," Kimberly replies. She casts her eyes around the floral department. "Do you think you'd like a vase to set out, or just flowers to leave?"

"Just flowers, please."

"Yes," says Kimberly. "Of course. That would be best. That sounds perfect. Just let me put something lovely together." Meg nods.

Kimberly is a whirl of activity as she moves among the displays of fresh flowers. Meg tries to picture Etta, what she would look like now. She wonders if Etta would have gotten married by now, if she would still be with Newton. *Probably not.* Maybe Etta would have made her a grandmother by now. *Grandma Meg.* The notion she's old enough to be a grandmother is bittersweet. *Might as well face facts.*

Her memory of Etta's face is slipping. She has a vague sense of a vivacious spirit, a confident presence. Her thoughts of Etta are defined through an awareness of her absence, more than a lingering relationship with her distant presence.

Kimberly is there again, handing her a huge bouquet of flowers wrapped in layers of plastic sheeting and paper to protect it against the weather. She passes the armful of flowers over as if it's a newborn and Meg is taking it for the first time. Meg imagines Kimberly will say, "Mind its head. Support its neck."

Instead, Kimberly says, "I think this will serve your needs very well. I used a mix of the sale roses, and I put in some other things to fill it out."

"Thank you," Meg says, reaching for her wallet.

"Those are on a special sale today," Kimberly says. "They're free."

Meg is confused.

Kimberly explains, "I remember you. I have a daughter who was in school with your girl. Darby was two years behind Etta. After your tragedy, Darby said how kind Etta was to everyone. She felt terrible about what happened. We all did. The whole town. The whole country. I remember Etta. And the flowers are on me."

"Thank you," Meg says again and leaves before she gets choked up.

Meg cradles the flowers in both arms and places them carefully in the back seat. She thinks of buckling them in place but worries the belt will crush them. She drives back to the house, fully expecting to meet another train. Instead, the lights all turn green, the road opens in front of her, and she's home in a few short minutes.

She doesn't bother parking in the garage. She tucks her head down to peek at the back door of the house. She gives the horn two taps to get Townes moving. She checks the time on the console. They should be at the cemetery by now. She honks again, looks for movement from the kitchen.

"Shit." She puts the car in park and pokes her boot heels into the snow on her way to the door. The door is still unlocked. The note she left is in the same spot. She snatches the note and stuffs it in her coat pocket.

"Townes!" she yells into the empty house.

Back outside she tries to judge the tracks in the snow to decide if Townes has been and gone, but she can't make sense of the marks.

She hops back in the car and rips into the street. Her tires spin on the hard-packed black snow. The car slides out of control. She turns the wheel, frantic to point the hood down the street. The windshield shows her the yard on the opposite side of the street. She slams on the brakes but the tires can't bite down, the brakes lock. The car smashes its rims into the curb with nearly enough force to cause real damage. She's jolted by the impact, jostled enough to hurt her neck, not hard enough to deploy the airbags. The flowers fly and slap into the back of her seat, tumble to the floorboard. She looks back at them, while the car sits crossways in the lane, thankful the street isn't too busy. She sees the head of one rose has popped loose and been mashed against the center console.

"Your brother can really be a trial," she says to Etta. Then she adds, "Also, I think it's best that you haven't made me a grandmother. I might not be ready."

# UNINTENDED STAKEOUT

Townes sits for long minutes, expecting to be discovered. He nibbles his nails, spitting the sharp bits into the seat next to him, keeping his eyes on the back of Army Coat as best he can. He has to lean around the shifting customers in the intervening booths. The effort he makes to see Army Coat is comforting. It tells Townes perhaps he isn't so easy to spot, crouching in the back booth, as he initially feared. Army Coat never turns in his direction. Townes stops biting his nails when there isn't anything left to chew. *Dirty, nervous habit,* he scolds himself.

He relaxes a little. He notices his hot water has turned tepid. Before it gets too cold, Townes unzips the section of his messenger bag where he keeps his favorite green tea in a Ziploc bag. He's in luck, one bag left. He lets the flow-through bag settle into his mug of water. He searches for his tube of locally sourced, pesticide-free clover honey. After two minutes, he bobs the teabag up and down in the mug, lets it drain, and sets it aside. He drops the whole tube of honey into the hot water, watches the tube dissolve and release its contents into the weak tea. It takes longer than usual, the water having cooled too much. He takes a spoon and stirs. He sets the spoon aside, brings the mug to his nose, and breathes it in. Finally, he drinks.

He feels the honey coat his tongue, tastes the rich, nurturing green tea. He thinks of Dory and smiles a private smile. He's calm as he watches the agitated shoulders of the man he came to find. He reminds himself why he is here: This man is a child snatcher. He doesn't know what Army Coat had planned for Esmeralda, but it can't have been anything good. Townes is the only one who knows the man is up to something. If he can find his name or address, if he can put his hands on some proof, then he can contact the authorities. Maybe he could give Charlie the information. It would be like they were a team. *Go Team Messenger!* He thinks it with as much high school pep as he can muster.

Then he starts again. *Why am I really here?* He answers himself: *You are here because of Etta. Because you did nothing for her when she needed you most. Because you have a pattern of not standing up until it's too late. Because you're tired of hiding. Because you feel guilty. Because you contributed to your sister's disappearance. Fear and guilt.* It's a hard truth to admit, even to himself, especially to himself.

Townes knows it's his ego that brought him here chasing after a dangerous man. It's a desire to earn self-worth through deeds, rather than based on a sense of superiority born of a rarefied state of mind, a fraudulent inner peace. He also sees he has confused his affection for Etta with his protection of Esmeralda. The psychological mashup is perplexing but hard to deny.

Townes sips his tea slowly, until it's gone. He drinks his juice slowly too. It is the sweetest thing he's tasted in an age. It makes his jaw ache and his teeth hurt. Townes sits with his empty mug and glass, killing time. His body is hunched in the seat, his cap pulled low, and his eyes keeping track of Army Coat.

Army Coat continues to wordlessly demand refills of coffee by waggling his empty mug every fifteen minutes or so. He continues to pull napkins from the chrome dispenser on his table and wring them until they come apart. Customers walk in, seat themselves in the booths between Townes and Army Coat. They order food, eat, pay at the counter, and leave. Army Coat stays put.

# MANO A MANO

Ruther looks like hell. *Six years must be a lot when you're already a fat old bastard with a mustache like a wet cunt.*

"Good. Good to see you again, Mr. Parker," Ruther says as he enters the interrogation room. "Please take a seat."

"I have to take a leak." Newton stays bent over, standing on the seat of the folding chair. *The Chair.* He chastises himself for not thinking of using the other folding chair to whack the camera. *My head isn't in the game today.*

"We can get that taken care of in a minute," Ruther says, eyeing Newton's new leg. He uses his face to indicate the leg, a twitch of the head and a flattening of the lip make the whiskers of his mustache actually bristle and ripple a smidgen, as if pointing toward the prosthetic. "I heard you lost a leg when you were away. I'm sorry to hear about your accident."

"It wasn't an accident." Newton steps down and drops into the chair again. "It was intentional: the idea of separating my leg from my body. But the more pressing matter is, I REALLY DO NEED TO PISS. I'm going to have another kind of accident right HERE IN THE CORNER."

"Okay. Okay. Please give me a minute." Ruther looks out the crack in the door and says, "Tell Davie to clear the bathroom. We'll need to get in there in a few minutes." He closes the heavy door with a click.

Newton doubts Ruther was speaking to anyone in the hall, suspects it was part of some cop mind game. Newton hops up and paces back and forth in the eight-foot run at the end of the room. It relieves some of the pressure on his bladder. Also, it defies Ruther's wishes for him to sit.

Ruther takes his place and knocks a thin manila file on the tabletop. "So, let's discuss how we both ended up in this room."

"You know, the usual way, I walked into my apartment with the intention of going straight to the bathroom. Because I had to take a leak. My door was standing open. People were rummaging through my apartment. And the next thing I know, my hands were being cuffed by jack-booted thugs." Newton stops moving and looks down at Ruther. "Which, by the way, interfered with me GOING TO THE BATHROOM."

There's a crisp knock on the door. Ruther reaches the knob without standing. Officer Wendy steps in and places a cardboard carton on the table. She closes the door behind her without a word. The box is packed with his backpack and other stuff from his closet, as well as his coat and phone, each sealed in its own clear plastic bag with a printed label stuck to it.

"Let's talk about this," Ruther says, his mustache indicating the box.

"I'll talk about some things. ONE," Newton counts off as he begins walking again. "That Officer Wendy and I went to school together. We were classmates. Did you know that? Did she put that in her report? Did she tell you what she said to me? She said she was a friend of Etta. She said that she hopes that I get the FUCKIN' DEATH PENALTY. I bet my lawyer would love to hear about that: illegal search and seizure by a cop with a grudge. She's a real power-hungry sicko, that Wendy. She said she hoped I died bad, like that one in Oklahoma or Texas or wherever the hell that was." He stops to see how Ruther is taking that news; Ruther looks irritated.

Encouraged, Newton continues to pace and talk. "TWO. When I was being tackled from behind I hit my face and received no medical attention." He points to the healing cut on his cheek. Ruther doesn't seem impressed. "You may not care that your fellow officers are attacking people in their own homes, but I bet my lawyer will."

Detective Ruther tries to get things back on track. "Mr. Parker. If you don't sit I will have you cuffed to the table."

"THREE," Newton continues, "I am supposed to get a phone call."

"Newton," Ruther warns, the color getting up in his face, his mustache like a cat's back.

"And FOUR. I'm not talking about any of that shit in the box until I get to take a leak." Newton stops and leans his back against the wall. Crosses his arms. Waits.

Ruther gives in. "All right. Let's take your tiny delicate bladder to the bathroom before you ruin your best panties." He opens the door for Newton. "To the left."

Newton happily hustles to the left. The hall is empty. All the doors along the way are closed. Next to a water fountain, he shoves into the men's room and has his dick out before he can cross to the urinal. Ruther follows him and leans against the sink to wait.

"Ahhhhh," Newton says as he finishes his business. He buttons up and flushes. At the sink he waits for the water to turn warm, letting it run a long time. He takes a page from Cranky Thomas's book and lathers and washes as if he's prepping for surgery, taking his time, seeing how long Ruther will put up with it.

"Okay. Okay," Ruther says when Newton finally shakes his hands over the sink and goes for the hand dryer.

"I can't hear you," Newton says. He works his hands in the blower until it times out. He hits the button again and starts to rub his hands some more. Ruther grabs the back of his arm and shoves him, using Newton's body to knock the door open. He gives him a push back toward the tiny interrogation room. Newton is pleased he's made Ruther angry, and he smiles as he saunters back into the room and takes his seat. He eyes his phone as he passes his belongings.

"Okay. Okay," Ruther starts again. "I drove here from downtown so we could have this talk. I'm supposed to be off-duty. I've been working for eight days straight. I've put up with your shit, because I didn't want to make this contentious. I should have known better. So now, you answer my questions and I will get you out of here."

"I'm sorry," Newton says. He sounds sincere. "It's no fun to be cuffed and threatened. It's not cool to be intentionally pitched around in the back of a squad car while Officer Friendly rams into every pothole he can find and then chuckles about it. No fun to be jerked around and left to sit in here for God knows how long. You understand?"

"I understand. I drove as fast as I could to get here. No one is trying to jerk you around. I needed to talk to the arresting officers before I could see you. You understand?"

Newton shakes his head affirmatively.

"Good. Good," Ruther says. "Now, let's chat."

"I will chat with you, Detective, but I need to make a call real quick. It won't take a minute."

"That can wait."

"Nope."

Ruther doesn't even try to negotiate. He leans over the box and digs with both hands until he finds the phone. "Here. Make your fucking call." Ruther pitches the bag with Newton's phone over. "But then you better quit tugging my dick."

"Privacy?"

"Fuck you, kid. Just make your call and let's get this over with."

Newton brings his phone to life. It's nearly out of juice. The screen shows he's got a message from Townes. Which is a surprise. It's probably about the memorial, so he ignores it. He swipes down his list of contacts and finds the number listed as Etta's. He realizes he didn't really need to look it up, it is still right there in his head. All he has to do is let his fingers start tapping numbers. He dials it, for the first time in years. Ruther watches him. It goes to a machine. Meg's voice sounds so much like Etta's, Newton feels the blood leave his face. He's instructed to wait for the beep, so he does. He waggles his eyebrows at Ruther. Ruther scowls back.

"Hey. This is Newton. I appreciate the invitation to the memorial. I wanted to attend, but something came up. I don't think

I'm going to make it. I'm sorry." He taps his phone to clear the screen and drops it back in the Ziploc bag, tosses it into the box.

"Who was that?" Ruther asks. It's clear he knows the answer.

"Etta's mom. Mrs. Messenger."

"And what was it about?"

"Don't I get a private phone call? I should get some clarification when my lawyer gets here."

"If you called this lawyer you keep threatening me with, yes. You would get to speak to him in private. Instead, you called the mother of your missing girlfriend. That interests me. You said you would talk after the call. The call is over. So talk."

"You sure you're ready for me to stop pulling your dick?"

"Talk."

"I called Etta's mom because she invited me to a kind of service she put together to honor Etta. I wasn't sure about it, but I decided to go. Truth is I swung by my place to get cleaned up, iron some slacks or something. Get ready, you know. But instead I found my place full of uninvited guests."

Ruther nods. His mustache seems smooth and satisfied. His old, cloudy eyes tip up to the camera in the ceiling. He says, in an official tone, "Detective Ruther here with Newton Parker who has been read his rights and has waived his right to an attorney." He looks to Newton to acknowledge his statement. Newton nods.

"You have to say it."

"Yeah. That's right. I don't need a lawyer."

"Okay. Okay. So, let's start fresh here. I appreciate your honesty about the call. You were invited to Etta's memorial. You actually hope to still make it. Maybe we can get through this, and I can give you a ride."

Newton likes the idea of getting out of here, but he'd rather lose his other leg than ride with Ruther. If he'd known Ruther was invited, he would have never considered attending. He stays quiet.

"I need to ask you some questions about Etta. I need you to think back, think back six years. These are questions you've already answered, I know. And I know it's been a long time. I'm just trying to establish some details. Okay?"

"I guess."

"Just take your time."

"I will," Newton says soberly.

Ruther flashes his eyes to the camera again. It makes Newton wonder who's on the other end of that thing. Who's watching right now? Who's Ruther performing for, besides a possible judge and jury?

Ruther takes a deep breath and begins. "On the day of Etta's disappearance, you two saw each other at school . . ."

Ruther replays Etta's last day, in every detail. He establishes that Etta had texted Newton to say she was taking the bus, that she couldn't meet him before school. Newton explains again that they sometimes met and grabbed coffee at the Dunkin' Donuts before school. On the day of her disappearance, he had driven, gotten there in time to run straight into school. He'd seen Etta between first and second periods. He couldn't remember what they talked about. They'd kissed. Although they had different lunch schedules, he got a bathroom pass from study hall and went to sit with her in the cafeteria. She threw Cheetos across the table at him, and he caught them in his mouth, smiled his orange teeth at her. She licked her orange fingers at him. He went over the scuffle Townes had with Andy Adair. Then he'd talked with Etta after the last bell. They'd planned to get together later that night.

"What had you planned to do?"

"I'm sure I asked her to hang out at my place. She said her mom might not let her drive. I said I'd pick her up."

"And you would have been home alone with Etta?"

"Yes. My mom worked different shifts, at two different jobs, back then."

"And so would you two have been studying?" It was clear what Ruther was getting at. They'd already been down this road six years ago. Newton had been self-conscious about it and had tried to lie. But now, instead of dragging it out, he just gave the answer Ruther was looking for.

"Who knows for sure what would happen. Sometimes we would study. Sometimes we would watch TV. Etta liked to come over and cook us dinner, play house. She would make a plate for my mom and leave it covered in the fridge. I mostly invited her over hoping for sex. We usually did some combination of those things, but sex was nearly always a part of my plan."

Ruther looks to the camera again. Newton thinks maybe Meg and Charlie, Etta's mom and dad, are out there watching him right now. Maybe Townes had texted him to tell him, warn him. *We were asked to come to the station. . . .* He suddenly feels embarrassed by what he just said. He wants to say more. He wants to make Etta's parents understand. He imagines he can feel her father's eyes on him through the camera, and he wants to say something true.

"You know, about Etta and me. I was a teenager. You know. It was all kind of a game to me. I was trying to get as much as I could. As much sex as I could get. The best sex I could get with the cutest girl I could find. I didn't take it all that seriously. Didn't take it seriously with Etta. Even when she went missing, it just didn't seem real. But over the years I learned something. I learned I loved her. At the time, I said I did. I told her I loved her, but I only half meant it. I took her for granted. It had come so easily, I didn't know how rare and precious it is to find love, to find someone. Now I know I loved her. She was the only one I ever felt like that about."

Ruther thinks about that for a minute. Thinks of what to ask next. "So you sat with her at lunch and made plans to get together at your house after school. And was that the last time you saw Etta?"

"Yeah."

"You didn't swing by to see her at her house? Right after school? Pick her up when she got off the bus?"

"No. That was it. I texted her a few times later on to see if we were still on. She never replied. I just assumed her mom told her she couldn't go. Maybe she and her mom went shopping. I didn't know. But I didn't have a reason to worry too much."

Ruther flips open his folder and looks over the page of notes inside. "Last night, four boys were attacked in a bar by a one-legged man fitting your description. Do you know anything about that?"

"One-legged men are a dime a dozen these days."

"Mmm-hmm. Okay. Okay. Well, the police report states the assailant was struck in the face with a bottle, cutting his cheek. I noticed that you have that cut." Ruther's lips and mustache point at Newton's head.

"Small world."

"Today, two officers assisted with a possibly violent tenant that was disturbing the peace. That would be you."

"Agreed."

"Officer Wendy, as you call her, her name is Zwick."

"Right. I remember now. Wendy Zwick. She was very squeamish back in the day. Could not handle the sight of blood. Strange that she became a cop."

"What does that mean?"

"It's a biology lab thing. You had to be there."

"Nevertheless." Ruther tries to get back on track. "When Officer Zwick noticed this yearbook." Ruther stands and pulls the Ziploc bag from the carton by one corner, lets it smack flat onto the table in front of Newton. "As you said, she went to the same school. She also saw this." He places the backpack on the table, shifts the carton to the floor. "You see here, this brightly colored backpack? It has Etta's name on it in two places. One here." He points to a scrawl of blue ink. "And another here." He indicates a name tag in the open pack that reads, *Property of Etta Messenger.* Newton remembers the way she wrote her name, slashing the two Ts with one quick cross stroke that read like a capital H. Her name always looked like the monogram EHA. He used to kid her about it.

"So the thing that got me called in, the thing that set off alarm bells with the arresting officers, is you seem to be in possession of Etta's backpack. A backpack she reportedly carried with her onto the bus. A backpack listed as one of the things she was carrying at the time of her disappearance." Ruther sits back in his chair; it groans in protest. "So. So if you didn't see her after she left school, if you have no idea what she did after she left school, how is it that you have her backpack?"

*So this is clearly IT.* This is the entire reason Ruther is here, to ask this one question. Newton notices how Ruther tries to keep the emphasis from his voice, tries to ask the question just as he asked the questions that led to it. But this is the one that matters. This is the question that people on the other end of the camera are waiting to hear asked, are waiting to have answered.

"Simple," Newton replies. He pushes the backpack across to Ruther as he says, "This is not the backpack Etta was carrying. This was the backpack I was carrying. The one she had was black. My old backpack. We traded. Weeks before. Maybe months. It was a thing we did. Like getting pinned back in your day. Or wearing one another's school rings or letter jackets or whatever. We traded backpacks because we were a couple. For fun, but also like a statement. Like a commitment ring. You understand? Like one of those Irish friendship rings you flip over. You're Irish aren't you, Detective? You know the kind of ring I'm talking about? You know the kind. Wear it one way, then wear it another."

"We call it a claddagh ring."

"Yes. Okay. With the hands and the heart with a crown. Well, we traded packs. I was carrying this. She had my old black one when she took the bus home."

Newton watches Ruther's mustache droop at the corners of his mouth. He asks other questions about the bong, about the one hitter, about the picture in Newton's wallet, about the yearbook left open to an image of Etta.

Newton explains, "The bong might as well be a vase. I never use it. I don't have any weed."

And: "I used to smoke that one hitter in high school. The whole wrestling team smoked. Etta even smoked with me a few times. But it wasn't for her, smoking weed. It was in that box with all the shit I pulled out for the memorial." He lies about that part. But it's a little lie and Ruther is barely listening at this point. All his hopes of making an arrest, all his dreams of closing this case for Charlie, for Etta, for himself are drifting away.

Newton explains, "The same with the photos. The memorial got me thinking about Etta. So I dug those photos and the yearbook out to look things over."

To give more veracity to his comments, he takes a chance and admits, "It was me at the bar. I fought those guys. To be clear, there were four of them, each one bigger than the next. I guess that had to do with Etta too. I've been thinking of her a lot lately, because of Meg's invitation. Because I thought I might be asked to say something at the memorial. Maybe just because I miss her so bad. I do, you know. I miss Etta. As much as anyone does."

Lastly he says, "And the loud music and threats at my apartment, it's all related. I'm one messed-up guy. I didn't have anything to do with whatever happened to Etta. Not that I know of. Not unless she ran off because of something stupid I did. Something hateful I said. I don't know anything more about it than you do. I have no insider information. If I did, I'd tell you. Truth of it is, if I did it, I would confess to have this whole thing done with. I'm sick of it weighing on me."

Ruther mostly grunts and mumbles. His eyes drop lower and lower as Newton speaks. When Newton finishes, Ruther says, "Okay.

Okay. Well, we will check out your story about the backpack. You just sit tight."

He lifts the carton from the floor and stuffs the evidence back inside. He opens the door to leave.

"You think I can still make the memorial?"

Ruther checks his watch. "You just sit." He closes the door behind him.

Newton doesn't see Ruther again. The officer with the drippy forehead comes in ages later with food from the vending machine: a bag of Gardetto's and a Dr Pepper.

He says, "I grabbed you a snack. I picked the stuff I like. I hope it's okay."

"Cool," Newton replies.

When Newton finishes, Officer Acne returns to escort him to the restroom. Newton is allowed in by himself.

On the way back to the interrogation cell, Newton asks, "Can you tell me what my status is? If I'm not being arrested, I want to get the hell out of here. I've been sitting here all day."

"I think you're free to go. The detective said your story held up. You need to wait a little longer so they can process you out."

"Fuck that."

"No. Seriously. Just a couple of minutes. I'll be back in ten minutes to help you out. Ten at the most."

True to his word, Officer Acne returns in less than ten minutes and walks Newton to where he had been processed in. A taller version of the same old man passes him his personal possessions, has him sign for them. He throws on his coat. Checks his phone. It's dead. He packs the other stuff in Etta's old backpack, the bong poking out the top, and pitches it over one shoulder.

"How the hell do I get home?"

"I'm going to drive you," replies Officer Acne.

"Hey, man. You've been cool with me. What's your name?"

"I'm Officer Davie Jernigtney." He reaches over and shakes hands with Newton.

"I'm Newton. If you don't mind, I'll call you Davie Jay."

"Everyone does."

They walk out together. It's early evening when they exit the station, well below freezing and going dark. The weather has taken a bad turn. Newton won't make the memorial, probably already missed it. *Maybe it's for the best.*

At the car, Officer Jernigtney apologizes for not being allowed to let Newton ride shotgun. "Regulations," he explains.

"But no cuffs, right?"

"No cuffs."

Newton slips into the back of the cruiser, buckles himself in, and rides home. The big car rides real smooth when you don't aim for every hole in the road. He leans his tired head back and stares out the window. He's mesmerized by the way the falling snow floats against the vast night sky; it looks as if the stars are falling slowly to earth.

# THE LONESOME MEMORIAL

Meg finds a place to parallel park right on Main Street, down the block from the cemetery. She smoothes her coat and buttons two buttons. *I'm nervous.* She places her gloved hand over her heart, feels the shallow rise and fall of her chest.

"My heart is racing," she tells the Etta in her mind.

"You did just nearly crash your car."

"Good point."

She opens the rear door and picks the flowers from the floorboard, carries them carefully. She locks the car, walks slowly down the block, the snow beginning to fall again. There are three steps up to the historic cemetery, tucked between the microbrewery pub and the wine bar. Her legs are hard to lift, as if she carries a weight on her back. She gets both her boots on the first stone step and pauses to rest.

She always loved this oddly tranquil spot. It's small and immaculately kept. Even in winter, the paths are clean, the headstones swept free of snow. Etta and she once sat at one of the stone benches and passed a cherry snow cone back and forth. That would have been the summer before Etta started high school, about a decade ago. *Time is such a strange thing, the way it slips past us, always surging ahead, even when it feels like we are standing still.* Meg feels her own mortality, her vitality sloughing off.

She takes another step, pauses again. She can see the spot toward the back where Etta's headstone has been placed, can see the area has been cleared, as if for a funeral service. She also sees no one else has yet arrived.

She takes the last step onto the stone pathway, damp with melting snow and crunchy with sprinkled salt. Her motions down the path are slow and deliberate: step step pause, step step pause, as if she's a young bride, walking the central aisle of her wedding ceremony. Step step pause. Willing herself to move slowly, with poise, not let her nerves get the best of her. Trying to feel the moment, to freeze it in her memory and hold it, as if trapped in amber, forever, for all time. At least all the time she has left. Step step pause.

Even at this pace, it only takes her a moment to reach her destination. She dangles the bouquet of flowers by their bound stems. The top of the bag they're wrapped in sweeps the hard snowpack. She looks around her. *So quiet.* A place separated, as if by magic, from the commercial district that surrounds it.

"So," she says. "Here we are."

She checks her watch. "The others should be here already."

"They aren't that late," Etta says reasonably. Performing her usual role as family peacemaker.

"I suppose, if Townes is walking, it could take him time. I'll give it a few minutes." Meg acquiesces to Etta's tone, trying to keep calm.

"And Dad never was good at keeping track of time. Focused on the task at hand, oblivious to the rest of the world."

"True. Punctuality was never one of his strengths."

They stand together in the comfortable silence. The dark limbs of the trees are hunched under the weight of snow, the warm weather earlier in the day not enough to melt their burden. Meg casts her eyes to other gravestones, the names of families that first settled the area recorded around her.

"Can you imagine?" Meg says. "A Messenger will be represented here, among all these important folks." Etta doesn't reply. Meg worked passionately to make it happen, but it's hard to feel proud, considering the circumstances.

Meg takes another look at the time: half an hour late. She looks back down the path to the entrance. She imagines Townes and Charlie walking in together. Talking together, shoulder to shoulder. All four of them together again. A family. Beat up and pulled apart.

Damaged and imperfect, but still a kind of family. *As good as any of these fucking families.* Townes isn't there on the path. Charlie isn't moving up the stairs. Even Newton and Ruther have decided not to attend.

"Well, shit," she says. "It looks like it's just you and me. Let's get this show on the road. What do you say, baby girl?"

"You're the one running this circus."

Meg unwinds the paper bags and plastic sleeves that Kimberly so lovingly put in place. It takes a while. She lets the wrappings drop to the ground, along with a dozen velvety, pink-and-red petals, bright against the dormant grass. One stem was snapped in the near crash. The flower hangs its heavy blossom like a head lolling on a broken neck. She lifts the bloom, tucks it back into the bunch, and allows the surrounding flowers to support it. She tosses the stem with the missing blossom into the cemetery, the bloom left in the car.

"There," she says. "Good as new."

She walks to the headstone. She reads her daughter's name. The granite is beautiful, magenta in color with dark mahogany flecks sprinkled throughout. It's a vibrant stone, strong, polished, hardy, and durable. It will last a hundred years. The letters are crisp, distinct, and bold. Not weatherworn and difficult to decipher like the names on the adjacent markers. Snow is gathering already in the bottommost edge of each recessed letter. She considers if placing the flowers on the stone or on the ground is better. She settles for the ground along the base of the stone. She steps back to take in the vignette.

Her breath catches. She weeps fat, silent tears.

"You know what I said, Etta." Meg wipes at the wet under her eyes; her fingertips smudge with watery mascara. "I bet I look like a raccoon." She digs in her purse for the Kleenex she knew she'd need. She wipes around her eyes again, blows her nose.

"You know, I said at the house we were cleaning, the one that belonged to that old French couple, that life is like a long, slow goodbye. That you had lived the best part. Not the part filled with compromises and disappointments. You remember, don't you?"

"Of course. It was just this morning."

"Well, I was feeling down. You know, a little blue, like your grandma used to say. I was wrong to say that. I think a long life beats the shit out of the alternative. Life isn't easy. Don't get me wrong. But as long as you're living it, there's a chance for good things. For moments of joy and fleeting magic.

"Like you, Etta. Like you were in my life. That's how I think of you. Having known you made your loss nearly unbearable. But if the loss was the price for the time I was allowed with you, for the life we had, the time we had, it's a steep, fucking price. It sucks. But I think it was worth it. I can't imagine my life without having spent a part of it with you. I guess a small part, a sliver, is all I get, and that will have to be enough." She moves up and touches her gloved hand to the gravestone. She says, "I love you, baby. I love you always."

She pivots on her boot heels, gathers the trash she let drop. She walks lightly down the path, feeling a little better. She doesn't even pause to see if Etta has a response. She knows how Etta feels. She shoves the plastic and paper into a trashcan when she hits the sidewalk.

Next door, at the wine bar, the owner greets her. "Welcome. Do you have a reservation?"

"Yes. Messenger, party of six," she says.

"Would you like to wait for the rest of your party?"

"No. They are running late. Weather."

"Oh, yes. I hear the storm is going to be bad. Well, come right this way."

Meg follows her to the largest table in the place, scoots in with her back to the wall, where she can keep an eye on the door. She takes the short menu and the long wine list and pretends to read. She thinks about her cell phone. She only uses it for work. Doesn't go in for all that texting stuff. She uses her phone for phone calls. She left it at home, plugged in its drawer. She wonders if maybe Townes has tried to call. Or Charlie. She'll have to check her messages when she gets home.

A waiter comes over. He's in dark jeans, a white button-down shirt tucked neatly into a brown belt. He's youngish and well spoken. He says his name, and she doesn't care enough to listen. He asks if she wants to wait for her other guests. He talks about the food specials, about good wine pairings. She orders something he suggests, not even aware of what. She wants him to go away and come back with something alcoholic.

She watches the couples sitting at the other tables. A few middle-aged couples, clearly married, comfortable, chatting lightly, telling old jokes, talking about the personal faults of their coworkers, family members, and close friends. Plotting the course of their children's lives.

She watches an older couple of women, holding hands across the table. A young man, mid-twenties, if Meg's guess can be trusted, likely on a first date, makes his best effort to impress the girl he's with. He talks a lot and loudly. He listens poorly, interrupts his date to get back to his point. When she doesn't seem engaged enough, he talks louder.

Human behavior makes her question the concept of evolution. We are all basic, uncomplicated animals. Needy. Perhaps with slightly better organizational skills and more elegant means of waste disposal than our ancestors. Advanced in our tool making, but basic in our social rituals. Of course, she knows Darwin believed in random variations causing species to evolve over time. And really, this guy's ineptitude in no way refutes Darwin's primary premise. *But still.*

The waiter returns with a plate of cheese and cured meats, a bottle of wine. He pours a bit in a glass. She tastes it. She's not wild about it but doesn't want to have to choose anything else. "It's fine."

He pours her half a glass and leaves. She fills the glass the rest of the way. She drinks the wine and eats. She watches the door. She fills her glass again. The young man's odds with his date continue to diminish with each word he speaks. The girl checks her phone under the table, texts a friend about how poorly the evening is going, even as the man thinks he is building a solid foundation for a nightcap back at his place.

She pours more wine. She nibbles slowly at the food. Charlie never arrives. Townes doesn't walk in to sit with her. Even Etta is absent. She sits alone but not lonely. She feels she accomplished something today.

She is getting very drunk. *What the hell.* She pours a last glass of wine to the top and continues to watch the people with normal lives come and go around her. She used to be one of those people. She doesn't envy them their normalcy. She's starting to feel settled in the life she's living, tragedy and all.

When the wine is gone, she asks for the bill. She pays for her food and buys two more bottles of the wine to take home. No one complains directly about her reserving the large table. She doesn't bring it up either.

The owner says, "Sorry the weather interrupted your gathering."

"I'm not," Meg says. "I had a lovely meal."

She tips the waiter well and leaves with her expensive bag of booze.

The owner opens the door as Meg unsuccessfully attempts to artfully twist and tuck her scarf.

"Thank you for coming. Hope to see you again," the owner says.

"Yes," Meg says. She's worried she'll slur if she says more.

"Can I call you a cab? The streets are starting to get treacherous."

Meg notices the snow coming down. The day has turned to night. "No. I'm fine. I have a ride coming."

"Very good," the owner replies.

On the street, the headlights of the traffic cast their bright beams, illuminating cones of soft snow.

# MACHINE-MADE COFFEE

Ruther walks into the room where Charlie's been watching the laptop. He sets the carton of evidence on the tabletop and says, "Well, that could have gone better."

"Better for who?" Charlie asks. He's getting a headache from squinting at the small, fuzzy screen, his eyes working hard to stay in focus without his glasses. He'll have to get replacements soon. And some sleep.

"I thought we had him." Ruther pushes his finger onto the screen, covering the image of Newton's head where he sits, looking relaxed and self-satisfied. He twists his fingertip like he's stubbing out a cigar.

"Yeah. And now?" Charlie asks.

Ruther straightens up, closes the laptop. "Well, I want to check his story. But I believe him. I hate him. But I believe him." Ruther pauses, stroking his mustache as he considers something. He amends his previous statement. "I don't hate him. I overstated it. I may have read him wrong. And I hate that I had it wrong. He's winning me over. I feel bad though. Those patrolmen thought they'd solved the Messenger case. I should have known it was too good to be true."

"Yeah," Charlie says again.

"Of course I'm sorry for you too. For your family."

"Of course. I know. It's okay. I know what you mean."

Charlie still looks at the place the laptop screen had been. He points to the void where the screen used to be, in order to indicate Newton. "I believe him too," he says, a little sadly. He looks at Ruther. "But I'm glad it's not him. That would have been hard to take." Charlie thinks abstractly about Etta's relationship with Newton. He had known she was sexually active. He'd never heard anyone say the words out loud. He supposes, as a father, he should be alarmed or outraged, but he's not. He says, "I think I understand where Newton is coming from. I was that age once too. We all were."

"I guess so," Ruther says, for lack of any other insight. "But if we believe Newton, that leaves us with nothing."

"Not nothing," Charlie says. "We know Etta was carrying a black backpack. It's not much, but it's something we had wrong. Now we have it right. That's something. It feels like progress. Don't you think? We are getting a better picture; things are slipping a little more into focus."

"Barely," Ruther says. "Just barely."

"I look at it this way: Things have been gridlocked for years. Nothing moving. Now, there is movement. Something could break loose." Charlie pushes his fists into the muscles of his low back. He's sore, starting to lock up.

"Listen," Ruther says. He pulls his comb out and fixes his mustache. "I'm going to borrow a desk, make some calls, take my notes, and do my paperwork. I'll have someone take you to the break room. I'll give you a lift home. Give me an hour. Okay? I'll try to hurry."

"That's fine. We missed the memorial you know."

"Too bad. I bet Meg will be disappointed."

"She'll be something," Charlie says, a rueful smile twisting his lip.

Ruther opens the door, puts a hand on Charlie's shoulder, leads him the right direction down the hall.

They pass Officer Davie-the-Welshman.

Ruther says, "We're probably kicking Parker loose. Can you make sure he gets home once the paperwork is done? I'll start the process."

Officer Davie nods his response.

Ruther keeps moving and Charlie keeps following. They exit the long institutional hall and enter an institutional room. Officer Harris is there.

"Officer. Can you show Mr. Messenger the break room? Get him settled, please?"

She nods crisply to Ruther. Then, to Charlie, she says, "It's down this way."

Charlie follows her through a long hall, down a few flights of steps, and into an untidy break room. The lights snap on as they enter.

"Okay, Mr. Messenger. You help yourself to coffee over there on the counter. Sorry about the mess. The snack machine and coffee machine are pretty good too. I don't have any more change, or I'd buy you something."

"Don't worry about it."

"Oh. There might be doughnuts in that box." She points next to the coffee maker.

"I'll be fine. I just need to sit. And thank you."

Officer Harris leaves him; the door pulls shut on its industrial, self-closing hinges.

Charlie wants to curl up on the floor and sleep, considers it for a moment. There's no pillow, no couch, no removable chair cushions. The low-pile carpet has been glued to a cement floor. Not comfortable enough for his old bones. His own couch would be perfect. He remembers Bootsy rudely waking him. He pinches his earlobe between his thumb and finger. It has a sore spot. He decides he won't get to sleep. *No rest for the wicked.* Besides, he better make a call, take his medicine, so to speak.

He brings his phone to life, dials up Meg. It goes to her recorded message. He imagines she's with Townes. Sitting in their old kitchen. Commiserating over the small turnout at the memorial. *Meg is angry and refusing to answer the phone.* He knows three of the intended participants never made it. He wonders if she invited others, some of Etta's old friends, the ones that Ruther might be calling right now to ask about the backpack. The phone beeps.

Meg. It's Charlie. They brought Newton in. They found Etta's backpack in his closet. He says they traded months before she disappeared. If that sounds right to you, call me. Ruther is checking with Etta's girlfriends. He wants to make some calls. So far his story checks out. I don't think he had anything to do with it.

He wants to say something else, doesn't have the right words. He ends the call, tucking his phone back in his coat. He removes his coat and throws it onto the nearest wobbly four-top table. His phone clunks against one of the corners; he feels foolish for pitching it.

At the coffee counter, he finds two glass pots, one under the drip basket, the other on a warmer. They are both nearly empty and look like they've been sitting for ages. He lifts the flap of the box of doughnuts and finds half of a glazed. Someone had bitten into it instead of breaking it. He leaves it. But the sight of the doughnut reminds him that he's hungry. He pats his front pockets, feels some change, pulls out a fistful and opens his palm flat to sort it. He only has forty-five cents, some of it in pennies. Not enough to get much from the vending machine. He rummages in the cabinet over the coffee maker and finds an old coffee tin with a note that reads: *Coffee Costs Money. Pay UP*. It's half full of change with a few singles crumpled on top. He takes what he needs.

*First things first. A little caffeine.*

At the coffee machine he jams coins into the slot, punches the buttons for large coffee, one cream. A cup falls into the holder with a hollow *thunk*. A pump comes on inside the big metal box; the cup is shot full of weak coffee, hot enough to scald flesh. When it's nearly full, another pump shoots three short blasts of pale cream into the coffee. He watches it swirl. He carefully pulls the thin cup until it springs loose. Coffee sloshes over the rim and burns the side of his fingers. He holds steady. He expected the burn. It's how these machines are made. Slowly, he tips the rolled, waxed rim to his lips and sips. *Horrible.* He thinks longingly of Jitters Café.

He pumps coins into the snack machine. He punches the letter-number combination for a honey bun. He usually avoids sweets like this, especially late at night, but the half doughnut was a disappointment; it got his mouth set for gooey baked goods. Charlie sips more coffee. The honey bun twists from its slot, drops heavily into the base of the machine. He reaches in. The flap grabs his wrist as he yanks the glistening hunk of dough out. It hurts. He expected it though. It's how these machines are made.

He takes a seat next to his coat, opens the confection. The thin wrapper sticks to the gummy sweet surface, comes apart in long strips that he has to pinch at with tweezer fingers before he can ram the food in his mouth.

He thinks of what Newton said about sex. He recalls he wasn't much different from Newton. He'd dropped his first serious girlfriend the moment he knew Meg had eyes for him. He wasn't trying to be cruel or mean to that other girl. His whole being had reacted to Meg in a way he'd never experienced. If there was a chance of being with her, no matter how slim, he'd had to take it.

Before Meg, Charlie had had a thing for blondes. He'd dated a string of them, starting his freshman year of high school and continuing until the moment he laid his eyes on the girl he would marry. For the most part, those other girls were interchangeable in his memory. The last one had braces that made her slobber when they made out. He can't remember any of their names. He imagines they are smart, interesting grown women now with families of their own. He should have been more aware of the people they really were, instead of taking them for granted.

He can still see Meg, hip cocked, long, tan legs coming out of cut-off jeans shorts. Just the same age Etta had been when she went missing. The image of that electric moment snatches his breath.

Charlie drops the piece of honey bun he's holding onto the remains of the wrapper. He looks for a napkin, doesn't see any. He licks his fingers. He takes his wallet from his back pocket. Like Newton, he carries an image of Etta with him. He takes it and feels the familiar hit of joy. He narrows his eyes as if he can squint tightly enough to see the past. He holds the image out as far as he can so his eyes can focus. Etta, tan, dark hair sun-streaked, and an appealing spray of freckles across her nose and cheeks. And that magnetic smile. A candid summer shot, after a long day tromping around the dunes. Maybe it isn't fair to keep thinking of her as that young girl. Maybe it isn't fair to either of them.

The lights in the break room snap off. Charlie sits in the dark, the picture still held out at arm's length, but he can't make it out at all. Not one detail. *Motion sensor.*

Charlie scoots his chair back and starts walking toward the door. The lights come back on. He returns the photo to its place for safekeeping. He finishes his sugary snack. He sips more coffee. It goes down easy.

The day the picture was taken, Charlie had suggested spending the day on the dunes as a family. They could hike for a couple of hours and spend the afternoon on the beach. Wrap the day up with a cookout on the deck of their vacation home. Townes had whined at the plan. He was tired. Wanted to go play putt-putt golf and sit somewhere in the AC and read his books. Charlie was openly disappointed, had said as much. He and Meg had divided their efforts, as they often did, in an attempt to make everyone happy. Charlie spent a nearly perfect day with Etta. Meg had shopped and sampled wine and let Townes have his space.

Charlie misses his family. He flips his coat over and finds the book Townes sent him. He drinks coffee, thumbs through the pages. After a time, he starts reading:

Everything has its own place and function. That applies to people, although many don't seem to realize it, stuck as they are in the wrong job, the wrong marriage, or the wrong house. When you know and respect your Inner Nature, you know where you belong. You also know where you don't belong.

The lights snap off again. Charlie sits in the dark with his thoughts. If the book passage is meant for him, then it is about how he had expected Meg to grieve for Etta in a way that was against her nature. How he had wanted Townes to be someone he wasn't.

Townes is a good boy. He's been through a lot. Because of Charlie's simplistic, single-minded drive to find Etta, Townes has grown into manhood without having Charlie around. Charlie wonders what he might have said to Townes at the memorial.

He speaks into the dark, empty room, "Thank you for the book, Townes. You're a smart kid. Smart and good-looking. Not so much a kid as a man. You might be the smartest person I know. You're much brighter than I am. But I know you've had a tough time and I worry about you. I care about you. I love you."

After more silence he adds, "Most of all, I'm sorry I've let you down. You deserved better. You deserve better. I've pressured you to be something you're not, but I'm done with that. I love you, just as you are."

*That was easy, with no one here.*

He needs to change some things, wants to be a father to Townes. Even find a way to partner with Meg in raising their son, if nothing else. He's let Etta's loss take everything, let some stranger take more than his daughter, take his whole life. *I failed. I failed to save Etta. I didn't keep her safe. What a stupid promise to make. I could have avoided most of the upheaval that followed Etta going missing. That really was my fault. My choice. It was selfish of me.*

He wants to cry, but his body doesn't work that way. He doesn't release feelings; he holds them.

He considers standing, waving his arms, throwing something at the light switch to activate the motion sensor. Instead, he leans over the tabletop, uses the book and his coat as a pillow, and rests his eyes. *Just for a moment*, he tells himself.

# INTO THE COLD

As Townes sits, scrunched down in the booth, the sky outside the diner becomes cloudy and overcast, the sun slowly sets, and snow begins to fall. Eventually, the elderly waitress returns with more hot water and Newton makes more tea with the used tea bag. He adds more honey; this time it melts fast. He's halfway through his mug of tea when Army Coat slides out of his booth and walks aggressively to the bathroom. Townes hears the force with which Army Coat opens the door, hears the door slam hard into the wall.

This is his chance to sneak out. He could leave cash on the table and be out the door and down the block in a minute's time. He could find a cab, catch the train, or even call Meg. The memorial should be over by now. But he doesn't know exactly where he is, couldn't give her directions. He thinks of those apps that allow parents to track their children in real time through a network of triangulated digital towers pinging off of cell phones. He wishes Charlie could look at his phone and find his location right that moment, could drive straight to him and take him home.

He stays rooted in place, thinking. It could be fear that holds him. He tells himself it's a conviction to see this thing through. *I'm the one who knows what this man is, what this man does. I'm the one who can protect people. Not because I'm special or capable. Far from it. But because I'm the only witness. It comes down to perspective. From the perspective of Esmeralda, I was in the right place, the right time . . .* He thinks these kinds of thoughts until Army Coat bangs out of the bathroom and goes outside.

Army Coat is leaving. Townes starts to scooch out of the booth, intending to ghost him. He tugs his cap, buttons his coat, pops his collar, and slings his bag over his shoulder. He's standing at the counter trying to pay when Army Coat walks back in, smelling like cigarettes. The scent is the same he smelled on his way in the door, but knowing it comes from Army Coat turns it sour in Townes's nose. The man with his reeking coat sidles up beside Townes and knocks him in the shoulder as he passes cash to the waitress.

The waitress finds the pair of golden reading glasses, worn on a beaded necklace like part of a geriatric Mardi Gras getup. She holds the cash up to the overhead light, looks skeptical. She turns the fifty-dollar bill over, then over again.

"Break that for me. Fast. I need change for the bus. Hurry it up. It'll be here in a second." She drops her skinny arm and looks at him, bending the bill in her hand. Townes can see Army Coat reflected in stereo in the individual lenses of the woman's cheap glasses: two rat faces, four eyes slick and dark as shards of night, and two open mouths full of sharp rodent teeth.

It's clear by the set of her puckered mouth that the waitress is considering telling him to go to hell. Something stops her tongue. Townes doesn't look at Army Coat directly, stares straight ahead. The old waitress makes change and dumps it into Army Coat's outstretched hand. He doesn't say thanks. He looks at the side of Townes's head, right at the place where he has a cut hidden under his cap.

Townes pretends to have the sniffles and reaches for a napkin from the dispenser on the counter. He snatches one and blows his nose, turning his face away. Army Coat leaves.

"Did you enjoy your hot water?" the old waitress asks him. She lets her glasses fall back on their beaded chain.

"Mmm. Yes. Very good. I made green tea."

"I saw." She takes his paper bill and his money. She impales his bill on a spike next to the cash register. The cash drawer pops open. She passes back a few dollars and a little change.

"Can you break these dollars?" he asks. "I might need it for the bus."

"Sure, sweetie," she says.

Townes takes the money. He leaves a five on the counter for the waitress. He goes to the door but doesn't exit. He sees the sign for the bus stop but can't see where Army Coat is standing.

The bus appears out of the dark, blocks his entire view of the street, and brakes loudly. Two people leave the back door of the bus. Army Coat appears from nowhere and mounts the front steps. Townes rushes to climb the back steps. He puts change in the slot and stands on the bottom stair where the other passengers can't see him. He stands until the doors close and the bus moves. He doesn't think Army Coat spotted him. He checks his breathing. *Too fast.* He counts and he breathes.

He steps up and sits in an empty seat, careful not to look around. He twists his messenger bag around to his lap. When he's maneuvering his bag, he glances toward the front of the bus. Army Coat is looking at him, too intently. Townes gives a slight nod. He looks back at his feet as casually as it's possible to look at one's own feet. Maybe Army Coat recognizes him from the diner, but not the train. Maybe he just looks out of place, riding this bus, in this neighborhood. There's a chance Army Coat doesn't remember him. *The struggle on the platform had been so brief.*

Most of the others on the bus are a mix of working-class blacks, Latinos, and a few older, pale faces. They wear layers of sturdy winter clothing, scarves, and caps. Among them are groups of school-age kids. Some carry backpacks like they're just leaving school or the library. Others bop their heads to the bass line thumping through their headphones. They pretend to ignore the world around them, but their bodies are too rigid; they are more on edge than the older passengers.

The bus stops and every person on the bus lurches in unison, brushing the person next to them. Townes's shoulder pushes into a lean woman on his right.

He says, "'Scuse me."

She says, "Don't you think twice on it."

Three older commuters stand slowly and step tiredly off the bus. Two young guys climb on at the front of the bus, talking as they enter, take seats next to Army Coat, block his view of Townes. A young kid, thirteen or fourteen, walks on by the back entrance among several older men in work coats. The kid wears pristine, buttery-yellow Timberland boots, laced loosely with the cuffs of his dark jeans tucked into them. He drops into the empty seat next to Townes, gives him a nod. He stretches his legs out in front of him. Proudly displaying his boots. The boys next to Army Coat stop talking. They turn their eyes on those boots. The kid next to Townes feels them staring. He doesn't move. His body becomes tense, wary, and hyperaware. If he had ear stalks, they would turn toward the other boys. Townes notes the working-age folks all keep their eyes down, try to mind their own business. Several school kids glance between the front of the bus and the back.

Townes recalls Stoddard's remarks about schools being shut down. He knows there are neighborhoods in Chicago where the blocks are divided among different gangs. He's heard kids are coerced to join a gang, just so they can walk back and forth to school. It's dangerous to cross into another territory. He wonders how many unmarked boundaries the bus is moving across as he rides.

The bus brakes for the next stop. Timberland stays put while a fiftyish black couple and a Hispanic woman with a bag of groceries leave through the back entrance. Three people, a Latino couple and a black man in a tailored wool trench coat, take their seats. The doors begin to close. Timberland scrambles out the back door before it can shut. The boys up front leap as the bus starts to move. They pound on the glass door. After half a block, they pull the cord and the bus stops. The driver is slow to open the doors. The boys rush out on the sidewalk, scan for Timberland, but he is long gone. The driver closes the doors and starts to drive as the pair of boys turn to remount the stairs. They kick the side of the bus. The bus driver's eyes are big as he uses the mirror to look back through the bus. Townes keeps his head down, tries not to gawk, to blend as much as possible. He does his best to act like it's just an everyday kind of occurrence. He guesses it may be in the lives of the other folks on the bus. The woman next to him clucks her tongue and shakes her head.

The bus makes two more stops. People get on. People get off. Townes bumps the woman next to him, and they repeat their previous exchange, verbatim. At the third stop Army Coat stands and steps out of the bus when the doors open.

Townes takes a lesson from what he's seen. He waits for the doors to close. He stands to see which way Army Coat is heading. He loses him immediately. He tugs the cord and the bus stops. The doors open and he steps onto the sidewalk. The sun is down, the wind is up, the temperature dropping, and the dark sky is spitting snow. Again he is grateful for the cap. He is grateful for Dory. He touches his cheek with his gloved hand where she kissed him. The bus pulls away. He tugs his collar up again, tucks his chin into his scarf.

Townes walks in the direction he just came from. It's a residential block, though it seems mostly abandoned. Few lights shine from the old houses, some have bars on the windows, some have bright spray-painted numbers or symbols on the front doors or on the sidewalks out front. Townes can't decipher if the spray-paint swirls are official marks to indicate a building to be torn down, sold, or that is too dangerous to inhabit. *What bureaucratic euphemism do they use? Blighted?* It could mean black mold is present, or walls are infested with vermin, or the basement packed with wild dogs, for all he knows. Or the Day-Glo symbols could be gang signs, boundary markers. Just as likely the marks are kids tagging for fun, though spray paint is illegal within the city limits. He doesn't suppose that would stop many people.

Townes stays to the long shadows. He has no notion where Army Coat is, which house he disappeared into, what street he turned down. Ahead, a streetlight flashes on with a buzz like a bug zapper, its cadmium sulfide photoresistor sensing the lack of light in the atmosphere. It casts a wide spotlight onto the dark corner, and Townes watches the flurries that herald the coming storm drift carelessly through the beam. The individual streetlamp is the only one that comes on. The way it shines on the desolate intersection looks like the set of an undiscovered Beckett play.

*What the hell am I going to do if I've lost him? How will I get home?*
Townes takes out his phone. Again the low battery message appears.
He realizes he's lighting his face in the shadow and turns the screen's
brightness low, steps closer to the trunk of a long-dead tree. He
remembers he never turned off his Wi-Fi. *Stupid.* He has nine percent
battery and very bad service. Only one dot out of five indicates his
level of satellite reception. His Wi-Fi shows moderately good reception
available. He allows a search; maybe he can hop onto someone's
residential service. The phone searches for the available networks and
finds only one: BabyCakes38. The battery drops to eight percent.

Townes taps on BabyCakes38 and he's on the network. He dials
up his ride-share app, assuming taxis wouldn't do much business in this
neighborhood. A car passes through the circle of cast streetlight ahead.
A few blocks away a police siren sounds one blast. The smartphone app
tells Townes that no ride-share cars are near him. He feels panic rising.
He's lost, alone, in a dangerous place, and the temperature is dropping.

He turns off his Wi-Fi to save the little bit of battery he has. He
stuffs the phone in his pocket. A dog growls nearby. It's answered
by another growl, low and dangerous. There is violent barking,
snarling, a yowl of pain, and silence. Townes starts walking. He
thinks about the homeless woman yelling at him for money for her
cell phone bill. It seems slightly less absurd now.

He approaches a building that looks like it might be an
abandoned garage or industrial business of some kind. It has neon
beer lights in two of the windows and a single exposed bulb over a
front door. When he gets closer he sees a sign that reads, *The Blue-
Eyed Devil.* Townes hears music coming from inside; it sounds like
R & B. Maybe the kind of thing his father would appreciate, would
know who the artist is and the name of the song, the year of the
album, the studio where it was recorded.

He moves through the dark toward the front of the place. Icy
snowflakes appear from the black night in front of him and hit him

directly in the face. The sound of the precipitation changes; it's turning to hard ice pellets and increasing. He squints down hard, but a few bits penetrate his lashes and sting his eyes. His foot catches on a ragged crack in the sidewalk, and he steps down hard on his sore ankle. He had forgotten about it. *It must be getting better.*

He peers through a diamond-shaped pane of glass in the front door. He sees Army Coat, plain as day, at the end of the bar. His is the only white face in the place. He jiggles his leg where it's cocked on the stool, like he's full of uncontrolled energy. His pants are covered in big pockets and are colored vaguely like a faded pair of World War II–era army fatigues. *Stupid.*

Townes, as a rule, tries not to be judgmental of others. The human condition being what it is and the stream of constant consumer suggestions blasted at Americans every waking moment make one's purchasing choices almost more a symptom of an affliction than a defining attribute of personal character. Drawing conclusions about people based on their clothing is a losing game. *A waste of time. And wrong-headed.* But in Army Coat's case, Townes makes an exception. He hates cargo pants. Refuses to wear them. Meg used to buy them for him, and he would return them. *Cargo pants are a marketing strategy for selling low-fashion military-chic to the masses. It's evidence of our country's continuing romance with war and violence, and they are worn by the weak-minded.*

As Townes stares, lost in thought, Army Coat pops a palm full of bar snacks into his foul face and takes a look around him, like he can feel Townes's eyes. Townes pulls away from the window. After a moment, he peeks in again. Army Coat is looking back at the bowl in front of him, pitching the parts of the salty snack he doesn't like onto the bar top, gathering another handful of the pieces he likes into one palm.

It's warm and close looking in there, but Townes knows he can't slip in unnoticed. He backs away. He searches the façade for a street number and doesn't see one.

He moves across the street, stands with his back to an alley, the snow starting to fall heavily now, a mix of big flakes and hard bits. Fat flakes settle on the circle of his arms as he holds the phone up to snap an image of the bar. He texts a quick note to the first person he can think of who might have an idea where the hell the place is. He sends the image of the bar too. Then he shuts his phone down and looks for a good place to settle.

He plans to give it an hour. No more. He'll check for a reply to his text. If nothing happens in that time he will start walking. To the east, the Loop casts lights against the undersides of the storm clouds. To the west, Townes knows, Charlie's house sits somewhere past Austin Park. Though which is closer, downtown where he can find a ride-share car, or Oak Park, where he has family? He thinks briefly of calling Dory, being invited to crash at her home. *Wishful thinking.*

Halfway down the alley, he opens a dumpster and finds a crushed box. He drags it out and sets it on a mostly dry spot along the alley wall, settles his ass on it, crosses his legs as if about to meditate, and puts the back of his coat against the cold, damp brick. *This*, he thinks, *is no way for a person to live.*

He considers the flow of his thoughts, now that he has let them run unchecked. He knows a few things. One is that he thinks of Army Coat as something *other*, not a member of the tribe. And in fairness, if the man is what Townes believes he is, then he's comfortable passing judgment. Army Coat is a sociopath willing to hunt children.

Townes also notes his brain is being strategic by defining Army Coat as *other*. He's preparing for a confrontation, preparing to be as brutal as is necessary, snapping off the switch that controls normal empathy. He recognizes, with a mild smirk at his own flawed humanity, the hypocrisy of judging Army Coat for his pathetic adoration of military culture while in the same moment preparing himself mentally for potential violence.

Townes knows there was a Western philosopher, he gets them all confused, who defined humans as rational animals. He also knows there's some writer, American, maybe Steinbeck or Faulkner, who said something like, all violence is due to man's failure as a thinking animal. Townes sees his own multiplicity toward the subject of violence. Man is the animal that feels one thing and thinks another. If there is any such thing as original sin, if there is a flaw that is built into humanity, it is the relationship between our emotional motivations and our capacity to rationalize our bad actions. Or, to turn it over in his mind, it's the capacity to use cold logic to rationalize the actions demanded by our hot blood. But he doesn't know. He's no philosopher.

All he can do is wait the hour he has set for himself and see what develops. He pulls his cap off, finds the ear flaps that Dory told him about, and pulls them out to flop over the sides of his head.

He takes advantage of the quiet, of the reasonably comfortable position, and begins to meditate. He needs to come back to his center. He breathes in deeply, filling his lungs with frigid air. He exhales slowly, obscuring his vision with a cloud of his own breath. He lets his eyes close and begins a slow inventory of the sensations and sounds within the reach of his body's senses. He notes the *tap tap* of the falling ice as it touches down on the dry paper surface of the cardboard. He continues on from there. Starting with his feet, his sore ankle, and moving on up his body, slowly, until he reaches the swollen lump above his temple.

When he's taken his incremental inventory, with as little commotion as possible, he finds his mala bracelet up the sleeve of his coat. He rotates the bracelet until his fingers find the knot. Then he begins the chant that is his evening mantra. He walks his fingers to the next bead and chants again.

# NIGHT RIDE

Ruther walks into the break room, already talking. The lights snap on, Charlie sits up, *The Tao of Pooh* sticks to the side of his face before dropping away.

"Sorry it took so long," Ruther is saying.

Charlie is frightened, disoriented in the unfamiliar place. His unfocused eyes frantically shift around to take in the surroundings: the vending machines, the institutional decor, the subterranean windowless room, and the electric hum of recessed overhead fluorescent tubes. He tries to push his glasses up his face, but they aren't there. Then it comes to him, where he is, why he's there.

"Were you sleeping?" Ruther asks.

"Just resting my eyes. What time is it?" Charlie vigorously scrubs his face with his hands. He smacks his lips, tastes the sour in his mouth.

"It's well past midnight. Let me give you a lift home."

Charlie nods. He stands and leans over to grab his ankles, lets his stiff back stretch out. He goes to the sink next to the coffee pot and cups water into his mouth. He swishes and spits. He rinses the sink. He moves his heavy legs, trying to make his knees pump. He slips his coat on, drops his book back in his pocket. He thinks briefly of Townes.

"I'm ready. Let's go." He's still groggy, but he keeps moving his boots and following Ruther upstairs and down long halls until they exit the building. The cold air is refreshing. By the time they get in the car, he's wide awake and his teeth are starting to chatter, his shoulders coated with a winter mix of snow and ice.

As the car moves out of the lot, the streets are pretty clear. The stoplights are bright red, the go lights are a vivid green. As they drive, the ice stops tapping off the car, the drifting snow slows and becomes peaceful, gentle, like a kiss before sleeping.

Ruther steers the car onto the interstate, passes through the tollbooth, and merges into the empty expressway without using his blinker. The Eisenhower is clear and salted. Charlie stares into the night. *It's been a long day.*

When Townes was little, he was a bad sleeper. He would get overtired, frustrated, and worn thin, unable to relax his little baby brain enough to drift into sleep. Meg would become exasperated trying to rock him, pat him, swing him, comfort him. He would close his eyes if he was in motion and then wake when Meg tried to lay him down. He'd scream and rage until he was red in the face, his throat sounding raw. None of the tricks that worked with baby Etta applied to baby Townes. Meg feared there were no tricks that worked on Townes.

Until Charlie discovered the solution. He'd buckle Townes into his car seat, belt him in the back of the car, and drive. Charlie would steer through the calm night; the darkness limited the visual stimuli; the gentle rumbling white noise of the hollow tires on the rough road soothed Townes's disturbed mind. Charlie would roll down the window and let the cool air circulate, running through his hair and easing his son. Charlie imagined it was like being back in the womb: the motion of the car, the sounds.

And Townes would sleep. Charlie would drive, sometimes long distances, out to the west where the suburbs suddenly gave way to farmland. Other times he'd make laps around the neighborhood, tracing random paths among his neighbors' homes. He'd catch snatches of activity as he passed the lit-up interiors of living rooms or bedrooms. Sometimes he'd see people jogging in the dark, teenagers kissing in cars, the bright eyes of wild animals looking at his headlights. It's a good memory. He had felt close to Townes in those quiet hours. He'd felt like a father to his son. *I miss that.*

Ruther lets the cruiser drift lazily across the empty lanes. Charlie almost says something, thinks Ruther has started to nod off, but when the car reaches the far left lane, it holds steady between the painted lines. Charlie turns his attention into the night, his eyes on the snow.

There was a time Charlie would have felt less comfortable sitting in a police car. His first time driving alone was in a stolen car. He was fourteen. One night, walking home from a pal's house, he'd found a car idling outside a walk-up medical clinic in a strip mall. The car lights were left on, doors standing wide. When he slid into the car, he initially intended to pull it into a spot, snap off the headlights and engine, leave the keys in the ignition.

Instead, he drove, took a spin around the block, then around town, used a drive-through to order a chili dog and a Mr. Pibb, waved out the open window at buddies riding their bikes. His friends' mouths gaped; he let loose with a loud hoot, a cackle, and a jubilant *honk honk* of the horn. He loved the freedom of being behind the wheel, the liberty to go where he wanted, when he wanted.

He braked too hard at every stop. He turned too wide at every corner. He flipped on the windshield wipers when he wanted to use the turn signal. Every car he passed, he assumed was a cop. He knew arrest was imminent, but no one pulled him over. After twenty minutes, the stress got to him; he returned the car to the clinic. When he got home, his dad tossed him around a bit. "You had your mother worried sick." He didn't confess to the joyride. He'd been late getting home and was grounded for two weeks, but it had been worth it.

Ruther banks up the off ramp, waits a moment for the red light to change at the empty intersection, but he's impatient and he's a cop so he flashes his lights and pulls across the road against the light. The snow is picking up, the flakes getting fat. Charlie knows that usually means the tail end of the storm is passing over.

Sometimes, Charlie imagines Etta had done something similar on the day she went missing: found an empty car on the curb, running, puffing hot exhaust into the winter afternoon. She decided she was sick of the cold, sick of high school bullshit and overbearing parents and her pesky little brother. She was sick of constant pressure for more and different sex from her boyfriend. She saw her chance, slipped behind the wheel, and drove away. He always pictures her driving south. Somewhere warm. Maybe Mexico. She'd study Spanish and teach at a language institute near the gulf. Or perhaps she passed straight through Mexico and stopped in Belize, took a job at a resort, made a life for herself living on large tips from rich American tourists.

Ruther puts the car in park in the middle of the narrow street. Charlie looks out and sees his home. They don't speak or move. They sit in the idling car for a long time, two men beaten up by the effort of living their lives day after day, decade after decade.

Charlie slips his hand around the door handle; he yanks it and the door comes open. He sets one boot on the snow-covered street. The cold air rushes in as the warm air moves out.

"Thanks for the lift," he says. "Be careful getting home."

"No problem, no problem. Hey, Charlie," Ruther says in a way that grabs Charlie's attention. Charlie looks back at Ruther, his face lit by idiot lights in the dash, his mustache rumpled and bent like the bristles of an old paintbrush. "I'm sorry," Ruther says. "I let you down today. I let you down again. This shit is hard on you. For me, it's hard, but it's a job. Don't get me wrong. I care. I care about you and Etta. Meg and Townes too. It's more than just a case, but I can compartmentalize. You though, for you it's different. I know that. I can't even imagine."

"I appreciate what you do, Ruther. You know that. I think of you as a friend. Really the only friend I talk to. My few old pals bailed out when things got hard. They didn't know what to say, how to help. It's okay though. I get it. I just gotta get to sleep. I'm wrung out."

"Yeah, I know," Ruther says. Then, as if he just remembered something, "Hey. I talked to two of Etta's old classmates. They confirmed Etta wasn't using her own backpack. That she and Newton had swapped. It was like he said, a kind of commitment thing."

"That's what I figured. It's good. It's good to know."

Charlie walks to his front door. Ruther drives away without waiting to see that Charlie makes it in. Charlie finds his keys, opens the door, and has to block Bootsy from running out to roll in the snow.

"Not now, Bootsy. You can go out in the morning." Bootsy is understanding.

Charlie dumps his stuff and ends up on the couch, Bootsy purring in his lap. He doesn't want to go up to his big bed. Doesn't like the feel of sleeping on the wide mattress without another body to share it with, without Meg. He leans over and unlaces his boots, kicks them off where he sits. He reaches to remove his glasses, once again finds he's not wearing them. *No wonder my head hurts.* He flops over and stretches out on the couch, bunches a throw pillow under his head. He closes his eyes, but his head won't stop.

Charlie is tortured by a sad realization: He can't remember his last real conversation with Etta. The only thing he remembers is they spoke the night before she went missing, in passing, about getting her car stuck at school. They hadn't said *I love you* or hugged. They hadn't held hands. He'd given her winter driving advice. Nothing personal or affectionate. The kind of exchange two strangers might have.

"Remember to be sure to accelerate and decelerate slowly when the roads are slick. Look in the direction you are turning, you know. And it's smart to keep the tank full of gas so the fuel lines won't get ice in them. We've talked about this before."

"Dad, I just got stuck. It was no big deal." Etta was annoyed with his advice and not capable of masking it.

"You can never be too careful. Park farther away if you have to. Just make sure you find a clear spot. Do you have salt in your trunk still?"

"It is right where you put it."

"And that little snow shovel?"

"Yes."

"Good then." He had walked away, not wanting to get too entangled by her growing frustration. They hadn't said goodbye.

Meg's memorial made sense to him. He wants closure, a substitute for never having said the right things. He never said, "I'm so proud of you, baby, proud of the person you've grown into. If I knew you back when I was your age, we would have been good friends. Being a dad is rough sometimes. Your kids outgrow your ability to parent at every turn. But even without much help from me, you turned out good. And I love you."

But Charlie had always been too protective, too worried about what could go wrong to celebrate the minor triumphs that made up Etta's young life. *Sure, she got a star on her fourth grade poetry book, but how the hell are we going to pay for the ballet shoes she needs? Yeah, it's good that she made the honor roll again, but there's a crack in the foundation that gets worse each year.*

Bootsy nuzzles her head into the crook of Charlie's arm, assumes her preferred sleeping position. As the calico falls asleep, Charlie knows he won't sleep more. *I shouldn't have napped, shouldn't have filled up on crappy coffee. I should have enjoyed Etta while I had her.* Those are his last thoughts before he begins to snore.

# HEROICS ARE FOR THE HEROES

Townes finishes his mantra and slowly allows his mind to come back to the moment, attends to his breathing. His eyes crack open and slowly adjust to the sparse light. The first thing he notices is a layer of light snow settled over his folded legs and resting in the gathers of his lap. His lower back is stiff from walking and from sitting in the cold on a hard surface for so long. He needs to move soon, maybe attempt a few yoga stretches.

Townes nearly forgot where he was as he meditated. During his agitated search for Army Coat, he had ignored many of the details around him. Now, his usual focus has returned.

The dark clouds have broken overhead; the snow stopped. The scene comes into focus. It's like the end of the world. Red shotgun shells, faded pink by last summer's sun, visible only inches away from where he sits, tucked next to the base of the brick wall. There are several flat piles, spread out in a loose semicircle around him, that may be the carcasses of small, crushed critters. Tufts of bristled fur stick out of the snow over each pile at irregular angles. There are, of course, busted beer bottles. Beyond the shotgun shells, a page from a porno magazine flutters its loose edge in the bitter breeze, a coy wave. Townes can see the image is of a girl wearing an Ivy League logo hoodie on her top half and nothing on her bottom half. She's curled on a bed, what looks like the bottom half of a dormitory bunk. The wind bends the image over into the snow where it slowly soaks up moisture. Next to the model, on the alley floor, a crushed can of Red Bull, some empty Takis bags, and the smoked-down nub of a Swisher Sweets cigar. Most everything is damp or frozen; most everything has snow on it.

He unfolds his legs, stretches them in front of him, smearing the snow from the surface of the cardboard box he rests on. He jangles his feet on his ankles. The hurt ankle feels bruised but not swollen.

The alley reminds Townes of images he's seen of abandoned neighborhoods in Detroit or Midwest towns after a tornado had hopscotched through and leveled every other building. He recalls the aftermath of the debacle that was Hurricane Katrina; a blanket of river silt had spread over the neighborhoods, mold slowly growing up the walls of every structure. This alley was not exactly like that, but a little, maybe, if the polluted snow were replaced with soft, organic loam. There was another place: that fake, lifeless town out West where they used to set off atomic bombs. Every structure abandoned or destroyed. No life left, no human activity.

As if to prove him wrong and draw attention to his exaggerations, a car drives down the street and past the mouth of the alley, mashing dirty tracks into the fresh snow. Three men exit the front of the Blue-Eyed Devil. They share a story, their laughter trailing off as they move out of sight.

When Townes turns his face back, he freezes mid-motion. He sees something there, deeper down the alley, on the edges of the cast light from the bar. It's a creature, low to the ground, flashes of reflected light from two red eyes. Townes draws his knees up toward his body, pulling his feet in close, his recent moment of clarity replaced by fear of attack.

The creature doesn't move or make a sound. It's injured, a matted coat of gray fur torn away in places to reveal the pink hue of raw musculature. It could be a large rat, an alley cat, even a tiny stray dog. It's hard to tell from this distance, in this light. It could be a city opossum, with a mean, pointed face and bald fleshy tail. Opossums have always given him the creeps. It's the kind of thing Townes used to dream about during the worst of his nightmares, a malevolent presence, just on the edge of comprehension, bent on inflicting undefined harm.

Townes reaches for the shotgun shell he knows is beside him, not moving his eyes from the deformed varmint. He takes the empty shell, lighter than he expected, and casts it at the creature. It strikes where he aimed, in the side of the thing's head, but the act elicits no reaction. The abomination stays put, coiled to strike, waiting for something. Completely focused on Townes.

Townes slowly stands; he stabs his eyes this way and that for any kind of weapon, anything to defend himself. He pats his pockets, spots a length of rusted rebar sticking out of the edge of his mashed box. He holds it threateningly, swishes it through the air a few times to demonstrate his prowess.

"Get going," he says. No reaction.

"Get!" he says louder. Still nothing.

From this fresh angle, the thing still doesn't look like a specific animal. It's a mutant, a hybrid from a soup of radiation poured into the sewers under the city.

He staggers on his stiff legs, his feet slip on the skim of crusty snow, but he keeps his feet. He moves closer. After just a few steps he sees his mistake. His eyes take in the details, but his brain is slow to give up on his original assessment. What he thought was a rabid beast silently stalking him is, in fact, a twist of wet newspaper. A fat Sunday edition of the *Chicago Tribune*, judging by its mass. It has been abandoned in the alley; the red plastic sleeve pulled over its girth like a thin condom on a deformed penis, meant to keep it dry during delivery, has ripped and pulled away in places. The plastic gives some sections the look of shiny, raw, red flesh, and the holes have the look of matted gray fur. He pokes it with the rebar to make certain.

He's relieved.

And he's done with this whole stupid escapade. He's out of sorts. He wants his bed, his stack of books, his meditation clock. Sleep is a vital part of his practice. He needs to sleep. He waited his hour. Or longer. Army Coat never appeared. It's time to get someplace warm, dry, and out of this alley as soon as possible.

He drops his length of rebar and snatches up his messenger bag. "My detour into fanciful adventure," he says to himself. "My diversion into daring action, my erroneous attempt to perform a penitent gesture has come to an inauspicious end."

He steps out of the alley and looks both directions before crossing the street. He walks into the eerie neon glow from the bar's nearest window, as if taking the stage in this existential play for the final act.

There are many tracks in the snow leading in and out of the Blue-Eyed Devil. He wonders if he nodded off as he meditated. It hasn't happened for a while, but it was common enough when he first began his regular practice, and it has been a long, stressful day.

He takes a gander through the window in the door. The room is less crowded, mostly older men lining the short bar top. Army Coat is gone. His barstool sits empty.

Townes takes the cap from his head and tucks the ears back into the lining. He feels the heat shooting out the top of his head. He smacks the warm cap back on. He shifts his weight from side to side, glancing up and down the block. He sees no other likely place to warm up. *I will go in. I will order something warm. I'm out of tea bags. Coffee. They will have coffee. A little coffee won't kill me. I'll figure out where I am, decide which way to start walking.*

As he takes the knob in his hand, he thinks, *I am still nothing but a fraud.* He dwells on the notion and is defeated by it. He can't follow Army Coat if he doesn't know where he went. He can't be held responsible for whatever harm the man causes the next vulnerable child he runs across. He's done his part. He's done his best. *I'm a fraud of the worst sort*, he thinks, but he accepts it and enters the bar.

He walks to the only empty place along the counter, the stool left by Army Coat's departure. The music is loud. The heat in the space is thick with smells of body odor and booze, some kind of deep, moldy smell underneath. The bartender, a white guy Townes hadn't seen when he peered in earlier, with choppy silver hair and bright blue eyes, steps in front of Townes and waits for an order.

"You have coffee?"

The guy doesn't answer. He twists and grabs a mug from under the back bar, reaches below the counter, and as if a master illusionist, manifests a steaming cup of coffee. He sets it on the bar amid the peanut shells and unwanted cracker bits Army Coat discarded earlier. The blue-eyed bartender doesn't offer cream or sugar. He just sizes Townes up and says, "Five dollars." He says it like he's daring the suburban boy to quibble with his price.

Townes doesn't quibble. He pays and takes his coffee to the farthest corner table next to the jukebox. All the fight is gone out of him. He just needs to sit a minute. Marvin Gaye's "Sexual Healing" begins to play. Townes knows this as part of the soundtrack of his youth, as dictated by Charlie. The song is a familiar detail in an unfamiliar place and Townes is comforted by it. He likes it.

He sips the coffee. It's bitter and old. It tastes worse than he remembers coffee is supposed to taste. He recalls the flask and taps his breast pocket where it's stowed. He surreptitiously pours the rest of the flask into his coffee. What did Stoddard call it? *Irish coffee.* There are no spoons, so he stirs the coffee with his finger and shakes it off over the floor. He sips some more. The taste is not improved, but it does warm him.

He drinks half the mug as quickly as he can get it in him and then starts humming along to the music, quietly singing the words to the chorus. He smiles a little. Feeling good. Glad the ordeal is over. Feeling foolish but pleased to have survived his ridiculous lark. A little slaphappy, a little soulful and groovy.

He fiddles around in his coat pocket and finds his phone; he turns it on and the screen shines dimly in his face. He swipes to his control screen and turns the brightness back up. He finds his folder listed as navigation. He taps his maps app. He allows the phone to search for his current location.

Something living, some creature, solid and aggressive, hits him hard from behind; his diaphragm punches into the table's edge. His mug tips and dumps coffee across the table, running onto the dirty floor. He drops his phone and sucks in air. The side of his face is mashed into the table, and something sharp and cold enters his upturned right ear. There is a bright point of pain, an audible pop as the tight skin of the wall of his ear is penetrated, and a hot trickle of fluid as his ear canal begins to fill with his own blood. *The creature from the alley got me*, he thinks. *The nightmare creature from my dreams.*

The ambient sounds of the room, the last chords of Marvin Gaye, are deadened as his ear fills to overflowing. Every noise seems to come from far away, as if heard from down a long hall. His eyes go wild. He tries to twist and thrashes, not thinking of consequences, just reacting, but he's held tight. His face scrubs around on the table, his cheek smeared with lukewarm coffee. His cap. The cap that Dory gave him flips off his head and absorbs all the coffee its fabric will hold. Hot breath pants on his neck, a body bending over him, a mouth near his shoulder. The mouth makes wet sounds as it moves into a grin and seeps reeking nicotine over his face. It says, "Hey, hero. Didn't I tell you we'd settle up one day? 'Member how I told you I'd take it out of your hide?"

Townes goes still. Army Coat has him. He feels the tip of the knife twist a little deeper into his ear, feels the blood flow increase. Then the knife is drawn back. The blade is held where he can get a close look at it. It is long, and strong, and whetted keenly as a scalpel. Townes mewls loudly. The knife draws back, a silver arc moving through the dark space. He sees it coming for the side of his skull. The blow cracks like thunder and sends a flash of light across his brain, like being swept by the blinding high beams of a big rig.

"You make a racket like that again, I'll crack your fucking skull. Now stand up."

Townes is yanked to his feet. A stream of blood runs down his neck and into the collar of his coat. His legs are loose under him, like walking across the center of a trampoline. Army Coat helps support his weight. As they pass near the bar on the way out the door, he calls to the bartender, "My nephew isn't feeling well."

The bartender grunts back.

Townes tries to work his cotton mouth into a desperate cry for help; the words don't form; the sound won't come. And they are outside, Townes and the man he came to find, walking crookedly down the center of the unlit street, like two drinking buddies at the end of a long night.

# A BRAND-NEW DAY

There's a white burst as bright as midday when Newton's eyes crack open. Overnight snowfall has coated the world outside his apartment in bright white flocking, making the reflected light streaming around his half-drawn curtains intense and unforgiving. He has slept long and hard and wakes refreshed. The emotional stress of the past several days must have worn him thin.

As he sits and absently rubs the raised scar that forms a slight curved lip around the front edge of his amputation, like the interlocking seams of a baseball, he feels calm. Better than he's felt in a while. Definitely better than he's felt since he received the invitation for the memorial he missed. Perhaps the missed event is the source of the quiet, contented feeling. He regrets the lost opportunity. *But I'm not angry about it. Not mad at Officer Wendy and Man Cop. Not even upset with that pube-faced Ruther. A little sad, but all in all, it was likely for the best to have skipped it.*

He slips off the bed and hops over to his clothes, still piled on the floor where he had stripped them off. He finds the correct pocket and takes out his phone. It's still dead. He plugs it in, rubs his hair around on his head, works the sleep from his eyes.

Things Cranky Thomas said the previous morning have stuck with him. The idea that Albert and Etta both saw something good in him, and that they would want good things for him, even if they couldn't be a part of it. It has the ring of truth. And coming from that ancient, inked-up, crotchety old shitter, it has the weight of life experience behind it, too. He respects his two missing friends. He thinks of each of them as smart, exceptional people in their own unique ways. He loved them. Maybe, if they cared for him, and he believes they did, then he should trust they knew what they were doing. It's a powerful emotional tonic, and he lets it soak in.

Newton thinks about how few people escape to the end of their days without some devastation. Most people suffer deep loss and personal pain. Most people mourn and heal and grow from the experience. They go on, fold those events into their sense of self, allow those events to shape them. When the process is over, they retain their core, their true self. He wants that too, to incorporate his anger and loss, let them be an aid to him instead of something he fights against, or more accurately, ignores until it bursts out.

It reminds him of learning to walk with his new leg. At first, he had hated it. Didn't want anything to do with it. Fought against the idea of anything replacing the leg he'd lost. He was loyal that way. He still cared for his old leg; how could he replace it with a new one so lightly? Why didn't the doctors, physical therapists, or other vets see that it was deceitful to take another leg? But he'd come around. He watched the other soldiers adapting to their replacement limbs. He started thinking of the new leg as a tool. Then, eventually, as an extension of himself: his leg. The affection for his GI leg didn't make him unfaithful to his missing leg.

He shakes his head. He's got to attend to some business if he hopes to keep a roof over his head, so he gets in the bathroom and starts getting ready. He peels the bandage from his calf and checks it out. It's a little slimy and pink, but not too saturated with blood. He takes that as a good sign. He should make a note on his phone to buy some ointment. He tries to see the tattoo, bending his neck back and cocking his leg out. It helps to lean a hand on the wall, but he can't get a good enough angle on it. He can't imagine how to make the mirror from the medicine cabinet useful either, short of ripping the door completely off. Destroying apartment property is the opposite of the impression he hopes to make on Mr. Heller this morning.

When he's clean, shaven, and dressed, he takes out his hiking shoes, ties one onto his prosthetic foot and the other onto his birth foot. He gets his leg on, considers taking his phone with him, but decides to let it charge.

In the kitchen, he puts an egg on to boil, does his pushups and drinks two glasses of cold water. He does jumping jacks until his shoe starts to twist around sideways on his prosthetic. He shifts it back into place, ties it down tighter, and peels his egg under cold water from the faucet. He mashes the egg down with the back of a fork, salt, pepper, butter, and down the hatch.

He has real direction, a goal, shit to take care of. It's a good feeling. Not for the first time, he realizes the real antidote to his recent emotional funk is probably getting a job, something to keep him busy. Some cash in his pocket would be good too. A career with a future would be ideal, but just a place to go with a paycheck would suffice. He puts on his coat and buttons it tightly. He unplugs his iPod dock and makes certain he has his keys. Then he walks into the bright morning and around to the management office, the snow making a dry crunch as it packs beneath his rolling gait.

After three knocks, Arthur Heller opens the office door with a steaming mug in his hand. He looks immediately worried.

"Don't be worried," says Newton. "I came to talk, please. To apologize. May I come in?" After a moment's hesitation, Mr. Heller backs into the office and opens the door wide for Newton.

"Take a seat then," he says, indicating one of the chairs in front of his cluttered desk. "Would you like some tea? The kettle is hot."

"Sure. Yes. Thank you," Newton says. He doesn't drink tea, but it is cold out, and it seems like the civil thing to do. He sits in one chair and sets the iPod dock in the other. He waits while Mr. Heller warms a mug for him, packs some loose tea leaves into a silver ball, and drops it into the mug with a clink, before pouring steaming water onto it. "Would you like some honey?"

*Some what? And don't call me honey* is Newton's first thought. Instead, he says, "No, thank you."

Mr. Heller sets the mug within reach of Newton on a clear spot at the edge of the desk. "Let it steep," he says. Then he steps his large body through the small space around the desk, until he settles into the high-backed leather chair.

"Well. You wanted to talk. Please, proceed."

"Mr. Heller. I'm sorry for causing you trouble and stress. I like it here. I know my loud music has been a problem lately. I wish you'd give me another chance, before evicting me. As a show of faith, I brought you this iPod dock, for safekeeping, until you feel you can trust me to have it." He watches the big man's kind face, sees he's moved by the gesture.

"I accept your apology. I do."

Newton draws breath to respond, and Mr. Heller goes on quickly to finish his thought, flashing one big, pink palm to stop Newton from speaking. "But I'm not the one you have to convince."

"I see," Newton says. "Mr. Beige?"

"Mr. Gray," Mr. Heller corrects him, a little sternly.

"Right. Sorry. Honest mistake. I knew it was a color name. I couldn't remember. Honestly," he lies with his most sincere voice.

"It's all right," Mr. Heller says.

"So, do you think you could walk me over to Mr. Gray's place and let me apologize to him? I'd like the chance to apologize."

Mr. Heller points at Newton's mug of tea. The mug has a photo of a frowning cat curving around its side. "Your tea is about ready."

"Is this your cat?" Newton asks. "Very distinctive," he adds diplomatically.

"No. That is Grumpy Cat. Don't you know Grumpy Cat? I love Grumpy Cat."

Newton takes a sip of tea. It burns his lip and tastes mostly like very hot water, but bitter. "Mmmm. Good." Then he adds, "I am not familiar with Grumpy Cat."

Mr. Heller makes a *tsk tsk*, as if to say, *You don't know what you are missing, but there is no point trying to explain the complex joy of*

*Grumpy Cat.* He sips his tea and lets the time pass. Newton follows his example. After what feels like many long minutes, Mr. Heller sets his mug down and says, "Let me give Mr. Gray a call."

Five minutes later, they are at an apartment identical to Newton's but a floor away with a different number. They knock, Mr. Gray opens the door immediately, keeping a bit of his body shielded and his hand on the knob, prepared to slam it shut.

"Yes?" He's wearing the same cardigan as the day before, the same house shoes, but different-colored slacks. There is the sound of a soft jazz saxophone quietly filling the space behind him. He waits, directing a sour-lemon face in Newton's general direction, while careful not to look him directly in the eyes.

"Mr. Gray. I'm sorry about the loud music. I'm sorry that I've been rude and disrespectful. I realize this is your home and you should feel safe and secure here. I know, I know. I have been horrible. My only explanation is I suffered a lot of loss in recent years, and I've been having trouble coping. I came to apologize and ask for a favor. I've been seeing a counselor and will continue to seek help. Will you, please, agree to give me another chance? We can take it a day at a time. A week at a time. At a word from you, Mr. Heller can serve my eviction notice and I'll leave with no argument."

"You punched me. What about striking me? Should I just forget that?"

"I'm especially sorry for that. Sorry."

"You suggested Mr. Heller and I were," Mr. Gray's eyes look up as he searches his internal thesaurus for the best word. "Involved."

Mr. Heller shifts around uncomfortably behind Newton.

"Yes. I did. I was trying to upset you. Distract you. Perhaps get you angry. It was foolish and rude. And childish."

"I'm not gay. Not that it would be a bad thing. I am attracted to women."

"No. Of course. Clearly. As I said, I'm sorry for what I said and did and leave it in your hands."

Mr. Gray takes this all in. He allows the door to open a little wider, lets his hand fall away from the knob. He stands within the opening to his apartment, his posture slowly improving as he considers, his shoulders pull back a bit as he realizes the power he's been given. He looks less damp, looks proud, smug. His cardigan sleeves don't seem quite so long. "So, you're willing to put your fate in my hands?"

"Yes. I'm sure you'll be fair. Also, I gave my stereo to Mr. Heller for safekeeping, until the two of you decide I can have it back."

Mr. Gray gets a nod from Mr. Heller. Then in the most presentational and magnanimous gesture Newton has ever witnessed, Mr. Gray inclines his head, bows a bit at the waist, and makes a sweeping gesture with his arm while snapping his fuzzy heels together. "You may stay in your apartment," he says. The saxophone behind Mr. Gray bleats like a startled sheep, then goes quiet.

Newton wonders if the little freaking weirdo is intentionally making it difficult for him, to see how much insipid behavior he will endure before breaking. "Thanks," he says. "Thanks so much." Then he pivots on his real heel and walks away before he blurts something insulting.

Mr. Heller claps his beefy hands together once, as if to seal the deal, and plods along on his thick legs behind Newton. After a few blessed moments of nothing but the sound of crunching snow and the *swish swish* of Mr. Heller's arms against his puffy vest, Heller calls, "Well, that went well."

"Yup. I agree. Very good."

"Would you like to come in and finish your tea?" Mr. Heller says.

Newton doesn't want the tea, but he goes in anyway and chugs the tasteless mess. "Refreshing," he says. He aims the empty mug at different surfaces around the room, not sure where to leave it.

"Oh, just leave it on the desk," Mr. Heller says.

Newton makes a clear spot on the edge of the desk, unable to locate the previous clear spot, sets down the cup, and says, "Thanks, gotta run," and he leaves.

He gets in the cold cab of his truck, now covered in snow, and pumps the accelerator a few times with his army leg, cranks the cold engine, and pumps the gas some more. The strange little truck was his father's old beater, used to haul yard waste and other crap: a 1965 Ford Econoline with the engine between the seats and three on the tree. A van up front with truck in the back. No power steering or brakes and tires nearly bald.

Newton's mother had demanded it during the divorce, just for spite. And it had sat behind the garage, slowly rotting, for years. When Newton came back after the war, he needed a vehicle, had no funds. He got it running. Learned to drive it.

It kicks over and starts to warm up. The wipers clear most of the snow from the windshield. He doesn't bother brushing off the rest. He rolls down the side windows, one at a time. The back window is covered in snow, but it will blow off. He uses his side mirrors as he backs out and coasts around to his assigned spot. He says, "Shit, it is so hard to be a nice person. I don't know how people do it."

"It doesn't cost you nothing to be nice," Albert says, big smile on his face.

Newton isn't convinced. Albert laughs at his stubborn streak.

Newton lets the truck idle and runs upstairs to grab his phone. It's half-charged. He taps his contacts and taps on Etta's old number. Like he was afraid would happen, the phone kicks him to the same machine as last time. He steels himself. He hears Meg again, doing her best Etta impression, a little deeper, much sadder, close enough to shock him, even though he was prepared. Her recorded voice says: "Hello. This is Meg. If you are calling about house cleaning, please call my work number." She gives the number twice, very slowly. Very sadly. "Otherwise, if it's about anything else, just leave a message. I'll get back as soon as I can." Then her machine goes, *BEEEEEP.*

"This is Newton again." He tries not to sound as flustered as he feels at hearing that voice, at thinking of Etta. "I wanted to call about last night. I'm really sorry I missed the thing. I wasn't sure you would get my last message in time. So, I wanted to explain. I'm thinking about swinging by to apologize in person. If that's okay? See you soon." He taps his phone screen closed.

He feels like there's something else. Some other thing he needs to do with the phone, but he can't remember. The buzzing stress is starting to bounce around his head again. The peaceful groove he had when he woke is quickly fading. He tucks his phone in his coat and marches out the door; he lets it slam too loud as he leaves.

# IMPRISONED

The first thing Townes sees as he comes to is the pointed profile of Army Coat sitting at the foot of the mattress. He's cleaning under his long nails with the blade of his oversized knife and wetly sucking his nasty teeth. He looks old to Townes, maybe the same age as Charlie, but malnourished and uncivilized. Townes wishes for Charlie to appear, to save him. But he knows he's on his own.

Townes tries not to move, tries to keep his eyes closed. He takes a personal assessment. He's on a bare mattress. The top of his head is against a cold metal headboard. His head throbs. The sharp point of a migraine bores into the soft tissue of his brain. There's substantial swelling on the side of his scalp, so severe his skin could split open like a busted zipper. *At least it might relieve some pressure.* The new injury is opposite the one from the train platform. *A matching set.*

The last thing he recalls is being led along a weaving course of alleys in the middle of the night. Army Coat stopped to piss on a fence. Townes tried to run. He only made it a few strides before being flattened from behind, and his vision went black.

Through the slits of his eyes and the tangle of lashes, he sees a small, dirty room. The room is gloomy, one primary light source, an incandescent bulb screwed into a porcelain fixture in the center of the popcorn ceiling. There is a window, too, at the far end. It gives a faint glow. Perhaps it's daytime. Townes risks rolling his head slightly for a better look. Army Coat smacks his lips loudly. Townes flinches and shuts his eyes tight.

There is background noise: a wooden spoon knocking on the bottom of a pan. Townes thinks how remarkable the human mind is; for all of its constant, useless churning, it stores a lot of information. What a distinctive sound that particular combination of objects and actions creates. He's read that the human mind can decipher the difference between the sounds of skim milk or wine being poured into identical glasses from fifty feet away.

Louder than the sounds of someone cooking is a TV blasting a show for kids. He hears an over-enunciated voice screaming from the speakers, *Swiper No Swiping. Swiper No Swiping. Swiper No Swiping.* He also hears children's voices, repeating the phrase in unison with the TV. He knows the show, something with a little Latina girl and her talking purple backpack. Programming intended to teach idiot Americans about the growing necessity to learn another language, a program to teach Spanish speakers to scream basic words in high-pitched English. He's comforted by the notion kids are in this place with him, watching cartoons. How bad a situation could he possibly be in, if children are watching Nick Jr. down the hall?

As if to underscore exactly how incomplete his reasoning may be, Army Coat's weight shifts on the bed. Townes feels eyes on him. He holds his breath.

"Hey there, sleepyhead," Army Coat says in an uncomfortably intimate tone, quiet and gentle as a lover. "Sorry if the rug rats woke you. They do love their shows in the morning."

Townes lets his eyes come open.

Army Coat turns his face slowly to stare. "Remember me?"

*He must have noticed a change in my breathing.* Townes doesn't intend to be obstinate. His first instinct isn't to struggle or fight. He just wants to, in his slow, introverted way, gather information to understand the situation he's found himself in. He doesn't respond to the question he was posed. This sets the other man off.

Army Coat lunges at Townes, grabs him one-handed by the throat. His grip is a vice cranked tight. He squeezes until Townes's air is cut off, until he chokes, until his windpipe loses its rigid, round shape. His tongue starts to poke out; his eyes bulge from his head. The pressure builds to bursting; the epicenter of pain is the swollen knot on the side of his head. A hand strikes him hard across the hollow of his cheek, sending a spray of stars across his vision. But at least he can breathe so he sucks down huge gulps of air.

Townes coughs and opens and closes his jaw a few times, like a fish tossed in the tall weeds of a riverbank. He can feel the caked blood from the puncture in his ear crack and pull in the hairs of one sideburn, can hear the scab crackle in his ear canal. Army Coat takes the hand off his throat. Townes remembers the knife. He's thankful the man dropped it on the bed rather than used it to stab him, or just as bad, pummel his skull again. He doesn't think his head will survive another hard knock.

"I asked you a question. You think you are too good to answer my questions? You look down on me? You think you are in charge here?"

"No. No. I think you are in charge." His voice is ragged and he coughs with the effort of speaking.

"Good. Because I'm in charge. I'm the one. Me." He thumps his chest. "Now answer me."

"Don't slap me again. Please. But I forget the question." He coughs some more and adds, "Could I have a drink of water?" He pulls his forearms up to fend off an attack that doesn't come.

"I wouldn't piss down your throat if your guts were on fire. But I'll tell you what I'll do. I'm going to stab you. You believe I'll stab you? You believe I will let you bleed out right here? This fat old mattress will soak up every last drop of juice in that scrawny body of yours. It will fill up like a tick and I'll drag it out back and light it on fire. I'll let the kids roast hot dogs over it. You believe that?"

"I do. I believe that." Townes lowers his arms, his voice a little less husky.

"Good. 'Cause it could happen as easy as slicing a sammich in half. The question I asked is do you remember me?"

"Oh. Yes. Of course. I heard you ask. I thought it was rhetorical."

Army Coat smacks his face again, with less heat. Townes can't get his arms up to block it, but he tries. At the same instant, he turns his head away from the blow. That makes the other man mad. He throws his knees up on Townes's arms, just below the place where his skinny biceps meet his slender shoulders. Pinned under the man's full weight, Townes is helpless. He squirms to test how trapped he is. He's careful not to move too much, afraid of another slap, punch, chokehold, or stabbing.

Army Coat pummels Townes's head where it's swollen. It sends a jolt around the base of his neck and shoots down his spine. The throbbing turns into a constant, unbearable pressure. He feels like he's going to vomit. The soles of his feet tingle as they release the sensation. Townes wallows his head to make space between his nose and the unwashed crotch of the man's fake army pants. Army Coat grabs a hank of hair on the top of Townes's head and yanks until Townes quits moving.

"Now. You think you're smart. I can see that. But who is really the smart one here? The one on bottom or the one on top?" He waits.

"On top," Townes answers dutifully. Trying to will his stomach to settle, his head to hurt less.

"Fucking bingo," Army Coat says. He lets loose of Townes's hair. "We are going to come to an understanding. I'm a reasonable man. I wasn't always like this. Hard times and tough situations make hard, tough men." His knees dig a little deeper into the meat of Townes's arms as he leans forward to watch Townes's facial expression. Townes, for his part, tries not to wince at the increased pain, keeps his face neutral. "You believe me? That I'm a reasonable man, don't you?"

"Yes." Townes nods as best he can.

"Good. And you believe I can cut you open and leave you here to die if I feel like it. You believe that too, don't you?"

"Yes." His throat is tightening in preparation to heave. He tries to relax the tight cables running along his neck. He can't make his breath draw right. *The last knock on my skull might have done permanent damage.*

"Good. We understand each other. Like men." He dismounts from Townes roughly, knocking Townes across the face with his knee as he goes. He flops his butt back in his original position at the end of the bed. He goes back to cleaning under his nails. Townes scoots around a little, trying to prop himself against the wall. Trying to find a way to be comfortable, but there is no such position.

"You thought you were pretty slick following me. But I saw you. You aren't as smart as you think. Not as smart as me. Not by half. Right?"

"Yes. Right."

"Say the whole thing."

"What? The whole sentence?"

Army Coat turns quickly to look at Townes, ready to spring on him again. He gives Townes a warning look, a look that says he better do what is expected and do it now.

Townes says, "You are the smart one. You are the smart one between the two of us. I am not as smart as you."

Army Coat shows Townes the side of his face again; his muscles visibly release. "Bingo," he says. "So here is how I see it: Yesterday you robbed me on the train. It was a modern-day train robbery. Like the old West. You are a regular Billy the fucking Kid. I was taking care of business. Then you stuck your nose in. You robbed me. You took money from my pocket. You took food from the mouths of my wife and my boys. Now what do you think is a fair thing to do with someone who robs you? Huh? What do you do with someone like that? Someone who sticks his beak where it doesn't belong? Someone who takes from your family?"

An image of Esmeralda comes fresh to his mind, and Townes wants to say, *If you're talking about that little girl like she's a commodity, I would say you're a sicko.* Or *Kidnapping children is not a job. Not a career path.* He hears the kids hooting down the hall, singing a song about a grumpy old troll. He wonders if they are kids this man has nabbed. If so, to what end?

"I said, what would you do with a lousy thief? Someone who robbed you?"

Townes thinks, *You're the kind of fiend they write fairy tales about, to teach children to fear the dark, to fear strangers.* And *If I were robbed, I'd think the person must need whatever was stolen, and do my best to be at peace with it.* He knows those answers will lead to more pain. So he says, with as little sass as possible, "I guess it depends on how serious the offense was."

"Okay. Now we are getting somewhere. And how would you measure the seriousness? Because remember, they used to hang people for robbing trains. That was considered justice. Stretch their necks right out, tips of their boots scraping little circles in the dirt. American justice. Given that fact, how would you measure the seriousness?" Army Coat is animated, almost gregarious.

"Well," Townes offers. He initially thinks of monetary value, but he's uncomfortable with that, so he comes up with, "Maybe how much it inconvenienced you?"

"Okay. So let's say it was very fucking inconvenient. Very extremely really very fucking inconvenient. What do we do about it? What would be the just thing?"

"I caused a big problem and you take that personally. I can see that. I'm sorry. I'm sorry I did it. Understandably, you take it seriously. But I don't think I can fix it. Some things can't be undone. You can't unring a bell."

"Bingo. I like that. You can't fucking unring a fucking bell. You caused me this serious problem that can't be undone. And by extension . . ." Army Coat says leadingly.

"By extension I have a serious problem to fix," Townes responds obediently. He glances around the shabby, sealed room to confirm the inescapable truth of the statement.

"You're fucking right." Army Coat says it hard, not playing at all. "Let me tell you a story. You got time for a story?" He waits half a beat. Long enough for Townes to think he should answer, long enough to draw a breath. Before Townes can speak, Army Coat says, "Sure you do. You'd love a fucking story. Every sad motherfucker loves a good story."

Army Coat adjusts himself, turns to face Townes, cocks one leg on the bed, leaving the other leg propped on the floor. His movements jostle Townes and get his stomach rolling again.

"Not too far from here, there was a big warehouse. Guys from the neighborhood worked there. Old men with grown kids worked there. Their grown sons worked there too. It was a photo processing plant. You're too young to remember probably, but it used to be you would take your little Kodachrome camera, feed in the film, take a picture, crank it, take a picture, crank it." Army Coat pantomimes the action, holds his hands out for Townes to see his imagined boxy camera.

Townes nods. His stomach works up some gas and he burps, catches and holds it in his mouth until Army Coat starts talking again. Too afraid a loud burp will be taken badly.

"You see, in the early seventies what was called the C-41 color negative development process was introduced. And when you cranked your film all the way to the end, you'd go down to the drugstore and stick it in an envelope, write your information on it, and drop it off. It would show up at a warehouse with big vats of swirling, stinking chemicals, and a bunch of men would turn that cartridge full of negatives into a pile of prints in the size and number you requested. So, when I finished high school I did what a lot of other people did. I applied for a job at the plant and started working. I can't tell you how many pictures of naked baby butts and summer picnics I developed. How many piles of happy families doing domestic things I tucked into folders and shipped back to Duluth or Omaha or Quinnipiac. Wherever the fuck those places are.

"But as I'm sure you've heard, the only constant is change. And almost as soon as I started working, the chemical companies started selling smaller and smaller units to drugstores or standalone Photo Huts. You see, people could take three rolls of bad snapshots at a raunchy bachelorette party, drop that film, and a few hours later have a document of every embarrassing, drunken moment. And that's what they wanted. They wanted it right now. Eventually the processing warehouse shut down. Obsolete. You know that word?"

"Yes. I know it."

"It means a thing has outlived its usefulness," Army Coat explains anyway. "I had my head up. I saw it coming. So I quit a year before the layoffs started, and I took a job managing one of those Photo Huts. But prices on those developers got so cheap and the units got so small there was one in every grocery store. All the Photo Huts closed. But I was smart and I could see the future was in video, so I scrounged a job at a dub house. Someone shoots a movie and they want to sell a million videos. Well, you gotta have all those copies made. Dub house. That was me. I did that."

Army Coat pauses, looks into the past, recalling a life he once lived. "Long story short, digital killed the dub house. New media killed the old media. Automation took manufacturing jobs out in an alley and put a bullet right behind its ear. And NAFTA helped bury the body. You with me so far? You see what I'm getting at?"

"I'm with you."

"What do you think? Sum it up, smart guy. You're a smart guy, right? So sum it up."

"Skilled labor was a career around here. You could raise a family on one income. Union job. The pay was okay, I guess. The benefits were good too. But it's not like that now."

"Bingo. When I was let go the last time, I bought up some old equipment and had my own business, dubbing for small companies. At the dub house I worked for, they had five hundred networked

VCRs in banks of a hundred. Big red lights to show they were recording. You'd take the master tape, which was a one-inch tape, and play it quick time. In half an hour you'd have five hundred copies. So I bought a bank of a hundred VCRs and went into business. You know, CEO bigwig speeches at trade conferences. Etcetera. I was an entrepreneur. Over the years a lot of companies started doing those things in-house. I eventually found myself dubbing skin flicks. I made connections in LA. Became the only distributor for hentai, which is Japanese porno cartoons. Giant swollen cocks shaped like party balloons. Sixteen hours a day all I heard was humping and moaning. Porn videos were a good mail-order business. That and dick pills. It was a golden age. But then even porn turned digital and started streaming, the economy tanked. My skills were deemed useless. Unskilled workers took all the jobs I was qualified for. Fucking immigrants. And, to come clean with you, I started selling drugs. Started using the drugs I sold. I was in a bad way." He brushes his palms against one another three times, turns them up, and blows them off, to show he's reached the end.

"That's the big story. I've been hustling for a decade. Selling the leftover inventory where I could. Moving to cheaper and cheaper housing. I ran out of money. Ran out of options. I was born near here. It wasn't so bad then. People had pride; they took care of one another. Before all these low types moved in. This country is on the decline. It's so obvious. Things get worse every year.

"On the upside, I got clean, got married. My wife, bless her, pointed out I still have equipment and the know-how to use it. Truth is, I tried to sell it a hundred different times, but nobody wanted it. That was good luck. Because she was right. I still have a few friends in LA. I started making calls, feeling out options. Then I saw on the TV America's got this glut of unaccompanied South American girls flooding our country. And I think, *It's time to go back into business for myself.* Supply and demand." He nods over to an expensive digital camera mounted on a shitty tripod, near the room's window. The window gives a pale glow through the patchwork of masking tape and newspaper that cover it and illuminates a twin mattress thrown on the floor. Townes swallows hard. It's clear what Army Coat had planned for Esmeralda. He wants to point out that Esmeralda was neither unaccompanied nor South American. But he knows better.

"You see, there is a niche market for mail-order video. But only the kinds of things you don't want the feds to catch you streaming. They've gotten good at following that shit back to its source. You see where I'm coming from. I kind of had a stroke of genius here. Don't you think?"

Townes looks into the face of a monster, the exact breed of man that had taken Etta. He's never wanted to hurt someone before. Never had the urge to plot violence. Not until now. He knows if he gets the chance to hurt this horrible man, he will. It is beyond his control. He won't be able to stop himself.

"So you see, I was about to start a new enterprise. It's humble, I admit. But Apple started in a garage. I made promises to people out in LA. People are counting on me to deliver. I took an advance to buy some equipment. I'm on a deadline. You messed up my launch. Cost me time. Time is money. But you are a white man," Army Coat is saying. "And I like to give other white men a break if I can. In this day and age, we have to stick together. I'm willing to let you go. Let it pass. Find a way you can make it up." He slaps Townes on his ankle to get his attention. Townes feels the tender throb of the sprain from the previous day. Feels his stomach start to let loose with something more than a belch. Army Coat asks, "Are you listening?"

"Yes. I hear you," he responds quietly.

"And you believe me?"

"Of course." But it doesn't seem real. The grave look on Army Coat's worn face tells Townes he means every word.

"You understand me. Right?" Army Coat pats one of the exterior pockets on his green coat. He pulls out a length of green, rubberized cable.

"Yes," Townes says.

"Good. Do you know what I have here?"

"No."

"I didn't think so. You've never hung your clothes out to dry, have you?"

"No."

"Well, you should. It's the best way to dry your clothes. Real fresh. Nothing like it. You gotta take this serious. I mean it. If you ever get the chance, you gotta put up a clothes line."

"Okay. I will. I'll try it."

"Good. You keep thinking that way. Keep pretending things are going to work out." Townes's body is tugged down so the back of his head is flat on the mattress. The other man slowly climbs back onto Townes. Townes lets him, doesn't think he could stop him.

"This." Army Coat dangles the length of green cable over Townes's face. "As I'm sure you've guessed, you smart son of a bitch, is premium clothesline." He straddles Townes again, mounts his knees on Townes's arms, thrusts his groin in close to Townes's mouth and nose. "What makes it premium is that it is thin and strong. It has a wire core with a rubber coating. It won't give, but it won't rust in the weather either. It is a fucking miracle of American ingenuity. You can appreciate that, right?"

"Mmm-hmm."

"Good." He folds the length of wire, forms it into a noose. He snares Townes's left wrist in the loop and tightens it down. He knots it in a complex way, leans his abdomen on Townes's face as he reaches to use a small key-lock to secure the other end over the metal-tube headboard. When he's done, he stands next to the bed. Despite being bound in an unknown location, Townes is momentarily elated to breathe freely again.

"Now you stay put. I gotta decide how you can make up for the trouble you caused. You see, the punishment has to fit the crime. My wife will be in to feed you soon. Don't want you to starve." He turns to leave. Townes feels immediate relief at the promise of his absence, but Army Coat pauses to taunt Townes.

"I'll miss you while I'm gone. You be polite to my wife. You be a gentleman or I'll hear about it. She barely speaks a word of English any fucking way. But you be a regular Little Lord Fauntleroy. Okay? Speaking of Lord Fauntleroy, you might want to try hard to get rich while I'm gone. I mean it. If you were rich, if you had access to cash, that might make this whole fucking thing a lot better for you."

Townes has no idea what the man is saying anymore, but he shakes his head that he understands, anything to make the man leave the room. His forehead has started to sweat. His face is hot. He needs to vomit. Army Coat walks out and closes the door.

Townes hears a lock snap. He puts his face in the mattress and starts to whimper. It grows rapidly into a wet, self-pitying blubber. He cries a cry that dredges the old heartache from the bottommost depths of his being, where it had happily settled and been mostly ignored. He sobs, spit forming on his bottom lip, his mouth rolling over the grubby mattress. The clothesline cuts into his wrist. He huffs out hot air and sucks in ancient mattress spores. He yowls until he's too exhausted to cry anymore. He belches up bile that burns in his throat and sinuses.

Sniveling slightly, he rolls into a sitting position, easing the pain on his wrist and shoulder. He turns his cheek down and wipes it on one shoulder, scrubs the tip of his nose on his shirtsleeve.

*All I want is to be home.* Not in the room over the garage, but in his old room, with Etta down the hall, with both of his parents, married and home. He wants to know Charlie is tinkering in the garage or in the front yard on a summer day, mowing a diagonal pattern into the lawn. Meg is making breakfast in the kitchen.

Not grapefruit, something homemade and hot. One of her meals with the power to make him happy from the inside out. He thinks of biscuits and sausage gravy, with Meg's strong coffee. Not the disgusting mess he witnessed at the diner. The real thing. Townes doesn't consume dairy, or processed sugar, or white flour, for that matter, but a hot cup of Meg's coffee with ample whole milk and two heaping teaspoons of granulated sugar would be the perfect thing to cut the sausage fat in the rich gravy. The thought of it makes his stomach gurgle and threatens to make him start bawling again. He's plain tired. Bored with being helpless.

Townes is done being a victim, done crying. But he doesn't feel the catharsis that can come from a long-needed sob. Instead he feels empty, used up, and abandoned.

# A MOTHER'S JOB IS NEVER DONE

This morning Meg doesn't give a shit what her selfish son thinks of her fucking smoking habit. After her customary two-cigarette morning at her bedside, she takes her ashtray from her drawer, a box of matches, and her remaining cigarettes right with her into the bathroom. She's hung over. Wine always gives her a headache. She's topless, wearing her tights and tall boots.

Last night, she drove safely home, despite having finished an entire bottle of wine. She had started undressing immediately. Dropping her nice coat on the table, nearly choking while removing the poorly knotted scarf. She unzipped her dress, letting it fall around her boots. She was careful not to trip as she stepped out of the circle of dress. Finally, she unhooked her bra, the real objective of her kitchen striptease. She left one bottle of wine on the table and took another upstairs.

The unopened bottle of wine is still there, on her bedside table as she moves to the bathroom. She had forgotten a corkscrew and had fallen asleep rather than walk back to the kitchen to rummage for one.

On the toilet she unzips her boots, tugs them loose, and kicks them aside, then lights another cigarette and smokes while she pisses. After she reaches back to flush, she's tempted to sit with her tights around her knees and smoke until her legs go numb from the toilet seat, but she's more ticked off than tired, so she makes the effort to stand and keep going. She tries smoking in the shower, shampooing with one hand and holding the cigarette out of the water the best she can, until it gets soggy and floppy and she can't draw through the filter anymore. She pitches the dead cigarette at the open toilet. It lands on the seat and sticks, spilling tobacco leaves from a tear in its side. *Something else to clean.*

Now, with two free hands, she soaps and rinses and applies conditioner briskly. She feels her pits and decides not to shave them or her legs. *Good enough.* She lets the conditioner sit.

The irony of her life smacks her in the back of the head as water runs through her hair. She gave up much of who she once was, of who she might have potentially become, to raise her children. Cleaning up after them, cooking for them, meeting their needs and the needs of her husband without often considering what her own needs were. And now, her big act of rebellion and independence as a single woman with only one grown child to look after: start a house-cleaning business so she can spend all of her spare time picking up after other people's wretched children.

To be honest, she didn't do it all for her family. She was compelled personally, internally driven, motivated by a sick cocktail of maternal hormones to nest, to nurture. Now she can hardly remember what goals she had given up for the sake of her family.

Except, she remembers her sophomore year in geography class they watched a video about the Appalachian Trail. It had moved her. Captured her imagination like few things could in those days. The overwhelming beauty of the land, communing like Emerson and those other Transcendentalists she'd been forced to read in English class. An idea had hooked her, that she would take a summer to hike the entire trail. She would sleep under the stars and build tiny campfires; she would bathe in ponds and creeks and rivers, bare naked, brown as a berry, proud and strong, standing tiny in the big world. The idea had taken root and grown. She'd dreamed about it. She'd secretly read about the trail and looked at maps. She'd visited camping and hiking stores and made lists of supplies she couldn't afford. She started going for long walks in the evenings with the notion that she was training. But she had lost interest by the time she met Charlie and his little ass in his tight jeans.

And now, well, it's too late. Not only is she too old, too tired, and too broke, but telling people you intend to *hike the Appalachian Trail* is taken as code for *I'm having a fling with an exotic nymphomaniac.* One fucking old white politician ruined a national treasure for an entire generation, but that is kind of what politicians do. Right? Take advantage of their positions to line their pockets and act as if they're entitled to whatever they want, regardless of how their greed affects the people they are elected to serve.

She has the impulse to run for office on a platform that reads: Mark Sanford of South Carolina owes each and every citizen the two dollars and thirty-four cents that working Americans have paid over the course of their lives to maintain the trail. Why? Because he has ruined the entire trail for everyone. *Typical selfish male prick. He owes me. Owes us all.*

She snaps off the water and waits a moment to let most of the water run down her body. She pulls her hair over the front of her shoulder and wrings it. She reaches for a towel, leaving the shower curtain closed to hold the heat, and wraps the towel around her head like a turban. She uses a second towel to dry herself; the rough, nubby fabric is scratchy and invigorating. She slides the shower curtain aside on its plastic rings, takes the towel, folds it over, and places it next to the tub to use as a bathmat. She steps out, into the cold house, naked as the day she was born.

As soon as she's dry, she lights another cigarette. She stands it on its filter end, watches the corkscrew of smoke trail off its ashy tip and drift slowly upward until it dissipates, as if it were never there. When she's done brushing her teeth, she lifts the filter back to her lips and smokes some more. It's hot in her mouth, and the mix of tobacco smoke and toothpaste tastes like she's smoking a menthol.

She smokes while she blow-dries her hair; she smokes while she puts lotion on her face, hands, and elbows. She holds the cigarette away from her lips long enough to apply bright lipstick, blots it, knocks the tobacco crumbs and damp cigarette into the toilet with the fold of Kleenex, and flushes the toilet. She walks into the bedroom and dresses.

She smokes as she walks through the hall, as she descends the steps, intentionally stinking up the whole house. *My house.* She finishes that cigarette and lights one more as she waits for the coffee to finish brewing. She sits and drinks coffee, two cups. Plays with the cap Townes refused to wear. She waits for Townes to wander through the back door. She runs the kitchen tap and swishes the cigarette under it, drops it in the disposal. She feels light-headed and keyed up with nicotine.

Normally, she would get Townes's grapefruit ready for him. *He can section his own fucking grapefruit.* She would also wait until he has eaten and left before she eats her greasy, meaty food, but today, she makes herself a microwave sausage biscuit before he even arrives. Takes big, steaming mouthfuls and sucks in air around each bite to cool it enough to chew. She throws away her trash and wipes off the counter. She pours more coffee in a plastic go-cup and sets it aside. She wants to march out and give Townes a piece of her mind. *Selfish. Little. Ass. Had to. Ruin. My memorial.* She realizes what she's thought and corrects herself. *Etta's memorial.*

She leaves her clothes from the previous night where she dropped them. She doesn't care if Townes realizes she was distraught, maybe drunk. She's a grown-ass woman and can drink and undress wherever she feels like in her own damn house. With whomever she feels like undressing with.

She heads to the coat closet to get bundled, slips into her warm, comfy winter boots. On her way back through the kitchen, she sees her answering machine flashing a big red number five. She moves to listen to the messages but hears the scrunch of a car pulling into her back drive. *Odd.* She remembers the man with the mange and the too-tight shirt, standing in a pile of red slushy. She wonders if she's about to be arrested but dismisses it immediately. She thinks it's Charlie, come to apologize for ruining her event. *Etta's event.*

She is sick of men. She's done with them. Why are they all so selfish and oblivious? What makes them think the women in their lives should cater to their every fucking need? Why do they never return the favor? To be faithful or honest or attentive? It would take a lifetime of daily sacrifice on Townes's part to repay her for all she's done for him. For all she still does for him. *He's a fucking grown-ass man for Christ's sake.* "Then again," she mumbles, "like father, like son, I guess." Charlie abandoned her after they lost Etta. The daughter she raised. Not him. Charlie didn't do it. She did. She raised Etta, lost Etta, and he is so pathetic in his mourning that he leaves her alone to raise damaged, strange Townes on her own.

She goes to the back door to investigate, fully prepared to give Charlie an earful. She snaps the deadbolt open and looks out the window set in the back door. First, she sees all the snow, sees more is starting to fall. It's frigid out. *The Transcendentalists were rich white guys who had the spare time to wax philosophical about savage man and his need for nature, and not one of them had to endure a day without a hot meal or one night of Chicago winter.*

Then she registers the strange-looking truck she doesn't know, with someone she doesn't recognize sitting behind the wheel, letting the engine idle, looking down at his phone. *It is definitely not Charlie.*

Her hand rests on the cold knob. She studies the profile over the distance as best she can through a swirling dustup of snow and the powdery film on the driver's side window. It's a young man. Older than Townes but still young. The older she gets the more difficult it is to judge the age of young people. They all look like idiot kids: newscasters, her gynecologist, politicians passing laws that ruin people's lives and tweeting pics of their wieners all over the globe.

But this kid is familiar. Then it clicks: Newton Parker. Another fucking man she asked to help honor Etta who couldn't be bothered to fucking show up. *He claimed to love her!*

She jerks the door open and stomps down the steps to harangue Newton with an unwelcomed diatribe, not because it's the fair thing to do, but because he is the one available at the moment.

# HARANGUED BY
# AN UNWELCOME DIATRIBE

When he drives onto Etta's street, Newton is deeply uncomfortable. Though he'd been here dozens of times, eaten dinner with the family a few times, he'd usually tried to arrive when he knew her parents would be away. Charlie was usually working and Meg was often running errands. Townes was always around, but he was in his cave playing video games in the dark with his headphones on, effectively avoiding Newton altogether.

He and Etta would have the run of the place. Sometimes they did homework. Sometimes they watched afternoon TV and made out. Once they took a shower together, directly across the hall from Townes. Newton feels happy at the memory. The intimacy of turning sideways to pass one another in the narrow tub, taking turns in the warm stream from the shower, their slick bodies brushing one another, kissing, water running down their faces, soaping one another's body. No sex, just a slow, provocative tease and a promise of more to come.

He feels guilty about that episode, nearly seven years ago, as he pulls slowly into the driveway at the back of the house. Not because it was a bad thing, but because it was a transgression of trust between Etta and her parents, and because he's returning to the scene of the crime to meet with Etta's mom. He wonders for a moment if he should make a full confession.

He puts the car in park and fishes his phone out; he checks to see if Meg has replied to his message. Finds no reply. While he's holding the phone, he recalls that he'd seen a text from Townes while he was in the police station.

He taps his text app and sees two new items. One reads:

This is Townes. My mom asked me to encourage you to go to the memorial tonight. You should go. Especially because something has come up, and I'm thinking I might be running late. Let my mom know for me. Okay?

The second is a photo. He taps it, is waiting for it to open when knuckles rap on his window. He pitches the phone into his passenger seat and finds Meg, bundled against the cold and glaring at him. She looks beyond angry.

He pulls the door handle, lets the door open a bit. Turns the engine off. Gives Meg a chance to step back and allow him to slip out. The cold air hits him the same time Meg starts in.

"You have some fucking nerve showing up here after you ruined Etta's entire memorial." She steps in close to him, the same height as him, eye to eye. He's forced to lean back against the truck's door so they don't bump noses. "You think you can take from our family and never give anything. You took our daughter." Newton's eyes go wide. *She's heard I was arrested.*

As she goes on, he gets a different impression. "The last year we had with her, she was always off with you. You hoarded her." She shoves him, his ass pushes into the door hard enough to click it closed. He hopes it's not locked, because his keys are still in the ignition. He gets his arms up between him and Meg to ward her off as she leans in closer, her voice rising louder and louder as the wind kicks up more snow. "You took the last year we had with her. And now you can't even do this one little thing? To honor her memory? You are worthless. Like all of them. Like all men. Charlie didn't show. Townes didn't show. You didn't show. GO! Just go! Go away. Drive away now! Go. Go now!" She beats on him, the whole weight of her abdomen pressed against his, and he lets her hit him, hammering with the sides of her fists. He figures he deserves it. He sees she's distressed and confused. He knows he isn't the reason for all of her anger, but somewhere along the way, he earned all of it.

"I'm sorry." He doesn't say he's sorry for being with Etta in the shower, or in Etta's room, or on the couch, but he thinks it; the thought passes through his mind as he says, "I'm sorry." He repeats it over and over, until she stops pounding on him. "I wanted to be here with you," he confides in complete earnestness. He speaks just loudly enough to be heard in the wind. "I did. I wanted to be here, but I was detained. I'm sure you heard. I'm pretty sure your husband was there. I mean your ex. Right? Charlie. Were you there, too?" At the mention of Charlie's name, Newton sees Meg's eyes widen, like she's interested in what he has to say, listening for the first time.

"Charlie? Tell me about what Charlie has to do with this. What was so fucking important he had to take this from me?"

"He was at the police station, I think. I'm not sure. I didn't see him. I just thought he was there." He realizes he has no idea if Charlie was there, so he changes tactics. "But I called. I used my one phone call to let you know I was being detained. I could have called my mom or called a lawyer. But I called you instead. And I drove here this morning to apologize. In person. You see? I came here to tell you I'm sorry. For the memorial. Why else would I be here now?"

"Wait. What do you mean? You were arrested? And Charlie was there? It was about Etta?" She pulls her collar up around her face and clutches her coat closed at her throat as a sharp gust of cold wind hits them.

"Yes. I was arrested, but it was a mistake."

"Come inside." She tromps back to the house. "You left a message?" she calls over her shoulder. He nods but she can't see. "Come inside," she tells him. He does as he's told.

The kitchen looks the same as he remembers it; a stainless steel microwave is where a black one used to be, but otherwise it's the same. There's a coat on the table, a dress and bra on the floor. He tries not to stare.

It's warm in the kitchen and smells of cigarettes and grease. Newton likes the smell. He unzips his coat as Meg walks to the answering machine and pushes the play button. A mechanical voice says the date and time, then Townes's voice says:

Hi Mom. Listen. I just left a message for Newton like you asked. I was on my way home, but I got sidetracked. I think. I don't know. A girl might be in trouble. A little girl. And I have to do something. If I can. I don't know. I'm going to be a little late. But I need to do this. Etta would have wanted me to do this, I think. At least, I want to do it for Etta.

Meg's eyes flick toward the back door. The machine beeps loudly, gives the date and time, and plays the next message:

Meg. It's Charlie. I'm driving with Ruther. He brought someone in about Etta. They found something at someone's place. I'll call when I know more.

Meg turns her attention to the man in her kitchen; she narrows her gaze and scrutinizes Newton. Beep. Date and Time. New message:

Hey. This is Newton. I appreciate the invitation to the memorial. I wanted to attend, but something came up. I don't think I'm going to make it. I'm sorry.

Newton thinks he sounds genuinely, painfully sorry, and a little nasal. Meg's eyes soften as they look into his face. Beep. Date. Time. Message:

Meg. It's Charlie. They brought Newton in. They found Etta's backpack in his closet. He says they traded months before she disappeared. If that sounds right to you, call me. Ruther is checking with Etta's girlfriends. He wants to make some calls. So far Newton's story checks out. I don't think he had anything to do with it.

Beep. Date. Time. Message:

I just wanted to call about last night. I'm really sorry I missed the thing. I wasn't sure you would get my last message in time. So I wanted to explain. I'm thinking about swinging by to apologize in person. If that's okay? See you soon.

Then the machine says, "You have no more messages."

Meg pulls a chair out from the table, crumples into it. She stares at the tabletop as she speaks. "I remember now. About the backpack. You traded. She was carrying a black one, right?"

"Yes."

"And you were carrying her backpack? The one with all the gaudy colors?"

"Yes."

"And all this time, I didn't think of it. The cops had bad information, a bad clue, a bad lead. Right. Do you think . . . do you think it makes a difference? Could it make a difference that they were looking for a bright backpack instead of a black backpack? I mean, why was it on me to know what backpack she was using? What clothes she was wearing? Didn't Townes see her last? Why is it my fault?"

"I don't see how it could make any difference. No one would blame you for something so minor. So . . . what do you call it? Trivial. Something so trivial when there was so much else to deal with." Newton timidly takes the seat across from Meg.

"But . . . but Ruther said the little details are important." Meg cries big round tears onto the kitchen table, silently at first, and then with deep inhalations of breath followed by uncontrollable, retching sobs. She stays hunched over, her shoulders quaking, making a puddle on the tablecloth, showing Newton the top of her hair, glistening with melting snow.

Newton stands to look for tissues, finds only paper towels. He tries to rip a few off. The roll pops loose and the spring-loaded holder smacks hard against the bottom of the cupboard. He sets the whole roll on the table where Meg can reach it. She's oblivious.

"There," he says. He sits across from her again. "For your nose and stuff."

She catches her breath. She makes a wad of paper towels and blows her nose, blots her eyes with the oversized clump. She looks at Newton, her eyes nearly swollen closed. She sops up her drool and tears from the table. After a minute of steady breathing, she says, "Townes." She says it in Newton's face like he should understand how important a statement it is.

"Excuse me?"

"I didn't see Townes last night. He hasn't come down for breakfast." She knocks her chair over as she runs to the back door and out into the winter storm. Newton follows. They cross the blacktop, pass his truck, and enter a side door into the detached garage.

"Townes!" she calls. She runs up some steps, Newton at her heels. In the tidy little space they stare at Townes's bed, empty. The bell sound chimes from his alarm clock, echoing loudly through the space, the snow coating the windows making the sound heavy in the room. She listens for Townes in the bathroom. She knows he's not there, but she checks anyway.

Newton stands where he is, takes in the room. A simple bed, made neatly. One pillow, centered at the head of the bed. There are stacks of books, three-foot-high pillars, running along two walls of the room. No bookcase. The chime from the clock blasts and he feels it pound his skull. Next to the alarm he sees a string of red-lacquered beads knotted with a gold tassel. He's not sure how he knows it, but he thinks it's Buddhist; it keeps track of meditation practice the same way the Catholics use a rosary.

In the bathroom, Meg runs her thumb along the bristles of Townes's toothbrush, finds them bone-dry. She feels the towel that hangs next to the shower; it's dry as a rib in the sun. *He hasn't been home all night. He never came home!* She leaves the bathroom.

"Townes never came home," she says flatly. Matter-of-factly. Newton thinks she's talking like either she's traumatized or in damage-control mode. Probably both. "I need to call Charlie," she says. Then she blurts, "Townes never came home!" She makes for the stairs.

She crosses the space back to the house and is in the kitchen by the time Newton gets the door to the garage shut against the wind. He remembers his text from Townes. He checks his pocket. *Not there. Shit.* He had pitched his phone into his passenger seat.

Thankfully the truck is unlocked. He starts the engine to get the heater running. When he taps his phone to life, he finds the image is of a bar at night. The sign is unlit, but the name is clear in the reflected light on the snow. He's never heard of the place, has no idea where it is. It looks like a hundred other neighborhood joints around Chicago. There's a text with the image:

> I got in a fight on the train. Not a fight exactly. But we kind of tussled. There was this oily guy in an army coat trying to snatch a little girl. I tried to stop him. He got off the train. I followed him here. It's a long story. I've got to keep an eye on him. Make sure he doesn't do it again. I'm scared. I don't know what I was thinking. You know about fighting, right? I might need a ride. Call me.

Newton's first reaction is disbelief. The Townes he knew would never throw fists with some stranger. Never. Not if he could avoid it. Never start a fight. He'd rather give up than fight back. He was a total wimp. No heart. No pride; just a sad little sniveling wussy. He was a target. People wanted to hit him, because he was so fucking weak. If this whole fight thing is true, Newton is impressed. It's the kind of thing Albert would have done. Jumped some stranger who was picking on someone. Albert was forever sticking up for people. It was one of the qualities Newton admired most about his friend, and now he finds it just as appealing in Townes.

He taps the phone and lets it dial Townes's number. It goes immediately to voicemail. The phone is turned off or out of battery. He leaves a message:

> It's Newton. Not sure why you sent me the picture. That's crazy about the fight. Really? Did you really jump some guy? That's crazy. Crazy cool. Your mom is all kinds of upset you didn't come home last night. I'm hoping you hooked up with a lady. Or a dude. I don't know your preferences. Maybe you impressed someone. Anyway. Call your mom before she has a stroke. What's her problem anyway? Is she always like this?

Newton ends the call with his last question ringing in his own ears. He thinks about it, how callous he was. *Of course she's upset, asshole.* She raised two children. Her little girl is gone without a trace, and now Townes doesn't come home, doesn't call. She's already lost one child. Of course she's a little nuts. She earned the right to be crazy. *Ass.* He regrets how he lets his mouth move faster than his brain sometimes. He vows to try harder.

Newton runs his windshield wipers to clear his view of the back of the house. He can see Meg inside, pacing, yelling into the phone. He knows he should tell her about the bar, about the text, but he's too scared to deal with her. He doesn't do well with his own feelings, much less someone else's. He decides to gather what information he can and call her later. Maybe he can repay her for the time he stole from her, from Charlie and Townes. Time he spent with Etta. Time they will never get back.

He flicks and pinches at the smooth screen of his phone. He Googles the name of the bar. The connection is bad. The page won't load. The storm is jacking with the signal.

He flicks and pinches at his phone some more. He tap taps a contact and the phone rings.

"Who the fuck is this?"

"It's Newton."

"What the hell do you want?"

Newton can't help himself. He says, "You spelled *foot* wrong on my tattoo. It reads EFF OH TEE OH: foto. One foto in the grave."

"Really?" Cranky Thomas says, completely unperturbed. "That's cool. I like it. Poetic. I should charge extra." Then he says, "Smart ass. Now what the fuck do you want?"

"Okay, does your phone receive digital images?"

"My phone receives phone calls. And I'm thinking of having that feature canceled. Because you won't stop calling me."

"Can I swing by and show you something? I need some help. It's a picture of a bar. I'm hoping you know where it is."

"Sure. What the hell? I'm up now. But bring coffee and doughnuts."

# PARENTING IS FOREVER

Meg goes straight to her phone and dials Charlie. She paces back and forth. She kicks her dress around on the floor. Charlie picks up on the fifth ring.

"Hello?" His voice is raw, half-asleep.

She doesn't give a shit how tired he is. She says, "Townes never came home last night."

She can hear Charlie moving his body into a sitting position. He croaks, "What?" His voice isn't working right. He clears his throat, tries again. "What?"

"I said: Newton was just here." She knows this isn't what she just said, but she sees context is necessary to aid Charlie's sleepy brain. He was never a fast waker. "Newton apologized for missing the memorial. It was very thoughtful, but I was pissed and I gave him a piece of my mind. He probably got most of what you deserved. He told me he was taken in for questioning. Is that right?"

"Hmm. Yes. Listen. I'm sorry."

"You should be sorry. But listen."

Charlie listens. Meg doesn't say anything. He says, "I'm listening."

"Good. You listen to me. You found Etta's backpack. Is that right? At Newton's place? Yes?"

"Yes. A squad was called to his apartment for a tenant issue. I didn't get the details, but the officers found some of Etta's things out in the open. Sounds like they got excited. They thought they had cracked the case. They called Ruther. He called me. Do you remember Etta's backpack? The one with the bright patchwork colors?"

"Yes."

"Was that the one she was carrying when she was taken?"

"No. I thought it was, but I remember now. She and Newton swapped for some reason. I don't know why. Love, I guess. She'd been using a black one, and Newton had probably been carrying the other one. I can't see her with it in my mind, but I remember they traded."

"Well, Ruther wanted to give us an answer. He thought Newton was it. He laid into him hard, but Newton was clean."

"That explains why you didn't show last night. And Newton and Ruther. But Townes didn't attend either. It was just me. I was the only one there for Etta."

"I'm sorry. Really. I am. Ruther sounded so sure. I thought we had something. I thought we were going to understand what happened to our girl."

"Well, that doesn't matter right now. Townes didn't come home."

"Are you sure?"

"You listen to me. Listen now. Townes is your child. I know Etta was your first. I know she's gone, and I know that broke you. She was my first, too. I fucking carried her in my body and gave birth to her. But we brought two children into this world. Two. You and me. Together. Etta is gone. We don't know where. If you were honest, you'd admit she's not coming back. But Townes. Townes is your son. Your spitting image. Townes is alive and he needs his dad. He needs you to take your head out of your ass. He needs you this minute. He didn't come home last night."

"I hear you. You're right. I came to a similar conclusion. I need to do better for Townes. I've neglected him. I basically abandoned him. Abandoned you too."

"That's great. And hell yes and amen. But I don't think you hear me. Townes is missing."

"I said I hear you."

"Well? What do we do? I don't know what to do. You know about this stuff. Call Ruther. Search. Call in the posse, circle the wagons. Find your son. Find your kid. You can't save Etta today. But you could save your son. Right now. Do it."

"Okay. Calm down please. Just calm down. He didn't want to go to the memorial. Maybe he just crashed with a friend."

"No. Listen to me. He called and left a message yesterday. On the way home. He said something about running late. Said he'd come across a girl in trouble. That he was going to protect her. That he would be late. I checked his room. He never came home. Not at all. He left on the train; the train didn't bring him back."

"Okay." Charlie says. He sounds convinced. He sounds engaged. He says, "If something happened on the train, maybe there was a report. Metra is a separate system from Chicago Police. I'll call Ruther to start looking. Okay?"

"Yes," she says. "Thank you," she says. "I need you," she says. She leaves it at that, with all it implies.

After a sober moment, she can hear Charlie getting to his feet. He says, "I'll call Ruther now. Get the wheels in motion. I'll get cleaned up. Without more to go on, the best thing is to see what develops."

"No," Meg says.

"I know. It's hard to wait. I know it feels like last time. I don't like it either. I'll call Ruther and get the wheels turning. I will. We'll have to see what turns up. If you think of anything else, call. I'll call you as soon as I hear anything. Anything at all. Okay?"

"Yes. I understand. Yes. But call soon. Even if you don't hear anything. Call me. Don't leave me like this. I can't take it. Not again."

"I will. I'll call soon."

Meg hangs up. She puts more coffee on, to keep busy. She wishes Charlie were here to sit with her, to hold her hand. Another person would be a comfort, but he's gone. Gone from her life like Etta. Gone. Gone like Townes could be gone.

# CHICAGO'S LEADING EXPERT
# ON DIVE BARS

Newton gets his old truck in gear and creeps his front bumper up to the edge of the street. He doesn't pull out. He's thinking how he didn't say goodbye, left Meg frantic and alone. He'd just made a solemn vow to turn over a new leaf, not say things without thinking first, not say things he doesn't mean. He wonders if it should apply to doing thoughtless things. Things like leaving the distraught mother of his missing girlfriend alone without a word of consolation. Leaving a mother with two missing children all alone without a kind word. He decides his vow should absolutely cover such things. *Starting . . . now.*

He watches the snow drifting down, the wind nearly gone, the sporadic flakes barely constituting a flurry. He hears the thudding scrape of a snowplow blade stuttering down the block. He looks back at the house in the rearview. The snow behind his car glows red from his taillights. The plow rumbles by and scatters salt from a spinning contraption on its rear as it passes. Newton takes his foot off the brake and the truck takes him to the Honey Bee Bakery.

Traffic is light, and Newton is able to follow the plow truck nearly all the way. He gets three Boston creams and two huge black coffees. When he takes the bag, he puts the open end over his face and breathes in the sweet fried smell. He pays and is at Cranky Thomas's kitchen counter before the coffee can get cold. Newton explains the general situation, about being arrested and missing the memorial, about going to apologize to Meg, about Townes staying out all night, about Meg being upset, and about getting the photo from Townes sometime the night before.

Thomas nods and swears and chews. Newton's eyes drift around the dusty room. He thinks of lying on the floor in the back, the needle carving the ink into his flesh. He feels blood pumping in his real calf, thinks of the phrase held there: *One foot in the grave.* He thinks of his other leg too, the one he lost. How he lost it and who he lost. Albert deserved better.

Finally, between doughnut two and doughnut three, Thomas seems to wake up fully. "You know, the Boston cream is not only the best doughnut ever . . ."

"But it's your doughnut equivalent," Newton interrupts.

"Shut up. I'm making a point." Thomas takes a grateful pull off the top of his coffee. "The Boston cream is not only the best doughnut ever, it is also the very best thing to ever come out of Boston." His fleshy brows crawl up his forehead expectantly, waiting for a response. "The *only* good thing to come out of Boston," he amends. Newton still doesn't respond. Thomas drinks more coffee, tumbles the last doughnut out of the bag into his curled mitt, and takes a huge bite. He seems disappointed. His expressive face hangs loose on its bones.

"Did you expect an argument? I'm not from Boston. I've never even been to Boston. I don't have a dog in that fight." Newton sips his own coffee.

"Just an observation." Thomas finishes his beloved pastry and sticks the tip of each wrinkled, bruised-looking finger into his old, puckered mouth with a loud smacking sound. Newton notes the contrast: the ancient, fading tattoos next to the pale yellow, vanilla-flavored filling. The childish, innocent glee of the action performed by the grizzled, liver-spotted old soldier. It makes him think people can survive anything life throws their way, given enough time.

"You know," Newton says. He uses his cup to gesture at the place where the doughnuts used to be. "My dad would have called those doughnuts *Berliners.*"

"Why the hell would he do a dumb-ass thing like that?" Thomas asks, smiling a sugar-induced smile.

"I guess that's what they call it in Germany. This kind of little doughy puck filled with fruit or cream. It's what my granddad called it, my dad's dad. He was born in Germany."

"Wow," Cranky Thomas says. "That is fucked up. Can't they do anything right over there? No wonder your family moved to America. Now, let's see this fucking picture." He sets down his cup, leaving the fat, cartoon-bee logo stamped on the cup's side turned in Newton's direction. He takes the phone when Newton offers it.

"Hmmm. Let me think," he says. He rubs his gray stubble and gawks at the picture Townes sent. The phone goes dark. "What the hell? What did I do? I didn't touch anything."

Newton taps the phone for him. The picture lights back up. Thomas coughs up something and spits in the sink next to him. "The Blue-Eyed Devil," he reads aloud. "Never heard of the place."

"Really? You sure?"

"Well, it does look like a place I used to go to near Cicero, on the edge of the Austin neighborhood, but that place was called the Peanut. It also looks like another joint called Luther's out near Bronzeville, and one called the Shandy Room up in Lakeview, and one called the the Jungle in the Back of the Yards neighborhood. Shit, man. They all look kind of like this. It could be Punchy's in Old Town." He takes a harder look at the place, trying to study the details, weigh it against the images in his mind. His face squeezes and relaxes, his features seeming to pump, trying to extrude the right memory. The phone goes dark again; he slides it across the counter to Newton. "Shittin' technology."

"You think this joint is where the Peanut used to be? Or one of those other places?"

"I wouldn't swear to it, but yep. It could be the same spot as the Peanut. I guess. The door is in the right spot; the glass block is beat to shit the same way. The sidewalk is busted up by tree roots in the right places. The Peanut used to have a few shitty shrubs along the front. If this Blue-Eyed Devil is the Peanut, the shrubs are gone. It all looks about two decades worse off, but with a new coat of paint and a layer of graffiti over that. Of course, all the snow makes it hard to say. Plus, fucking cars in the way. Could you give me a smaller, crappier photo to look at? But the old Peanut would be my guess."

"Can you write down the address or something?"

"No."

"But you're pretty sure?"

"Fuck, man. When you get to be my age, it all kind of runs together. You'll see."

"I doubt I'll live that long." Newton tries to tap the bar's name into his phone again. His search engine never stops loading. After a few minutes of waiting, staring at the phone and drinking coffee, Thomas pipes up to say, "But I can ride along with you. I think I could find it. If you want me to come along, I mean. I bet I could find it. If it's important to you."

"Yeah. It is. It's important to me. I should do what I can to sort this out. You serious about coming along?"

"The fuck else am I going to do today?"

Newton nods, to both concede Thomas's point and accept his offer in one concise gesture.

Fifteen minutes later, they have filled the truck with gas and passed through the tollbooth to merge onto I-88. The toll way is damp but clear of snow, and the traffic has reached a normal capacity for midmorning, midweek. Newton checks his mirrors and pulls from the far right lane to the far left lane. "Texas Sweep!" he declares, as he always does when he makes that maneuver. He settles into the lane, the median barriers rushing by at his left. He takes a glance at Thomas. Thomas seems lost in thought.

The cab starts to get warm and Newton turns down the rattling blower on the old heater. The tires throw a spray of wet through the hole in his floor pan under the heel of his real foot, making his pants damp. Given enough time, it will soak his sock and squish into his shoe. The road noise, the sticky sound of the tires perpetually peeling themselves from the damp pavement, moves itself from the background of Newton's consciousness to the foreground. The sky is cloudy in a way that diffuses the light and hurts Newton's eyes. He fiddles for his sunglasses, slips them on. The glasses are too dark for the low light and he can barely see. He yanks them off his head and tosses them back where they came from. He squints against the glare, listens to the sounds of the creaking suspension, and follows the road to I-290.

"*Ich bin ein Berliner*," Thomas says loudly.

"What?"

"*Ich bin ein Berliner*," Thomas repeats happily. "You speak German, right?"

"Not really. My granddad does."

"You know about *Ich bin ein Berliner* though? Right?"

"Not that I know of."

"What the hell do they teach you kids in school?" He pauses as if he expects a cogent reply. He appears disappointed when Newton doesn't respond. "Well," Thomas explains, "in the early sixties sometime, sixty-two or sixty-three. I don't know. I was a kid. JFK was president. John F. Kennedy. You know who the hell I'm talking about, right? The first Catholic president of the United States of America?"

"Yes. I know JFK. Democrat. Hot wife. Cute kids. Shot in the head. National tragedy."

"Right. That's the one. So JFK goes to West Berlin and gives a speech. He throws out a few phrases in German to get the crowd going. You know how politicians do."

Newton is only half listening. He sees a curving trail of red taillights snapping on ahead. He carefully begins to decelerate, trying not to slam down his brakes on the wet pavement.

"One of the things he says in that speech, right there along the Berlin Wall . . . You know about the Wall, right? The Republicans believe Reagan knocked it down with his conservative laser eyes. But he didn't. No lasers were involved. One of the things Kennedy says is, '*Ich bin ein Berliner.*' But he's speaking German in his crazy-ass Boston accent. Can you guess what it means?"

"What what means?"

"Pay attention, will you? When Kennedy said '*Ich bin ein Berliner.*' I just said that."

"Umm, I am from Berlin?"

"Right. Yes. He says, 'I am a Berliner.' Which means?"

"That he was from Berlin?" Newton taps the brakes to slow the car further; they are coasting along with the idling of the engine now. He downshifts to first; the engine lugs down hard; his lap belt mashes his innards.

"No, that he was a tasty cream-filled doughnut. You see what I mean. Kennedy was a very popular figure, and all these krautheads were gathered to see him."

Newton casts his dead gaze on Thomas at the minor slur to his ethnicity.

"No offense on the whole krauthead thing."

"It's okay."

"So," Thomas continues, "all these West Germans gathered in this great blond-headed sea in front of the stage, and JFK says, '*Ich bin ein Berliner.*' You said your German granddaddy told you a Berliner is a filled doughnut, right? So Kennedy told that adoring crowd, 'I am a tasty filled doughnut.'"

"Only in German," Newton adds.

"Yes. In German." Cranky Thomas is cranky his stolen observation isn't having the effect he had hoped. "I guess some things just don't make sense taken out of context."

"Yeah," Newton says. He's too busy watching the traffic, which is starting to pick up speed, to care much about Thomas's witticisms. He has the presence of mind to question if it was a good idea to make this trip with Thomas. For the first time, maybe ever, he thinks of Thomas not as an interesting soldier who's seen some things or as a good man to talk to, but as a tired, lonely, fusty man full of dusty old stories.

The car in front of Newton stops completely, and he has to stand on his brake and clutch at the same time. His truck slips and fishtails under him, but he doesn't hit anyone. The eyes that Newton sees looking back from the rearview mirror in the car ahead of him are apologetic. The car creeps forward so Newton has room to straighten the truck out so it's square with the lane. They sit at a dead stop.

After a minute, Cranky Thomas says, "I was wrong earlier. Boston cream isn't the only good thing to come out of Boston." He's serious about it. Newton guesses he means Kennedy, but he doesn't know how to respond. He supposes being sad and contemplative is a natural affliction of old widowers.

Thomas stays quiet until traffic starts to move. Newton is thankful for his silence and guilty for thinking harshly of the old man. The traffic eventually starts rolling; Thomas indicates where to exit the interstate.

Newton drives where Cranky Thomas instructs. They almost immediately leave the commercial shops near the interstate to cruise low-rent neighborhoods amid working-class family homes, brick two-flats, small frame houses, and countless brick story-and-a-half bungalows. They drift through a stark industrial area as they near the south end of the Austin neighborhood and pass a row of large Victorians turned into multifamily housing, in desperate need of maintenance. Here, there are dilapidated row houses, a significant portion of them with windows boarded and no apparent signs of working electricity. Other buildings have metal bars on the windows. They pass a series of massive corner apartment blocks, and they pass a multitude of brick three-flats and low-slung apartment buildings with the open courtyards piled with dirty snow.

Along the way, Thomas explains several times that he used to take the Lake Street bus to get to the Peanut, take it a certain number of stops then walk a couple of blocks. He finds navigating from the exit ramp confusing. Making things worse, the streets are mostly narrow; many of them are one-way, lined, sometimes both directions, with busted-ass cars; and less than half the streets are clear of snow. From the looks of many of the streets, they haven't been cleared for weeks. It takes more than ninety minutes to find the Blue-Eyed Devil. They drive past it the first time without noticing, too busy expressing their regret over all the once-glorious structures now left to rot.

"If it weren't for all the snow and American cars, I'd think I was driving through Afghanistan," Newton mutters.

"Or any city that's been in a war zone," Thomas adds.

A few blocks later, Thomas catches a street address and knows they've gone too far, has them turn and go back. It is basically where Thomas remembers the Peanut was. They stop the car in the street and stare at the entrance.

"Well, what now?" Thomas asks.

"Good question." They sit a while longer, the billowing exhaust settling heavily around the truck until they look like they are parked in a cloud.

"Doesn't look like they open until two," Newton says.

"Want to go get some lunch and come back?"

"Yeah. Good plan," Newton says. "Being lost makes me hungry."

# FOLLOWING BREAD CRUMBS

The phone makes a sound. Charlie answers before it completes one ring.

"Yeah?"

"It's Ruther. An incident report was filed with Metra. An unnamed man tried to take a girl from an inbound local train when it stopped at Cicero. Townes interfered and tackled the suspect. Townes was struck in the head by the pommel of a heavy knife, but seemed fine and refused treatment. The kidnapper got away. The witnesses made Townes out to be a real hero."

"Townes did that?"

"Yes. The report is clear. He saved that little girl."

"Townes did? My Townes?"

"Yes. Your Townes."

"Do I have it right then? There was no name for the suspect, no earthly idea who the hell he is? And if Townes saved the girl on an inbound train, why would he leave a note in the evening that he'd found a girl in danger? It doesn't jibe. He would have been headed home by then."

"I know. Maybe he was making an excuse to skip the memorial. You said he didn't want to attend."

"True. Maybe. I suggested the same thing to Meg. She nearly bit my head off. Besides, he didn't come home. He always comes home. He likes his little, solitary cell. He doesn't stay out all night. He doesn't hang out, or date, or party. He doesn't socialize. He doesn't randomly become a crusader for justice." Charlie thinks about it. Tries to picture Townes as a man of action. The image won't form.

"What if," Ruther suggests, "Townes spotted the same guy on the train? What if they crossed paths on the return trip?"

"That makes as much sense as anything. I have trouble believing Townes got lucky enough to survive a fight in the first place, but I feel certain if there was a rematch, he'd come out on the losing end."

"I bet you're right."

"Well. What's the next move?"

"I've got a call in to Metra dispatch to see about talking to the officer who took the report. Maybe we can get a better description. Find out more. Get a sense of Townes's state of mind."

"Call me as soon as you hear anything. Yes?"

"Of course."

"I better call Meg." He cuts the line.

"Charlie?" Meg's voice sounds calmer.

"Hey, baby," he says naturally, reflexively. He uses the tone he always used when trying to comfort her. There is an awkward pause. He recovers with, "I got a little information from Ruther. He says Metra filed a report about Townes. On his ride into the city yesterday he stopped a man from taking a little girl from the train at Cicero. There was a fight. It got physical. Townes was struck in the head. The report says he was fine. Refused treatment."

"He's fine. You're sure he's fine?"

"The report said he was fine."

"You can't tell with head injuries. What if he was concussed? He could have passed out somewhere."

"But he left you that message hours later. I think he was fine. He always had a hard head."

"Like father like son," she says. Charlie can hear the strain in her voice.

"Yeah, I guess." Charlie lets the worry creep into his voice. "Anyway. All we know is that on the way home, Townes left you that message. Ruther wonders if maybe Townes saw the same perp on the return trip. That's the only thing that makes sense. Anyway, Ruther is trying to talk to the Metra officer."

"Okay. What can we do? Isn't there something we can do?" Meg scowls at the thought of the backpack, how she had been frantic to help when Etta went missing. How she had been so interested in progress, in helping, that she misremembered that detail. *It could have made a difference.*

"We wait to hear more. Have you tried to call Townes?"

"Of course, I tried. It goes straight to voicemail, like it's been turned off." She's lonely. She wishes Etta would talk to her, have another conversation like when they were cleaning together. She's afraid Etta won't come to visit anymore, now that she's been put to rest.

"Hang in there, Meg. I'll call as soon as I hear anything. You do the same. Okay, baby?"

"I will," she says distractedly. He cuts the connection.

There's a memory fluttering in a back corner of her mind, like a moth bumping against a light fixture. A backpack. A black backpack. She has seen a black backpack, like the one that used to be Newton's, the kind Etta was carrying when she and Townes stepped off the bus six years ago, but she doesn't know where.

# CRISIS OF FAITH

Townes sits up slowly. He's stopped feeling sorry for himself by the time the salty tears have dried, crusty and cold on his lashes. He thinks about how to get the hell out of here. He asks himself what he knows. *Well, I know my wrist is going numb. My shoulder is losing feeling. My head hurts and isn't likely to start feeling any better. My throat is raw. My eyes are dry and itchy. I also know complaining isn't going to help.*

Townes has spent a lot of time learning to focus his mind, to breathe and quiet the chatter in his brain. While other kids have been living in dorms, doing keg stands, and sitting in auditorium lectures, he has been honing his practice. He uses all that preparation now, willing his brain to calm, to still itself. In the absence of any other kind of control, he can, at the very least, control his bodily rhythms, his own chaotic thoughts, and the rate at which air moves into his lungs and is expelled. He takes that much control.

Calm now, he uses his free hand to wipe the snot from the tip of his nose and rubs his wet fingers on the mattress top. He scoots his body closer to the headboard to take pressure off his wrist. He tugs at his bindings. There is no give, no slack.

He sees the other mattress on the floor, a few pillows thrown around, the camera aimed down. He feels dirty being in the same room with the equipment, Army Coat's intentions having left a sickening psychic residue in the space. He sees the lone light bulb, the window with the newspaper taped over it, the locked door. From where he sits, he can see screw heads in the window casing. There isn't anything else in the room. His bag isn't there, neither is his coat or his phone. He notes his prayer beads, his wrist mala, is gone, replaced by the double twist of clothesline. It was probably ripped and broken when he was ambushed in the bar or tackled in the alley. Briefly, his hopes rise at the idea that someone from the bar might have called the authorities. But the Blue-Eyed Devil didn't look like the kind of place where people were in the habit of calling cops. It looked like the kind of place where people went to avoid cops. In the bar, his face mashed flat to the tabletop, his cap had fallen into the spilled Irish coffee. The hat Dory had given him. Gone. All gone. Nothing he sees can be used as a tool to get out of the snare, or the window, or the locked door.

From the other side of the door, Townes hears a loud commercial: "Foot Pal is like a pet for your feet. It's a PILLOW! YAY! It's a SLIPPER! YAY! It's a snuggly, funny PUPPY PET! YAY!"

Again, he hears the sounds of many children, screaming a high-pitched and heavily accented "YAY!" along with the commercial. When the commercial is over, the kids start to argue in Spanish. A woman scolds them. The arguing continues. Because he makes out the phrase "Foot Pal" and the word "*azul,*" Townes guesses the kids disagree about which color of Foot Pal puppy is best.

Over the next several minutes, Townes paints a picture from the sounds that come down the hall: That wooden spoon he had pictured earlier is scraping something gummy from a pan. He sees it as fried potatoes with onions and peppers, with loads of salt, butter, and black pepper. A wedding ring clicks against a glass; a hand sets the glass in a deep stainless-steel kitchen sink, runs water. More things go in the sink: plates, cheap flatware, and the thin-walled pan from the stovetop. The TV goes to the intro of a show with characters who speak in British accents.

A few minutes pass with only the sound of the TV, then bare feet pad down the hall. The lock on the door clicks, the door opens, and a small woman in a black tank top and yellow SpongeBob pajama bottoms walks into the room. She carries a plate of food and a glass of water.

Townes tries to smile and nod, get a read on her state of mind, maybe find a sympathetic ally. She shoves the plate of food roughly into his free hand. She plunks the water glass on the floor next to the bed where he can reach it. She turns her haunches to him and rolls her round ass out the door. Townes sees she has what looks like dried oatmeal on one butt cheek, or dried barf. She pulls the door firmly closed, locks it tight.

He crosses his legs, making a place to set the plate. It is scrambled eggs with diced vegetables, some chunks of avocado, and a splash of salsa. Townes doesn't eat eggs anymore, but he's hungry, and he needs his strength. There is a fork shoved into the pile of food. He takes a small amount of food on the fork, lifts it to his mouth, and eats. He doesn't gag. If he doesn't think of it as the violently mixed ovum of a creature caged and forced into a short, hard life, then it's not bad. Pretty good, really.

He scrapes the plate clean. Drinks all of his water; it has a sulfur smell. His head starts to feel better; his mood improves. He's pleased at his new inventory of tools. Both the plate and the glass could be broken and used to saw through his bonds. The fork might work too, to gouge his way. Maybe the end of the fork's handle would remove screws from the window casing. He can't tell if they are flat-head screws or Phillips-head screws, but he'll know soon enough, if he can just get loose. Breaking the plate and glass will draw attention, so he starts with the fork. He stabs it into the knot. The tines find purchase around and through a void in the knot. He twists. It tightens the noose around his wrist but doesn't damage the knot. It takes effort to yank the fork back out. He stabs at it again, harder this time. One tine scrapes his wrist.

He hears the little woman's bare feet coming back. He pulls on the fork. It's jammed. The lock clicks open. He pulls harder; his hand slips from the handle. The door opens. He gets a firm grip, pulls the fork out, puts the tines in his mouth as if he's taking a last bite, draws it out slowly, and tries to have a satisfied look on his face as he says, *"Delicioso. Gracias. Gracias."* His Spanish 101 is coming back to him. He nods and tries to coax a response from the woman.

She has long, black hair pulled into a ponytail trailing over the front of her shoulder. With her left hand she snaps her hair behind her. Townes see she's carrying a kitchen cleaver in her other hand. He throws the fork at the plate in his lap with a loud clatter, so there is no chance she feels threatened.

She gathers the plate, glass, and fork and carts them out of the room, leaving the door wide open. The TV is loud now. A whiny British girl says, "Charlie. But I like to wiggle my toes in mud, Charlie." The woman comes back in the room, the cleaver in one hand, a key in the other. She waves the flat, square blade loosely in her grip. He thinks she's going to throw it or drop it, but she just gestures with it, shooing him toward the wall. He moves as far away as his arm will allow. She unlocks his wrist, loosens the place where it is snared snugly against his thin skin.

"Go piss," she says. It's not clear she knows what the phrase means. The delivery is wrong. The inflection is strange, like a memorized password called into the next foxhole in a World War II movie, but he takes her meaning.

He rubs the grooves from his wrist as he walks out the door, pumps the blood back into his fingers by making a fist over and over. He sees the light from the TV at the front of the apartment; he sees four pairs of small sock feet. The woman shoos him the other direction, toward the back of the apartment. He passes the open door to a small bedroom with two cribs on one wall and a desk piled with dismantled VCRs along the opposite wall. The next door is a bathroom. There are two more doors beyond. One is likely another bedroom, and the other a door to the outside at the end of the hall. He notes the deadbolt has a key in the lock.

She stands at the open door and watches him pee. He tries to turn his back to her as best he can. She hustles him back to the room before he can wash his hands. When he walks into the room, there's a crash from the front of the apartment, then a scared child crying.

She waves the blade at him, saying, "*No se mueva*. Not move. You stay."

She puts the cleaver near his nose and eyes him hard. The blade smells like onions. She waits for a response as children begin to argue. He nods infinitesimally, afraid of the sharp blade. She leaves the room, slamming the door but not locking it. Townes considers a sprint down the hall to the back door, but the thought of being tomahawked in the back by the cleaver gives him pause. Instead he takes the chance to walk over to the window. He feels sick as he passes by the small mattress, thinks of kicking over the camera, but chooses not to. In the window casing, the screws have the deep, rounded + of a Phillips-head screw.

There is a loose corner of newspaper. He bends it back and looks out. It tears a bit more. He's on the second floor of a multifamily complex of some kind, a two-flat or fourplex. Rickety stairs lead down from a small deck to a snow-covered yard that opens onto an alley.

"Hey!" The woman is in the doorway, cleaver in hand. Her accent makes the common word sound foreign. Her stance is low, knees bent, muscles bunched. She is keyed up and ready. Townes has no doubt she could snap and do him severe harm. She is a scary woman.

Townes holds up his hands in a calming gesture. The woman waves the cleaver at the bed. He piles back on, puts his own hand back in the loop of the clothesline. She snaps the little lock closed and checks to see that he's cinched tight, pulls hard enough for it to ache. A moment later he's back where he started: alone in a locked room, with a sealed window, lashed to a bed frame in a bad neighborhood, and with no way to improve his situation. *No hope.*

His stomach begins to rebel against the unfamiliar protein and spicy salsa. The salsa had a metallic aftertaste. He worries it had gone bad. The uncomfortable pressure in his gut could be the first stages of food poisoning. A belch bursts from him and he blows the smell away.

He sits for hours, shifting around, getting depressed and more desperate. During the long span, he takes account of his failed heroics. He berates himself for the ludicrous escapade he willingly chose to launch into. What possessed him to think getting involved with Army Coat was a good idea? He sees how preposterous, self-serving his scheme to follow a dangerous man into an unknown place really was. Life isn't a game. People die. They go missing, as easily as slipping off a step and breaking your neck. Why would he embark on such a stupid plan? *I'm just a dumb kid. Same as ever.*

*My brain.* He'd let his mind have too much free rein. *But why?* The desire to impress Charlie. *But what else?* An impulse to disrupt the carefully constructed world he'd built, breath by breath, over the past many years. *But why do that?* Because he was calm, but not at peace. He was coping and existing, but there was, at the center of his being, a living embryo of guilt; it began to throb when he saw the little girl on the train. It grew and spread with actions of his busy, fevered thoughts until he couldn't control the impulse to act, taking on a life of its own. Ultimately, he knows the answer can be boiled down to one phrase: *unresolved issues.* The life he'd built kept it at bay, but the anniversary of Etta's disappearance and his mother's constant yammering about the fucking memorial had stirred everything up.

There was more. *What other feelings contributed? The kiss!* At the memory, he reaches with his free hand to brush his fingers over the place Dory's lips touched him. He does realize that the new level of affection, the respect he witnessed in her face when he shared what he'd done, and the kiss had motivated him to take the local train instead of the express. He had told himself it was to protect some theoretical victim, but it was at least as much about seeking a new way to impress Dory. *Simple. Basic. Human. Longing for companionship, for physical contact. A primitive mating dance.* He hates to feel so common and vulnerable to the whims of his heart. Exposed. He lashes out, punches his own thigh with frustration. It hurts. But the pain focuses him.

If he had kept to his routine, caught the right train, hadn't been sidetracked dealing with his mother's demands. *If if.* He recognizes the trap he's falling into. Inattention to his practice led all the way from the safety of his normal, hermetic, suburban life to incarceration, tied to a dirty bed like a hostage tourist in the jungles of South America. He sees now the only possible answer is a return to his practice. Not a rejection of it. Not a continuation or an amplification of the chaotic ramblings he's allowed to flow freely through his thoughts.

There's a scientific principle at play. He can't recall the specific law or the person who posited it, but it argues that in a closed system, at each stage of energy transfer, entropy increases. And isn't every thought we have just a microscopic electrical firing of the synapse in the mind? He has allowed the forces of entropy to run unchecked for twenty-four hours. *And look at where it has gotten me.*

The Buddha once said something like, *Just as a snake shedding skin, we must shed our past over and over again,* and that is exactly what Townes needs to do. Let go of guilt. Forgive his mistakes, even the senseless blunders of the past day.

At the foundation of all of his attempts to live a meditative life is a belief that his own external existence is a projection of the thoughts he puts into the world. He reaches an elegant conclusion: *The only possible option, sitting here, on this bed, tied to this headboard, with no avenue of escape, is to take control of my interior landscape and project it outward until my reality takes on a more pleasing shape.*

Having reached a new decision, he aligns his body for thoughtful meditation. He sits in such a way that his back is erect, his posture not slumping, his shoulders not too rounded, so that if anyone discovered the scene, they would find him looking focused but relaxed. He doesn't forcefully ignore the sound of cartoons from up the hall, but he is able to push it to the back of his mind. He begins his meditation.

# REALIZATION DAWNS

Meg works up a sweat just moving across to the garage, going as fast as she can through the loose snow. She opens the garage door, unlocks her trunk, and finds her tote full of supplies and keys. She hooks the right pair of keys and slams the trunk. She leaves the garage door open and trudges down the block.

Her sidewalk needs to be shoveled, but the next house down has been cleared. She stomps the snow from her boots on the clean stretch of sidewalk. Across the street an older man is shoveling snow. She throws her hand up in greeting. He gives her a reluctant wave, a sour curl on his lips. He judges her uncleared sidewalk, she thinks.

*Fuck off, old man.*

It only takes a few minutes to get to the house and unlock the rear door. She doesn't bother removing her shoes. She heads straight to the basement. Each step down the dark stairway, the air temperature drops a degree. At the bottom of the stairs, she tugs the chain to the pull light. She quickly walks to the locked storage cage with its shelves of abandoned items. Amid the camping gear, on top of the folding cot and under the empty cat box, she spots a black backpack.

It's unremarkable. It could be any black backpack. It looks full, packed to the point of bursting. She knows, like she's been visited by a ghost, that she is looking at Etta's missing backpack.

She takes the lock in her hand and yanks on it, as if she can pull it off with the sheer magnitude of her need to be in the cage. The lock doesn't budge. She pats her coat for her phone. She left it at the house.

"Shit, shit, shit," she says. She pounds up the steps and back up the block. She doesn't bother to lock up.

She wonders about the backpack: *How did it end up there? Has it been there this whole time?* She neither has the answers nor knows how to get them.

In her kitchen, she finds her cell phone. She uses it to call Charlie.

"Did Townes make it home?" he asks.

"No. I found something. I knew. I knew. I knew I'd seen it, but I couldn't remember. Then it came to me."

"Slow down. What is it? Do you know where Townes is?"

"No. But I found Etta's backpack."

# ULTIMATUM

Townes reaches a deep meditative state and lingers there for an unknown duration. He may have stayed there in the dark, buoyant pool of his inner sanctuary for an hour or more, if the conditions in the noisy, rancid building had been more conducive to serene contemplation. The slamming of a door, forceful enough to feel the shock through his shoulders where he rests against the bed's headboard, pulls him abruptly from his calm state. As his eyes crack open, he's immediately agitated.

There is loud talk coming from the front of the apartment. A man's voice, deep and angry, is lecturing someone. Townes assumes Army Coat has returned. There are the muffled sounds of the kids too. He fears Army Coat has arrived with another little girl. He pictures Esmeralda, but with mint-green fingernail polish, the kind his sister used to wear. His stomach churns and he burps up acid; it burns raw in his throat. The woman's voice takes a turn, making a forceful counterpoint to whatever Army Coat is saying.

"I'll be back," he retorts. "Warm me up a plate of food, will ya? Do something useful around here for once."

The door is unlocked and Army Coat looms into the space.

"So. Did you get rich while I was gone?" Army Coat asks as he enters. "I told you to get rich. I hope you tried real hard to be rich. Did you? How did it work out for you? Good?"

"No. Not good. I'm still not rich." Townes humors the man.

"Well, shit. I was afraid of something like that. I got your phone here. I know you yuppie types have your info on here. Your PayPals and your bank cards and your whole fucking life. If you can get me in your phone and dial me up say, two thousand dollars. No. Make it five. Five thousand dollars. Then I will let you go. I'll even stick you in a fucking cab and have it drop you at a Starbucks so you can spend your last six fucking dollars on a mocha-latte-chino with whipped cream and drizzles of sweet shit and sprinkles of crunchy shit."

"I don't have that kind of money." Townes shifts around on the mattress and something sharp jabs him in the thigh. He moves until it stops poking him. His hand feels numb. He worries about the blood flow. His fingers are taking on a blue tint. "I'm poor. My parents are poor. My dad is a brick mason. No work through the winter. My mom cleans houses. That's all. They have no money. I'm a deadbeat. I mooch off my parents."

"Really? What are they, Polish? All the fucking Polack women I know clean houses while their husbands work in the trades. You don't look Polish to me. But shit, it's hard to tell. Let me ask you a question: At a family reunion, how many of your people does it take to screw in a light bulb?"

"Yes. Really. Not rich. And no. Not Polish."

"I figured you'd give me a sob story. But you owe me. You robbed me. You stole my money." He pauses for a response. Townes keeps his lips pressed tightly together.

"I had a chance to think on your situation. And I came up with a solution. You lost me one girl. You help me replace her lickety-split. Sweet and simple. You see the problem is, I'm old and ugly and little kids see me and their stranger alarm goes off. So I got to thinking, you're young and not ugly. You don't look one bit threatening. You could help me get the talent I'll need to set this business off right."

Army Coat grins like a diseased mink. "I don't mind telling you, it is a big load off my mind coming up with this good plan." He flops on the end of the bed with Townes, pats Townes's foot as if it were a favorite hound dog. He looks over to his video camera, imagining all the money it will make him.

Townes looks over too. He sees an amalgam little girl that is Etta and Esmeralda, a manifestation his mind has given birth to, the implied victim of Army Coat's sick scheme. He sees her as clearly as if she were there in the room with the two of them.

Townes discards his idea of focusing on his practice, on shaping the external world from the inside out. He needs to stop this man. Not to impress Charlie or Dory, but because he is the only one who can do it. With absolute clarity, as if he'd just read the most important line in a novel, he knows how to do it. He has the right tool at his disposal.

"With your help," Army Coat is saying, "I know I can find one better than the one on the train. Don't you think?"

"I wouldn't know." Townes concentrates on implementing his plan. He might get stabbed for his effort, but he doesn't care. For his whole life, everything in his head has felt too complex, so complicated, but this is simple. A child of his conjuring needs his help. He will find a way to help. Whatever the cost. Simple. Clean. Pure.

"You could show some fucking enthusiasm, pal. A fucking *thank you, sir,* would be nice."

"Really?" Townes doesn't filter his hate.

"Yes, fucking really. What the hell, man? Did your fucking balls drop into your sack? You were in here crying like a bitch. Shit!" Army Coat reaches to his belt and slips his knife out.

"Thank you," Townes says. He realizes his mistake. Antagonizing this sociopath is a bad policy.

"Thank you, what? Goddamn it. Thank you, fucking what? I was in a good mood. You really have a way of rubbing me raw. Thank you, fucking what?" Army Coat points the knife at Townes, looks down the blade like he's lining it up to strike at Townes's right eye.

"Thank you, sir."

"Bingo. You bet your ass, *thank you, sir.*" He quits aiming the knife but doesn't put it away. "I'm a fucking realist when it comes to money. The specialty video market demands young girls. If I don't fill the need, someone else will. What should I do? Let the opportunity pass by? Hell, no. That would be bad business. I am not a bad businessman. Do I look like a bad businessman to you or a good businessman?" Army Coat straightens up and poses, juts his chin, and adjusts a pretend tie at his throat.

"You look every bit the successful businessman." Townes tells the preposterous lie convincingly.

"I do, don't I? As a man of business, I sell the thing that is in demand. You have to see that. That is just facts. I see an opportunity and I grab it with both hands." He snatches a fistful of air out in front of him to demonstrate his point.

"It's like I'm one of those technology queers, what do you call 'em? Early adapters! Or early adopters? Fuck. One of those guys who see the value in some new tech bullshit. We are on the ground floor of Google or Facebook or that one with the tweeter birds. I'm trying to make my fortune. You know some of those assholes retire at thirty and buy a sports team and an island and a robot butler? It's crazy what money will get you. You understand where I'm coming from? I have aspirations. I have a fucking five-year plan." He looks to Townes. Townes avoids his gaze but nods once.

He ticks it off with his hook finger. "To finish my original point, I will make my money off of you one way or another. I'm going to go eat. When I come back, you're going to fucking make a decision. You are going to tell me how to get money out of your family, out of your phone, or by helping me find a new sweet girl." Again his gaze shifts toward the expensive digital camera and dirty mattress.

"What if I say that won't happen? None of those things will happen."

"Well," Army Coat says in a reasonable tone. "You can ignore those options at your own risk. I'm a realist. I deal in facts, you know? If you don't come to terms with your delicate sensibilities, maybe you'll be the star of your very own snuff film. You know what that is?"

"A recording of someone being killed."

"Bingo. That's another niche market for video. Not a big one. But maybe I could recoup my losses over time.

"You'll be a star," he went on. "But only after you're dead. They got a word for that, don't they? Course they do. They got a special word for every fucking thing."

Townes despises the man, looks down on him, wants to put an end to him. Smash him like a fat fly buzzing around his favorite meal. He almost says something snarky. He wants to talk back, but he holds his tongue.

Army Coat scoots down the mattress and uses his ass to shove Townes. He sits in the crook of Townes's raised arm. He twists his neck around and talks quietly. It's clear to Townes Army Coat enjoys being in control, feels confident in his superior position. "Like I said, I'm going in the next room to eat. I'll make you a deal. I'll chew slow, to be considerate, because I pride myself on being a considerate person. I am a well-mannered motherfucker. Ask anyone. But I'll be back pretty fucking soon, and you best have made up your mind. Do you want to get out of here alive and free or dead and rolled in an area rug for the landfill?"

The door slams and locks. Townes says, "Posthumously, you ignorant asshole. The word for when something happens after a person's death is *posthumously*. You fuck. You inbred, backward, evil, degenerate, drug-addled lump. You mentally deficient pervert."

The manifestation of the little girl, Esmeralda, shuffles her boots, backing deeper into the corner. He can see she's afraid, so he stops mumbling ineffectual insults and begins the job of getting them the hell out of there.

# UNWELCOME REVERIE

Thomas successfully aims them toward a corner diner a mile or more from the bar. They order greasy food on chipped plates and drink bottomless cups of black coffee. Thomas seems tuckered out. Newton is reminded how old Thomas is, how out of the ordinary this kind of thing must be for Thomas these days. The lines in Thomas's face are deep crags in the slant light from the front window. Bags under his eyes hang loose, the weight pulling his bottom lids down and revealing a raw, red rim. His skin is dry, crusty in places, and it has a gray tint like window glazing.

Newton says, "Thomas, man, thanks so much for helping find that place. You're a standup guy. You did me a true solid. I never would have found it without you."

"You betcha." His voice grinds like metal on metal. He pitches back a bit more coffee to get some lubrication.

"You okay? You look a little green around the gills."

"I'm old. And my head is too full of ghosts. That's all. You wouldn't understand." Thomas goes back to picking at his food.

"I might," Newton says. "You ever need to talk, I can listen. I may only have one good leg but I got two good ears. With minimal permanent hearing loss."

"It's nothing, kid," Thomas says like the matter is decided, then he starts talking. "When I first moved back with Tommy, I ran around with a chubby girl from Georgia most nights. I'd leave Tommy on the neighbor's couch. Drive these streets with my hand between that girl's plump thighs. Sometimes we'd go in some bar and drink till they closed. Sometimes we'd buy a bottle and drink in the car. We'd park and screw in the back seat. It was stupid. One of us always had a seat belt buckle jabbing us in the hip." He smiles at that. Then focuses his hangdog eyes in the middle distance, his mouth turning down hard, his meaty brows spreading out across his forehead. "Some mornings I wouldn't get back home in time to get Tommy to school. The neighbor would do it for me. That neighbor was a good family woman. No one really expected much from a man raising a child on his own in those days. Everyone expected me to be out trying to find a woman to marry so she could raise little Tommy. That's just how people thought back then. I got a lot of credit just for keeping him. More credit than I deserved. No one expected me to know how to cook or clean or kiss skinned knees or any other kind of domestic thing, and because no one expected me to be capable, I never thought to try. Women in the neighborhood kind of took up the slack.

"It was like that for years. I was trying to drink and fuck enough to forget about my dead wife. Forget the war. Forget dead friends." He gives his head a sharp shake, and his skin sways on his skull. "Eventually that big Georgia girl realized I wasn't too serious about her. She took her fat sweet ass on down the road and sat it on the next fella's lap. I never blamed her much."

Newton nods and listens and sips his old coffee.

"Anyway. She left. I got my tattoo business going so I could stay in one place. Be around more for my kid. For our kid, me and Anh. I regret those years. I could have handled things better." He finishes talking, stares out the window, watches a specter of himself cruise by, scooched down low to half conceal the tipping of a bottle. Handing off the hooch to that round girl whose laugh was like cool water burbling over smooth creek stones on a hot Southern day.

Newton follows Thomas's lead and watches the street out the cracked plate-glass window. The wind off Lake Michigan is picking up. It sweeps off the wide, flat surface of the water and is rammed, squeezed, and compressed between the tall buildings downtown. Moments later it blasts into West Chicago like air through a jet engine. It's not snowing, but all the dry, dusty snow that the wind can find is curling and crawling down the center of the potholed street. It looks like a living thing, the snow, the way it whips and tumbles down the block, like twisty snakes in a wrestling match.

His mind drifts along with the snow. The week before, Newton had been drinking at some bar near his place, and the TV news had done a puff piece on a local artist who was drawing attention to poor street maintenance by filling neighborhood potholes with complex, colorful tile mosaics. Newton would be the first to admit he doesn't get art. He doesn't care about it, has no interest in learning about it. If anything, he is openly biased against the arts, but he'd found those street mosaics impressive. The colorful facets sparkling bright as cut jewels next to the salt-powdered asphalt.

On Newton's first day back in school after Etta's disappearance, he'd been sitting in a rudimentary art class. It was a graduation requirement he'd put off as long as he could. That day he'd been instructed to cut sheets of colored construction paper into triangles. The teacher, Mrs. Patel, was a much beloved Indian woman with a voice that had never completed its transition to adulthood. She had given squeaky instructions to the class with practiced enthusiasm and a rote demonstration that is characteristic of teachers nearing retirement.

The idea, as Newton understood it, was to take the little pieces he'd cut and assemble a paper mosaic of some sort. The end product was to be the likeness of any animal of his choosing. He'd been told when he raised his hand to ask, "No. I'm so sorry, Mr. Parker, but a motorcycle is not a wild animal." Mrs. Patel got a laugh from the class. Newton wasn't sure it wasn't at his expense. He was considering asking to see the school counselor, faking emotional distress to get out of the paper-cutting bullshit when Detective Ruther and two patrolmen banged on the classroom door and pulled him from class. Newton had been grateful initially as he was escorted through the deserted halls, but during the interview, conducted in the empty lunchroom, it became clear Ruther was running out of leads and thought scaring Newton, catching him off balance, might cause him to slip up, say something stupid. Perhaps Newton would spontaneously remember he had killed Etta and blurt out a full confession.

"So you and Etta are in love then?" Ruther had asked. He sat across a long lunch table with little built-in, floating, round seats. He had a pocket-sized notepad sitting out, the pages tattered from being flipped back and forth too many times.

"Yeah. I guess so. We are dating, aren't we?" Newton answered with an equal combination of candor and defensiveness. His hands, resting in his lap below the tabletop, began to clasp and twist one another.

"You were dating. She's not here to date now. Is she?"

"No," was Newton's sullen response.

"I spoke to two people that said you and a freshman named Cindy something got very friendly toward the beginning of the school year." Ruther's mustache puffed out proudly at dropping that bomb.

"So what?'

"Well, weren't you and Etta dating? Because if you were, it throws cold water on your whole mournful boyfriend act."

"Does it? Does it throw cold water? I can be in mourning even if I was running around on Etta. Can't I? You piece of fuck. Etta and I were taking some time off. We were on a break, you know. She wanted space. Cindy and I hooked up a few times. It was no big deal."

"You're kind of hot shit around here, aren't you? Some kind of wrestling jock? King shit of pimple town, huh? I saw your name in the trophy case. A bunch of times. How many times?" Ruther started the insults slowly and conversationally. The patrolman behind Ruther smirked. The one behind Newton shuffled his big, square shoes.

"I don't know how many. Several, I would say. Is that a crime?" More handwringing, Newton's voice openly snide.

Ruther ignored Newton. "I bet you're used to getting your way. The administration makes allowances for student athletes. Helps them with their grades so they can stay on the team. Maybe teachers are encouraged to waive a few assignments when the team is traveling. Overlook bad behavior. Am I right?" Ruther's mustache was drippy at the edges of his mouth, like he got it wet drinking warm soup from a bowl.

"I don't know? You tell me? You're the detective."

"Okay. Okay," Ruther said. He slapped his palms on the tabletop and leaned his foul facial hair so close Newton thought he could smell salty chicken broth. "I will tell you. I am right. I got your fucking number. I interviewed your classmates. They think you're an entitled little shit. With equal emphasis on the *little* and the *shit*."

Newton started to get red in the cheeks, his neck muscles started to flex, and his hands quieted, clenched into hard fists.

"They tell me you're the kind of kid who feels you deserve what you want. How you want it. When you want it. They say you're the kind that might just snap if someone tells you you can't have something. You are a shooting spree waiting to happen. You are a killer looking for an opportunity."

"No!" Newton said, coming to his feet, putting his face still closer to Ruther's. The patrolman behind Newton put a hand on his shoulder. Newton shrugged it off. Ruther shook his head once so the officer wouldn't interfere. Not yet.

"If Etta said she was done, you would lose it, wouldn't you?" Ruther stood too, awkwardly, his legs jammed between the table and the ridiculous seat. "You might manhandle her. Show her what's what. You deserve to get what you want, how you want it, when you say so. Right? How dare she leave you? How dare she make eyes at other boys? Smarter boys. Tall, handsome boys that will have a life after high school. Doesn't she know she belongs to you? Like a shiny, curvy, high-performance car. She is your property. You have the pink slip."

"No!" Newton planted his fists on the tabletop.

"She wanted to take a break. Get some space. And you conned her back. But she finally wised up and told you it was over for real. And you got mad."

"That didn't happen."

"You weren't going to take that from her."

"You're making shit up. That's all."

"And you took care of it. Right. You put an end to her independent ways. Permanently."

"No!"

"That's how it is for the school's wrestling hero. Right? I mean, the school might help to cover it up. I mean they help when you have bad test scores or get busted for smoking weed in the parking lot, drinking a beer under the table in the lunchroom. Right? If you got caught screwing Cindy Rottencrotch under the bleachers during gym, they would let you off with a warning. Boys will be boys. Right?" Ruther snatched up his notebook and riffled the pages, pretending he found notes to back up his claim. Tapped a page triumphantly, if fraudulently. He was pushing this kid's buttons, and it was so easy.

"NO!" Newton bellowed.

"Why not when you hurt your girl? Right? Maybe the whole world would help you get out of it if you wrung her neck like a damp dish towel."

"I SAID NO! NO! NO!" Newton pounded his fists on the table. The patrolman started pulling him back. Newton tried to climb over the table, hooked one knee on the edge. He fully intended to grab Ruther by the ears and pound the back of his skull against the hard, cold floor.

"Got quite a fucking temper there, don't you? You got enough temper for someone twice your size. Pretty hard to control too, I see." Ruther kept taking digs, hoping Newton would yell something out. The officer behind Ruther moved up, ready to intervene.

"Fuck off. Will you?" Newton stopped struggling and was pushed back onto his seat.

Ruther hadn't had anything to throw at Newton that day but wishful thinking and conjecture. No hard evidence. A weak theory with no proof, other than a working narrative and a deep dislike for Newton. Newton's alibi for the time Etta went missing had held up. Completely solid.

"I think maybe I should get back home." Thomas's voice slowly registers in Newton's brain.

"Huh?"

"I'm feeling off. You think you can take me over to the Metra stop so I can ride on back to LaGrange?" Newton's ears itch from too much blood. They must have turned bright red as he recalled Ruther's failed interrogation. He scrubs his ears and digests what Thomas has said. He can feel his usual nasty edge coming back. The feeling of peace he'd woken with washes away in a wave of hot anger. He wants to hit someone. To Thomas he says, "Yeah. Sure. No problem. You ready to go?" He starts to throw a little cash on the table.

"I'll get the meal. I feel bad about leaving," Thomas says.

"Don't worry about it, Thomas. You were a big help. I never would have found the place without you." Newton means it.

"You remember how to get back there? Right?"

"Sure."

They pay the ancient, bent woman at the register and they mosey out to the truck. They get it running and tool off to the nearest Metra stop. Newton parks and walks with Thomas up the stairs to the platform. They check the schedule, trace along the lines and columns with their eyes. Newton checks the time on his phone.

"Looks like twenty minutes to wait. I'll stick with you."

"You can go."

"I'll wait." They sit on the one bench that has all its slats intact and huddle against the strong wind.

After a few more minutes, Thomas says, "Can I call Tommy to have him pick me up?"

Newton passes over the phone. Thomas stares at it, looking for buttons. Newton pulls one glove off with his teeth. Brushes his chilly finger over the screen and brings up the phone, taps the numbers for Thomas, passes the phone back. Thomas talks to his son. When everything is settled, Newton puts the phone back in his pocket.

Newton removes his other glove and offers the pair to Cranky Thomas. The old man refuses them. "What do I look like? A sailor? I'm not a fucking puss. It's barely below freezing out here. Brisk."

Newton is happy to hear Thomas sounding normal. He slips his hands into his gloves. His fingers feel no warmer, but the gloves do cut down on the sting of the wind. He makes a fist and punches it into his cupped hand. He alternates like this for a while, feeling the sharp edge of his knuckles in his palm, feeling the blood flow in and warm him.

"Hey, soldier. You take care over there. Don't get in too much trouble trying to help your friend. He wouldn't want you to get hurt on his account. You understand me?"

"Yeah. I understand."

"And when you know what you want on that leg of yours, you come on over. I'll give you the friend price. And no one ever, fucking ever, gets the friend price."

"I will, Thomas. Thanks." Newton reaches down and smoothes his hand over the place where the new inscription floats in his skin. It's still tender, but not bad. He can live with it.

When they hear the train coming, Thomas stands on his long legs, stomps his feet to get the blood flowing. "Sometimes I wonder whatever happened to that girl from Georgia. I could use some good company like that."

"So could I. Maybe she has a much younger sister. Much, much younger. We could double-date. What was her name?"

"That's what I've been trying to remember, and I'll be fucked running if I know."

The train rolls in, the doors spring open, Thomas steps on board and doesn't look back. Newton hops down the cement steps two at a time, feeling his power leg taking his weight, feeling his heavily engineered knee do its job. He's strong and mean. He feels like his old self.

# CONFESSION IS GOOD FOR THE SOUL

Townes knows the little girl he imagines in the corner is only crossed neurons and fragmented memories coming together to keep him company, to keep him focused. His brain has conjured her to give him a message, remind him he has a tool at his disposal, something he'd overlooked. Specifically, she is a visual hallucination, a benign presence, and the best company he's had since leaving Second Story Books. He likes having her there. And besides, visualizations are easy. He can make her whatever he needs. Reality isn't nearly so pliable.

"*Hola. Soy Townes,*" he says to his new friend. He assumes this Esmeralda speaks only Spanish, like the real girl from the train. Making a game of speaking to her helps to direct his frantic thoughts. He reaches his free hand across his body to his far hip pocket and pats it. Finds what he seeks.

In his mind's eye, Pretend Esmeralda brings her smooth brows together, perplexed. He wonders if his name is confusing to her. *It certainly confuses plenty of adults.*

He tries to be calm, not to let the deep concern he has show in his face, in his voice. He draws one word out of his memory at a time, in his slow, halting, poorly enunciated, and badly constructed Spanish. "*Lo siento. Siento que te tienen miedo. Ayuda. Que te ayude.*" He thinks he's said he is sorry and wants to help.

Her eyes relax, eyes the color of Etta's; her head nods. She has a dark bob haircut that emphasizes the roundness of her cheeks and makes her head look like one big, adorable circle. Her back is in the corner, her legs curled up beneath her, her toes tapping nervously. The place where her busted buckle fell from her boot is evident.

He keeps speaking while his fingers grip the sharp shoe buckle he'd shoved in his pocket yesterday, the buckle from the little girl's boot. Her gift to him, as if a boon from above, and the key to his plan.

"Can I tell you a story? Esmeralda?" She shifts her eyes to him. "Do you speak English?"

She shakes her head and says, "No." She says it with no Spanish accent, with his sister's teen voice.

The buckle is caught on his pocket. He scoots down, makes his hip lie flat. But doing so moves him so far his fingers can't grasp the buckle.

"Okay. That's okay." He smiles as kindly as he knows how and keeps talking to his guest, to keep the panic down. "I don't speak any Spanish really. I studied it in school, but that was a while ago." He's aware of the TV down the hall, the sound of a fork knocking into a plate. He is running out of time. He breathes in. He breathes out. He contorts his body so his pocket can meet his hand, thrusts his hips up to change the angle of his pocket.

He says, "I had a sister once. Her name was Etta. She looked like you when she was young. I mean, I only know from photos. Pictures. You understand. Because she was my big sister. She had nice round cheeks. Just like you, when she was your age. And little straight bangs too."

The little girl has a wide, innocent face as she tries to make out his words. *The face of an angel.*

His fingers work into his pocket again, find the buckle, tug it out slightly. He can feel his heart rate increase. He needs to keep talking. He remembers almost confessing to Dory, almost sharing his biggest secret. That's all he can think of now. This could be his last chance to get it off his chest.

"I want to tell you something. Something I've never told anyone in the whole world. It's a secret, so keep it to yourself. Can I trust you? It's *un secreto.* Okay?"

She nods.

"Six years ago. Six years today. *Seis años.* Six years ago my big sister, Etta. *Mi hermana* Etta. Etta was taken, or she left. Or she was hurt. Whatever happened, she is gone. And the last thing I did, the last time I saw her, I might have driven her away." He's surprised by the emotion in his own voice. He's lived with the idea that Etta's absence is his responsibility for years, but he's never articulated it. The tip of his finger curls into the center of the buckle, takes a firm grip.

Esmeralda looks like she wants to hug him, in the sweet way a little child can. *"Esta bien,"* she says in his mind. *"Esta bien."*

*"Gracias."* Tears are gathering in his eyes, threatening to spill out. He feels pathetic, confessing to an empty room and weeping at pretend kindness. But not so pathetic that he wants to stop.

*"Gracias,"* he says again and goes on talking. "We went to school that day. It was a weekday. A snowy day like this. I had a bad day at school. I blamed her. I thought she made my day worse. I don't know why. Just felt that way. Sometimes, if you're not careful, your mind will run things for you, instead of you running your mind. Do you understand? And that day, my head, my emotions were in charge." He closes his eyes. His voice gets louder. The tears start to roll around his cheeks into his ears. He has to sit his ass down on the bed, his low back unable to hold the position.

"The school bus, *escolar autobus*, it stopped at our house. I got off the bus, I fumbled with my keys and marched up the steps of our front stoop. I opened the door, I stormed in, and I locked the door behind me before Etta could get inside. I heard the autobus pull away. I threw my shit on the floor next to the door. Etta started pounding on the door. She slapped it. She beat her fists against it. She kicked it. She had a key. I know she had her own key, but she was mad I'd locked the door. She was mad I hadn't left it open for her. You see? You understand?"

Little, sympathetic, imaginary Esmeralda nods that she understands. Townes throws his hip out again and yanks on the buckle, pulls it half out before it catches on the soft material of his pocket again.

"Brothers and sisters fight sometimes," he says.

She nods like she has spontaneously acquired full English fluency.

"All of Etta's banging on the door, it made me mad. It enraged me. I hadn't fought back at school. This was my sister. She was supposed to love me. She was supposed to have my back. And I thought, I don't know, really. I was angry. So she was kicking the door and I jerked it open. I stepped out and I shoved her. I was careful, sort of. I shoved her toward the side of the stoop, toward the huge drift of snow gathered around the shrubs. I didn't want to hurt her, not really. Not too much. Was careful she didn't slip down the hard steps. You understand? *Comprender?*"

She says, *"Sí, yo entiendo."* As he knew she would. He hears a plate being dropped into the kitchen sink. He's out of time. He has to finish.

He says fast, "In my mind it's pretty comical. The kind of thing we might laugh about now, if Etta were here. I opened the door and shoved her. She was all waving arms and feet in the air. She went over onto her back into the snowdrift and was swallowed. Gone. Her backpack was full of books, and once she got off balance: poof. Like a magic trick. She was out of sight for ages, then she popped up, sputtering, caked in snow like she'd been dusted with powdered sugar. Like a pissed-off beignet. She yelled, 'You little cunt. What the hell. I'm going to . . .'" He remembers he's talking to a little girl and adds, "Excuse my language."

Esmeralda seems to take no offense, so he continues, "And I slammed the door on her. I smiled. I remember how happy I was. I smiled a big, wide smile that made my mouth hurt. So proud of myself. I slammed the door. Left her to scream. Left the door locked to slow her down. And I walked up to my room, locked my bedroom, and wedged a chair under the knob, started to play video games with my headphones on. I never saw her again."

Esmeralda empathizes; he can see that in his mind.

He says, "Esmeralda. Thanks for listening. It's good to get it off my chest. And thanks for your buckle. *La bota?* Thanks for leaving it for me." With that, he gives one last yank and frees the buckle from his pocket.

"That fucking son of a bitch!" Army Coat's voice rips through the apartment, through the entire building. There is no question the comment is pitched down the hall for Townes's ears. He is the son of a bitch. He is the object of Army Coat's sudden, violent outburst. "I'll be back, asshole!" Then a door slams and rattles the cheap windows.

The children around the TV wail into the startled silence the man leaves in his wake. Esmeralda quickly crawls back to a deep corner of his mind so he can work. Townes is left alone to wonder what he could have done to Army Coat.

# A MAN ON A MISSION

Charlie listens to Meg. He says, "You go back to the house and wait with the backpack. Don't let anyone near it. Don't touch it. Take your phone. Call the real estate agent. Find out if there's a key to the cage. If there isn't, I'll open it when I get there. Okay. I'm on my way."

Meg listens. She agrees.

It takes Charlie time to rummage through the tools he keeps stacked and stored on the locked back porch. He finally finds his long bolt cutters. He runs out to his car, remembers his phone but forgets his keys. He runs back in; the front door is unlocked. He finds his keys. He gets the engine running and glances back at the house, sees he didn't close the front door. Bootsy is standing on her back paws, front paws on the glass of the storm door, yelling to come out. Charlie leaves the car running, goes back to the house, pushes Bootsy into the entry, and locks the door. He slows down enough to push the storm door until it latches. He jogs back to the car, tucks behind the wheel, and angles out of his space.

He takes his phone and calls Ruther.

"Charlie, have you heard from Townes?"

"No, but listen to this. You know how I said maybe knowing about the backpack was a development? It was at least a new piece of the puzzle?"

"Yeah. I know you said it."

"Well, Meg found the backpack. It's in a basement on the same block as our house. It's locked in a storage cage. It's been sitting there for years. Right on our own block."

"Hot damn. Is she sure?"

"Yeah. She seems pretty sure. It's there. It's there."

"Tell her not to touch it."

"She can't get to it. She's sitting with it until I can get there."

"You don't touch it either. Send me the address. I'll get a crime scene unit there as soon as I can."

Charlie agrees and hangs up. He doesn't ask about Townes. Doesn't think to ask if Ruther has heard anything about his son.

# BARSTOOL PHILOSOPHER

When Newton parks and saunters into the dim interior of the Blue-Eyed Devil, unraveling his scarf and tucking his gloves in his coat pockets, the small bar top is full. There's an ass on every stool, the TV is loud and tuned to, surprisingly, *The Queen Latifah Show*. He wedges his way between two old men hunched over their glasses, not speaking to one another, and draws a twenty-dollar bill from his wallet. He flaps it when the bartender turns his way. He gets a nod of recognition, but the bartender finishes serving his regulars before moving in Newton's direction. Newton watches Queen Latifah laugh at some story Quincy Jones has just shared. "I know that's right, I know that's right," she says.

"What can I get you?" The bartender is white with choppy hair the color of steel wool. It looks like he cut it himself with a buck knife. He's got big arms stretching against the sleeves of his black T-shirt. White letters printed across his broad chest boast: *Chicago, America's Deadliest City.*

Newton notices how dirty the place is, how the bar rag tossed on the back bar is growing black mold. He says, "I'll just take a beer in a bottle." He guesses that's safer than drinking from one of the scummy glasses.

He expects a follow-up question, but the bartender reaches down and bends the cap off a Budweiser without hesitation. Newton pays and takes his change, leaves a single as a tip. Before he walks away he sees how bright and blue the bartender's eyes are in the dark bar. He wonders if the bar is named for him, for those eyes. Thinks maybe he's the owner of the joint. He sits at an empty two-top and nurses his beer real slow, waiting for some sign of Townes or the man he described.

Newton counts seven black men past retirement age. Two younger black men huddle together, sharing stories. They twist in his direction and give him a quick assessment. Then they ignore him. Similar to the reaction Mara had given him a couple of nights before. Once in a while they laugh real loud, and a few of the gray heads turn their direction. Not annoyed, not interested, just drawn by the commotion. There are also two younger Hispanic men with their heads together, shooting the shit in Spanish. Everyone still has their coats on, but most are unbuttoned, and there are lumps of gloves and scarves pitched upon the bar top every few feet. A red stocking cap is on the ground behind one of the old black men.

Newton starts to shuck his coat off, toss it back over the chair. It feels good to be out of the wind. It's by no means warm in the place; as a matter of fact, the bar feels and smells like the only heat is radiating off of unwashed bodies. He decides to keep his coat on, keep all his possessions under his close control. It's safer that way. When his beer is gone, he checks his phone. No reply from Townes. No messages at all. He punches up the image of the exterior of the bar he now sits in and rereads the message:

I got in a fight on the train. Not a fight exactly. But we kind of tussled. There was this oily guy in an army coat trying to snatch a little girl. I tried to stop him. He got off the train. I followed him here. It's a long story. I've got to keep an eye on him. Make sure he doesn't do it again. I'm scared. I don't know what I was thinking. You know about fighting, right? Call me.

The picture was taken at night. He reads the time at the top of his phone's screen and does the math. *Almost fourteen hours since Newton took that fucking picture.*

He leaves his empty beer bottle to hold his place and takes a leak in the tiny bathroom. It's about as filthy as he would have expected, but it smells worse. When he goes to wash his hands, he finds that only the cold water tap will turn and the sink is pulling away from the wall dangerously. A quick inspection reveals it's being held in place only by a brittle iron drainpipe and two skinny water pipes, not secured to the wall at all. He dries his hands on the front of his coat. When he's done, he peeks out the front window and down the block at his truck, sees the mouth of the alley across the street, and guesses it's where Townes stood to take the image.

Back at the bar, he grabs up the old man's red stocking cap and hands it to him.

"Dropped your hat," he says.

"Mmm. Thank ya," the old man replies. He rolls the cap over his head and goes back to staring at the foam in his glass.

Newton pays for a second beer, sits back at the table, and dials up Townes. The phone rings several times, then goes to voicemail. Townes's voice sounds calm, confident, and mature. When the beep comes he says, "Yeah, man. This is Newton. I got your message. I came looking for you. Your mom is worried. You missed the memorial. Don't worry though. Me and your dad missed it too. I guess it'll have to be rescheduled. Your mom was pissed though. I'm at the bar now. The one you sent me. The Blue-Eyed Devil. I'll hang for a little longer. Call me."

Newton sips his beer and watches the people in the bar. There's no one with an army coat. No one he would describe as oily. Though no one he would describe as not oily either.

Queen Latifah says, "We have a surprise. Your talented daughter wanted to drop by and say hello. Rashida Jones." The actress walks out. The camera pans the audience reaction. The whole crowd hops up, except a couple of big black ladies who refuse to be pressured. They keep their seats and clap with their hands held over their heads. When the camera points back at Queen Latifah, she repeats, "Rashida Jones!"

The couple of younger black men stop talking and watch the father and daughter reunion on the screen. One of the black guys says, "Damn!" The other one bumps his fist in agreement. They laugh real loud. They slide off their stools and button up, put on caps, stuff hands into gloves as they pass Newton's table. Newton feels his adrenals spit a little juice into his blood as the young men separate, each passing on a different side of his table, on either side of his body, brushing his shoulders, pinning him in, if only for a moment. Then they move into the comparatively pure white light of the snow-covered neighborhood.

He can't imagine Townes walking into this place, especially at night, when the crowd would tip younger and louder. When the unemployed men who pass their summer days standing on breezy corners, defending their territory, trolling their blocks, or lounging on their stoops might make this kind of place their hangout for the long winter. Then again, the Townes he knew in high school is long gone, grown, changed. Maybe he doesn't know Townes at all. *Hell, I'm not the same person I was a week ago.*

He has to admit the place makes him nervous, and he came here half looking for a fight. He's shot people dead for his country, been shot at a dozen times, walked up on known insurgents, kicked in doors to rooms he knew were full of armed men, *lost my goddamned leg for the love of Christmas.* Maybe because of his accumulated experience he knows this is a neighborhood where a fistfight can turn into a stabbing or a bullet in the back. He knows you don't start something in this kind of bar unless you're prepared for it to go all the way. If you get stabbed or shot out here, the cops and the ambulance aren't likely to get to you before you bleed out. That's the kind of place it is.

It's the kind of place Albert might have fit in. Albert was so big few people would start anything, and he was so easygoing, funny, and warm, no one would have a reason to. He misses his friend, misses things about that other life across the globe. Distant now. Almost like he saw it unfold on a flat screen mounted over some bar, rather than lived it every day. His phantom limb throbs with pain he can't fix, as if to verify his past.

Newton slams his second beer and belches. He's sick of waiting. He peels the paper labels from the brown glass. He checks his phone a few times. He calls the home number for Etta. Meg's recorded voice barely worries him this time. He says, "After I left, I got a note from Townes. I knew you were upset so I tried to follow up on it. I'll forward it to this other number for the house-cleaning deal. Okay? I'm at the bar in the photo now. I guess I'm going to ask around about Townes." He hangs up the phone feeling like he's made a big mistake. *This whole thing is a wild goose chase.* He's sick of it. Sorry he got dragged into it. He listens to Meg again, repeats the cell number in his head until he can dial it. He forwards the image of the bar and the message from Townes to Meg's cell phone.

He checks the bars on his phone that indicate Internet service; he has a strong signal. He searches on the name of the bar. The first entry is about a drive-by shooting that took place in the fall, on the sidewalk outside the front doors. Three young black men shot by unknown assailants. It isn't an article. Not like the kind of lengthy pieces written about Etta. A couple of factual sentences. More dead black boys. More black-on-black crime in a neighborhood known for that kind of thing. No big deal. No news there. They may have never printed it except they had a snapshot to go with it, rusty-red blood spray across an unswept sidewalk littered with brittle fall leaves and curls of busted brown glass. He wonders if his white leg was given more attention than Albert's whole brown body after the explosion. If they had a good photo of his mangled leg, with smoking wreckage of a Humvee in the background, would he have made the news back home? He knows he wouldn't have. People didn't want to know about the wounded or the dead. It interfered with binge-watching *Breaking Bad.*

There are no other search entries that list the bar. No ads. No reviews. No descriptions on local business sites, food sites, bar sites.

No ratings. Just a shooting out front. That's how this place is best known. That is the totality of the Blue-Eyed Devil's web presence.

Mara and her tight sweatshirt come to mind. He imagines her sitting here, across from him. He bets she would be nervous in a spot like this. He bets she's never been to this part of the city, never seen a neighborhood like this. She might not realize these kinds of places exist just miles from where she goes dancing with her drunk friends. She's uncomfortable being here. She scoots her chair around the table to be closer to him, he puts an arm around her shoulder, and she snuggles in, feeling safe. She saw him beat the living hell out of those big frat boys. She knows he can handle himself. She may have acted unimpressed, but now, in this place, she can appreciate the kind of man he is.

Again he wonders at his fixation on Mara. He doesn't know her. Doesn't know how she grew up, what she knows, how she feels, what she thinks. She's just some cute thing to project his fantasies onto. Dreams of being loved, being wanted. Loved like Etta used to love him. That's all it is, nothing more.

Newton shuts his phone down, stuffs it in his pocket. *I'm done with this fucking bullshit.* He steps to the spot the young men had vacated a few minutes before. The bartender is busy chatting it up with one of the young Mexicans. They are talking about sports, debating the benefit-cost ratio of the Bears' quarterback. Newton settles onto one of the stools to wait. It takes a long time, and Newton is tired of sitting; he's about to leave when the bartender walks his way with another open beer in his hand. Newton shakes his head, starts to say he's looking for a friend. Before the words form, an oily white guy in an army coat takes the stool next to Newton.

The bartender sets the beer in front of the new arrival. The two exchange chin nods.

"You want another one?" The bartender directs the question to Newton. Newton looks at the oily guy, sees him flash his dull teeth, at once a grin and a challenge. Newton knows this guy thinks he's the toughest man Newton has ever seen, an apex predator among the sheep.

In fairness, Newton has rarely fought anyone particularly formidable, maybe never. The guy keeps his eyes on Newton, his mouth working like he's hiding a secret in the back of one of his rotten teeth, rolling it around with his tongue until he's ready to spit it out. The guy has a sly, dangerous vibe that makes Newton nervous. Newton likes that. It appeals to his recklessness.

Newton smiles his own smile right back and says, "Yeah. What the fuck. I'll have another one. I'm just getting started."

The bartender does his trick of materializing a beer from thin air, bends back the cap, and lifts it off the bottle's mouth before placing the beer in front of Newton. Newton takes a long pull, sets the bottle down, and waits for things to develop.

"Hey, bring me some of those bar snacks will you?" the Oily One calls at the bartender's back. Then to Newton, "I never seen you here before." His eyes turn up toward the TV set. The cast light from the screen shifts to a bright commercial for a new Muppet movie, and the Oily One's upturned face is bathed in golden light, his expression rapt, as if in a moment of religious ecstasy.

"I'm supposed to pick up my truck from the body shop around the way," Newton improvises. It's like a chess game, he thinks. The Oily One is up to something. He knows something. Is trying to get a read on Newton. Newton has countermoved nicely. They sit while the Oily One contemplates his next move, his mouth hanging open as he gawks at a series of commercials.

"I see," he says. "So you live nearby, I guess?" he asks when the broadcast switches back to the talk-show format.

"No. No. Not these days." Newton deflects the question. The bartender returns with a Solo cup full of skinny stick pretzels. The other guy reaches for the cup and pulls the whole thing over, starts snapping the pretzels in half and tossing them in his mouth. Newton catches a glimpse of something around the guy's wrist as he nabs a second handful of pretzels: a bracelet of red-lacquered beads, little black characters stamped into each bead, tied on a thin gold rope with a tassel. A smaller version of the one Newton had spotted in Townes's room. Newton tries not to get caught staring, but now he knows deep in his bones: Townes is in trouble.

"Can I have a few of those?" Newton nods at the pretzels.

"Free country."

Newton takes a few pretzels. He eats them one at a time. They taste stale, damp, and coppery, as if they had been stored in an open container in a refrigerator. But the beer does a good job of clearing the taste from his mouth. While he eats, he thinks about the coincidence of this guy sliding up next to him. He wonders if the bartender gave him a call, but he doesn't think that's it. That's not the answer to the puzzle.

The Oily One lowers his voice but doesn't seem overly concerned that people might hear. He's taking a new approach at feeling Newton out. He turns his legs Newton's direction and splays them out so Newton is sitting between his knees. The Oily One's crotch shoves uncomfortably close. He leans into Newton's space. "This neighborhood isn't too safe for the white man these days. You make yourself a target just sitting here. When we Europeans immigrated to this country, we were industrious and hard-working. Not like these blacks and browns. They don't have a culture of work. They take siestas. You know what a siesta is?"

Newton knows what a siesta is, but he wants to keep the Oily One talking until he knows the score, so he gives his head a negative shake.

"Siesta means they take a nap every fucking day after they eat lunch. Can you imagine? We'd still be living in caves and eating bark if whites believed in taking naps instead of working. The Industrial

Revolution would never have happened if *we* thought like *them*."
He nods his head down the bar at the nonwhite men. He eyeballs
the side of Newton's face when Newton shoots his eyes down the
bar. The old man in the red stocking cap looks back at him, his
expression neutral.

"I see." Newton leans a little away from the other man. "You're
right. You make a lot of sense. I never heard it put that way, but
when you line it all up like that, it makes so much sense."

"Bingo. When our people traveled from Europe, they made
something of themselves. They built a fucking country. These ones,
they come in illegally, breed like rats, take all the jobs, then don't
do good work. It undermines our reputation as the greatest nation
in the world. You ever hear of American Exceptionalism?" Now the
Oily One is getting into it, forgetting what game they are playing.

"No. Tell me," Newton encourages him.

"It means America is special. A special country, by God. It used
to be true. No one would ever argue that it wasn't true. But now
we are getting watered down with browns and blacks. And some
of them other kinds. The tiger moms with their precious mathletes
and their little violin prodigies. All kinds of towel heads. And those
Muslim women are the worst of all. Oh my God, those women
aren't allowed to drive in their own countries. They come here, get
a license and a big SUV, and they nearly kill someone every time
they get on the road. I went a month last year when every fucking
time I was on the road some Muslim woman stopped short in front
of me, cut me off, ran a stoplight, or made some traffic violation."
He grabs Newton's sleeve to make sure he's listening, his voice
getting loud and agitated. "I saw this Muslim woman with a car
packed full of baby Muslims run right through a busy intersection
when she had a red light. She hit three cars. When the cops came,
she swore it was someone else's fault. I almost stuck around as a
witness but I had places to be." He yanks Newton's sleeve some

more. "Muslim women have come here to kill us, one car wreck at a time. It's a coordinated conspiracy to undermine our social fabric. Yoga! Fucking yoga is part of the conspiracy. I finally had to sell my car. I think I was on a Muslim hit list. You can say it's crazy. But I'm convinced. I've seen behind the curtain."

He pauses to eat more pretzels and watch more commercials. Newton takes the opportunity to shove his stool back a bit, buy a bit of space. When Queen Latifah brings out her new guest, the Oily One turns back to Newton.

"What was I saying? Anyway. The point is the more of them, the less exceptional we become. It is a proven fact. You know we will be the minority in our own country soon?" He reaches out and pokes Newton's shoulder for emphasis. Newton doesn't stop him. But he wants to. Wants to aim a knuckle at the asshole's temple and knock him clean out.

Instead he says, "You are shitting me." He doesn't bother to put any melodrama into it. There is no need. The Oily One is on a roll.

"I'm not. I'm not shitting you. Not at all. And it's not long. A few years. A few years and there will be more of *them* kind than *us* kind. Did you know Chicago is nearly a third full of Mexicans?"

"I didn't know."

"Besides, you know Black Obama has opened the fucking borders and just let a flood of those mud people come up all the way from Central America. I saw it right here on this TV. Lots of kids. Lots of teen girls. Shit. If you think about it, with half the whites being feminazis and refusing to make babies and half the white men being fairies. Shit. Straight white men, the kind of men that built the whole damn planet, men who invented the airplane and landed on the moon, men like us, we are an endangered species."

"I think you're right."

"Bingo. I'm right. You bet your ass I'm right. You go fifteen minutes from here and every other white man you see is a butthole maniac, can't wait to poke you right in the ass. They are ruining the whole country. Too many queers means not enough pregnant white women. That's why they're outpacing us now. It's a national tragedy."

"It is. I couldn't agree more." This time the other guy seems to hear the derisive tone in Newton's voice. He swigs his beer and sets it down hard; foam shoots out the mouth and runs in a frothy sheet down the side of the bottle.

"You aren't one of the gay boys are you? Where do you live? Huh? You never said. You aren't from Boystown are you? Maybe Andersonville? You ever hang out at a place called the Closet or Little Jimmy's? Huh? You ever march shirtless in the Pride Parade wearing nothing but a rainbow-striped Speedo? And why call it a Pride Parade? What are they so fucking proud of? That they are degenerates?" He's yelling now, really angry about the mainstreaming of homosexuality. The old faces along the bar turn his way, not shy about being seen but careful not to get involved. "Did you know you can fall in gay love and gay marry in half the states in the country now? I bet you knew. I bet you like a nice hard cock, don't you? Really gets you excited." The guy examines Newton's reaction closely, tries to read his expression, find a confession there, an admission of gay guilt, but Newton doesn't give him what he's looking for.

"Who? Me? Are you kidding?" Newton doesn't like having the tables turned on him. This strategy of accusing others of being gay is something he'd done since grade school. Whenever he wanted to fight, he knew he could use it to agitate someone. He'd seen it used a hundred times in the military, especially by the older drill sergeants during basic training. It was a tried-and-true technique, and he had never realized how ugly it was. No wonder he wasn't popular in that bar the other night, the way he was throwing around the homophobic craziness. No wonder Mara wouldn't warm up to him. He added it to his list of things he should never do again.

"Well, good." The Oily One drinks his beer down, hoists it toward a trashcan behind the bar; it clatters in on top of other bottles already there. The bartender looks his way and gives a nod. The Oily One wipes his damp hand on the front of his army coat and nods to the bartender.

"See that one? The bartender. I come here because he's the only white business owner for a mile in any direction."

"He seems real nice."

"He's an asshole. But he's a white asshole. And that is why you need to get out of here before dark. It's all right during the day, but at night you need to be gone. These young blacks around here will shoot you and take anything you have worth taking. Then they'll shoot each other to decide who gets to sell it. The Mexicans will steal your car and have it stripped before you know it's gone. They'll rent it out like an apartment and let all their fucking cousins move in. They will take a good sharp knife and slash your throat from behind." He looks at Newton with a predatory gleam.

"I appreciate the advice. I do. Thanks. I plan on being long gone as soon as business is taken care of."

"You mean business with your car? Right?"

"Yes. My truck."

The bartender sets down a new beer for the Oily One. He doesn't ask if Newton needs one. Newton wants to get out of here as soon as he can, can feel things are coming to a head. He's lingered enough but he needs to figure out how to find Townes.

The two of them turn back to the bar and drink. On the screen over their heads, Queen Latifah mentions the guests who will appear on her next show. She thanks Quincy Jones, Rashida Jones, and the author of a gluten-free cookbook.

"You come here a lot then?" Newton asks.

"Hmm. Daily, I'd say. My place is right up the block and it's full of screaming babies and Spanish babble. I can't stand my fucking wife."

"Your wife is Spanish?"

"No. Not Spanish. Mexican. White women don't know how to treat a man like a man. You know that. You've banged white women, haven't you? Besides, just because I'm racist doesn't mean my dick is. My dick is an equal opportunity employer." He flashes his rotten teeth at his own joke.

"Good one," Newton says with a fake chuckle. "And you two have a lot of kids?"

"I got twin boys. Otto and Pablo." Newton notes the strange juxtaposition, the German name more bizarre next to the Mexican one. He fears he and this lunatic share common ancestry. "They are snot-nosed toddlers now. Plus two nieces my wife watches."

"Really? Kind of a daycare?"

"Yeah. Daycare. Kind of like that. It's money." He grins again, real sly, as he brings the beer's mouth to meet his lips.

Newton thinks about the claims Townes had made. That he jumped this guy on the train. That the guy had been trying to take a little girl. Newton wouldn't put it past Oily One. Not at all. The Oily One has an evil air around him. Newton sees for the first time that Oily One has a cut on his head.

"You say you live right up the block?"

"Mmmm. Yeah. Right up the block." He abruptly moves and Newton's hands come up to protect his head, but the Oily One just slips off the back of his stool and puts his hand out to shake.

"I'm Walker," he says. He clamps hard on Newton's hand and pumps it up and down twice. Then, before Newton can ask, he says, "Just Walker," and pumps his hand again.

"What's your name?" Walker asks.

"I'm Thomas," Newton improvises.

Walker cocks his head like he heard something he wasn't expecting, is about to speak. Draws a breath and holds it. He doesn't speak. He releases Newton and glides lazily back toward the restroom. When he turns, his coat swings open and Newton can see a skinning knife in a rugged sheath mounted on his belt. Down the little hall, Walker pats his big storage pockets on his army surplus coat. Then he disappears into the bathroom.

It punches Newton in the side of the head: *The message he left for Townes. The one he just left half an hour ago.* That's what brought Walker into the bar. Walker has Townes's phone, listened to the message, came right down to check out the situation. Newton had left his real name in the message. Walker knows who he is and knows he's a liar. Newton is certain of it.

Newton takes out his phone and scrolls his recent calls, taps on Townes's number as he edges down the hall to the bathroom door. He hears a phone ring. It makes a chime sound like the alarm he'd heard in Townes's room. On the other end of the line, someone answers and listens, doesn't speak. There's the sound of breathing and sucking teeth, like Walker put the whole phone in his rancid mouth.

Newton knows in his bones that if he stays put, if he tries to play this game any longer, keeps leaning on the bar and trying to be chummy with this psycho, it will come back to bite him. He'll end up with that knife in him, dumped down some back alley.

He's got to get out now. He fast-walks back to his stool and shuts down the phone. He pitches money on the bar and heads out. The bartender ignores him, but the man in the stocking cap nods his farewell.

Newton loops his scarf around his neck and buttons up as he pushes out the door. He slips on his gloves and jogs over to his truck. He pats his pockets for his keys and can't find them. He pats his pockets more, turns back toward the bar. Before he can get too concerned, he realizes he has the keys clutched in his hand. He gets the engine running and pulls down the block as fast as the cold truck will move. When he's gone a couple of blocks, he whips the truck around, has to hop it up on the curb to get the big old beast to complete the turn. He parks a safe distance back from the door to the Blue-Eyed Devil and waits for that shifty bastard to come out so he can follow him home.

# A VIOLENT CONVERGENCE

Newton doesn't have to wait long. Walker bursts out of the Blue-Eyed Devil, turns his drab-green back to Newton, and shuffles away. His walk, the lazy way he scuffs the toes of his boots with each step, is an embarrassment to the ragtag military ensemble he wears. It offends Newton as someone who was forced to march in an organized way, in time to the soldiers at his front and at his back. Proper marching is a choreographed event, meant to efficiently move large numbers of troops safely.

Newton hears the echo of his drill instructor in his own thoughts. Sergeant Turner believed, with every patriotic fiber of his gung-ho being, that proper marching was the key to victory in any military engagement. "War is won on your feet and on your stomachs," yelled directly at the side of Newton's head, was an example of the motivational speeches Turner liked to deliver to his men. Newton never liked the sergeant. The feeling seemed mutual. As a result, Newton was a regular target of the sergeant's forceful lambasting.

Sometimes Newton had become so enraged he'd seriously considered hooking a noose over Sergeant Turner's head, cinching it down quickly, and watching him thrash until all the kick was wrung out of his body. Albert and he had discussed the fantasy quietly, to cheer one another up, but the sergeant was scary, and Newton never dreamed he could get away with it. Maybe never really meant it. Not a hundred percent anyway.

Sergeant Turner had had a raw scar running from the corner of his mouth in a red swell down beside his chin. There was constant speculation about the wound. Many recruits believed it was shrapnel from an IED. Newton liked to think the sergeant, dressed in only red, white, and blue boxer shorts on a hot summer day, had tried to use a chainsaw to carve a stump into the shape of an American eagle. The chainsaw had kicked back, gouging a deep line in his face and leaving his left profile looking like a marionette with a clap-jaw mouth. For Newton, that scenario had the absurd ring of truth.

Sitting in the cold cab of his old truck, the truck that had been his father's, watching his white breath come out in ragged puffs, he can hear Albert's quiet laugh at his back. It was a sound Newton could always depend on, on those days of long marches and later, when they were deployed together.

Drill Sergeant Turner's face would materialize next to Newton's ear and bellow, "You march like a hooker with a busted high heel and a case of gonorrhea. Straighten that shit up, soldier. You hear me? Pick up your fucking feet." Then he'd be gone, jogging up and down the line, barking ridiculous insults at volume, all while carrying a full pack and barely breaking a sweat. Newton could barely catch his breath to keep moving. He had to grudgingly admit, the boxy tyrant was an impressive physical specimen.

From behind him, Albert's low laugh would tumble out, and he'd say, "That is one mean puppet-looking motherfucker." And just like that, Newton would let his anger go. Albert always put things in perspective.

In the end, when Newton graduated from boot camp and gave his snappiest farewell salute to the sergeant, he felt the respect the gesture implied. He and Albert both agreed they were glad they hadn't murdered Sergeant Turner. It was a comforting thought, to know he was out there. It was even more gratifying to think he was chewing some new recruit's ass while they were free and clear of him.

Now, Walker crosses the intersection, angling off to the west, his black boots kicking chunks of polluted snow ahead him. Newton works the shifter on the steering column until it pops into first gear and lets the clutch off softly, easing into the street. He rolls slowly up the block. The mirrors show him he's the only one on the road.

When he gets to the corner, he turns the direction Walker went. It's a narrow street, cars along both sides, barely room for the wide-bodied, blunt-faced old Econoline. With the application of some focus and skill, edging the truck around the jutting bumpers of poorly parked cars, he finds a way to keep moving through. There's no Walker in sight.

When he reaches the first alley, he stops and peers first one way, then the other. He still can't see Walker, but in one direction he finds a trail of black snow hunks cast about the alley among the dumpsters and disemboweled trash bags, as if someone destructive just kicked his way through. He can also spot fresh boot prints punched into the softer, virginal white drifts created by spiraling wind gusts.

He parks the truck in the first spot he can find, three blocks away. He takes just enough time to be sure the truck doors lock. He turns and moves fast on his fake leg, falling into a productive gait, a military double-time march. He takes the corner down the alley and breaks into a full run, scanning for Walker. Finding no obvious sign of him, he sweeps the alley floor with his eyes. It's easy enough to follow Walker's trail to the back door of a tall brick building. The boot prints lead up a set of back stairs to a dilapidated wooden porch that stands on long, half-rotten, scabbed-together two-by-four legs. Clearly not pressure-treated lumber, clearly not up to code, and precariously jammed into the soft earth, no footings visible. *It's a deathtrap.* Unfortunately, it hadn't collapsed as Walker pounded up it.

• • •

Townes hears Army Coat stomping up the back stairs. His big, clumsy feet bang into the storm door. Glass breaks on the back deck, the lock on the back door clicks, and the door slams open hard enough to drive the knob into the cracking plaster. The lock snaps closed again. By the time Army Coat unclasps the latch and enters the bedroom, Townes has concealed Esmeralda's boot buckle in his closed fist and pulled his legs up until his body is a tight ball curled against the headboard.

"Who is Newton? Huh?" Army Coat barges in and holds Townes's phone, aims the blank screen toward Townes's face. "You sent him a fucking text? You brought him here. Looking for you. Looking for me. What did you tell him? Did you call him?" He rushes at Townes, pushes the phone's screen against his forehead and mashes it into the tender cartilage of his nose. Townes is too startled to speak. He makes an animal yip and scrunches down, trying to hide his head like a turtle.

"You're going to tell me, or you're gonna eat this phone." Army Coat grabs Townes's face, his strong fingers smelling of beer and urine, and uses them to force Townes's jaw open. The bitter corner of the phone knocks hard into Townes's front teeth. Townes opens wider, without any intention. The phone moves between his teeth, ramming into his mouth, forcing his tongue back, filling the entire void. Townes shakes his head, pulls away from the violent insertion. Drool runs out of the edges of his mouth. Army Coat pinches his nose so he can't breathe. Townes's eyes stream tears. He tries to yell some reply but can't move his mouth or move his tongue, can't find his breath. He gags reflexively; his throat clenches for another try.

"You like that? You like the way it tastes?" Army Coat jabs the phone in deeper before jerking it away. He walks out of the room, slamming the door behind him and not stopping to latch it. He screams as he stomps away, "I'll be back. You better be ready to talk. Or you're dead. I don't care about the money. You're dead."

Townes hacks loudly, deep, shuddering clucks that make his sides ache. He's trying to suck air into his lungs as bile and half-digested *huevos rancheros* rise up to shoot out his mouth. He leans forward, aiming most of it at the floor next to the bed. He spits the taste from his mouth, pinches the burn of spicy salsa and stomach acid from his nostrils. He settles back into a position that will allow him to finish cutting his bonds, marinating in the smell of his own sickness.

He remembers his practice. He breathes. He calms his heart; he tries to slow his mind and think clearly. Think of one thing at a time. Not what may come in the future. Not his mistakes of the past. Just right now. That is all anyone can really control.

Once he feels relatively calm, he thinks of Esmeralda, of Etta, and of all the other incarnations of little girls that are in danger as long as Army Coat is walking around free.

"It'll be okay. Um. It'll be good. Um. *Va estar bien.*" The phrase comes to him. He isn't sure it's right, probably the wrong form of the verb, poor conjugation. *"Va a estar bien,"* he says a little more competently. He says it to himself as much as for Esmeralda's benefit. But the Spanish phrase coaxes her forward in his consciousness.

The buckle has cut a groove into his palm, and it's painful to release. He's careful as he maneuvers it into position. He begins an infinitesimal sawing motion. He can hear Army Coat talking at his wife in harsh English, hear her replying in harsh Spanish. He can also hear children crying. After a long exchange, the house quiets down. A dog barks next door, maybe stirred by the commotion.

His bindings are nearly cut through. If he had to, he could yank his wrist hard enough to break the clothesline. He could dash to the back window, try to use the space heater to shatter the panes, bust the skinny cross-pieces from the lower sash, crawl through fast, and run down the steps. But he won't. That way is too risky. And he knows he'll only get one shot.

The buckle's sharp edge snaps the last of the wire center. He feels the pluck of it strum through the buckle. His body starts with excitement. The buckle slips from his cramping fingers and falls to the bed next to his thigh. He hears Army Coat call from the front of the apartment.

"Here I come. You best be ready."

*Hide the evidence. Don't get caught. Not yet.* Townes bounces on the mattress, shifting his weight until the buckle is hidden by his leg. The motion causes the remaining green rubberized coating on the clothesline to pop, his wrist coming free. Townes sits loose on the bed; his hands fall into his lap. His captor is beginning the short stomp down the hall. Townes remembers the knife, knows when Army Coat reaches the room and finds him like this, the knife will come out and find a place tucked neatly between Townes's ribs.

• • •

Newton knows some things. For instance, when entering a hostile urban structure, it's important to gather as much intelligence as possible. It's vital to have backup. It is preferable to have superior firepower evident as you enter the premises. Newton has no firepower and no backup. He lets himself hear Albert's laugh at his back, thinks of how he didn't have the chance to save Albert, to say goodbye. He misses Cranky Thomas's ill-tempered commentary. His cantankerous presence would give Newton steel in his spine, and his advice made of equal parts wise and wiseass might make Newton's next move clear. *I hope he made it home safely.* With neither of his running buddies to watch his six, the least he can do is take a look around before blundering in. Maybe let someone know where he is, in case things turn ugly.

At the top of the rickety back staircase to Walker's place, a broken storm door stands open. Jagged angles of glass cling to the bent frame like clear shark's teeth. Beyond it is a solid wooden door, filthy and perhaps getting wood rot along the bottom gap. A new deadbolt stands out against the door, like a polished stone in a puddle of mud. The longer he stares, the less he likes the look of the back entrance.

He walks over to a pile of brick fragments, dumped loose in the backyard, maybe the remains of an old garage floor or chimney stack that tumbled over and was only half-cleared. He picks up one of the smaller chunks, just to have something in his hand. A short span of chest-high cyclone fence separates the front yard from the back. He grips the top and throws his body up and over, landing with his biological knee and his manmade knee working in perfect concert.

Newton hears a dog bark, maybe inside the house, maybe from next door. He puts his body near the wall to make it harder for anyone peeking out the upper windows to spot him. The dog stops barking. He moves into the front yard, out onto the sidewalk, and across the ankle-deep snow still covering the residential street.

He sets his chunk of brick on the roof of a car directly across from Walker's front door. That's the place to go in, a frontal assault. He needs a way to get the door open. He pulls his phone from his pocket and zooms in on the building's address. He snaps a picture and texts it to Meg. He takes another image of the whole house, listens to the swooshing sound that indicates the digital bits are on their way. He aims his camera down the street to the corner, where he sees a pole for a street sign. The sign is ripped off. He zooms in on it, takes that picture and sends it too. Then he taps a message: *Followed a guy named Walker from the bar to this place. He had Townes's phone and bracelet. I think Townes is here. I'm about to find out.* He sends it. He drops his phone in one pocket and palms his hunk of crumbling old brick.

He goes through a quick checklist: He scoped the place out and decided on a point of entry; he found a weapon; he sort of called for backup.

He pats his pockets, pulls his wallet, and removes the cash and ID. He stuffs his valuables into an inside breast pocket and zips it closed. He smacks the closed wallet against his gloved hand. He's nervous.

"Nothing to do but to do it," Albert says to him.

"I've got a bad feeling about this. I might not walk out of this one."

"Do the odds get better if you put it off?"

"No. But maybe this Walker will relax a bit. I don't know. Based on his teeth, he probably spent a little time smoking crack. Maybe he'll get high if I give him a minute."

"That's some wishful thinking," Albert says with a good-natured chuckle. It makes Newton feel a little more relaxed.

"Wish you were going in with me. This greasy guy may be too much for me."

"I wish that too," says Albert. "There's always the kid, Townes. He'll help if he can."

"I don't see it happening. I'll be going solo," Newton says. "Well, I'm going to walk around the block one time. Take a long look at the place from all angles. You know, gather more intelligence. Then I'll pull the trigger."

Albert laughs again. "You might as well gather all the intelligence you can. You usually run below average."

Newton has to laugh at that, because it's true. He appreciates the pep talk from Albert. Is glad to have him around. He does as he told Albert he would, begins to move around the block, trying to look casual, just someone trudging through the winter, hunched against the oppressive cold.

As he moves past Walker's house, he sees it's a two-flat with one front door: a main floor residence with black iron bars over the windows and the second floor place where Walker entered from the back. Newton can see two buzzers next to two mailboxes.

He thinks about Etta. He wishes she would visit him, take a circuit around the block with him, dodge the upturned edges of sidewalk, and hold his hand. Maybe they could stop to kiss now and then. *If she were here now, what would she say?* He tries to imagine but has no luck, can't make his head form the words.

He realizes that Cranky Thomas gave him contradictory advice: *Don't get lost in your own head; instead, deal with reality.* And: *It's important to live with the memory of those you've lost, spend time with them to honor them, as if they were still with you.* It would be easy to dismiss Thomas as a foolish old man for preaching his opposing views, views that practically cancel each other out. Instead he thinks the advice was smart and true. Not only that, he feels to go on living while having conflicting beliefs might be the very best definition of living. Messy. But true. *Or maybe I'm just scared and tipsy.* The thought of those beers makes him realize his bladder is full.

He crunches through the snow and around the corner. The alley looks different from this end of the block. The potholes are filled with asphalt patch; the dumpsters are rolled into their spots; no random garbage bags are thrown around; no dirty diapers are tumbled onto the ground for the rats to eat. It looks like someone ran a snowplow, removing the worst of the accumulation. He guesses this neighborhood is like many neighborhoods: a mix of good, hard-working people and others less good.

He passes the back of Walker's house. The back room on the second floor has a window completely covered with newspaper. He checks the other windows. They sport old, crumpled venetian blinds. *The room at the back. That's where Townes will be. If he's there at all.*

"Only one way to know," says Albert.

"Only one way to know," agrees Newton.

Newton finds a spot to pee. A sharp wind cuts through the street, lifts a light skiff of snow from the roof of Walker's home into the air. It spreads in the sky like the contents of a cremation tossed from a cliff to scatter on a sea breeze. Newton watches the hard, crystalline dust turning and catching light until it falls into the shadows. He tucks himself away and keeps moving.

When he gets to the street he had driven down a few minutes earlier, he watches a rusted and dented seventies-era Ford Gran Torino painted to look like the one from *Starsky & Hutch* slowly navigate up the block. He steps into the street to watch it creep safely past his truck, leaving a cloud of heavy fumes in its wake.

He turns two more corners and picks up the pace. His legs stride out like they were made to work together, efficient and smooth, strong, balanced, sleek, and unstoppable. He glides down the unshoveled path to Walker's building. He sees the names on the mailboxes. One reads, *Garcia*. The other is just marked with a numeral 2 in red marker. It's an ugly mark like a fresh gash, and Newton sees Walker's hand in it.

"Here goes nothing," he says to Albert. Albert laughs his laugh.

• • •

Meg is standing in the basement, facing the storage cage. Looking at the backpack that had once belonged to Newton. The backpack Etta had worn the last time anyone saw her walking the earth. Her phone blips in her hand. She sees a text come in. *Charlie again. Or maybe the fucking real estate office is finally returning my call.*

She regrets not bringing a pack of cigarettes. She could use a smoke. She resuscitates her phone, taps her SMS feed, and opens the message, not from Charlie, from Newton. Three images of a place she doesn't know in a neighborhood she would likely avoid. And a note:

> Followed a guy named Walker from the bar to this place. He had Townes's phone and bracelet. I think Townes is here. I'm about to find out.

Her breath catches up high in her chest. For no rational reason, she drops her phone. She lets it go quickly, like it's electrified, and watches it tumble down. She tries to correct her mistake but knows she's too slow to snatch it from the air. She sticks her foot out to stop it from shattering on the floor and accidentally punts the phone with the toe of her snowy boot. She watches as the phone slides under the wire frame and into the locked enclosure with the backpack.

"No! Fuck me! No!" she yells. She slaps her torso onto the dank floor and shoves her arm under. She only has room to reach in up to her forearm. Her fingers stretch and fiddle in the air. She gives up, lays her cheek on the floor, and sucks in the musty smell.

She thinks of Townes and hops straight up. She looks around for a tool to get into the cage. *I can't wait for Charlie to get here. It could be too late. What if Townes is in trouble?*

She sees nothing handy. She rushes toward the wooden steps, intending to head back to her house, but under the steps she spots a rack of tools. Her hands reach for likely objects, and she arrives back at the locked cage with an old lawnmower blade, green with grass stains, and a carpenter's framing hammer.

Setting the edge of the blade on the hardened steel U of the Master Lock, she bashes it with the hammer. The blade slips off and cuts her palm where she grips it, but she doesn't let go.

"That's not going to work." She reassesses. The latch the lock runs through is secured by a single bolt and nut. And to her deep satisfaction, the nut is turned out, her direction. She just needs pliers.

"Fuck it," she says. She lifts the blade again, holds it perpendicular to the shaft of the bolt, and angles it until its edge bites into the nut. She raises the hammer and swings it with desperate strength. Several things happen as a result: The hammer glances off the blade, and on the downswing, it hits her in the side of the ankle. The blade cuts the meat of her left hand. She can't hold on, and the blade clatters to the ground, along with the hammer.

"God fuck it!" she squeaks.

She flaps her hand and sucks on the gouge. She reaches her hand into her boot to rub the place where a knot is starting to rise over the tender bone. On the ground, she sees the end of the bolt next to her foot, the nut still attached. She straightens, her pain forgotten. The latch is mostly free. She lifts the heavy hammer and uses it to convince the latch to let loose. It is convinced in three swings. She shoves into the storage cage. She reaches past the backpack and takes her phone in her hand. She dials Charlie's number by heart.

"Charlie. Newton found Townes. You have to go there now. Forget about the backpack. I'm sending the information." She begins to listen to his reply but then cuts him off midsentence. "We know Townes is alive. We know he's in trouble. We don't know what this fucking backpack means. Not yet. Go save the child we still have." She forwards the photos, hangs up and is at a loss for what to do next. She knows she shouldn't touch anything. She sits on the cold floor, her eyes on the backpack, and hopes for the best.

• • •

Charlie takes the first exit off the interstate. His car *ding ding dings* that he is almost out of gas. He pulls onto the shoulder and opens his texts. He sees the pictures as they load. He reads the note Meg forwarded from Newton. *Meg is right.* The backpack got him focused on Etta. He was willing to let Townes's situation go, let it work itself out. He got so focused on Etta so easily, he ignored his only son. Townes was his baby too, once. Townes has been reaching out to Charlie, sending him the book, needing his father. And Charlie has been blinded by his stubborn commitment to find Etta at any cost.

He forwards the texts to Ruther along with a note that reads, *Call Me Now.* His car jumps back into traffic. He crosses over the interstate. The car reminds him again that he needs gas. He ignores it and shoots down the ramp to merge into the eastbound stream of commuters. He drives fast and recklessly with the phone at arm's reach.

When Ruther calls, Charlie says, "Did you get the texts? Do you know where that is? I don't see a street name."

"I don't know. I'm calling a guy who should know. I'm trying to look up this Walker. If he's the same guy from the train, he might be in the database. Previous arrests, sexual assault, maybe around Cicero based on the Metra report. I'll be in touch."

"Soon," Charlie says. He swerves around a car driving slowly in the fast lane, stomps on the gas, and drives straight to Cicero.

• • •

Townes is determined to stop Army Coat. To do so, he has to save himself. He reaches for the sharp buckle and launches himself off the bed. He has no plan. Maybe get a jump on Army Coat. Maybe use the buckle's corner to poke a hole in the guy's neck before he knows what's happened. Then out the window.

Army Coat knocks the toes of his boots against the baseboards as he comes down the short hall. He gets within a few paces of the bedroom door when the phone rings at the front of the apartment. Army Coat stops his advance. The boots turn and walk away. The phone stops ringing.

"What?" Army Coat demands. Townes listens. "Oh, yeah. I know you are doing me a big favor. I'm making good progress on the video. Don't worry. I'll get you the first hundred copies in a few days. You think you can shoot me that next payment now?"

*This is my chance.* If Townes flips the mattress over on the floor, maybe he can use a length of the bed frame to wedge against the door, slow Army Coat down. Or use it as a weapon, a club, or a spear.

"Too much noise," he says to Esmeralda, who doesn't understand him but seems pleased to be included.

At the window, he rips strips off a section of newspaper. Peers down into the barren backyard with its construction debris and precarious stairs. The rickety, thin boards of the long supports remind him of cricket legs. He considers using the corner of the belt buckle as a screwdriver, working the screws out of the window so he can sneak out quietly, but he knows he has no time.

"All right, goddamn it, you fucking prick," Army Coat yells, apparently not winning the negotiations. "I'll wait on the money. But you have to send it the second the videos arrive."

Townes sees the door is a bit ajar. He makes a decision. He creeps to the door, inches it open. He can't see Army Coat, but he can hear when he pushes the button to turn off the cordless phone. Townes leaves the room and turns the corner. He passes the video dub room, the bathroom, and a closed door. He gets to the back door, sees the deadbolt is locked, the key missing. He tries the knob, rattles it. Locked solid. He looks for the key. It's nowhere obvious. *Not here.*

"The fuck you think you're going?" The voice beats against his back as Army Coat stomps the length of the hall. Townes turns to face the man. He doesn't yell. He doesn't cuss. He doesn't make idle threats or raise his hands to defend himself.

He says, "You'll never lay a hand on another child," not too loudly, just to himself.

Army Coat pitches something at Townes's head. Townes jerks aside. His phone flies past his left ear and shatters against the door behind him. He feels pretend Esmeralda push her body closer to the back of his leg.

• • •

Newton starts to jam the buzzer for the upstairs flat but decides to check the door first. It's not latched. He eases quietly in. He removes his scarf and hangs it over the newel post at the base of the stairs. He looks over at the door to Garcia's place. He sees movement at the peephole. He makes a smile and a nod at the door.

He drops his coat off his shoulders and hangs it over the knob of the newel post, covering his scarf. He leaves his gloves on, clasps the hunk of brick in his right hand, and takes his empty wallet in his left. He stomps up the stairs, making more noise than is needed. At the top of the landing sits the ancient carcass of a fifties-era refrigerator; the chromed, pot-metal pull handle is pitted and flaking. The once-white, lozenge-shaped monolith has gone to rust and dusty, oxidized paint.

He hears stomping and screaming coming from the other side of Walker's door.

Newton eases around the refrigerator, bangs on the door to the apartment. While he listens to the raised voices inside, he holds up his empty wallet, waves it at the peephole, and tells Albert, "Wish me luck." Albert holds his breath.

• • •

Army Coat forces Townes to the ground. One hand snatches the hair on top of Townes's head. The back of his head is mashed into a dirty puddle of snowmelt. In his other hand, Army Coat has the blade, the point riding on Townes's Adam's apple when he swallows.

His assailant lets out a relieved laugh. "Ho, ho, ho," he says. "You nearly made it. Didn't you? I'll give you credit. You surprise me. I thought you were going to curl up and die in there. But you got your second wind. Didn't you? You got some balls down there. Some fucking *cojones*."

Army Coat calls back down the hall to his wife, "This one has *cojones*."

"Now where were we? Oh, right. You tried to rob me again. Taking money from my pocket. Again. So what I'm going to do is stick you with my knife. Real slow I'm going to stick you, let it slip in and wedge you open, nice and pretty. But if you tell me about your buddy Newton, right this second, maybe I will reconsider. You might live through this." He draws in air to say more but stops at the sound of someone pounding loudly on the front door.

Army Coat perks up and twists around tall to see what's happening. Townes can feel Esmeralda, can imagine tears running around her cheeks and dripping down. Esmeralda weeps for Townes, because he's too scared to do it for himself. The thought of her gives him hope. He winks at the place she might be standing, tries to smile the best he can.

A familiar voice calls loudly through the door, "I found Walker's wallet at the bar. It was full of money. So I dropped by."

"Don't open the fucking door, you ignorant cow," Army Coat screams at his wife. But it's too late. She ignores her husband. The door comes open.

• • •

Newton enters the room, still waving the wallet he'd flashed at the peephole. He pitches it to the short woman who let him in. She grabs it from the air and flips it open.

"Townes?" Newton yells.

"Fuck you doing?" He hears Walker before he sees him running with his head down, a knife swinging in one pumping fist. Newton pivots toward the threat. He brings his arm over in a wicked baseball throw and hurls a chunk of sharp red brick at major league speed.

It hits Walker on the top of the head. Walker sits on his ass at the mouth to the wreck of a living room. A wound opens on his head, and a stream of blood traces his right sideburn and runs down around the front of his throat into the neck of his shirt, slowly soaking in. His eyes are open but unfocused. Newton takes advantage of the lull to scan his environment.

The little Latina is gawping at her husband, holding the empty wallet loose in her hand. There are a few kids, quiet, as if in shock. Finally, at the far end of the hall, Newton spots Townes. He climbs to his feet and comes down the hall, edges past Walker, and acknowledges Newton with a nod and a thin smile. He keeps moving right out the door like a man with an agenda.

Newton catches movement. He watches Walker's eyes. They are starting to focus, come back to reality. They look in the direction Townes is exiting. Walker stands slowly, the knife still in his hand. Not looking too sure-footed but dangerous enough.

The little Latina breaks the spell and starts to scream in Spanish. She steps over and hits Newton on the arm and shoulder, the wallet still clamped in one balled fist. Four little kids, two girls and two filthy little pale-skinned boys, all start yowling.

Walker takes a couple of steps forward, finding his balance. Newton shoves the woman over to get space to work. He moves forward fast, but the knife comes at him. He backs off, circles around. Walker matches his footwork. Recovered now, the blood flow staunched. A shiny black mass of blood is starting to skin over in Walker's hair, like the hard shell of a cockroach.

Newton tries to move in repeatedly, testing Walker's guard. Each time the knife nearly finds Newton's chest or eyes. They circle a bit more. The kids are silent. The woman stays where she landed. Newton can hear Townes reach the landing at the base of the steps.

*It's time to go.* Newton drops his guard, lets Walker come in close with the knife. Walker lunges, the knife goes for a kill stroke at Newton's throat. Newton does a nice sidestep. Walker misses, leaving his side exposed. Newton's hard fist comes in under Walker's arm and breaks a rib with the first strike. Sour air erupts from

Walker's mouth, the knife flails and catches Newton's left fist across the curled fingers, ripping through his best gloves. He pays little attention.

Newton beats his fists into the man's midsection. Walker tries to hit Newton with his fist, tries to swing the knife again. Their fists collide once and glance off; the knife cuts the air. Newton shifts and advances as Walker backs away. He jabs and catches Walker in the eye. The Oily One drops the knife.

Newton keeps advancing. His fists drive like pistons; they shake the sick meat of Walker's body; they rattle his innards. They pound out a rhythm until the circle of Walker's ribs begin to lose its natural curve. When Walker's body crumples like a building that's imploded, falling in on itself, Newton reaches over to take his empty wallet from the woman, but she yanks it away. *If looks could kill,* he thinks. He lets her keep it.

• • •

Townes stands at the base of the stairs, listening to the scuffle above. There's a heavy, definitive thump. Newton walks out of the apartment smiling. He waves down at Townes, blood making his gloves look wet.

"Fancy meeting you here. You want a lift?" Newton sounds happy, relaxed, and friendlier than Townes has ever seen him. He seems truly glad to see Townes.

"That'd be great," Townes calls back.

Newton edges past the refrigerator and starts down the steps. There's renewed screaming in Spanish and the wife comes out the door. Army Coat is using her as a crutch. He throws his knife at Newton. The knife knocks off the banister to land on the steps. Newton bounds back up the stairs, looking excited for round two. He glances at the knife as he steps around it.

"Look out!" Townes warns him.

Townes sees the refrigerator topple straight toward Newton's skull, set to drive him through the steps like a sledgehammer striking a finishing nail. Newton springs back to avoid getting clocked but loses his footing and lands head down on the steps, the rounded treads knocking against his spine as he slips down. The massive appliance crushes his leg. The concussive impact in the tight stairwell sounds to Townes like a bomb going off, like being slapped hard on both ears.

Newton is pinned in place. He looks scared. The refrigerator starts to slip farther down his body, threatening to crush his hip girdle, squeeze his guts out the top of his head like he's a tube of toothpaste. He jams his hands onto the top of the fridge, halts the creeping juggernaut's slow compression of his body. Townes sees that he can't hold it; he's got no strength left.

Townes crosses the distance in three strides and jams his shoulder against the weight, digs his feet into the old stair treads, uses all the strength in his legs. Together, they manage to shift the weight to one side.

Army Coat steps away from his wife, starts down the steps. Townes hears him coming. He sees Army Coat is holding his ribs, each jolt down the stairs causing agony. The wife screeches, giving her husband orders, pointing, and cajoling.

"*Matalos. Matorlos a todos.*" Esmeralda understands her and moves her presence closer in Townes's mind.

Townes and Newton, straining together, are able to get Newton free. He flips over and elbow-crawls, like in basic training, down the last few steps but is forced to leave his mangled GI limb behind.

Garcia's door opens, and an old man in a flannel work shirt and house shoes says, "*Venir en. Entrar. Entrar.*" He makes room. Newton gets upright on his one leg, his empty pants waving like a battlefield flag, and hops toward the open door.

The mean little Latina is leaning over the rail, screaming frantically. She hurls Newton's wallet like a Molotov cocktail. It slaps the wall near the front entrance. The slow, unrelenting thump of Army Coat gets closer and closer.

Townes reaches for Newton to get him into Garcia's apartment. There's enough time to get inside, lock the door, call the cops. Wait for them to arrive. *Wait. Barricaded and scared.* Townes begins to help Newton, resigned to cower until help arrives. The woman screeches again in Spanish.

Townes remembers the cleaver. He thinks of the deranged couple chopping through Garcia's door to get at them. Stabbing and picking with that long knife until it pokes through. Chopping anything that gets in their way. He imagines how frightened Esmeralda will be, how horrible to lose her. He lets go of Newton and waits at the base of the steps, putting himself between his friend, all the Esmeraldas, and the maniacs who want to hurt them.

• • •

Newton stands in the mouth of Garcia's apartment; his gloved hand on the doorframe leaves a bloody print. He watches Walker taking one step at a time, the knife now back in his hand. He watches Townes a few feet away yank Newton's special leg loose from the refrigerator. The calf-shaped housing has been busted, smashed between the massive weight of the appliance and a step's edge.

Townes backs away with his trophy, letting Walker come. When Walker steps onto the landing, Townes gives him a serious look. He says, "You take one more step, and I'll end this." It sounds a little Hollywood to Newton's ear, but Townes means it.

Walker sucks at his front teeth; he assesses Townes. He doesn't find panic and doubt. His wife screams more Spanish at the back of his greasy, bloody head. Her nagging pushes him forward. He raises his knife, going for a quick kill. Not enough energy to drag it out.

Townes is fully in the moment, watching Army Coat come. There is no past guilt driving him, no concern for future consequences or rewards. There is just this raw instant, only himself and Army Coat. Townes's grip on the prosthetic tightens.

The blade flashes, moving fast, ready to rip open Townes's soft middle.

If Townes misses, or if he's late, he will be gutted.

He is all that separates this nightmare from the little girls of this world.

He stands his ground.

He focuses on his target. He swings Newton's leg by the ankle.

The angular knee strikes Army Coat square in the temple. Army Coat's eyes don't have time to register the blow. The cold point of the knife touches Townes's flesh through the side of his shirt, leaving a long, raw scrape.

When Army Coat falls this time, it's definitive. He's a loose pile on the ground at Townes's feet. The ringing clatter of the knife dropping on the wooden entry is all Townes hears, the final bell at the end of a prizefight.

Then he hears Newton behind him exhale slowly and say, "Holy shit."

# A FEW LAST WORDS

The past weeks have brought an uncharacteristic warm spell, melting snow and coaxing trees to put out green shoots and bulbs to push out tentative blooms. Only the most sheltered heaps of snowpack managed to survive the heat, the runoff turning the ground soggy and the whole world wet. But it couldn't last, not in February. Not here.

In typical fashion, as Meg finalized plans for the event, a cold front turned and dropped into Chicago, bringing frigid Arctic air, the most severe of the season, complete with bitter, slashing winds that could kill a person within thirty minutes of exposure.

Meg shivers and turns her face to the sky, trying to divine the intention and timing of the snowstorm that gathers above.

"Well, we might wrap this up before the snow comes. If the boys are on time."

"What are the odds that the boys will be punctual?" Etta asks rhetorically.

Meg grunts her pessimism into the cemetery.

The footpath is tidy as always, the spot separate, isolated from the surrounding commercial district. Normally this makes her feel at peace, calm. Today, the shocked warm ground is releasing wisps of curling fog into the cold air, like a smoker's sensuous exhale. For the first time, the dead under her feet make her uncomfortable. Again, she glances to the entrance to see if Charlie has arrived. *Not yet.*

Etta's headstone is swept clean, the granite darker than before, the rich mahogany flecks dominating the stone in the presence of so much moisture. Meg is relieved her daughter isn't in the ground, surrounded by decaying bones, rotting flesh, and decrepit, illegible grave markers.

"You know what you're going to say?" Etta asks.

"No," Meg replies. "I'm going to wait and see how the spirit moves me."

• • •

Charlie backs his car into a spot on Main Street.

In the weeks since Townes's incident and the recovery of the backpack, Charlie had willed himself to be patient, to take things one day at a time. But it hadn't been easy. When Ruther had shared his suspicions Etta had been taken over the border, Charlie started packing for a drive to the great white north. Realization slowly dawned that he had no specific destination, no passport, and no information. He'd eased off. His years of effort had gotten him no closer to his daughter. He'd filled his life with busywork, making pretend progress. He'd failed at every turn. For all his vigilance and spent energy, it was Meg who had found the only concrete lead. *She always was the smart one.*

He pushes his replacement glasses up his nose. They are familiar and foreign at the same time. He'd found frames like the ones he'd crushed: black, reliable, and timeless. At the last moment, he'd chosen a clear acrylic version. They sit on his face the same but cast an odd light at the edges of his eyes. He constantly feels something is there, brushing at his attention, like passing through a cobweb.

He checks himself in the lighted vanity mirror on his car's visor. His reflection belongs to someone else. The clear frames bring out the smattering of silver taking hold in his sideburns. The glasses were a poor choice and make him feel pathetically trendy, like an old man trying too hard.

He spots a patch of Bootsy's fur on the collar of his winter coat, brushes at it with no effect, lets it go. He's self-conscious about his looks, which is new for him. He'd always considered these mirrors a place for women to check their lipstick. He'd never felt the urge to use one. He smacks it up and slips out of the car.

He carries a bunch of flowers. The florist had described them as "fragrant Oriental lilies, boasting multiple blooms on each stem to create a luscious bouquet." Charlie nodded and took his word for it.

He walks up the steps, salt crunching under his boots, and spots Meg toward the back of the small memorial plot. His heels clomp on the hard path. She hears him coming and turns, her red lips spreading into a warm, welcoming smile.

When they come together, they embrace firmly. When the hold breaks, they grasp one another's gloved hands.

"Glad you made it," she says.

"Me too."

• • •

Newton parks the truck on a side street at the far side of the brewpub. His hat, gloves, and scarf slide off the slick engine housing between the seats as he stomps the brake. He yanks the parking brake, puts the column shift in neutral, and lets the engine run. He unbuckles his lap belt and stretches to shake out his winter gear where it had landed in a puddle of snowmelt, returns the items to their perch on the hot engine. He's in no hurry to go. His mind is on other things.

Earlier that morning Newton had dropped by Fresh Hell Tattoos to touch base with Thomas. He walked on his replacement leg, bringing doughnuts and coffee, which was the SOP. He found Tommy waiting at the base of the steps.

Tommy confided, "Dad is sick. He wouldn't want you to know. He's got the skin cancer. He's old and mean but not in great shape, you know."

"I'm sorry. They can help him, right? Get him going on treatment?"

"We don't know. They're limited by his age and health. By how far along the cancer is. By what the local VA is capable of. They call it stage three. The cancer. Which is bad. Could be worse. But pretty bad."

Newton's body braced for another loss; his muscles tightened; his heart began to race. "What can I do?"

"Keep hanging out with him. He likes you. He loves me. Has always done his best. But he's not cut out for the dad shit. Never was. I'm a grown-ass man now, so I understand. I'm not bitter. Not anymore. He's a soldier and feels at home around other soldiers. Part of him is still over there, where he met my mom. Where we left her. That's the truth of it. And being with you makes him feel at home. I think I remind him too much of Mom. I can see his eyes turn sad when he sees me." Tommy reached over to shake Newton's hand. They were about the same height, same build.

"If you come around and keep him company, that would help."

"Sure."

Tommy went back in the garage. Newton stomped upstairs to watch Thomas shove doughnuts in his mouth and swallow them without much chewing.

In the cab of the rattling truck, an old, familiar rage heats him from the inside out. *I hope God in heaven has a big mushy face I can cave in real nice if I ever meet that trifling bastard.* He puts the rage away, saves it for another time. Since the fight with Walker he's been attempting to cultivate a kinder, gentler Newton.

After Townes put Walker down, they were joined by Ruther and two squad cars. Charlie showed up minutes later. Mrs. Walker was arrested and hauled away in cuffs, screaming and spitting as the cruiser drove away. Soon after, an ambulance arrived. They carted Walker out, still alive but unable to wake. A city worker who looked like a harried J. Lo in a bad suit showed up and spoke Spanish in calming tones to Walker's sons and nieces. They all held hands and left together.

Newton and Townes were eventually taken to an emergency room, where two male nurses who smelled like cigarettes gave them a once-over. On one table, Newton got stitches in a line across the front of his fist. On the table facing him, Townes was issued bandages on his ear, wrist, and side. Townes smiled at Newton, evidently pleased they had survived, like comrades, like soldiers, like brothers in arms. Newton found it bittersweet. There was a jolt of utter contentment at being above the ground, followed by respect for Townes mixed with a swell of guilt over Albert not being around.

He turns off the truck, grabs his stuff, hits the sidewalk, and lets the harsh reality of winter focus his mind.

• • •

The express train drops Townes at the Main Street station, only a few blocks from the cemetery. He tugs his cap down as he waits for the train to pull away and the pedestrian gate to lift. Dory bought him a replacement for the cap he lost. She put it on his head as he left the shop an hour ago, kissed him on each cheek. At the memory, his eyes close and he grins languidly. This must be what love feels like, like slowly sinking into a deep, soapy tub of hot, buoyant water. The gate lifts and he sleepwalks down the block.

He recently curtailed his meditation practice. Still, he feels at ease. Centered. Calm. He doesn't owe it all to Dory, though extending affection and having it returned is the most potent emotional elixir he can imagine. Dispatching Walker had been a magic spell. He won the respect of Charlie and Newton. The only one not particularly moved by his escapade was his mother. She's irritated with him for being reckless and seems to believe that constantly frowning at him will discourage future, half-cocked misadventures.

Most significant to his mood is the contents of Etta's backpack. It contained the stuff you'd expect: schoolbooks, folders, class papers, a dirty gym uniform with the name *Messenger* printed across it. There was her old flip phone that could yield pertinent text messages. And house keys. Only Townes understood the significance of the keys.

His last seconds with Etta had been crappy and rude. He'd locked her out of the house. Still, she could have used her keys, could have come in. It was a reasonable assumption, all those years ago, that she would do that. She hadn't. He still doesn't know why. No one does. But now, he's capable of forgiving himself for shoving her, knowing she chose not to come in of her own free will. He hasn't found the courage to confess his fight with Etta to his family. He can't imagine what purpose it would serve.

When he gets near the cemetery, he sees Newton coming toward him on the sidewalk. He waits at the entrance. They exchange distracted greetings and walk toward Etta's headstone side by side.

• • •

Gathered in an arc around Etta's symbolic resting place, the four of them look to one another, hesitant.

Meg clears her throat and says, "Well, I appreciate everyone coming. I really do." She glances into each set of eyes that watch her. "This is a commemoration rather than a memorial. It's a chance to say what we think about Etta, about her life, her absence, our struggles." The men nod solemnly. She's at a loss for what more to say. They stand reverently, shuffle their feet on the hard ground as the first flakes begin to fall. She says, "Charlie wants to say a few words. Right?"

"That's right," he says. "I wanted to give you the latest from Ruther. We already know the backpack was in a storage cage. We now know the place was owned by an old couple. Turns out they were Canadian. Last name Roy. Moved here from north of Vancouver. They had a daughter, Chloe. Looks like Chloe died around her twentieth birthday. It's difficult to piece it all together. Ruther is looking into the details."

Meg places her hand on the shoulder of Charlie's work coat.

Charlie pushes his transparent glasses up his nose. "Ruther is careful not to say more than he knows, but we know the wife, Delphine, was sick when Mr. Roy moved them back to Canada. We don't know the exact dates because the house was left empty, the utilities weren't canceled." Charlie pauses, trying to get things straight.

Meg pats him, urging him to continue.

"There was something new found in Etta's backpack. A flyer. The kind you see stapled to utility poles. It'd been ripped loose, torn at its top edge, folded over a few times, and shoved into a textbook. It reads, *Free Kittens to Good Homes*. It has the Roys' old address. It's looking like Etta got off the bus but didn't go in the house. Instead she went to see some kittens. She never left that house. We think she was kept there. Kept on a cot, locked in that storage cage. She was in that basement while we were searching for her. When they moved, our best guess is she went to Canada."

"But why?" Meg asks. Townes and Newton keep quiet, listening closely.

"We don't know. The good news, there was no sign of foul play. No blood. The ground is too frozen to dig around the property, but there's no evidence the yard had been turned. So, that's good. Roy's whereabouts are unclear. Ruther's working with the Canadian authorities, trying to get some traction. It isn't much."

"But it's more than we used to know," Meg says.

"Yeah, it is," Charlie acknowledges. He steps toward the headstone with his daughter's name chiseled into it. He turns his back on it and faces his wife and son. Faces the young man who loved his daughter. He says, "I'm no good at saying important things. I never was. I always assumed people knew me, and that was enough. Knew I loved them, knew when I was hurt. But I made a mistake. Many, probably. The biggest was not talking." He lifts the bouquet of flowers and looks at the white blooms, snow tapping into the cellophane wrapper and sticking.

"I was focused on getting Etta back. I never appreciated the things I still had. The people I still had. Meg," he says, looking at her. "I love you and should have told you so. But I let Etta's loss spread out and drown my whole life. I didn't know how to tie off the wound."

"I know it, Charlie. But we are all still standing. We are here. We're together."

"Townes, you too. You know? The same goes for you. I should have been there," Charlie says. "Thanks for trying to connect. I'm sorry you had to be the grownup. But I'm ready to try harder if you'll give me a shot."

Townes nods and looks down at the snow gathering on the toes of his shoes.

"Newton, I appreciate you going after Townes. And I'm sorry you got dragged through the mud at the police station."

Newton silently accepts Charlie's apology.

"One last thing: the older I get, the more I understand the best thing I will know in life is the love of family. You're what really matters." He hands the flowers to Meg. She's surprised but accepts them, confused and touched by the gesture.

"Etta isn't here right now," he explains. "But you are. And you deserve to get flowers. You deserve to be taken care of once in a while." He gets back in line and waits.

Newton steps out. He says, "I don't do public speaking. I don't like it much. But Etta was a good thing in my life, a life that has been filled with a lot of terrible shit. She believed in me back then. Because of that, I'm making an effort to believe in myself."

Meg's eyes are getting wet; she wipes her nose with her gloved hand. Townes gives Newton a friendly smile. Charlie watches as Newton takes out his wallet.

Newton gets his photo booth images and carefully tears off one framed section, hands it to Meg. He tears the next for Charlie then gives one to Townes. He tucks the remaining picture back in his wallet.

Meg holds the small image cradled in the palm of her gloved hand: Etta's mouth half-open, caught midsentence, and Newton with his forehead tipped toward the lens. "Thanks, Newton," Meg says, her voice low and rough. She steps out in front as Newton moves back to his spot. She carries the flowers in one hand, puts her other hand to her chest. "I'm overwhelmed. I'm feeling like Etta is here with us. Earlier I was looking at this weather. See those blue flowers poking out there? They have a little plastic spike with their name rammed in the dirt. It says it's called glory-of-the-snow. I'd never heard of it until I read it." She points out the flowers for the boys. "You could think that flower is going to die because it bloomed too early. Or you could think, that flower was so determined to live it poked itself out the first chance it got. And just look. Look how beautiful it is, if only for a few days. And you can bet your ass that little flower will try to keep going, try to live through the coming storm. I've been thinking of Etta as being dead because it was easier than believing she is out there, somewhere unknown, in trouble. That was wrong. If she had a chance to keep going, she would have fought for it. You know. And that's a good thing." She sniffles and wipes her nose again. The snow is getting thick, sticking to hats and shoulders, blowing into eyes. The four of them move closer to one another as wind and snow twist around them. The walking path becomes obscured.

"Townes," Meg says, "you told me this gravestone was a dumb thing. Now is your chance. You have anything to share before we get someplace warm?"

Townes stands in his place in the world, thankful for the people around him. He considers his desperate quest for a perfect peace through meditation. *Maybe it was a fool's errand. Finding how to be happy is a lifelong effort, not the kind of thing you can check off your list in your twenties. It's the kind of thing you uncover as you go along.* He trembles at the cold soaking through him. The wind shifts and brings a sound like laughter. He clears his throat and says, "This was a good idea after all. And I can't think of anything else to say." He cocks his arm so his mother can take it. He leads her out of the cemetery, picking his way by feel. Charlie follows, proud of the family he has. He nods to Newton, who saunters along beside him.

# ACKNOWLEDGMENTS

Thanks to those early readers who gave their time and attention to my manuscript at an unseemly stage: JamieLou Thome, Danielle Morency, Jessica Craig, Marina Penalva, and Caroline Tetschner.

Gratitude to all my magical agents; but especially Anna Soler-Pont and Leticia Vila-Sanjuán.

My affection for the Eastside Crew continues to grow with time. Thanks for the support.

Genuine appreciation to my new friend and editor, Benjamin LeRoy.

Ana Quevedo, *Muchas gracias por su consejo con respecto a las secciones deespañol.*